W9-CBN-636

WITHDRAWN

FOUR BEFORE RICHARDSON

Selected English Novels, 1720–1727

FOUR BEFORE RICHARDSON

Selected English Novels, 1720–1727

Edited by

William H. McBurney

UNIVERSITY OF NEBRASKA PRESS · LINCOLN

PR
1297
.F68
1963

Copyright © 1963 by the University of Nebraska Press

All Rights Reserved

Library of Congress catalog card number: 63–9095

First Printing April 1963

Second Printing February 1964

MANUFACTURED IN THE UNITED STATES OF AMERICA

117267

1582

For
Professor George Sherburn

11 7267

1582

For
Professor George Sherburn

Foreword

THE HUNDREDS of novels which crowded the bookstalls of St. Paul's Churchyard, Little Britain, and Paternoster Row in early eighteenth-century London have now largely disappeared. Many were undoubtedly read out of existence, while others were allowed to perish because of changing tastes in fiction. Some, fortunately, survive today in English and American collections of rare books, though critical indifference continues to condemn them to a literary limbo. Like the apparitions (and examples of true love) in La Rochefoucauld's maxim, very few people have ever seen them, and they are denied even his cynical consolation of being widely talked about. The novels of Defoe are a possible exception.

During several years of research in this neglected field I came across some novelistic ghosts which seemed worth reviving. For this anthology four have been selected from almost four hundred publications between 1700 and 1739. At first glance they may seem less substantial than their modern counterparts, which is to be expected since they appeared when the genre was just beginning to materialize. More specifically, all four were printed between 1720 and 1727. This chronological concentration is a coincidence, but perhaps inevitable, for the third decade of the century saw the first real English development of the form. A more deliberate factor in their selection was that each, in various ways and to varying degrees, anticipates the works of the important mid-century novelists, Richardson, Fielding, and Smollett. They are thus representative of their own age and interesting forecasts of the greater age to come.

Such a selection cannot illustrate all trends, even in a limited period, and specialists may object to certain omissions. Defoe is excluded because most of his novels are easily available. Mrs. Aphra Behn's works belong to the seventeenth century, and have also been reissued recently. One of her plots, however, reappears in eighteenth-century guise in *Luck at Last*. Mrs. Mary Manley of *New Atalantis* notoriety is less a novelist than a literary gossipmonger. The strange fictions of Mrs. Penelope Aubin are tempting, but Mrs. Eliza Haywood offers much the same material in a more interesting prose style. Her most extensive biographer, Professor George F. Whicher, would not have agreed with my particular choice from her voluminous production. I hope, however, that the reappearance of *Philidore and Placentia* after two hundred and thirty-six years will send students to Whicher's pioneer study and lead to further exploration of her works.

The four works presented here are arranged in a progression of technical skill and general interest, although my introduction suggests interrelations. All texts are taken from the first editions and are reproduced without omissions. (The infrequent suspension points indicate an uncompleted remark by a character.) Punctuation, capitalization, and paragraphing have been modernized; and spelling has been adapted to accepted American usage. There are a few exceptions to these rules, such as passages in which eighteenth-century spelling or syntax preserves the flavor of the original and is still acceptable, and passages which defy modernization without extensive alteration. Obscure words, terms, and allusions are explained in footnotes.

It is a pleasure to thank the libraries which own the original texts: The Newberry Library (*Luck at Last*), the British Museum (*The Jamaica Lady*), and Harvard College Library (*Philidore and Placentia* and *The Accomplished Rake*). I also wish to thank Professor George W. Stone, Jr., for permission to use information from my article on Mrs. Mary Davys, *PMLA*, Vol. LXXIV (1959). To Mr. Edward M. Riley, Director of Research for Colonial Williamsburg, Williamsburg, Virginia; Lieutenant D. R. Hahne, U.S.N.; and Professor Lois G. Morrison of San Antonio College, I am indebted for valuable information and suggestions. My former colleague, Professor Michael F. Shugrue, as well as Professor Don S. Woodmency of Wisconsin State College at La Crosse, have given technical assistance and timely support. The dedication of the anthology to Professor George W. Sherburn is only slight acknowledgment of my great and continuing gratitude.

Contents

INTRODUCTION   xi

Luck at Last; or, The Happy Unfortunate   1
   by Arthur Blackamore

The Jamaica Lady; or, The Life of Bavia   83
   by W. P.

Philidore and Placentia; or, L'Amour trop Delicat   153
   by Eliza Haywood

The Accomplished Rake; or, Modern Fine Gentleman   233
   by Mary Davys

Introduction

WHEN MR. SPECTATOR, on April 29, 1712, warned his "fair Readers" of the perils of the month of May, he urged them "to be in a particular Manner careful how they meddle with Romances, Chocolate, Novels, and the like Inflamers, which I look upon to be very dangerous to be made use of during this great Carnival of Nature." In retrospect, this mildly satirical dismissal of the novel seems doubly ironic, since the Sir Roger de Coverley papers have come to be considered a novel in embryo, and since the warning occurred on the eve of the first important flowering of the novel in England. Yet it foreshadowed a critical attitude toward early eighteenth-century fiction which still persists.

In *The Rise of the Novel* (1957), Professor Ian Watt admits that he has not made more than "incidental reference to the earlier traditions of fiction, nor to the more immediate precursors and contemporaries" of his central figures, Defoe, Richardson, and Fielding. Since his valuable study is "necessarily selective," his omission is understandable, but it is also symptomatic of a general tendency elsewhere to admit the existence of immediate precursors and contemporaries while treating the great novelists as though each had, somehow, developed autonomously.

For this state of affairs, perhaps the novelists themselves are to blame. Defoe was aware that his reading public included "the airy nice peruser of novels and romances, neatly bound and finely gilt," but he paid lip-service to the Puritan distrust of deliberate fiction. Richardson was influenced by the same dubious prejudice. *Pamela,* according to the title page, "has its Foundation in Truth and Nature," and is "divested of all those Images, which, in too many Pieces calculated for Amusement only, tend to inflame the Minds they should instruct." Even Fielding was aristocratically careful to select for praise only established foreign novelists such as Cervantes, Scarron, Le Sage, and Marivaux. Smollett's contempt was, as usual, universal when he had Melopoyn in *Roderick Random* sneer at "a secret history, thrown into a series of letters,

[xi]

or a volume of adventures such as those of Robinson Crusoe and Colonel Jack, or a collection of conundrums, wherewith to entertain the plantations." All shared a common contempt for English fiction and for their more humble fellow practitioners, whom Fielding in *Joseph Andrews* termed "those persons of surprising genius . . . the modern novel and Atalantis writers."

Between 1700 and 1739 the novel was a sub-literary genre, produced by Grub Street for a popular market and increasingly dominated by the booksellers as noble patronage declined under the Hanoverian monarchs. Yet, without a body of fictional publication sufficiently large, diffused, and (within admitted diversity) well-defined, it is hardly likely that the later authors would have found the novel worth the negative tributes of satire or repudiation. Nor is it likely that they would have turned to the genre as a means of expression if it had not already shown itself to be vigorously suited to the tastes of a large and expanding reading public. Two facts are evident: they had read novels before they wrote them, and the products of "those persons of surprising genius" formed the only immediate native fictional background that they had. If one turns to the scores of histories, secret histories, lives, adventures, memoirs, accounts, and tales which appeared in the first four decades of the century and examines them with any degree of literary tolerance or antiquarian interest, it is evident that the main lines of eighteenth-century fictional development were implicit when Defoe was still a Tory spy, Richardson a printer's apprentice, and Fielding a schoolboy at Eton.

In 1692 Congreve made a useful and often-quoted distinction between the romance and the novel in the preface to *Incognita*. However, the two terms continued to be used interchangeably throughout the eighteenth century. "Romance," technically, was applicable only to the seventeenth-century French heroic romance and its English imitations. It is customary to say that this type of fiction was discredited by the ridicule of Boileau in *Les Héros de Roman* (1664). This may have been true in France, where the *roman* soon gave way to the shorter *nouvelle* but various factors in Restoration England caused a time-lag of ten or twenty years in fictional tastes and in immediacy of translation. Nor was the official text of Boileau's satire put into English until 1710. Evidently Addison's Leonora did not read it, for her modish library, as cataloged in the *Spectator*, No. 37, included five of the most voluminous French romances as well as "A Book of Novels." An edition of Sir Charles Cotterell's translation of La Calprenède's *Cassandre* was issued, "very much corrected," in 1725. And Horace Walpole in the second preface to *The Castle of Otranto* (1764) stated that he had attempted to blend "the two kinds of romance, the ancient and the modern," that is, the heroic romance and the novel.

The heroic romance by no means disappeared from the literary scene but, by the time of William and Mary, English taste had caught up with the French fashion of the *nouvelle,* which was, as Professor George Sherburn has noted, "the true source from which the later long novel emerges." For evidence of this new, important, and continuing influence one may turn to two collections, *Modern Novels,* printed for Richard Bentley in 1692, and *A Select Collection of Novels,* edited by Samuel Croxall in 1722 and expanded in 1729. Bentley's twelve volumes include forty-eight novels, thirty-seven of which are admitted translations from the French. Croxall's six volumes offered to "Her Highness the Princess Anne" thirty-three novels; twenty-nine were translations from French, Spanish, and Italian originals. As the continued dominance of Continental fiction indicates, there was little significant change in taste between 1692 and 1722, other than an increase in Spanish novels.

Although French influence was often deplored, it could not be denied. Gabriel de Brémond and Mlle de la Roche-Guilhem, who appeared in both collections, are seldom mentioned in English literary histories, but the aims of such authors were quite compatible with early eighteenth-century English tastes. Writing in 1656, Jean de Segrais, for example, declared that the aim of the novel was to picture things as we usually see them; in 1692 John Dunton praised works which offer a lively, natural, and particular description of "what is in Man, and what is ordinarily done by Men of all sorts"; and in 1705 Mrs. Mary Davys experimented in *The Fugitive* to see "whether it was not possible to divert the Town with real events, just as they happen'd, without Running into Romance." The *nouvelle,* then, was easily naturalized and its techniques assimilated into English fiction. The same is true of the picaresque narrative which appeared in the seventeenth century and intermingled with the native rogue or criminal biographies. Less obvious but no less pervasive was the influence of the Oriental *conte* which, after the translation of Galland's *Les Mille et une nuits* in 1706, was put to many uses by Grub Street.

The causes of a discernible increase in native English prose fiction about 1720 are elusive. Translations, or reissues of translations, from the French did not decrease numerically, despite the temporary decline of the novel in France during the troubled regency of Philip of Orleans. This coincided with the establishment of the Hanoverian succession and the relative calm of the long period of governmental control by Walpole. Whatever the political causes, the reading public was ready for a change. As the preface to *The Most Entertaining History of Hyppolito and Aminta* (1718) noted, "The Press has so long been employ'd with Controversies about Politicks and Religion, that in Reason it may be suppos'd that a great part of the Nation is quite surfeited with so often repeated and inculcated Arguments on both Sides." In any case, the first important cycle in eighteenth-century fiction began in 1719, rose to a peak in 1727–1728, and declined after 1730 with the deaths of several prolific authors, to begin again after 1740 with the fresh impetus provided by the first novels of Richardson and Fielding.

Although diversified, the fictional publications of this early period have various similarities. First, there is comparative brevity, which Mrs. Mary Manley in *The Secret History of Queen Zarah* (1705) declared was "much more agreeable to the Brisk and Impetuous Humour of the *English* who have naturally no Taste for long-winded Performances." There is, too, the use of interpolated stories, a device common in Continental fiction from the time of Cervantes but also a reflection of the eighteenth-century taste for "variety," which was to be the bane of the novel long after Richardson and Fielding had demonstrated the superiority of an integrated plot. Type-names and stock situations, often borrowed from the theater, are used, but all four of the novels presented here have English characters and profess to use the contemporary scene.

Of particular interest are the novelists' justifications for writing fiction and for using the novel form. Three describe their works as trifles—"only a novel," "the first fruit of my scribble," "an offering not worthy of acceptance"—and thus modestly echo the critical consensus that the novel was an inferior literary type. Arthur Blackamore, the author of *Luck at Last,* tries to dignify his work by pointing out that novels have much the same design that poetry has: "to profit and delight the reader." The author of *The Jamaica Lady* follows this familiar Horatian dictum with more satiric intent and goes further in trying to separate his novel from the works of his contemporaries which, he says, are either translations or abridgments of "some larger history." (For the latter category he may have in mind the popular "secret histories" of the Tudor courts.)

In *Philidore and Placentia,* as in most of her productions, Mrs. Eliza Haywood is too busy or too unabashed to theorize. Elsewhere, she insists that her work has a "good Moral use" and that it is "a true Description of Nature," terms which are not always identical in her fiction. More typically, she "pretends no farther merit than an aim to please" and contents herself with the frank title-page description of the work as "A Novel." Mrs. Mary Davys, however, in the general preface to her *Works* (1725), disassociates herself from histories and travels on the one hand, and from the French type of fiction on the other. To save the novel, which she defines as a probable feigned story, from pointlessness or tedium, she outlines a theory based on dramatic techniques. In the dedication of *The Accomplished Rake* she declares that she is "in a vein of writing something new," but she cannot, in fact, be credited with the first application of dramatic rules to the composition of prose fiction. Her theories closely resembled those formulated by her favorite playwright, Congreve, some thirty years earlier when he employed the unities of time, place, and "Contrivance" in *Incognita.* However, no English novelist before Fielding was so extensively influenced by the theater as Mrs. Davys, and the preface to her *Works* is one of the few thoughtful statements by a practicing novelist in the early eighteenth century.

In general, it was a period of undirected and exhaustive experimentation. The novelists wrote in the fiercely competitive air of Grub Street. The rivalry of Continental fiction, and continued critical disdain, made necessary or inevitable structural brevity, careless style, stereotyped descriptions, and repetitious multiplication of those types of fiction which pleased the most obvious tastes of the reading public. Negative benefits were, however, received from the general imitativeness. Since novelty or sheer variety remained the chief criterion of fictional excellence, each imitation strove to surpass its original model. This soon tended to exhaust the possibilities of the type. As a consequence, the popularity of specific works was less lasting and fictional vogues, discarded by upper-class readers, passed down through the social strata with increasing rapidity. Such acceleration of popularity prevented any stagnation of the novel, such as the heroic romance had experienced in the later seventeenth century, and to some extent eliminated the dangers of a similar discrediting. At the same time the process promoted a wider reading public and helped both bookseller and author to discover the preferences of this augmented group.

The great age of the eighteenth-century English novel had not yet arrived, but a broad and necessary foundation was laid.

Luck at Last; or, The Happy Unfortunate (1723) is the least sophisticated of the four novels, despite the fact that Arthur Blackamore borrowed his plot from a short fictional piece by Mrs. Aphra Behn which was published posthumously in 1698. *The Wandering Beauty,* however, lacked the salacious verve of the more typical works of "the divine Astrea," such as *The Fair*

Jilt, and Blackamore, by extensive alterations and additions, has transformed her Peregrina into a figure who closely resembles Pamela. His prose style lacks the faded elegance of Mrs. Behn's work and the development of the story is uncomplicated to an unusual degree. After the initial flurry of Latin tags, there is nothing to distract the barely literate reader who may have been attracted by the modest price of one shilling and by the affinity of the novel with popular religious tracts such as *The Practice of Piety*, with which John Gildon had sneeringly associated *Robinson Crusoe* as part of every old woman's legacy to her posterity. Whether or not Blackamore took orders is unknown, but the novel might serve as a sermon exemplum on the subject of virtue and patience rewarded. At the same time, Sylvia's rendition of the ballad of "Chevy Chase" ("a very melancholy ditty, but fittest for a person under her circumstances") underscores the second and equally popular appeal of the plot, the combination of various motifs from ballads and chapbook redactions of medieval literature—the runaway bride, the lost child, and the Cinderella story.

However, to dismiss *Luck at Last* as a poorly written mixture of popular religious and romantic strains is to underestimate the novel and to overlook the continued vitality of its themes in the eighteenth century. The lost child is pivotal in Steele's *The Conscious Lovers*, which was presented a year earlier. The forced marriage of youth and age is the key to many contemporary comedies, and the title of Richardson's *Clarissa* ("Particularly Showing the Distresses that May Attend the Misconduct Both of Parents and Children, in Relation to Marriage") echoes Blackamore's concluding judgments on parental tyranny and filial obedience.

The real weakness of the novel is the character of the heroine. Sylvia is first seen as a pert and resourceful heiress, importuned by Stertorius, the superannuated beau of the comedy of manners. After her escape and the gypsy interlude, she suddenly becomes an exemplar of modesty and humility, and apparently comes to believe that she is the beggar-maid she has pretended to be. Her rise from scullion to gentlewoman and her further elevation as wife of Philaretus are as predictable as they are unconsciously smug. Sylvia's blushing and panting, her strict observance of social rank and household hierarchies, her pride in the various promotions ("She now began to take a little state upon her as requisite to her post"), her prayers in leisure moments and after Philaretus's proposal, and the calculated stratagem to secure double affection from him by revealing her parentage are crudely anticipatory of Pamela's actions and attitudes.

As Ian Watt says of *Pamela*, so, too, *Luck at Last* "bears everywhere the marks of its romance origin . . . but it is romance with a difference." The name of Richardson's heroine may have come from Sidney's *Arcadia*; "Sylvia" also has pastoral overtones and may even derive from Shakespeare's *Two Gentlemen of Verona* in which Silvia runs away to escape a rich and foolish suitor. The resemblance is strengthened by the dream-vision of Philaretus who sees his Sylvia revealed, to the accompaniment of music, as "holy, fair, and wise."

This romantic aspect is, however, balanced by a pervasive sense of realism. The enumeration of servants, the amounts of alms received, the value of the chaplain's living, the dowry proposed by Liberius, and the country entertainments for the wedding are significant. The coach-and-six and the entourage of "twelve servants in noble liveries on horseback" at first seem to be Cinderella touches, but they become real when placed beside the billiard table and the "bowling green just at hand." The author states that the lady Gratiana was modeled on Mrs. Judith Bray of Virginia, the recently deceased mother of his patron. And one wonders about the appearance of David Bray when Philaretus is described as being "something swarthy," an unusual attribute for a Prince Charming. If Blackamore's characterization is not always consistent or the action always probable, he had nevertheless hit on several devices for bringing realism to Mrs. Behn's short tale.

Other qualities of the novel were undoubtedly of contemporary interest. For example, there is the universal benevolence not only of the main characters but also of ale-drapers and brokers, farmers, passing gentlemen, village beldames, and the vividly portrayed band of gypsies. It may be argued that these jolly beggars are as old as the Robin Hood ballads and, to some extent, their main function is to provide comic relief and a mild touch of bawdy. However, Blackamore manages to make them real by circumstantial detail and by use of beggars' cant. His primary emphasis is not on their roguery but on their basic kindness and the literal and figurative harmony within their democratic community. Such sympathetic treatment faintly anticipates Fielding's gypsy band in *Tom Jones,* and even Partridge's escapade.

Equally significant are the moral and social implications of the main plot. The parent-child relationship is analyzed in Sylvia's soliloquies of self-justification, the Esom innkeeper's story, the portrait and reconciliation scenes, and in the final summation by the author himself. Similarly, the attention given to the Theophilus episode (a precursor of Mr. B——'s proposal that Mr. Williams marry Pamela?) brings out Blackamore's ideas on the fallacy of rigid class distinctions. The entire action takes place in rural settings and there is a hint of later sentimental endorsement of the country in Sylvia's decision not to go to London. Finally, the attempt to give a picture of conjugal felicity instead of ending the novel at the altar is fairly unusual at the time.

The fact that *Luck at Last* was reissued in 1737, on the eve of *Pamela,* shows the continued currency of Behn's and Blackamore's work. It also indicates that there was an audience for such relatively unsophisticated narratives. If we did not have Richardson's statement that the plot of his first novel was based on a story he had heard twenty years earlier, we might suspect that he had found it and many of his ideas closer at hand in fictional form.

The ironic title of *The Jamaica Lady* (1720) and the promise of "Intrigues, Cheats, Amours" invite the reader to think in terms of such picaresque narratives as *La Pícara Justina* (1603) and *La Garduña de Sevilla* (1634), which were popular in the early eighteenth century. Perhaps Bavia is a descendant of these Spanish female rogues, but the author has thoroughly naturalized her and he claims in the preface that she is an actual person, a statement which details in the novel seem to verify.

If *The Jamaica Lady* had some of the lure of the picaresque and of the popular key-novel, it gained even more by the use of colonial as well as English settings. Interest in the West Indian colony had been evident since Ned Ward's *Trip to Jamaica* appeared in 1698 and ran through eight editions by 1702. Possibly the novel is the work of William Pittis, a friend of Ward; at any rate, there are a number of interesting parallels. Aboard Ward's ship is a wife in pursuit of her husband who has married "a Tawny Fac'd *Moletto*, a Pumpkin colour'd Whore," much like the novelist's Holmesia. Similar, too, are the bad-tempered captains and the comic Irishmen. Bad weather at Deal in both works is attributed to "the Prince of the Air"; during both passages, parlor games are played; and tempests arise just after the passengers have, in Ward's account, "well moisten'd our Drouthy Carcasses with an Exhilerating Dose of Right Honourable Punch." Jamaica is described as the "Dunghill of the Universe," and the climate seems to be especially harmful to female character, for "A little Reputation among the *Women* goes a great way. . . . An *Impudent Air* being the only *Charms* of their *Countenance*, and a *Lewd Carriage*, the *Study'd Grace* of their *Deportment*." In short, Jamaica is a place where ladies like Bavia and Holmesia can "be *Wicked* without *Shame*, and *Whore* on without *Punishment*." This climatic theory of behavior was still current in 1771 when Richard Cumberland had Belcour, the warm-blooded hero of *The West Indian*, exclaim: "O my curst tropical constitution!"

If *Luck at Last* anticipates Richardson's novels, *The Jamaica Lady* brings to mind those of Smollett, particularly *Roderick Random*, in which the hero is a surgeon's mate on a third-rate man-of-war under Mackshane, an Irish surgeon, and the harsh Captain Oakum. Smollett's purpose was, of course, savage satire rather than a "pleasant relation," and he drew upon personal experience for his material. However, in *The Jamaica Lady* we may note the beginning of a stockpile of nautical types and situations with which life repeatedly supplied eighteenth-century English fiction.

To the modern student of the novel the real interest lies elsewhere. In the manner of the picaresque tale it is relatively formless—a simple succession of intrigues and cheats. This generic weakness is increased by the presence of two *picaras* with the resulting dangers of divided narrative focus and duplicated adventures. Half of the book consists of four interpolated narratives. However, these *récits* are not entirely extraneous as is often the case in Aleman, Scarron, and Le Sage. Three are concerned with the two female rogues and reveal considerable literary skill in their stylistic variations.

The false account of Bavia's life, given by her emissary, is in the highly romantic style typical of Mrs. Haywood's novels. In capsule form the narrator presents many fictional clichés—the unfaithful husband, the long-suffering wife, the lustful sea captain, the threat of the Grand Signior's seraglio, and the concealed jewel, together with such Haywoodian trademarks as the indignant aside ("Perfidious crocodile, to weep o'er the prey thou art just going to devour!"), the verbatim repetition of involved conversations, and the description of the heroine's swoon. The effect of this deliberate burlesque is heightened by the appearance of the fair Bavia in a guise so grotesque that Captain Fustian is startled into blessing himself.

The true story of Bavia's background and Jamaican intrigues is told by the surgeon's second mate in a contrasting manner, which is both clinical and pompous ("she had as great a carity of virtuous fundamentals, as she had of formosity"). Frutesius reprimands him for this, in much the same prose style. Holmesia's career is presented by Pharmaceuticus with neoclassical elegance, a style which contrasts with the sordidness of its details. The fourth story, the cuckoldom of Phlebotomus, is told in the stage Irish accent used by Farquhar's Foigard in *The Beaux' Stratagem.*

The novelist's outstanding achievement is the figure of Captain Fustian. In outline he is the stock sea dog, unpolished, opinionated, and alcoholic. However, he is particularized by his gullibility, his taste for luscious tales, his fondness for minuets, his humane opposition to the flogging of the slave, and his parental affection for "Compy-boy" which leads to the comic chase around the steerage-table. It is clear from an allusion to Bavia as an enchanted Dulcinea that the author was familiar with Cervantes. Captain Fustian is an early example of the lovable quixotic character soon to appear in Fielding's works and in Smollett's Lieutenant Tom Bowling and Commodore Trunnion. The caricature of Bavia also brings to mind the descriptive method of Smollett, as well as Fielding's Mrs. Slipslop.

The actual intrigues, cheats, and amours are not very clever, and interest flags after the ship arrives in the Downs. This latter part, however, does contain a number of details which anchor the adapted picaresque firmly to English soil. Two years later, *Moll Flanders* was to take "a country ramble" to various ports where, like Bavia, she visits "a house where we saw a good quantity of prohibited goods." In Moll's case, the cloth is black Dutch silk rather than East Indian chintz, but the result is much the same.

The author of *The Jamaica Lady* did not produce a *Moll Flanders,* perhaps because he was more interested in the comic and amorous aspects of his narrative. For other reasons, he did not rise to the level of Fielding or Smollett, though he occasionally approaches them in such scenes as Quomina catching Fustian's head in the door, the captain's fight with Bavia at Deal, the sailors' horse ambling into every alehouse with Holmesia, and the nocturnal confusion at the inn near Dartford. Amusing and masculine knock-about farce was clearly ready for more talented use.

Turning to *Philidore and Placentia; or, L'Amour trop Delicat* (1727), the modern reader is plunged into an apparently very different world, but it is a world familiar enough to Mrs. Eliza Haywood's female readers during the 1720's. Mrs. Haywood, born in 1693 and briefly married to the Reverend Valentine Haywood, from whom she eloped in 1721, came to the novel by way of the theater, following a pattern already well established by Mrs. Aphra Behn, Mrs. Mary Manley, and other ladies who had, in her phrase, exchanged "the Needle for the Quill." Her dramatic career was unsuccessful but in 1719 with *Love in Excess; or, The Fatal Enquiry: A Novel* she discovered as lucrative a fictional vein as Defoe had, earlier in the same year, with *Robinson Crusoe. Love in Excess* had six editions by 1725 and Mrs. Haywood's career was assured. Her industry and ingenuity were equal to the evident demand. Thirty-nine novels printed between 1719 and 1736 have been attributed to her, as well as eight translations from the French.

She soon became part of a literary circle which, although outside Pope's "circumference of wit," included Richard Savage, Aaron Hill, and Mrs. Susannah Centlivre. That she knew Defoe and perhaps collaborated with him is indicated by the tangled history of the Duncan Campbell pamphlets, and in 1724 she dedicated a novel to Sir Richard Steele. However, Pope soon blasted her growing reputation by making her the heroine of the *Dunciad*, the prize awarded to the infamous bookseller, Edmund Curll, after one of the more obscene contests which celebrate the coronation of the King of Dullness. The poet was perhaps justified, for her *Secret History of the Present Intrigues of the Court of Caramania* (1727) contained an audacious attack on Mrs. Henrietta Howard, his neighbor and friend. Mrs. Haywood had already ventured into the dangerous territory of the scandal chronicle with her *Memoirs of a Certain Island Adjacent to the Kingdom of Utopia* (1725), in imitation of Mrs. Manley's *New Atalantis*. She escaped her predecessor's imprisonment only to stand in the pillory of the *Dunciad*, an eminence which has become her one assured position in English literary history.

Mrs. Haywood survived the exposure and reappeared before the reading public in 1742 with a series of novels in the new manner of Richardson and Marivaux. She largely maintained this moralistic pose until her death in 1756 at the age of sixty-three, by which time she had published at least that many fictional works. The later period was probably a severe penance for the dashing authoress of the 1720's but it did win her, posthumously, the praise of Mrs. Clara Reeve in *The Progress of Romance* (1785) and, more recently, the title of "the chameleon of English novelists."

If Mrs. Haywood proved herself a chameleon in taking on a more sober hue after 1740, in her early and more important period the word "salamander" is more appropriate. The short novel of burning emotion was her chief stock in trade, and she was called the "Great Arbitress of Passion" who commands "the throbbing Breast, and wat'ry Eye." The same eulogizer declared that, after "Pathetic *Behn*, or *Manley*'s greater name," she "clos'd the fair Triumvirate of Wit."

There is considerable truth in this praise, for she was one of the last (and in the novel, the best) of the latter-day Restoration female rakes. However, neither Mrs. Behn nor Mrs. Manley is mentioned in her works. In *The Tea Table* (1723) she associates herself with Mlle de Scudéry, the celebrated author of *Le Grand Cyrus*; Jean Regnauld de Segrais, whose name was linked, literarily, with that of Mme de La Fayette; and the Comtesse d'Aulnoy, who had been Eliza's French counterpart. Her real inspiration came from these and other writers such as Mme de Villedieu, Mlle de la Roche-Guilhem, and Mme de Gomez.

In *Philidore and Placentia*, therefore, the reader finds sentiments from mid-seventeenth-century France mingled with ideas from the reign of George I. It deals with "Venus tout entière à sa proie attachée," but there is more than the consuming Racinian *amour-passion* or the *amour-galante*, which pervaded the *nouvelle*. Although Mrs. Haywood utilizes, and mocks, both of these traditions, her chief emphasis is upon the newer vogue of *amour-tendresse* currently being expounded in the Parisian salon of Mme de Lambert and to be noted, in England, in such works as Steele's *The Conscious Lovers* (1722). *Philidore and Placentia* is a novel about "most Enthusiastick adoration," but the adjective was not invariably a flattering one in the eighteenth century. As the subtitle makes clear, it is a novel of love carried to extremes, a theme which reached its epitome in Hugh Kelly's comedy, *False Delicacy* (1768).

In 1726 Mrs. Haywood had published a work entitled *Reflections on the Various Effects of Love,* which contained examples "Collected from the best Ancient and Modern Histories, intermix'd with the latest Amours." This book was probably in her mind when she began *Philidore and Placentia* the next year, for it presents three plots with several variations on the theme of love. First, there is the Philidore-Placentia version which is *amour-tendresse* in its most exalted form. Philidore's fantastic Platonism precipitates the dilemma but the real psychological focus, as in all of Mrs. Haywood's works, is the heroine and her agonies of self-division, which lead to the desperation of her attempt to seduce Philidore—a scene unique in eighteenth-century fiction in its motivation, though Lady Booby and Joseph Andrews come irresistibly to mind. When Philidore declares that he will obey Placentia "in all things which I can do without forfeiting that respect which it is not even in your power to banish from my soul," we sense the gasp of utter surprise and expect her to exclaim, with Fielding's lady: "Intolerable confidence! Have you the assurance to pretend that when a lady demeans herself to throw aside the rules of decency, in order to honour you with the highest favour in her power, your virtue should resist her inclination?" Instead, Placentia faints, and, however insincerely, Mrs. Haywood strikes a Richardsonian note.

"The History of the Christian Eunuch," which opens the second part of the novel, presents the second variation. Here the author returns to her more familiar material, to flaming passion, which is also piquantly carried to extremes. However, the Bellamont-Arithea affair repeats, in a more exotic setting and with a more sensational ending, the relationship of the title couple. Bellamont is literally and figuratively a slave and, once again, the woman is the aggressor. Noteworthy is the parallelism of Placentia's garden with "many fine little close arbors where one might lie and in the noon of day enjoy a midnight's shade," and

Arithea's baroque alcove where she enjoys, in negligee, "the benefit of the freshest of breezes at the noon of day." Even more revealing are the luscious scenes in Placentia's bedroom and the seraglio
chamber where Bellamont, too, is commanded to sit by the couch
where his "submissive passion" is encouraged.

Placentia's predictable encounter with the sea captain, like
that of Bavia in *The Jamaica Lady*, affords a third variation—
physical lust. After delays, threats of suicide with a penknife, and
various *trop délicat* arguments about the nature of true love, the
heroine is brought to a standstill. "We will hereafter," resumed
he, smiling, "dispute on the niceties of that passion. My present
business is the gratification of it, and you must strangely differ
from your sex if I hear you not, some time hence, confess that
the fury of my impatience is a more agreeable testimony of love
than that cowardly submission and resignation you seem to praise
at present." This is an ironic comment on Placentia's earlier experience with Philidore, and one hears the distant accents of
Lovelace. Fielding's Mrs. Heartfree in *Jonathan Wild* had also
read novels like *Philidore and Placentia*, even if Fielding pretended that he had not.

The final touch is the Tradewell-Emanthe affair, a bourgeois
version of upper-class devotion and the most *romanesque* of all.
The merchant's son has never spoken to the lady's maid, but,
finding her a fellow slave in Baravat ("a place where I so little
expected her"), he resolves to buy her freedom with his ransom
and remain in captivity himself. And Emanthe, who has no real
recollection of Tradewell, upon hearing his tale, immediately
"testified by her countenance that her heart would be no farther
than the modesty of her sex obliged reluctant to the impression
he wished to make." Her alacrity is both a relief and a telling
footnote to the false delicacy of her mistress.

Stripped of their romantic settings and high-flown language,
all three tales deal basically with supposed misalliances, but it is
disparity of fortune rather than of rank which separates Placentia and Emanthe from their lovers. The underlying mentality
is middle class, and the walnuts that stain the "native whiteness"

of Philidore grew on the same tree that provided Sylvia with her disguise in *Luck at Last*. The sybaritic rich uncle is a brief glimpse of the enterprising English merchant who was soon to reappear as the "little nabob" in Sheridan. In fact, Thomas "Diamond" Pitt died in 1726, the year before Philidore left the East for London with his newly acquired fortune.

Further evidence that Mrs. Haywood was aware of contemporary trends is her attempt to incorporate elements from the works of Defoe. Mrs. Penelope Aubin had already tried this unlikely fusion in several novels with gratifying success. Much of Philidore's story after he leaves England is obviously borrowed from Defoe—the seizure by pirates; the marooning on a desert coast with only a sword, a gun, and some biscuits; the encounter with natives who run away but return to provide food; the "furious tiger" and other wild beasts; the decimation by disease; and the hero's linguistic abilities are to be found in *Captain Singleton*. Less specific are the storms, shipwrecks, and Turkish captivity which occur in *Robinson Crusoe*, as well as Bellamont's desire to return to England to have "the free exercise of my religion," which parallels Crusoe's pious decision not to return to Roman Catholic Brazil. Defoe would also have approved of Mrs. Haywood's denunciation of the Grand Tour as "the common error of the age."

Such underlying realism is disguised by Mrs. Haywood's prose style. Highly wrought letters burning with love, jealousy, or despair were inserted in her novels upon the slightest provocation and here she offers five examples. The maxims, sprinkled over every page, were also a Haywood habit, and *précieuse* logic-chopping appears in passage after passage: "The truth is that he saw not that she loved him because he wished not she should do so. With so pure and disinterested a zeal did he worship this goddess of his soul that he desired not to inspire her with a passion which, as their circumstances were, could not but be uneasy to her."

Even more clear is the influence of the English heroic drama, which was still sufficiently popular in 1730 to merit Fielding's ridicule in *Tom Thumb.* "For what unknown crime am I thus punished? To be rejected, rejected by my slave!" exclaims Placentia. "But I'll retrieve my peace. I'll banish the deceiver, the imposter, the cursed destroyer of my peace and fame." Any collection of Restoration plays easily produces similar rant. Thus, Zempoalla, when rejected by Montezuma in *The Indian Queen*:

> What shall I do! Some way must yet be tried;
> What reasons can she use whom passions guide!
>
>   *   *   *
>
> Here, jailer, take—What title must he have?
> Slave, slave! Am I then captive to a slave?

At times Mrs. Haywood's prose rises almost to the level of concealed blank verse, as when Placentia assumes the manner royal and cries: "Search the whole kingdom; inquire of all you meet. Who brings him obtains my favor and an ample recompense! What, are you stupid, or deaf to my commands? Begone! Let me not see a soul of you remain behind." The author did not have to seek far to find a model for such effusions, since she had written a tragedy, *The Fair Captive*, in 1721, complete with grand visier, Janissaries, eunuchs and noble slaves.

Certainly she was capable of penning most luxurious rants, but she had also tried her hand at comedy with *A Wife to Be Let* (1723), in which she acted the title role. Beneath the heroics of *Philidore and Placentia* probably lurks more sly wit than she is usually given credit for. The description of Philidore stealing out to the coach-house to "embrace the cushions on which she sat, kissing the step on which she trod" is surely written with tongue in cheek. We need only recall Tom Jones and Sophia Western's muff. Placentia's reception of "Jacobin," lying "on a couch with a studied but most engaging carelessness," the result of spending "the best part of the day consulting what look and habit would become her best," is as old as Potiphar's wife. It was also as recent as Congreve's *The Way of the World* (1700) in which Lady Wishfort finally decides to receive "Sir Roland" lolling on the couch in her dressing room. Emanthe, too, would make a fine Foible in the same play. "There is no doubt, madam, but he may be found. Comfort yourself therefore, and depend on certain intelligence at my return."

The entire novel might have become a comedy of cross-purposes magnified to intercontinental dimensions as Placentia and Philidore set sail simultaneously for Persia and England to prove their suitable poverty and wealth. Mrs. Haywood must also have been aware that she could go on indefinitely, since Placentia, by her brother's gift *and* her advantage of birth is ultimately superior to the hero who, to be consistent, should once again flee to spare her any "uneasiness." However, the "Great Arbitress of Passion" had written the number of pages required by her publishers. "Thus was the mighty scruple over, and this fair lady's delicacy was no longer an enemy to her inclinations." We can imagine the smile with which she laid down her pen, pleased and amused at the variety of readers she would please and, perhaps, edify with her fictional reflections on the various effects of love.

If Mrs. Haywood owed much to the heroic drama, Mrs. Mary Davys shows an equally astute adaptation of the characters, situations, and tone of contemporary comedy. This indebtedness alone, however, does not explain the merits of *The Accomplished Rake* (1727), which stands out as one of the few mature English novels to appear between 1700 and 1739. Both her background and her reading public must be considered.

She was born in Dublin in 1674 and married the Reverend Peter Davys, headmaster of the school attached to St. Patrick's Cathedral and a friend of Swift. After his early death in 1698 the young widow went to England and lived in York for some years before she made her literary appearance in London in 1716 with a comedy, *The Northern Heiress; or, The Humours of York*. Its moderate success led her to write a second comedy which was never staged. She shrewdly decided to abandon literature as a major source of income and opened a coffeehouse in Cambridge.

The university atmosphere was congenial, since she was the widow of a schoolmaster and clergyman, a woman of literary

inclinations, and, to judge by her works, a person of hearty and
somewhat masculine temperament. This business venture, which
isolated her from the literary vogues of the capital, shares with
her dramatic apprenticeship the molding of her career as a novelist and probably saved her from the imitativeness and excesses of
the period. All of her works were published by subscription, a
procedure rarely used for fiction, and to judge by the list appended to *The Reform'd Coquet* (1724), her student-customers
were her financial mainstay. The list includes three duchesses
and the more interesting trio of John Gay, Martha Blount, and
Alexander Pope, but, from various remarks we may deduce that
the fashionable coffeehouse "loungers" and "both the grave and
the young clergy" paid tribute to her wit and her punch by sub-
scribing to her projects, making critical suggestions, and providing
material which she incorporated in her work.

As noted earlier, Mrs. Davys was unusual among her harried
fellow novelists for developing a coherent theory of novelistic
technique based upon the drama. She could not have chosen a
more fortunate model, for the theater provided her with the important elements that were missing from most early eighteenth-
century fiction—integration of main and subplots, characterization
through dialogue, clarity and conscious wit in prose style, and
division of the novel into clearly realized scenes.

By the time she wrote *The Accomplished Rake,* Mrs. Davys
had tried her hand at various literary forms—comedy, familiar
letters, a *nouvelle,* poetry, disguised autobiography, and two
novels, *The Lady's Tale* and *The Reform'd Coquet.* All of these
were included in her *Works* (1725). According to the author, *The
Reform'd Coquet* was planned in some detail before execution
and its resemblance to a five-act comedy, with some touches of
melodrama, is striking. *The Accomplished Rake* was evidently
conceived as a companion novel. Though less geometric in its
actual structure, it shows even more clearly and extensively her
dextrous blending of the concurrent strains of comedy of manners
and of sentiment.

Only Farquhar is alluded to directly, but the work, upon close inspection, is an intricate mosaic of borrowings. Sir John Galliard is based partly on Etherege's Dorimant in *The Man of Mode* and partly on the reformed rake made popular by Cibber's *Love's Last Shift*. The coxcomb, Sir Combish Clutter, derives from Etherege's Sir Fopling Flutter, and in the 1756 edition of the novel his name was changed to Sir Trifling Flutter. However, the idea of pairing him with the boorish Squire Clownish Cockahoop resembles the Witwoud-Petulant combination in Congreve's *The Way of the World*. Cockahoop's song is like that of the drunken Sir Wilfull Witwoud, while his willingness to strike Belinda had been seen on the stage in *Love's Last Shift* when Sir Novelty Fashion draws on Mrs. Flareit. The same play may have inspired Sir Combish's egotistical wooing of Belinda (Sir Novelty and Narcissa), as well as Betty Dimple's virago attack on her seducer. The Sparkish-Alithea-Harcourt triangle in Wycherley's *The Country Wife* is the source for several scenes involving Sir Combish, Belinda, and Galliard, while *The Plain Dealer* provided a precedent for the disguised lady, "Mr. Venture-all." Dolly Galliard is a faint copy of such country romps as Congreve's Miss Prue and Vanbrugh's Miss Hoyden. And in their opening interview Nancy Friendly and Galliard echo verbally a scene between Congreve's Millamant and Mirabell. Less identifiable adaptations may be noted in the resourceful valet, the garrulous maid, the bickering of cuckold and wife, the Mall scene, and the playhouse scene which was to become traditional in later eighteenth-century fiction.

The Beaux' Stratagem, which Mrs. Davys had imitated in her *Northern Heiress,* was unquestionably in her mind during the composition of the novel. Galliard's footman, Dick, is described as posting home "like Scrub in the *Stratagem* with a whole budget of news" and his carousing with the tapster at the Black Swan in Holborn is obviously indebted to Farquhar's scene between Archer and Scrub. If the banter on the Mall between Galliard and the prostitute about "trifles" is a coincidental echo of Archer's "purest ballad about a trifle," the coincidence is curious indeed. That Mrs. Davys should like Farquhar is not strange, for he, too, was a transitional writer, bridging the mannered immorality of the last age and the newer sentimentalism of Cibber and Steele.

Her announced purpose was the presentation of a full-length portrait of a "modern fine gentleman." Thus, with an aim similar to that of the *Spectator*, she embarked on a novel which is at once satiric, didactic, realistic, and humorous. If, as Walter Allen speculates, "Sir Roger and the others exist on the threshold of a novel that was never written," possibly the story of Sir John Galliard is the form it might have taken. At any rate, the periodical essay was one of the ingredients that went into Mrs. Davys' novel and some of its flaws result from her attempt to anatomize the four "characters" of men—the coxcomb, the fool, the knave, and the man of sense. This explains the apparently intrusive prominence of Sir Combish and Squire Clownish, the fop and the fool, while Sir John Galliard exemplifies the two latter types.

In some respects, her hero is a double silhouette rather than a fully developed character, but he does come alive, and not always in a pleasant way. Even after he finds "a sudden alteration in his breast," he remains more human than even modern readers may wish as he condescendingly admits his guilt and loftily reprimands the wronged Miss Friendly ("I would not have you give yourself airs"). Even the neglected heroine is nicely characterized, first, as the "young, brisk, airy" coquette and, after her disaster (under circumstances which Richardson did not disdain to use in *Clarissa*), as a properly resentful young woman who, nevertheless, agrees to marry her despoiler, if he will legitimatize their child. Mrs. Davys was too sensible to repeat the fawning forgiveness of Cibber's Amanda in *Love's Last Shift* or the sensational absurdity of Mrs. Haywood's *The Lucky Rape; or, Fate the Best Disposer*.

Structurally, the novel shows considerable skill. The main plot deals with "the struggles betwixt [innate good] nature and a loose education" in the hero, a conflict which leads to the rape and then to reformation. Four secondary stories are interwoven—the affair of Lady Galliard with Tom, the footman-steward; Galliard's affair with the lady disguised as a beau; his attempted seduction of Belinda; and the exposure of Sir Combish's villainy by Betty.

Each of these subplots might have been developed into an independent novel, particularly the one involving Lady Galliard, Tom, Tom's wife, and Dolly. Beginning with seduction in a country manor house; proceeding through mysterious departures, discoveries by dark lantern, overheard conversations, forebodings and dreams, death by poison; and ending in revenge-rape of the daughter in a London brothel, it has all the elements of a very lurid Gothic novel. Nor is the Betty–William–Sir Combish triangle without interest, especially in its sympathetic view of the servant class, though Mrs. Davys chooses to call it a tragicomedy and has the betrayed country girl rave in mock-heroic style.

However, each subplot is linked not only to the general picture of low conduct in high life but also to the development of her hero's character. Lady Galliard's affair turns her son, after a scene of Hamletesque revulsion, into the path of debauchery. Tom, her reluctant partner, is a young man who has squandered his patrimony (a monitory counterpart of young Galliard), and his attempted revenge for his wife's death involves both Dolly and Sir John. The affair with "Mr. Venture-all," the lady in search of an heir, seems little more than an opportunity for a passage or two of *double-entendre* but, ironically, the illness of her child by Sir John puts Belinda in his coach and clutches. The Belinda episode reaches its climax with her denunciation of the hero as the base-born spawn of a footman. This remark seems so likely, in view of the Lady Galliard–Tom relationship, that he realizes the extent of his dishonor. And Betty's story of her loss of virtue through the wiles of a noble seducer parallels Miss Friendly's misfortune and causes Sir John "inward qualms" which, in combination with Belinda's remark, make his return to Miss Friendly more plausible than the usual fifth-act Cibberian *volte-face*. Even the minor episodes in which Sir John is set on fire by crackers and more seriously "burned" by Bousie's prostitute serve to turn his thoughts toward Galliard Hall and Nancy. It must be admitted, however, that the second half of the novel is padded to allow time for "the little macaroon" to be born and grow into the epitome of Sir John.

Mrs. Davys states on her first page that she will record nothing but plain fact in the fundamental part of her story, and the facts are amazingly plain. Her account of a rake's progress is much more vivid and plausible than the hot-house adulteries of the scandal chronicles. Despite her use of type-names and her didactic intrusions, the main characters are fairly complex and credible. With few exceptions (such as the anecdote of the whore devouring the rumps of roasted fowls, which is probably jestbook or university humor), the episodes are plausible and tied to reality by references to familiar London landmarks.

Also noteworthy is her prose style, which largely succeeds in breaking away from the stilted and impersonal prose which had been dominant since the days of the heroic romance. Many passages catch the accents of fashionable conversation and, if Mrs. Davys lacked the ability of Congreve, at least she had the will to be witty rather than merely sensational. The novel opens with an announcement of firm artistic control: "Young Galliard, who is to be the subject of the following leaves, will (with his own inclination, and a little of my additional discipline) be a very exact copy of the title page." Thus the author as conscious artist enters the novel the first time before Fielding. It is the "additional discipline" that elevates a familiar tale of rape and repentance above its analogues. At the same time it reveals a personality much like that of Fielding, for Mrs. Davys was evidently well read; sturdily perceptive of reality, which she chose to regard as comic rather than tragic; indulgent of human weaknesses, and yet convinced of the truth of religion and of man's innate goodness.

The Accomplished Rake was her last novel. She died in 1731, as did Defoe, the master, in another manner, of the new literary form. Swift called Mrs. Davys "a rambling woman with very little taste in wit or humor," but his remark, like Pope's attack on Mrs. Haywood, was based on pique rather than a just estimate of her work. *The Dictionary of National Biography* states erroneously that Mrs. Davys flourished about 1756, the date of the second edition of *The Accomplished Rake*—and the date of Mrs. Haywood's death. If she had lived until then, Mrs. Davys would surely have surpassed her fellow novelist. The concealment of Sir John in the closet, the drugged rape, and the abduction from the masquerade reappear as key episodes in the three novels of Richardson, and she was one of the first writers before Fielding to exploit extensively the English scene. A "rambling woman" she may, of necessity, have been, but with her "little taste" she brought a measure of commonsense and humor to the novel which had been largely dominated by sensationalism and extravagance.

LUCK AT LAST

OR

The Happy Unfortunate

Nil Desperandum.————Hor.
————*sunt hic etiam sua Praemia Laudi.*   Virg.
Post Nubila Phoebus.

LONDON

*Printed for H. Parker, and Sold by T Warner, at the
Black-Boy, in Pater-Noster-Row   1723.*

NOTES TO TITLE PAGE

In 1737 the same sheets were reissued by Thomas Cooper with a new title page as *The Distress'd Fair, or Happy Unfortunate: Being a Secret History of the Transactions of a certain Lady, Who privately withdrew from her Friends: Whose being reduced from one of the most flourishing Stations of Life to the lowest ebbs of Fortune, and the inconceivable manner of her being extricated therefrom, afford many extraordinary Incidents and surprising Events; as also, several useful and sublime Reflections.* In this edition, the dedication is omitted and the address "To the Reader" is shortened. The story is said to have been recounted to the author by a confidante of the heroine.

The first two Latin tags are from Horace, *Odes*, I, 7, 27 ("Never despair") and Virgil, *Aeneid*, I, 460 ("Here too is the meed of honor"). The third ("sunshine after clouds") may be proverbial or a coinage of the author.

Between 1713 and 1732, Thomas Warner was connected with the publication of at least fifteen pieces of prose fiction, including three works by Defoe. I have found no other mention of H. Parker as a printer of fictional pieces.

Dedication

To the ingenious Mr. David Bray, Merchant, of Virginia.[1]

Sir: That I give you title of "ingenious," I hope can be no offense, since all that know you must allow that title to be your due. You have formerly known me better than to imagine I would write this out of flattery, after the common method of most modern dedicators. For had my talent lain that way, I had probably fared more successfully in some particular affairs when I was in America. What Juvenal, the famous satirist, says upon another occasion, *Librum si malus est nequeo laudare*,[2] I think (pardon the vanity, if it be such) I may with some reason, and a very little alteration, apply to myself: *Virum si malus est*, &c. And this joined with your own experience of me, I am almost persuaded will induce you to believe this dedication designed for truth and not for compliment.

Several years are now passed, since I had the honor to be first acquainted with your worthy parents and, by consequence, to have some familiarity with yourself, being then a minor, the growing and only hopes of their family, and living more directly under their roof. I need not recount to you the effect of that acquaintance, nor how a closer correspondence was cultivated between yourself and me as you grew up. I am confident it is so fixed in your memory as not easily to be forgotten. I do not hint this as an argument of merit, but only as a motive to induce you to a favorable acceptance of the following sheets.

'Tis true the contents of these papers are nothing else but a novel; yet give me leave to remind you of the poet's expression

[1] David Bray (1699–1731), the only child of David and Judith Bray, was born in James City County, Virginia, and buried in Williamsburg. His father and grandfather had been prominent in local civic activities as justices, sheriffs, and vestrymen, and he was appointed to the Council at Williamsburg shortly before his death. Apparently he had been one of the author's pupils at the Grammar School, or perhaps he had been privately tutored by him.

[2] Juvenal, *Satires*, 3, 41 ("A book, if bad, I cannot praise").

that *Inest sua gratia parvis*.[3] And a simple nosegay from a poor peasant presented to his rich patron has frequently been recompensed with abundance more than an equivalent.

Besides, though it is only a novel I present you with, a novel may certainly have its peculiar use and virtue. Especially, while it is innocent in self, modest in its expression, interspersed with good morality, and directed to the promotion of goodness. If I understand the nature of novels aright, the design of them in general is much the same with that of poetry—to profit and delight the reader. Though whether this piece has hit the mark and attained the end was proposed by it, I must leave to your judgment. I am sure the design was laid upon no sinister view, and if there has been any failure in the prosecution of it, my fortune has been like that of Phaeton, to fall in an attempt that was above my strength.

But however this performance may appear in general, I flatter myself there is one particular character in it will not be displeasing to you; I mean that of the Lady Gratiana, because it so nearly resembles your late excellent mother in her parental care and Christian generosity that I think you can hardly read it without recollecting the alacrity and cheerfulness with which she used to supply the wants of her necessitous, sick, or distempered neighbors. I myself have known the time when she trod those paths and am sensible that if she did not outstrip Gratiana, it was wholly owing to the want of opportunity.

But not to revive too much in your memory the loss of so dear a parent, give me leave to commit the *Happy Unfortunate* into your hands. And if you shall be pleased to give it a perusal at your leisure hours and a candid admission into your study, at least for the sake of its author, you will oblige, sir,

Your most obedient, humble servant.

A. B.[4]

Vauxhall, Nov.
17th, 1722.

³ "Little people have their own charms." This quotation is probably proverbial, as is the following remark about the peasant's simple nosegay (which was also used by Christopher Smart in *Jubilate Agno*, line 510).

⁴ Arthur Blackamore, Master of the Grammar School of the College of William and Mary in Virginia until his removal in 1717 for repeated and "scandalous acts of drunkenness." A letter from the Reverend James Blair, then head of the college, to the Bishop of London gives a wryly sympathetic account of Blackamore's "endeavors of amendment" and inevitable relapses (see *William and Mary Quarterly*, XIX [1939], 372–375). He is probably the same Arthur Blackamore who was a matriculant in Christ Church, Oxford, on May 7, 1695, aged sixteen (Joseph Foster, *Alumni Oxoniensis, 1500–1714*, I, 132). Whatever his evident defects as an English prose stylist, he was certainly a Latinist of some ability, for he gained considerable local reputation by his poem, *Expeditio Ultramontana,* which celebrated Governor Spotswood's exploratory trip into the Appalachians in 1716 (*William and Mary Quarterly*, VII [1898–1899], 32–37). His first fictional work, *The Perfidious Brethren, or, the Religious Triumvirate: Displayed in Three Ecclesiastical Novels . . .* , was dedicated to Governor Spotswood from London in 1720. *Luck at Last* seems to have been his only other novel. He planned, upon leaving Virginia, to take orders and possibly his picture of the Hertfordshire chaplain, Theophilus, is evidence of his reformation; the dedication of the novel from Vauxhall in 1722 is, however, not very encouraging. I am greatly indebted to Mr. Edward M. Riley, Director of Research for Colonial Williamsburg, for most of this information.

To the Reader

To apologize to the world for a book I think wants no apology I have ever esteemed both foolish and unnecessary. 'Tis foolish, because no manner of reason can be given for it; and it is unnecessary, because the world needs not to be courted to what they will be pleased to like. I am not so vain as to think the whole world will approve the following performance. But I own myself (with the ape in the fable, who thought her brood the handsomest) to have some liking for this piece. And for that reason I am apt to persuade myself there are some of my fellow animals which may have the same taste. Various are the reasons which induce me to this belief. But among the many, take this one. I find several of my acquaintance like the same meats, drinks, and recreations which I do; and, I pray, why not the same books? I am sure the printers and booksellers would have but a sorry trade on't at that rate, if they did not. And authors would quickly be in a starving condition, though 'tis not much better with them as it is. The T–lands, A–gils, and W—tons[1] have found their several patrons, and why may not Sylvia? The impressions of those writers would have gone off but very slowly, and their poison would have been less diffused, had none approved their principles but themselves. But they had their accomplices to propagate their books; and perhaps I may find two or three acquaintances will be as zealous to encourage mine. Which, if they do, I shall not doubt a good account from the publisher. Two or three staunch friends are a sufficient stock for an author to set out with, and if they but cry him up lustily, ten thousand to one, like a snowball, they gather plentifully in the running.

But, however, lest perchance the following sheets should want some introducer, because in this stage of life our hopes are often frustrated, it may be necessary to give the reader some account of what he is to expect.

[1] John Toland (1670–1722), John Asgill (1659–1738), and Thomas Woolston (1670–1733) were well-known writers and free-thinkers.

The subject of the following pages was a lady of good birth and parentage, young, beautiful, and virtuous, but unhappy in the too-great severity of her father, which occasioned almost infinite troubles, both to herself and parents. This caused her to leave her father's house and betake herself to the life of a vagabond, till Fortune, kinder than her father, threw her into a considerable family, in which she so well behaved that from the meanest service she was, by degrees, advanced to the highest employment in her master's house. And being by this time become a companion to her mistress, her virtuous attractions so much enamoured a young gentleman of rare endowments, besides a vast over-grown estate, in the country where she lived, that he thought her a match deserving of himself, and accordingly married her, even before she had made any discovery of her parents.

I have put this history with all its various circumstances, as I heard them, into the clearest light and language which I could, and with this only view, *viz.*, to show that, however unfortunate some persons may be in the affairs of life, the utmost exigencies can be no sufficient arguments for despondency. For that a sudden turn may be, and an unforeseen Providence may so direct all things, that the worst of evils may become our greatest good.

If the reader likes the performance and it has any effect towards the end I proposed in it, I am satisfied. But if it fails of success, meets with dislike and the frowns of the many, let 'em know I designed it well, as a motive to patience and all other virtues from the encouragement they met with in the person of Sylvia. And thus, reader, farewell.

Luck at Last; or, The Happy Unfortunate

Since the beginning of this present century, near the pleasant vale of Esom[1] in the rich and fruitful county of Worcester lived one Sosander,[2] a gentleman by birth and education and of a plentiful estate. As his fortune had set him above the major part of mankind, so having sufficient time and opportunity, he strove to exceed them all in the rarer gifts and accomplishments of his mind. Though in his housekeeping and common method of living he was esteemed near and frugal, yet his hand was very diffusive. And if his table was narrow and confined at home, he had a large and expensive family abroad that were all maintained, or at least put in a way to maintain themselves, by his liberality. Having but one child in the world which he could call his own, and that a daughter, to inherit his estate, his poorer neighbors

---

[1] Evesham, fifteen miles southeast of Worcester. The region is still a famous fruit-growing district. In Mrs. Behn's *The Wandering Beauty* the heroine is said variously to be from Cornwall and Somersetshire. She is Arabella, eldest daughter of Sir Francis Fairname, and is wooed by Sir Robert Richland, who is approaching his "Climacterical Year." Her mother urges the match and Arabella feigns acquiescence. She runs away, exchanges clothing with a country wench, takes the name of Peregrina Goodhouse, and ultimately finds refuge with the family of Sir Christian Kindly, whose infant daughter she cures of an eye disease. She is made gentlewoman to an older daughter, Eleanora; is wooed by a chaplain, Prayfast, and rejected when he learns of her supposed origin; and marries Sir Lucius Lovewell, a neighboring gentleman who is attracted by her beauty and virtue. After the wedding she asks to visit her "humble" parents and contrives to have Sir Lucius meet Sir Francis and her mother. A reconciliation is speedily effected. Her father gives her a substantial dowry, and she learns that her aged suitor died, by nice coincidence, on the day of her marriage. All return to Sir Lucius's estate, arriving on the eve of the wedding of Eleanora Kindly. See *The Works of Aphra Behn*, ed. Montague Summers (London: William Heinemann, 1915), V, 447–468.

[2] As a teacher and classicist, Blackamore has altered Mrs. Behn's type-names with particular aptness: Sosander—helper of men; Gratiana—charming; Stertorius—snorer; Liberius—liberator; Angelica—heavenly; Theophilus—lover of God; Philaretus—lover of virtue. Both Sylvia and Chloe have pastoral connotations, and Canidia, the artful gypsy, is named in Horace, *Satires*, I, 8, 23 ff.

[9]

were as children to him and he took as much delight in providing for their good as in any other enjoyment whatsoever.

As Sosander was thus happy in himself, so was he also in the excellent qualities and equal disposition of his lady Gratiana (for that was her name), and she was a gentlewoman of uncommon excellencies of admirable sense, great skill in physic, strict virtue, and extensive charity like her husband, though she showed it in a different manner. For, as he took care to employ and encourage those that were well and would labor, so she made it her business to inquire out and look after those that were sick and could do nothing for themselves. For such, her closet was the common magazine, and one particular apartment near her house, allotted for that purpose, was almost a continual hospital. There she heard the griefs of such as came to her for advice; there she saw their wounds dressed, and administered to them according to their necessities.

After this manner, in a continued course of doing good, Sosander and Gratiana had lived for several years and were pretty well advanced in age when their daughter, Sylvia, arrived at her seventeenth year. Sylvia having been educated under such incomparable parents and having such bright examples always before her, it was no wonder if she trod in their steps, but especially her mother's. The force of example was nowhere more conspicuous than in this young lady, insomuch that she was now become the growing hopes and darling of the country round about. Under the direction of Gratiana she had so improved herself in the knowledge of physic and surgery that Sylvia could perform as well in the absence of Gratiana and very frequently did, with the same alacrity and cheerfulness. To these gifts of a happy disposition which were very evident in this young lady, Nature had been extremely liberal, having bestowed upon her body a beauty comparative, for I dare not venture to say equal, to that of her soul.

The fame of this, joined to that of her father's estate and the prospect she had in reversion, drew several young gentlemen to her father's seat to try their fortune in the way of courtship. Among the rest of Sylvia's admirers was one old gentleman who was not much short of his grand climacteric, being turned of sixty,[3] but of a vast estate and an intimate of Sosander's, that was enamoured with her. This senior, instead of Sylvia, made his addresses to her father. And could parents fetter the affections of their children as they can their persons, perhaps he had taken the right course. But as natural inclination cannot be forced to truckle to anything it has an aversion for, he did but beat the wind and raise a tempest to the detriment of Sylvia and no advantage to himself.

However, Sosander liked the notion—upon what view it is uncertain though 'tis probable upon the account of his great riches—and Stertorius, for that was his name, obtained a promise from him that he would lay his commands upon her if she should prove refractory. 'Twas strange, considering Sosander's sense and the little value he set upon riches himself, that he should make such a promise, and that he should persist in it, considering Sylvia's youth and the hoary head of Stertorius, is quite amazing. But, certain it is, he did persist, though it proved the greatest blemish of his life and what occasioned him a dear repentance with a long continued series of disquiet, both to himself and, till then, his most happy lady Gratiana, who all along dissuaded him from encouraging so unequal a match.

Stertorius, having full liberty of bed and board at Sosander's, omitted no opportunity of laying close siege to Sylvia, while she, poor creature, did all she could to avoid him. Though she respected him as a gentleman and an acquaintance of her father's, she could not endure him as a sweetheart. There is a kind of antipathy between youth and age, and the latter can never be made agreeable to the former for the sake of itself.

[3] A climacteric was supposed to be a critical stage in life, especially liable to a change in health or fortune. According to the *Shorter Oxford English Dictionary*, some held that all years denoted by multiples of 7 were climacterics, others only the odd multiples of 7, and some included the multiples of 9. All agreed, however, that "the grand climacteric," the sixty-third year (7×9), was especially critical. In Mrs. Behn's novel it is fatal to the heroine's unwelcome suitor.

It would have put a Stoic into a fit of laughter to see how the amorous Stertorius behaved under these circumstances, how he aped youth and strove to appear as gay and airy as a young man of twenty. His passion for Sylvia had inspired him with a sort of activity, though it was very awkward and against nature, and he continually haunted her like an evil genius, pursuing her from place to place but to no more purpose than if he had sat still. She was deaf to all his persuasions and proof against all his attacks. She looked upon him with abhorrence and like a death's-head, fitter for his grave or to be made a scarecrow than the embraces of a young lady. Notwithstanding, he still prosecuted her, and indeed it was a severe prosecution she underwent till she found herself obliged to treat him with a great deal of roughness before he would desist.

"Stertorius," said she, "I know not what you mean to be thus troublesome and interrupt my quiet, since all your endeavors shall be in vain. Can you imagine I will bury myself alive, or choose a bed of ice to lie on? 'Tis a contradiction to think I will, or throw myself into the embraces of the man I hate. I tell you, Stertorius, you may set your heart at ease. I will not love you and, though my father should approve, you never shall have my consent. This, if you please, I will give you under my hand, provided you can read it without spectacles. Fie, fie, Stertorius, go think of something else. You have other business of greatest moment. Mind that, for the sexton has got the rope in his hand and stands prepared to ring your passing-bell."

Having said this, away she went out of the room, leaving Stertorius in the utmost confusion, till having recovered himself, though horribly affronted, he went to find out Sosander, who was at that time walking in his garden, and related to him what scurvy treatment he had found from Sylvia. Sosander was extremely angry at the disappointment of Stertorius and the affront [that] had been put upon him, but promised soon to curb her insolence and bring her to a better temper. Stertorius being a little pacified, Sosander desired him to withdraw out of the garden, while he called for Sylvia and gave her a paternal lesson.

Stertorius was departed when Sosander, ringing a bill for one of his servants, commanded Sylvia to be called to him, and she came as soon as called, though her mind anticipated the meaning of it. At her approach Sosander, with a stern countenance and in a haughty commanding tone, thus began. "Mistress," said he, "what's the meaning I am thus opposed by you? Is this your obedience? Is this the reward of all my care?"

"My dearest father," replied Sylvia, "I am not sensible of my offense."

"No," said Sosander, "nor you are not sensible how you have maltreated Stertorius, but I will make you ask his pardon for it. I'll warrant you have got some young rake in your eye that will spend all I can give you and bring you to beggary. You want such a husband, madam, do you? I think I am something older than you, and should know better what is fitting for you. I tell you I am your father and I have pitched upon Stertorius for your husband. Him you shall have and none other. This is my resolution and I command your obedience."

At these expressions of her father, Sylvia was drowned in tears and, falling at his feet, besought him that he would hear her, but all in vain. He was obstinate in what he had resolved and deaf to all her entreaties. Though he had never found Sylvia to oppose his will or disobey him in anything before and though this was beyond what parents ought to do, to command their children's affections in a matter of such consequence, yet being quite bewitched with the dazzling grandeur of Stertorius and the benefit his daughter might reap by marrying him, though at the expense of her contentment, he resolved to make her passive in this, as she had used to be in all other things. And as she continued still upon her knees, he left her, only saying these words before he went: "I command you henceforward to encourage Stertorius and to love him. Have him you shall, whether you will or no; and therefore prepare yourself for his embraces on this day seven-night."

These last words of her father and his abrupt leaving her had almost cast Sylvia into a swoon. Certain it is, they were more cutting than any could be said and had thrown her into despair if she had not been a person of more than ordinary sense. As it was, they put her into such an agony that she could not forbear the following expressions. "Is it possible that any young creature can be so unhappy as I am? That my father, who is good to all mankind besides, should be his daughter's enemy? Is this an action of humanity? Is this the duty of a father? He has brought me up, 'tis true, and for that I owe him duty. But duty does not oblige to impossibilities. I cannot love Stertorius, and ought my parent to constrain me to it? I have an aversion to him, and there's no uniting of antipathies. But my father will have it so. They must be united in him and me. Alas! Unhappy Sylvia! You must cast yourself into the hated embraces of an old lecher or disobey your father. 'Tis a hard dilemma. O Heavens, what shall I do? Are we not all born free? Have we not the liberty of bestowing our affections where we please? And am I alone excepted? Must I bestow them where I would not? Will it be disobedience if I fly for it? It can't. No parent ought to be so cruel. This is to provoke their children and since 'tis so, I'll leave 'em. I had rather they should never see me more than see me in the arms of old Stertorius."

Just as she spoke these words, Stertorius entered the garden and, seeing Sylvia there, he went up to her and would have renewed his addresses to her, but she desired him to excuse her at that time, being very much indisposed, assuring him, to cover her design the better, that she would wait upon him and hear his proposals at a more convenient season when she should be well. This answer made Stertorius begin to think what her father had said to her might have taken effect and, begging pardon for interrupting her in her retirement, he turned down another walk, while she went directly to her chamber.

Being there by herself, for there was no person in the whole house whom she durst entrust with a secret, she considered what she had best to do. Whether to confine herself under pretense of indisposition or, by appearing, expose herself to the importunate addresses of Stertorius was a matter of some doubt. Upon mature consideration, the latter seemed best—to appear and run the risk of Stertorius rather than, by being sullen, give them any occasion for suspicion of design in her.

About three or four hours had now passed when she came in play again and Stertorius was presently at the old trade. Sylvia, certainly knowing that her father had promised her to Stertorius, upon the next attack resolved to capitulate rather than undergo the fatigue of a siege till she had gotten all things in readiness for her escape. Accordingly, that evening Stertorius fairly putting the question to her, she answered that she should submit herself to her father's pleasure and that his consent was hers. Upon this Stertorius, already secure of Sosander, took it for granted that she consented and, embracing her in his loathed arms, he gave her several kisses, though each of them was one more than she desired or approved.

And now Stertorius was to wait upon Sosander and to communicate to him what had passed when, having begged pardon of Sylvia for leaving her, he departed with free permission. Sosander was very much pleased at the news Stertorius had brought him and the obedience, as he esteemed it, of his daughter. And between 'em they agreed on the day for the wedding, appointing it the same Sosander had set to Sylvia in the garden.

The trouble of courtship being now happily over with Stertorius, as he thought, nothing remained but to prepare for the wedding. And because preparation was to be made at Stertorius's seat, as well as at Sosander's, he resolved to return home the next morning. This he communicated first to Sosander and afterwards to Sylvia, making a thousand excuses to her for his absence at that time, which he needed not to have done had he been acquainted with Sylvia's design a little better.

When Sylvia heard his resolution she inwardly wished the night were over, and, though she permitted her delicate body and charming lips to be hugged and kissed by him with a seeming willingness and as an earnest of what was to come, she wished him gone ten thousand times and at the farthest Indies rather than in her sight. The morning being come and breakfast over, Stertorius's coach was brought to the gate. Then, taking his leave of them all, but especially Sylvia, and promising to return in three or four days, he mounted and drove away, leaving Sosander extremely pleased at the conclusion they had made and Sylvia alike glad at the absence of Stertorius.

Soon after the departure of Stertorius, Sosander and his good lady Gratiana, that had never yielded to this match but in compliance to her husband's resolution, began to consider what preparations were necessary upon this occasion. And having determined that, they allotted each to the other their proper province. He was to take care to provide for the entertainment, while she was employed in equipping her daughter in the most agreeable manner that was possible, suitable to their own character and the quality of the person to whom she was espoused.

Accordingly, Gratiana was wholly taken up in setting her house in order and preparing of wedding clothes for Sylvia, while Sylvia thought of nothing more than an escape and was contriving a set of rags to escape in undiscovered. Her mother was not more busily concerned to fit her for her nuptials than she herself was for a contrary design. While her parents thought to fix her, she, like mercury at the approach of fire, was resolved to fly and expose herself rather to a merciless world than the embraces of Stertorius.

But to endeavor her flight in a garb that was anything tolerable was a method not proper for her to follow, lest that some feature of Sylvia might be discovered as she passed and entirely destroy her project. A deeper disguise was therefore needful and beggar's weeds, by her, were thought the proper. But to procure them it required some time and was a matter of no small difficulty.

In a treacherous world where three cannot keep counsel but when two are away, she thought it not convenient to entrust anyone with her design or to employ any other confidante to procure her what she wanted. The management of the whole lying thus upon herself, she made it her business privately to gather up all the rags she could find about the house and convey them into her chamber, where she sat up several nights after the family was gone to bed and patched them together in the likeness of a cloak to cover what other tatters she could scrape together and facilitate her escape.

While she was thus at work and contriving to get off, Stertorius returned, according to his promise, and stayed there till the very morning before they were to be married, to the great disappointment and dissatisfaction of Sylvia, who had got nothing ready as yet but that cloak, a few old dirty head-cloths, a straw hat, and a staff to walk with upon occasion or help her to counterfeit the cripple.

The stay Stertorius made was very uneasy to Sylvia, and she often wished him anywhere rather than near her. At last, having seen the forwardness all things were in, after many endearing expressions of his affection to Sylvia and some returns from her, he returned home, in order to come again the next morning for the consummation of the nuptials.

But Sylvia was resolved to disappoint him in his expectations, if possible, by the help of what disguise she had got together, since she could procure no more. Accordingly, when it was dark, and while the whole family was employed in getting ready for the solemnity of the next day, she took an opportunity to convey her masquerade dress privately from her chamber to a summer house at the lower end of the garden, from whence she might make her escape while the rest were asleep, by means of a back door.

And here Fortune seemed to favor her design and oppose the happiness of Stertorius. Her father, mother, and the whole family had been very much fatigued with the business of the day, and being got to bed, they slept soundly. Sylvia was the only waking person in the whole house and it was her business to be so, if she designed to be successful in her enterprise.

The clock had now struck one, when Sylvia prepared for her march and, putting on the worst clothes she had and an old cast-off nightgown over them, she stole out of her chamber (which she locked and put the keys in her pocket) so quietly that she was heard by none, till she came to the parlor door that led to the garden. But here she had like to have discovered her design by an unlucky accident. As she was taking down the bar, not being used to such work, it chanced to fall and had certainly alarmed the family but that she continued without motion for a while, excepting what proceeded from her frequent sighs for fear of a disappointment.

After some time, finding all quiet, she ventured to open the door without the least noise, and gently pulling it after her, she crept so softly down to the summer house that she was not descried of any. Being got so far, she quickly rigged herself in her new-fashioned dress, daubing her face with some walnut leaves she had prepared for that purpose, and out she went. But what a figure did she then make! The lovely complexion of her face and hands was changed into a dingy yellow; her head was muffled up with dirty clouts; and her shoulders, that deserved the richest attire, were garnished with a heap of rags. With her staff in her hand, she looked like a pilgrim, which indeed she was; and her straw hat supplied two offices: of a mask and an umbrella.

It was now about half an hour past two, when she left the garden, locking the door after her and throwing the key over the wall. Her fear had now given her wings, insomuch that she dispatched a great deal of ground in a little time and was got a vast way from home, quite out of her knowledge, before sunrise which, at that time of year, was about five.

About an hour after she came to a little village which, upon inquiry, she found to be ten miles good from her father's. However, though she was much tired, she made no stay there. Though she could willingly have rested herself, she was afraid to call at any house lest, perchance, she might happen on some person that had been a patient to her mother and might possibly discover her. By this time her tender feet, not being used to such journeys, were so galled she was forced to make use of her staff to hobble along the road.

Having left the village a mile or two behind, she was suddenly alarmed at the noise of horses and a coach approaching and, finding 'em to come towards her, she stopped to observe 'em, little thinking who was so near her. Seeing a numerous retinue both before and after, in very rich liveries, her curiosity prompted her to look into the coach, when, to her great surprise, she beheld Stertorius, set out in the most splendid manner and big with the expectation of the treasure he was that night to be put in possession of. Sylvia saw him and 'twas enough. She bid him farewell in her own thought and wished herself better fortune than to see him again.

Sosander and his lady Gratiana both rose very early that morning to give the finishing orders and settle all things for the reception of Stertorius. About seven, Gratiana, thinking that Sylvia had overslept herself, sent a maid to call her but no Sylvia answered. When this was told to Gratiana, she went herself and, having knocked several times without any answer, she began to suspect the worst, that Sylvia might have died suddenly or something like it, but she did not imagine that she had made her escape. Upon this, having inquired for the key and heard nothing of it, she ordered the door to be broken open. There was the nest, but Sylvia was gone. And here, what a confusion was she in! She knew not what to think or what to do. The whole family was quickly alarmed and the ungrateful news immediately flew to Sosander, who was no less surprised at it than his lady Gratiana. However, while she yet continued in Sylvia's chamber, where she had thrown herself upon the bed in a most disconsolate condition, Sosander entered the room and, finding what he had heard to be true, he endeavored to comfort Gratiana.

Then she, that had never been known to say anything to her husband disrespectfully before, began to upbraid him. "O cruel man," said she, "this is your doing. You have undone me; you have bereaved me of my child and brought an eternal scandal upon us." These words of Gratiana so enraged Sosander that he vowed he would spare no cost to find out Sylvia and make her know he was her father and, leaving Gratiana where he found her, he departed to give such necessary orders as might reach her before she was gone too far.

By this time Stertorius was arrived at Sosander's, and several

other gentlemen from different quarters to be present at the marriage. They were all amazed at the sudden disappointment, but
Stertorius (as it is the usual effect of an excessive grief) was struck
perfectly dumb. He appeared among them like a statue and was
hardly seen so much as to move.

While Sosander ordered all his servants out in search of Sylvia
and to make diligent inquiry after her throughout the neighborhood, some of the gentlemen, that had their horses ready,
offered their service to ride further and find her, if it was possible.
This accident had dismally changed the face of affairs in Sosander's family. The house that, a few hours before, was designed for
a place of mirth and jollity was suddenly turned into the seat of
melancholy and the mansion of mourning.

During the time of this confusion at her father's, Sylvia
trudged along as well as she could, never out of her way, because
she knew not where to go, neither did she care as long as she
went not homewards. She resolved to go where Fortune should
direct her, which she hoped would prove kinder to her than her
father.

Sosander's servants having diligently searched the neighborhood and the gentlemen having rode several miles about to no
purpose, they returned with the dissatisfaction of not having
found the person they went in quest of. Then, not being willing
to add to Sosander's grief, they took their leaves of him and
Gratiana and departed. Stertorius was the last that went, yet he
did, towards the evening, full of vexation and confounded with
shame of the disappointment.

As night drew on, Sylvia began to be under some concern,
how she should dispose of herself to get a lodging. Then, happening to see a company of beggars sitting under a tree in a field by
the wayside, she made up to them, whom she found carousing
heartily upon what they had gathered at several gentlemen's
doors, and with full pitchers before 'em, which they had sent for
from an alehouse just at hand. To join herself with these, Sylvia
thought would be the best way she could take to get her a lodging and to travel unsuspected. To this end as she approached

them, she saluted 'em kindly and demanded if she might be permitted to sit down among them.

"Yes," says one (a huge sturdy fellow and who proved to be the director of them all), "if you are fat. Have you got any money? For we never admit any stranger into our society without garnish."[4] Sylvia, being both hungry, dry, and weary, was willing to repose herself and asking them what they demanded, they said a shilling, which she readily paid and was presently admitted to participate of their fare which, though a perfect medley, she eat more contently of, and it went more pleasantly down, than all the cates and viands at her father's would have done in the company of Stertorius.

After supper, they replenished their pitchers and melted down Sylvia's shilling, according to their mode of expression and the laudable custom of those communities. And now they began to be as free with Sylvia, as if she had been an old acquaintance, or one of them and of a long standing, not in the least suspecting that she was anything else but what she appeared to be.

Their liquor being at an end, they began to think where they should go for quarters. Having found by inquiry at the alehouse where they fetched their drink that a good honest farmer, which used to entertain such guests, lived about a mile off, it was resolved, *nemine contradicente*,[5] to steer directly thither. Then packing up their awls,[6] they marched away and Sylvia among 'em.

Being come to the farm, according to their direction, a courier was dispatched to the house to beg the liberty of the barn for that night and, having a grant, they entered upon the premises and took possession. They were a jovial crew before and, Sylvia being added to them, they just equalled the number of the Muses.

They were all in and the key of the barn door turned upon them when, having straw enough, they prepared their bed, which was to be in common, men and women to sleep together promis-

---

[4] *fat*—rich; *garnish*—a levy upon a newcomer to be spent on drink for the entire group. The entire beggar episode is Blackamore's addition.

[5] No one disagreeing.

[6] All their possessions, perhaps originally a pun.

cuously. This raised a great deal of concern in Sylvia. She could hardly persuade herself to this. But considering she was now engaged among 'em and that, when at Rome, she must do as the folks at Rome do, with some reluctance she took up her lodging with the rest.

As for the company, they were four to four, *viz.*, four men and an equal number of women, and so great was the harmony among them that each man had his doxy already. This proved to be very lucky for Sylvia, or perhaps she might have found some inconveniency.

Having spread their bed and made 'em bolsters, which were of smaller trusses of straw tied very neatly up, they strowed their great patched coats and the women's gowns upon them for coverlets and laid them down with as much content as if it [had] been on the best feather bed and in the richest palace in the world. The rest went two and two. Only Sylvia had no mate and that was her satisfaction. So she wrapped herself up in her cloak and lay on a parcel of straw at a little distance from them.

As there are no persons live more merrily than beggars, so it was a custom among these never to go to sleep without some vocal music. Accordingly one of them, and that had the best voice among them, sung "The Jovial Beggar" and when that was ended, another minded to try Sylvia, put upon her to sing next. But she excused herself and pretended she was not well.

"Not well!" said the king of the company. "You young slut, you have no mind to sing. But I shall be with you presently, if you don't."

Sylvia was proceeding to excuse herself that task when the fellow made some motion of coming to her and, perceiving that she must expect a great deal of impertinence if she did not, she complied. The song she sung was "Chevy Chase," a very melancholy ditty but fittest for a person under her circumstances.[7] Though the words Sylvia had pitched upon were not so accept-

[7] Several versions of the beggar's song are available in collections of eighteenth-century ballads. The popularity of "Chevy Chase" is evident from Addison's praise in *Spectator* No. 70 (May 21, 1711).

able to her jolly companions, her voice was surprising, and they were charmed with it, though she industriously strove to conceal her skill and made a great many slurs on purpose. They thought her singing above anything they ever heard. Upon this they began to suspect she was some runaway from her parents or guardians and not an indigent, as she pretended; or, at least, that she had been well educated, though she might, at that time, be fallen under some misfortune. However, they made no further inquiry till the morning, when an accident happened to confirm their suspicion.

When they had done singing, they composed themselves to sleep, and so did Sylvia. But not lying very easily and turning often, she threw off her cloak, which unveiled her under-habit and disclosed a neck and breast like alabaster, though her hands and face were of such a dingy color and so vastly different they did not seem like parts of the same body.

Towards the morning Sylvia fell into a sound sleep and overslept herself till it was broad day. Then one of the fellows, getting up before the rest, chanced to spy her as she lay; and, his curiosity prompting him, he drew near to view her which he did with admiration and wondering who that beautiful creature should be. He was fully convinced that the complexion of her hands and face was only borrowed and that she was a person not inured to the sun or to undergo any hard labor. Her apparel, though it was her worst, was such as any gentlewoman might appear in and discovered that she was, or had been, of good fashion.

Having satisfied his own curiosity with this sight, he retired as softly as he could to wake some of the rest that they might behold her. But before he could do that with the management that he desired, Sylvia herself awaked and seeing one of her company up, who she suspected might have seen her asleep and without her cloak, she blushed exceedingly. Then getting it on with all the speed she could, she rose and walked about the barn in some disorder. By this time the whole gang began to move and were quickly up, not wanting much dressing. And the farmer's servant came and unlocked the door to let them be gone.

While they were packing up, the discovery that had been made of Sylvia was whispered about among the whole company. And thereupon, the superior of 'em took the liberty to ask her some questions, such as what her name was, from whence she came, and what necessity had compelled her, being such a likely young woman, to betake herself to that way of living? Sylvia, having expected those and such like questions to be put in her travel, was nothing to seek for an answer. She told them her name was Chloe, that she came from Cornwall, that her parents were people of substance where they lived but that the cruelty of her father had sent her from home to seek her fortune.

"I thought some such thing," quoth the fellow that had discovered her asleep without her cloak, "by the fine clothes you have on under those rags and, as I do not take you to be one of us, so neither do I believe you to be so far from home as you pretend. And let me tell you, if you design to lie hid under this disguise, you must get you some other trappings. I have known gentlemen have taken up with some of our women upon the road before now and, if that should be your fortune, as you are pretty enough for anybody, these clothes may chance to discover you."

These words of the fellow's had put Sylvia in the utmost confusion and made her blush excessively. But after a little time, taking courage and knowing what he had said to be true, she thanked him for his advice, wishing she could get some accoutrements more befitting her unhappy circumstances.

Sylvia waited not long for a solution to that difficulty, one of the women telling her presently they could furnish her among themselves, and that, as they pitied her condition, each of them would contribute their quota. Sylvia thanked them for their kindness and accepted their offer, when a gown, petticoat, shoes and stockings fit for a gentlewoman beggar were mustered in a trice and given to Sylvia out of their wardrobe, which they used to carry at their backs.

But here another question arose, *viz.*, how she should dispose of the clothes she brought out with her? This was solved in a moment, by telling her that about ten miles off lived a broker with whom they were used to deal; that whenever they had any clothes given them too good for their own use, which happened sometimes, they sold them to him; and that he took care to get them what they wanted, as shirts, shifts, and other linen proper for their vocation.

Upon this, Sylvia consenting to be disrobed, the men went out of the barn and left the women to themselves. While they were equipping their new disciple according to art and putting her in the best disguise they could, one of them, for that purpose having gathered some walnut leaves, they rubbed her neck and breasts with them, making them all of the same complexion as her hands and her face. This done, they robed her according to the mode of beggars; and each of them undertaking to carry something of what she had put off, they bundled up her clothes in several parcels and, putting them in their wallets, they went out to their companions.

Being now ready for their march and having sent one of their company to return the farmer thanks for his civility, they departed. They had not travelled above a mile before they came to another little alehouse and here they resolved to muster and determine what walk each should take that day and where they should meet again at a stated time in the evening. This motion, though it something disturbed Mrs. Chloe (for that was now her name among the beggars) yet, as she could not tell how to help it, she was obliged to be quiet. She was very much afraid of losing her clothes, but she thought it the best way to conceal her apprehensions.

After having eat their breakfast and guzzled some pots of ale, the first resolve they came to was that their place of rendezvous at night should be near the broker's, beforementioned. The next was one of the women should accompany Chloe and, because she might be tender-footed, especially having got untoward shoes on, go directly to the place where they were to meet at, only begging as they went along, to instruct her in the trade. The third and last resolution they made was that the rest should separate, some one way, some another, but be sure not to exceed six at the place appointed.

And now while Sosander and Gratiana were lamenting the loss of their daughter, she was wandering she knew not where, like a vagabond and in the company of one. Though messenger after messenger were sent out after her, while in this disguise none of them, though they had been intimately acquainted with her, could have known her.

The gang was now dispersed and only Chloe and her companion left together, who crept along a snail's pace towards the end of their journey. And indeed that was the fastest Chloe could go, for, if she was galled the day before when she had her own soft and easy shoes on and such as were exactly fit for her feet, she was foundered on this, with such as were too big as well as uneasy to her. She had hardly proceeded four miles onward on her journey that day before she was so lame and halted so by compulsion that she needed nothing of art, which is common among beggars, to set her off and make her pass for a cripple. Her expedition had made her one already and she, so lately happy Sylvia, was now become an object of pity by the unusual hardship of little more than one day's travel. However, she made what shift she could to get along by degrees, though she was often forced to sit down and rest herself, almost continually groaning for the agony she underwent.

The noise of these had reached the ears of a gentleman at a distance as he rid along, who, being of a tender disposition and generous withal, made up toward the place from whence the sound proceeded and seeing Chloe and her companion, he demanded what was the matter?

Then her companion (a cunning gypsy and who had learned her trade thoroughly) made this reply. "Sir," said she, "the poor creature you see in this miserable condition has been sick for several months and at last the distemper is fallen into her legs, so that she cannot move but with the greatest pain. She is my sister's child and both her parents are dead. I live but three miles off and have nursed her till we are both ready to be starved, having sold all that I had to maintain her in her sickness, and now am forced to bring her out to see if we can find any well-disposed persons to bestow a small matter upon us and keep us from starving." At these words, she burst out into tears, which flowed so naturally they had almost extorted some from the gentleman, whose eyes had been intent upon the supposed Chloe all the time she was speaking and perceived plainly that she was in exceeding pain.

Chloe all this while had industriously concealed her face, when the gentleman desired her to look up to him which she did with so much modesty that he was greatly taken with it as well as the exact symmetry of her features, and commiserating her misfortune, he pulled out his purse and taking two guineas, "Here," said he to the supposed aunt, "take these and go no farther but carry your niece home again. Get what is necessary for her, and God bless you together." Having said thus, the gentleman rode away, pleased in himself that he had assisted such, though they were but seeming objects, while Chloe's companion was much pleased that she had choused[8] him of such a booty.

It was not advisable to remove immediately from the place where they were, lest the gentleman might watch their motions. So they stayed about half an hour till being satisfied that he was gone, they proceeded though Chloe's pain was not at all mitigated but rather increased by her concern for such barbarous imposition upon the gentleman. From that very moment she determined to leave her new-found companions as soon as they had disposed of her clothes and she could get a convenient opportunity.

The sun had just passed the meridian when they drew near a gentleman's seat, where they perceived a great many beggars at the gate. Then says Chloe's companion, "To be sure this is a good house and we will call at it." And though it was against her inclination to make herself so public, Chloe was forced to yield. When they were come to the gate, Chloe rested herself at the rails while her companion thrust herself into the thickest of them.

[8] Cheated, tricked.

When several questions being asked, as usual among those people, she gave them such answers as she thought fit but she desired them not to trouble Chloe, for that she was a poor sick creature hardly able to speak.

It happened that day was the annual commemoration of the gentleman's wedding, on which he used to distribute a dole of money, bread, and meat to all poor people that would come, whether neighbors or strangers. This was his constant custom on that day and even before himself sat down to meat. They had not been long there before the gates were opened and the gentleman appeared, who presently ordered them to be served with four pounds of meat and a loaf of bread, while himself distributed the money, half a crown to each, with his own hand.

As the supposed Chloe drew near to receive her part, she recollected the gentleman, that she had seen him often at her father's, that he had both seen and conversed with her. This put her into such a panic fear that she trembled every joint, which the gentleman perceiving and that she walked very lame demanded what ailed her, when her companion, that was ever ready at an answer, answered for her. "Sir," said she, "this poor girl has been afflicted with an ague these four months and she has it now upon her." Then the gentleman presently doubled her money saying, "Poor creature, I wish thee better," and departed.

'Tis natural when people are under apprehensions to be afraid of shadows and create themselves ten thousand needless troubles, phantoms of a distempered brain and for which there may be little or no reason. Because she knew the gentleman, though he did not know her, she feared lest some of his servants might have seen and discover her. This thought made her very uneasy and spur her companion to be gone. And here, what the apprehension of danger can do was very evident for, though she walked in the greatest misery, yet she mended her pace and, Stoic-like, resolved to brave her pain.

By this means they were quickly out of sight of the gentleman's house and about four miles from the place of rendezvous, when happening to meet an empty cart which they found was going that way and somewhat beyond, they agreed for a pot of drink, mounted, and away they rode. This lift on the way brought them first to the broker's, where they inquired for their companions but none of them being yet come, they went to an alehouse just by, leaving word for them to be directed thither as they came.

The people at this house had been used to such guests and tasted what good customers they were. For which reason, as soon as they came, they were put into the best room and had all the attendance that could be imagined and as if they had been the best of gentry. At this place Chloe that, whilst she was Sylvia at her father's house, had often been employed in surgical operations and nicely observed her mother's management in like cases, was forced to try her skill upon herself. Accordingly, she first caused a hot bath of several herbs to be made, with which she bathed her feet, that were now prodigiously swollen as well as galled. Then spreading some plasters of comfrey root,[9] for want of other salve, she applied them where the skin was broke. This application in a little time mitigated her pain and gave her some ease; the swelling likewise abated with the pain.

By and by the company they expected began to drop in one after another, till they were all come. After usual salutations passed, the first inquiry was, what success? "Success!" cried one. "Very bad, I think. For, my heart, though I have walked at least a dozen miles, I have got but poor eighteen pence all the day except an old coat here, that I believe will not fetch us above three shillings."

"That's pretty well," said another, "for I am sure I have trod more ground and have not got half so much."

"For my part," went on a third, "I never found money so scarce in my life. I got but seven pence three farthings all this day, and out of that I spent my pint with an old acquaintance, who told me some bad news: that our trade declines apace at London, that the beggars betake themselves to selling of things

[9] A member of the borage family, formerly esteemed as a vulnerary.

up and down for want of other encouragement, and that he believes we must be forced to work for our living in a little time,
because the money goes abroad so fast there will be none left.
But however," continued she, "I have got some victuals which I
believe will serve us all, and that's some comfort."

Chloe's fellow traveller and herself sat still all the while and
spake not a word, till the rest that had taken their circuit had
given in their accounts which, upon the foot, amounted to above
thirteen shillings among them, besides the old things and the
victuals. At last, she that had been manager for Chloe produced
the loaves and the two pieces of beef and clapping them upon
the table, "Look here," said she, "here is good peck." "Aye," said
another, "so it is and let us order it to be dressed. We have no
need to eat cold broken scraps when we may have hot meat and
can pay for the dressing." Continued she, "We have got something to wet our whistles into the bargain: a brace of yellow-boys[10]
and three half-crowns besides." While they all sat wondering at
what she said and how they came by them, she related all that
had passed and how she had imposed upon the gentleman upon
the road. "Well," said the king of the company, "since you have
had so good luck, we will have a couple of cacklers to eat with
our beef. But first, down with the money. Put it into the common
stock." The women, knowing that to be the law of their society,
readily did it and, laying down two guineas and half a crown,
Chloe also threw down her two half-crowns to accompany them.

A fund being thus raised of three pounds and as many shillings, it was deposited in the hands of their treasurer, when the
landlord was called and supper ordered, one of the guineas being
committed to him by way of caution with strict charge that when
it was come in, he should give them notice. And calling for
brandy, ale, pipes, and tobacco, they tippled and smoked plentifully, while their supper was preparing.

During the time a motion was made if they should not send
for their broker and dispose of their cargo of clothes, which being

---

[10] Gold coins, such as guineas or sovereigns.

resolved, one of them called him forthwith. When he came, the first parcel they exposed to sale was the supposed Chloe's apparel, for which he allowed them five pounds and some odd shillings, which he paid upon the table and wrapping them up, he carried them home with a promise to return presently.

While he was gone, they delivered the five pounds to Chloe, keeping back the odd money, which they told her would be spent for the good of the company and should serve as an acknowledgment for the clothes she had received from them. And as for anything else she wanted to be furnished with, they told her, she needed but speak to the broker and he would get them for her against the morning. Here Chloe's feet putting her in mind, she told them she wanted other shoes and stockings, and accordingly it was resolved they should be got.

When the broker returned, they sold a second parcel, which consisted only of clothes [that] had been given them that day for about four and sixpence, which was delivered to their treasurer for the public use. Here they put the broker in mind of Chloe's wants—that he should procure her a pair of shoes and stockings, such as were whole, soft, and easy, because her feet were sore with travelling, which he promised and departed with his second bargain. At his return, which was very quick because they had invited him to supper, he brought them such as they had ordered and as fitted Chloe, which she paid for out of her own money, and both were satisfied.

By this time the table was spread with as much decorum as persons of quality and, supper being ready, it was brought in, when they sat down without any ceremony and eat as heartily as if their drinking before had created them an appetite. Only Chloe eat but sparingly and, as for drinking, she had an aversion to it. This made her dislike their company and [she] resolved, if possible, on the morrow to give them the slip. They had drank so plentifully before and at supper that their victuals and guinea concluded together, which the landlord reminding them of, another was deposited in his hands forthwith. This replenished their vessels, whilst the cloth was taking away, when the master-beggar began a health to the gentleman Chloe and her companion met upon the road. This they drank with several huzzahs and in twelve go-downs, which they compelled even Chloe herself to take.

The largeness of this draught, as well as the disagreeableness of the liquor, joined to that of the company, had such an effect that she was really sick, and her discomposure was visible to the whole society, who, calling up the landlord, gave directions that Chloe should be accommodated with a bed by herself and what she could desire, out of the public stock. As the benefaction they had obtained through her means had been liberal, they could not but allow her liberally out of it, specially for the restoring of a person that might be more serviceable to them. Notwithstanding, Chloe put them to no charge but only that of a separate bed, than which nothing could be more grateful to her and which, with the permission of the rest, she presently went to, with only the woman who had been her companion all the day to see her in bed and help her thither, if there should be occasion.

Being thus rid of that troublesome rabble and in the place (which was only a closet) where she was to lie, she addressed herself towards bed. Then slipping off her upper garments, which she could do very easily and as snakes do with their skin because they were not very fast to her, she was obliged to Canidia (which was the woman's name) to help her with the most troublesome part. Her bodice, which had never been unlaced from the time she had seen Stertorius till then, she could not manage and therefore desired her, when Canidia, observing them and the fine linen she wore, "My dear," said she, "we have forgot one thing."

"What is that?" said Chloe, sighing.

Then Canidia replied, "Some other bodices, head-cloths, and shifts."

To which Chloe answered, "That should have been done and, while I am in bed, I wish you would manage for me."

Canidia promised and, procuring another shift for Chloe in the house, she put it on, and taking hers with her bodice away, she lodged them in private till she could get the broker out from the rest. By and by she found an opportunity and, tipping the wink, he and she went out together and managed so warily that Chloe quickly had choice of what she wanted and money to boot.

Chloe being now in bed and supplied with all that she desired, Canidia and the broker returned to their company that by this time was all in *alt*[11] and had got a Roman fever, as they call it, upon them. Nor was Canidia and the broker very far short of them. Drunken persons are like those in a dropsy. They are still craving, though they have enough, and every drop is an augmentation to their disease, till their vitals are seized and they are laid either dead or asleep. And this was the case of these jovial companions who, though they did not drink themselves dead, yet they had much better have been asleep, for they drank till they were mad and the effects of that are sometimes more grievous than death itself.

The clock had now struck two, when the broker enticed one of the doxies home with him and she agreed. They had both stolen out and were gone before her mate began to miss her, and this was the prelude to a scene something comical. The beggar that had lost his mate was inflamed with drink and jealousy and nothing would serve him but he must fetch her back. And the rest, fired at the resentment of the affront done to their companion, resolved to assist him, though with the demolition of the rascal's house. Such an injury was not to be borne and had it been the greatest man in the world, at that time they would do themselves justice. Though the landlord persuaded them all he could to desist and let the woman have her will for once, nothing could assuage their fury or prevent their arming themselves with such weapons as they could meet with to carry on the designed war and the investing of the broker's castle.

Being provided with staves, prongs, a fire-fork, and a brace of spits, men and women, out they sallied all together but not without a great deal of noise which alarmed the neighborhood to such a degree that men, women, and children were all up presently—

[11] An exalted state of mind, intoxicated; literally, a high musical note.

and a certain long-staff officer among the rest, who followed them with a party to watch their motions. The first assault they made upon the broker was with a volley of pebbles against his windows, which he little valued so long as they were without doors. The curtains of his bed were a sufficient fence against those attacks, till he might accomplish his design and he did not desire to keep his bedfellow any longer.

This shower of stones having none effect, they prepared for a nearer assault and were already in the act of breaking in upon the ravisher when the constable coming up with a posse, though it was but a small one, demanded who was there, and gave orders to apprehend them. This being a terrible sound and such as usually carries horror with it to persons of their vocation, they immediately desisted from their enterprise and taking themselves to their heels, happy was he or she that could run fastest. Nor did any of them dare to see what was become of Chloe. The place being thus made quiet, Mr. Constable returned to his home without any farther inquiry, leaving the broker to his enjoyment without molestation.

Chloe, or Sylvia, having slept very well all this time, at last arose about seven, imagining by the silence of the house that they were all asleep. But coming down and inquiring for them, the landlord related to her the whole adventure and how the rest were fled upon it. Then Chloe expressed some concern lest she should be brought into trouble. Upon this account the honest ale-draper bid her fear nothing for that he could vouch for her, adding withal that he was sorry for nothing so much as the loss of such good company. "But," says he, "they have left above five shillings over the reckoning behind them which I pray you to take, and if ever they happen to come this way, I shall be glad to serve them." Here he returned Chloe the money which she at first refused but, being pressed, she took it and would have been going, but she knew not where, but the landlord would not permit her till she had eat her breakfast and bringing her out the remainder of the fowls that were dressed the night before, he set them before her. After having eat a little and drank once after it, she gave him thanks and departed, satisfied in herself that she was thus discharged from her company and resolving never to list herself under theirs or any such banners for the future.

In this condition Sylvia wandered up and down the country for several days without inquiring which way she went and behaved herself with so much modesty that she seldom asked a charity but she received something and never failed of the liberty of a barn to lie in wherever she petitioned for it, though that was not above twice or thrice and that only when she had not the opportunity of getting a lodging for her money.

After many a weary step, with pensive thoughts and deep-fetched sighs, at last she arrived at the borders of Hertfordshire, lying next to London and not many miles from that metropolis, when happening to see a great company of horsemen upon the road with two coaches and six, Sylvia's curiosity prompted her to ask one of the retinue who those persons were so splendidly attended, who answered they were the judges just come from London and going to the assize at Hertford. "And is this Hertfordshire?" said she. "No, child," replied the man, "but if you go about a quarter of a mile farther, you will be in it." And having said this, he rid away with the rest.

Sylvia, perceiving that she was not many miles from London, had a strong conflict with herself whether she should continue in the country or make up to the city.[12] She had a longing desire to see it, but then so many difficulties did occur which she could not get over easily as often turned her when she was upon the brink of a resolution to go. She had been always used to a country life, to breath the fresh air and she was apprehensive lest the foggy air of the city might disagree with her. She knew that it was an expensive place and that her money was short and would not support her without begging, which she imagined would not be safe for her when there was so great a resort of all countries

[12] In Mrs. Behn's work, Peregrina rambles north into Lancashire and so avoids her pursuers, who have ridden toward London.

and she might probably meet with some of her own. With these and such like considerations she turned the balance and followed the road the judges were gone before.

And now, as it were by the finger of an overruling Providence directing, she was almost at the end of her travels. About noon she had got near seven miles into the country and at the entrance of a little village, seated upon the side of a pleasant hill that arose with a gradual ascent to the top where stood a noble pile of buildings that overlooked the country all about and was the mansion of a gentleman named Liberius, who was a person truly deserving, being of known sense, probity, and integrity, of a vast estate, a generous soul, courteous, affable, hospitable to strangers, and a master of all the excellent endowments that are requisite to make one truly great, insomuch that he was an ornament to the gentry, the delight of the middle sort, and the idol of all the poor about, to which latter his gate afforded daily relief.

The first person Sylvia spoke to in this village was an ancient woman that sat spinning at her door, of whom she asked an alms. The woman, looking upon her and perceiving that she was young, told her she ought to work. "Alas! mistress," said Sylvia, sighing deeply, "that I would willingly do, could I get employment and I am now travelling the country to find some." This answer of Sylvia was spoken so feelingly and with so much concern that the old woman could not forbear gazing at her. At last, "Girl," said she, "there are a great many sluts go about the country begging under the pretense of seeking work and when it is offered they will do nothing. From whence do you come?" Here Sylvia owned her country, thinking herself now far enough from home, and her name, giving the woman a satisfactory answer to all the questions she put with so much modesty that she was taken with her and, directing her to the great house above, she bid her go ask relief there, which she did not need to fear at that time of day, among the other beggars. "But withal," said she, "when you have got your victuals, come back to me and I will see to find some work for you. And if I cannot immediately, I will find you lodging till I can and you may get some broken meat every day at that gentleman's among the rest. Besides," said she, "I will speak to the porter myself, to take some care of you."

Sylvia thanked the woman for her kindness and went to Liberius's gate as directed, where she found thirteen or fourteen more of the same fraternity among which, though with some difficulty, being an entire stranger, she got a share. Having sped there, Sylvia returned directly to the woman that had invited her, who, asking her if she could spin and being answered that she could, immediately set her to work and kept her employed until the evening.

That night the old woman took Sylvia for her bedfellow, as indeed she was during her stay with her, there being no other bed in the house. And Sylvia, having perfectly recovered herself, began to sleep as well as ever she did at her father's. Sylvia's hostess having recommended her to the porter as she said, she was a constant attendant at Liberius's gate about dinner-time and was constantly supplied.

It happened at this time that the only son of Liberius, a child of four years old, was grievously afflicted with sore eyes to such a degree that they despaired of cure, having tried the skill of all the oculists and physicians far and near. This was no small grief to Liberius and his lady Angelica who prayed continually for his recovery till at last her prayers had this effect, by means of Sylvia.

Sylvia had chanced one day to tarry at the gate a little after the rest of her companions were gone when the nurse brought out the young Liberius, that being his name, to walk before the gate. And Sylvia, seeing the child, looked very wishfully upon him and demanding of the nurse what was the matter with him that he was so muffled, was answered he had sore eyes.

Upon this Sylvia requested she might just look at them, and having liberty, she did, the nurse holding him in her arms. Having made her observation, Sylvia said, "Mrs. Nurse, I daresay, I can cure this child, with God's blessing."

"That," said the nurse, "is sufficient of itself without any other means. But will you pretend to do more than all the physicians can?"

"Well," said Sylvia, "I am almost sure I can do this, if my good lady will permit me to try, and I wish to God you would tell her." The nurse promised her that she would, and bidding her stay a little, she went in with the child to her lady and related what the beggar at the gate had said.

When Angelica heard it, she ordered the woman to be called in, which was accordingly done. Sylvia being now before her, she demanded if she had skill in sore eyes, to which she answered she thought she had, and if her ladyship pleased, she would tell her a method to cure Master. Angelica bidding her go on, Sylvia told her how to make an eye-water, which she hoped would do; and the lady (who herself had some skill in physic, though she had never heard of that recipe before) approving, Sylvia was dismissed, with thanks and a promise of encouragement, if the success answered.

The composition was quickly in a readiness (for what is there that may not easily be procured, when money is not wanting?) and applied with good success. In two or three days' space, the child was so much bettered [that] the Lady Angelica began to hope a perfect cure. She then thought a woman's receipt might outdo the most eminent doctors, and was fully satisfied the learned do not always perform the greatest cures.

During the whole time, from the first prescription till the child was well, Sylvia never failed to put up her petitions to Heaven for a blessing upon her endeavors for him; and the event was corresponding.

Angelica having found so much benefit by Sylvia's advice already, she thought it proper to consult her farther, lest, perhaps, there might be some occasion for an alteration of the prescription, according to the malady. Wherefore, sending for her, she said thus, "I know not what you are, nor from whence you come; but this I know, that my child is in a fair way of recovery, by your means; and I desire you to see him daily, and give such directions, as you shall think proper to accomplish his cure. I have given orders you to be admitted when you will, to see him, and you shall have your victuals in my kitchen." Sylvia was very thankful for her civility, and only desired she might direct what the child should eat and drink, almost promising success upon that condition.

In a month the young Liberius was perfectly recovered to the very great joy of his parents, and the universal satisfaction of the family. The Lady Angelica, in particular, was so transported that nothing could be more; her very transports, for the present, made her forget the thoughts of gratitude to Sylvia, and the frequency of her visitors, to congratulate her upon the recovery, took up all her leisure hours.

The child was well, and there seemed to be no more occasion for Sylvia to be let in, without a farther order from Angelica; so the servants began to slight her, and one of them took the liberty to say her post was at the gate and Sylvia accordingly receded.

About a week had passed and Sylvia was still neglected, when one of the physicians (that had the child in cure, and been forced to desist, finding all his skill to be baffled by the distemper) chanced to come that way, and calling in to pay his respects to Liberius and his lady, he inquired after the health of their son. Being answered that he was well, the gentleman was surprised, as thinking it impossible to be. "Certainly," said he, directing his discourse to the lady, "madam, you do but say so, for I never saw such a case before. For my part, in all my experience, I never found such an obstinate humor in any child's eyes before; and if he is cured, I think that miracles are not ceased, for, I do assure you, the very retina and all the tunics[13] of his eyes were affected."

Here Angelica calling for the child, he was brought, and the doctor was fully convinced of what he had been told; when acknowledging a deficience in his skill, he begged the lady would discover the means.

"No, Doctor," said she, "I must not do that without the consent of the person that communicated the secret to me. But if you

---

[13] Membranous sheath lining the eye.

please, you shall see her, for it was a woman, a poor indigent creature, that begs at our gate, and now I think on't, I have forgot to reward her for it."

"Madam," said the psysician, "a person that can do such a cure does not deserve to beg, and I should rejoice to see her."

Then a messenger, being called, was sent to the house where Sylvia lodged, who finding her, delivered his message from Angelica. The will of Angelica was a law to Sylvia, and she no sooner heard the message, but she went directly.

Sylvia had but just entered the room when said Angelica, "Sir, here is the person; this is my doctress."

These words, as they occasioned Sylvia to blush exceedingly, so they spurred the doctor to gaze upon her more earnestly. At last says he, "I do assure you, madam, you have chosen a very pretty one; and if this young woman has performed the cure I see before me, her skill in these affairs is not inferior to her features. But pray, sweetheart," says he, speaking to Sylvia, "how long have you been a doctress?"

"Sir," said Sylvia, "I am a poor ignorant person; I do not pretend to understand much of these things, but I can assure you I have known some great cures the same receipt has done and I bless God it has had success now. I am sure I am obliged to my good lady here, and to all her good family, and should be glad to serve them, though in the meanest degree."

Here the doctor had the same curiosity, as others before him to inquire after her name, country, parentage, and the reason she took to this way of living; and Sylvia giving him some plausible account, he rested satisfied. When he demanded of her the method she had prescribed for this great cure, she referred to the Lady Angelica for that, who knew the management as well as herself. Upon this Sylvia was dismissed with a promise from Angelica that she would reward her, at a more convenient opportunity. When Sylvia had departed, the doctor took the liberty to request the favor of Angelica to let him know what method had been used with the child, which she readily condescended to; and having expressed his approbation of it, and recommended it to her use upon the like occasion, he took his leave.

Presently after the doctor was gone, Sylvia was again sent for by Angelica, who gave her a gratuity for what she had done, and offered to receive her into the family and entertain her as a scullion, if she should like that post better than the begging trade, and would accept of it. Sylvia, who had never been used to rambling, accepting the condition with utmost gratefulness, Angelica gave directions to have her clothed, according to her post, which she promised should be bettered, as she behaved herself in this.

The so lately nice and beautiful Sylvia was now become a scullion, the most dirty employment that belongs to any family; and she, that had been used to command her father's domestics, was now to be commanded by a greasy cook and at the beck of almost every one of the most menial servants.[14] However, such was her humility, so great was the condescension of her temper that she could submit to any, even the most servile office, rather than repine or show herself disaffected to those that seemed to be her superiors by their place.

This winning behavior of hers, in a short time, recommended her to the esteem of all her fellow servants, but especially the cook's, to whom she was so obsequious and tractable that Mrs. Cook esteemed herself happy in having such an underling, and offered to instruct her in the mystery of cooking, the nicety of which, though Sylvia understood to perfection, she seemed desirous to learn of her and needed not abundance of instruction to furnish her with the practice.

Sylvia had not been quite a year in this employ, when it happened the cook sickened and died. During the time of her sickness, the management of the kitchen was incumbent upon Sylvia, who performed with such dexterity that the cook was not at all missed. Liberius's table was as richly furnished as before, and

[14] Mrs. Behn has Arabella-Peregrina enter the Kindly household at the highest servant level, though she would occasionally "lend her helping Hand to the Cook," preparing "the Quidlings, and other Sweet-Meats."

with rather greater art, insomuch that both himself and his lady were extremely pleased with Sylvia's performance. When the cook died, as they thought Sylvia as proper as any, they resolved that she should succeed and, agreeing with her according to custom, the care of the kitchen was committed to her trust.

This new promotion made Sylvia begin to spruce up a little, to make her look tight, and the complexion of her hands and face to alter. This last they attributed to the alteration of her diet and condition; and from the appellation of plain Sylvia, she was now saluted by the name of Mrs. Cook, pretty Mrs. Cook, and the like; not to mention, that she was sometimes obliged to receive a kiss from some of her fellow servants, who would have extorted it if she had not complied, and esteemed her proud if she had refused. Such affronts as these she was frequently obliged to put up, and with an unwilling willingness she did.

Sylvia had not been long in this employ before she discovered an education more than ordinary; and her sudden skill in cookery had almost betrayed that she was not bred up to that only, but that her qualifications reached farther.

It happened one day Liberius had invited a great many gentlemen to his house and a very splendid entertainment was to be prepared, when her master sending for Sylvia expressed these words, "Sylvia, I depend upon your judgment for the care of my kitchen this day. I have invited several persons of quality, and I would not willingly have my table outdone by any. Show your skill at this time, and I shall thank you."

It was not Sylvia's temper to say much, and therefore she only said she would do her endeavor and departed, having all things ordered her for the entertainment. This unexpected company had occasioned a very great hurry, but yet it did not discompose Sylvia in her temper. Though she had now been accustomed some time to the fire, yet it had not made her fiery and of the usual disposition of cooks. Her temper was calm and meek and, like the turtle, she was without gall, so that it was difficult to raise an emotion in her. Notwithstanding the suddenness of the thing, Sylvia managed with that discretion that all that belonged to her part was performed to admiration and received the applause of those that did participate of it. As for Liberius and his lady Angelica, they were both so pleased with Sylvia's performance that they thanked her in public for it and looked upon her as a prodigy among servants.

Among this company there happened to be one gentleman that had travelled Worcestershire and imagined he had seen Sylvia somewhere, though he could not recollect the place. But when Liberius gave an account of her indigence and in what condition she came to his family, considering that one apple might be like another, he desisted any farther questions.

When the company was broke up and gone, Liberius sent for Sylvia, and bidding her continue her diligence, he gave her ten shillings, with a promise of his and his lady's favor for the future. This was such a spur to the industry of Sylvia that she made it her whole study to please, and she fell not short in anything she designed. Liberius and Angelica were exceedingly pleased in a cook, and she was as well pleased in her master and mistress; and her fellow servants were all of them pleased they had now a cook who never refused them any liberty and was willing to serve them upon any occasion; and from this Sylvia received no little satisfaction. There was not one in the whole family but was willing to lend her a hand upon any emergency.

Use makes perfect, and Sylvia having been by this time inured by the hardships of servitude, was become so dextrous that she went through it with content and cheerfulness, neither murmuring herself or giving any occasion to others to murmur at her.

Among the other good qualities of Sylvia it was observable that when her business was done she was very reserved, and usually retired into her chamber at all convenient opportunities; and this had been taken notice of by some that had more curiosity than they needed, being prompted thereby to watch her motions and, if possible, to discover what she did there. This they did several times, but what did they find her doing? Nothing but what themselves ought to have done, and not to idle their time away in unprofitable pastimes. When Sylvia was retired from her kitchen and in her chamber, her usual posture was to be on her knees, either praying to God for a blessing on her endeavors, or praising him for mercies already received. By degrees, when they found her retirement was purely acts of devotion, they gave over watching.

This curiosity of theirs had one extraordinary effect. It augmented Sylvia's credit with Liberius and Angelica, who quickly were informed of her usual custom; neither did it lessen her in the esteem of her fellow servants, who, though they did not follow that practice themselves, they could not but approve it in her. Though people may be bad themselves, there is such beauty in virtue as must raise our admiration upon the sight of it and will force us to own that it is good, though we do not think fit to follow it.

Sylvia had continued in this post upwards of three years with universal applause, when Marcella, gentlewoman to Angelica, happened to be married and leave her lady very abruptly. The marriage of Marcella had been carried on so privately that her design was a perfect secret to the whole family, except Sylvia, until her wedding day; and to her she had communicated it, having before reposed some confidence in her.

On the morning she was to be married, Marcella addressed herself to Angelica, desiring her liberty to be absent two or three days upon some business she had to do and recommended Sylvia to attend upon her in her stead until she returned. Angelica was a kind good-natured lady and loved to gratify her servants, as far as she reasonably could, and this made her comply with Marcella's request, not doubting but Sylvia, who she found could turn her hand to anything, might serve her turn until Marcella came back.

Marcella was now gone, and Sylvia supplied the place both of the gentlewoman and the cook, and gave Angelica such satisfactions, particularly in her new employment, that she thought her equally deserving that post. But as yet she had no thought that Marcella had left her service until at last a letter came from Marcella to her lady, informing her of the true occasion of her stay, when Angelica communicated it to Sylvia, speaking to this effect: "I find Marcella has left my service, and I am not concerned, if it be to her advantage, though her departure has been something abrupt. She has not put me to a nonplus so long as Sylvia is with me, and if Sylvia will supply her place, I shall confer it on her, for I can get a cook more easily than I can a gentlewoman I like so well as you." Sylvia humbly thanked Angelica for the honor she did her and promised to do her utmost to merit her favor.

Thus Sylvia, from a scullion, was promoted to be the lady's gentlewoman and declared to be so to the whole family, who were well pleased at the promotion, and all congratulated her upon it. Sylvia, who wanted no encouragement from Angelica, was quickly furnished with an habit proper for her post, in which she demeaned herself with that decorum that the real gentlewoman appeared in her carriage, if she had not been one by her birth. She now began to take a little state upon her, as requisite to her post, though with all the modesty imaginable and never forgetting that she had been under command herself.

The becoming behavior she showed in her attendance upon Angelica made her really esteemed by that lady, and the pleasingness with which she delivered any commands to the inferior servants created such a love in them, they were all ready to obey her dictates as if they had been the direct instructions of Liberius or Angelica. This rendered her condition comfortable to herself and easy to all about her.

Sylvia had not been in this post (*viz.*, gentlewoman and companion to Angelica, which her lady allowed her to be) above a year and an half, before Angelica happened to be afflicted with a violent fit of sickness, which had very near carried her off, but for the care and diligence of Sylvia. A most terrible fever had seized Angelica, and was accompanied with the worst of symptoms, insomuch that the physicians despaired of her recovery. Seven days and nights had passed before there was any glimpse of hope. During all that time, Sylvia was very rarely out of her lady's chamber (only upon business, and to return immediately) and never out of her clothes; but almost continually upon the watch at the bedside, or if she chanced to doze a little, just to refresh sinking Nature, it was upon a couch not far off, in the same room.

In the absence of the physicians Sylvia had undertaken to see their prescriptions duly administered, and no one could have executed that office better than she did, even in the judgment of the doctors themselves, who very often inquired the symptoms of the distemper from her.

This care and diligence of Sylvia's had been taken notice of by all that were near Angelica during this time, but more particularly by Liberius, and was one of the main steps to her future fortune, Liberius, from that time, having such grateful resentments of her that he resolved to reward her in a remarkable manner.

In some weeks Angelica was perfectly recovered to the no small joy of her whole family, but especially of Liberius, whose very soul was so wrapped up in the charming excellencies of his dearest lady that it is a question whether he would have survived long, if she had been ravished from him by the inevitable and unerring stroke of Death.

When Angelica was thus well, Sylvia and the family were restored to their former tranquility. Sylvia resumed her province, which had been a little neglected upon this occasion, and all things were quickly reduced to their usual state and decorum.

Liberius had always kept a chaplain, and at this time there lived one with him, a gentleman he valued, and whose advancement in the world he desired more than any other who had lived with him before. And indeed his qualifications did merit the esteem of Liberius, for he was really a gentleman of excellent behavior, honest principles, and a good share of learning, the last of which he knew too well, and his knowledge of it proved very prejudicial.

At this time an ecclesiastical living of £250 *per annum,* about two miles off, became vacant by the demise of the late incumbent, and the presentation was fallen into the hands of Liberius, who never wanted any solicitations from his chaplain on that occasion.

Their living with him was a kind of a state of probation, and to have continued with Liberius for the space of one year was sufficient to entitle to the first presentation in his gift.

Upon the first account of this vacancy, Liberius in himself had determined it for Theophilus, which was the chaplain's name; but he did not declare himself until two or three days after, having a project of another nature in his head to communicate, which he was not willing to do without the approbation and consent of his lady Angelica.

His design was to give Theophilus the living and, if possible, to induce him at the same time to make courtship to Sylvia as a person he thought most deserving of a good husband, and to make a compensation for the seeming inequality of her birth, to offer him a portion, with her, of £700 as a token of the esteem, proceeding from gratitude, he had for her.

This thought of his Liberius communicated to Angelica, to whom Sylvia was become so dear [that] she had but one objection to offer against it, *viz.*, that she did not care to part with Sylvia. She willingly agreed to her husband's designed generosity, if the matter might be accomplished and Sylvia not go from her. This difficulty was easily removed by telling Angelica they should continue still in their house, and that neither of them should be removed from their posts. Upon this, the lady consented, and the next thing Liberius had to do was to break the matter to Theophilus.

Liberius had now prepared the instruments of presentation for Theophilus and signed it, when sending for him into his study one morning, he ordered him to sit down, and both being seated, Liberius began. "Theophilus," said he, "I respect you, and the reason I have sent for you is to convince you that I do. I suppose you know that I have a living now in my disposal." Here he stopped, and when Theophilus answered that he did, Liberius proceeded. "That I designed for you and have already drawn up your presentation to it. I am very well satisfied in my choice, and I do not question but those to whom I recommend you will be equally pleased." Here Theophilus having received the instrument from the hands of his patron with all the demonstrations of gratitude imaginable, and thinking that was all Liberius had to say at that time, he was retiring, when he was bid to stay, Liberius telling him he had something of equal importance to communicate. And here enumerating the many excellent qualities of Sylvia, his lady's woman, and extolling her to the utmost, he at last made a proposal of £700 with her, for a wife, if Theophilus would accept the offer, adding withal that what he did was out of respect to her virtues and in gratitude for the services she had done in his family.

Theophilus was surprised at this motion of Liberius, and his stomach began to rise, though he did not think fit to express his thoughts immediately; and therefore he only answered that what he had been pleased to offer was in relation to a matter of the greatest consequence and ought to be maturely weighed, that he would consider of it, and wait upon him with his full resolution in a little time.

Liberius was well enough satisfied with this answer, and Theophilus was dismissed, inwardly fuming at the affront, as he esteemed it, [that] had been put upon him by his patron, to offer him a wench that nobody knew from whence she came, but probably from the dunghill. That she was herself a beggar but the other day and rambled from door to door for her daily sustenance, and in all likelihood was some bastard was such a heartburn to a gentleman of his qualifications as could hardly be borne. However, for fear of an after-clap, he resolved to make sure of his living before he returned his answer, and Liberius was consenting that he should.

Having settled all those matters according to his mind, the resolutions of Theophilus upon the point of marriage was easily delivered: that he had not, as yet, any thoughts of entering into that state, but if he had, Sylvia would not be the person he should choose to settle his affections upon, for the meanness of her descent; though he could not but own her person to be agreeable, her virtues many, and her behavior without exception, he thought himself to be deserving of a gentlewoman with all those requisites, and a fortune, at least equal to what had been offered by Liberius. This last was enough to make him reject Sylvia without considering that persons of the greatest birth have, sometimes, been upon their shifts, and that those who raise themselves by their own proper merit rise upon a surer foundation than those who build themselves upon the merit of their ancestors.

Though Liberius did not expect such an answer from Theophilus, he expressed no show of resentment and dismissed him, saying, "I did not know but a pretty virtuous woman, with such a portion, might have been acceptable to you; but since it is not, I have a greater respect for Sylvia than to desire you to act against your inclination."

Sylvia, poor innocent gentlewoman, all this while had not the least knowledge of what had been transacted by Liberius, and consequently could have no resentments of Theophilus's contempt, though, if she had known the whole, it is a question whether she would have regarded it, having exercised herself so long in the practice of humility that she could bear any disdain with patience and had as great an aversion to pride as Theophilus could have to the supposed meanness of her birth.

This project being fairly over, Liberius and Angelica continued their usual favors toward Sylvia, and Sylvia had the command of the whole family, who delighted to be commanded by her.

During this time it happened that a young gentleman, Philaretus by name, aged about 25 years, and lately come to an estate of several thousands *per An.* upon the demise of his father and a great-uncle, was become acquainted with Liberius and had been invited to several entertainments at his house among other gentlemen, at one of which he chanced to cast his eyes upon Sylvia in the company of her lady, Angelica.

At the first blush he discerned something in her that was charming, insomuch that he was suddenly smitten; but he concealed his passion for the present until he might make some inquiry into her circumstances and get an insight into her temper, which, from the ingenuity of her countenance, he conjectured could not be bad.

Philaretus, as he was born to a good estate, so his education had been according to it. Nature had furnished him with regular limbs and a well-proportioned body, and nothing of art was wanting to embellish them. If his apparel was not extravagant and according to the mode of those who seldom pay their tradesmen, it was becoming, modest, graceful, and such as the greatest need not to be ashamed of.

If his complexion was something swarthy, yet his features were exact, his countenance manly, with an air of greatness and goodness, sweetly intermixed; and while *that* bespoke him to be something above the common herd of mortals, *this* was the index of his soul, and the discoverer of the bright inhabitant that dwelt within.

But what adorned him most were his internal excellencies, no less conspicuous in his conversation than his outward were in his person. Wherever he appeared, there was the gentleman, the linguist, the historian, the lawyer, but more particularly the civilian and the divine ready upon all occasions, and whenever he pleased, he could exert himself accordingly.

These were the qualifications that recommended Philaretus to Liberius and had made him already acceptable to the best and wisest of those that had the happiness to know him. These were the best viaticum or provision he needed for travelling among his friends and could make him welcome at any gentleman's, without another to introduce him.

Having seen the lovely Sylvia, though but once, he could not rest until he had satisfied his curiosity by another visit to Liberius and, accordingly, the third night following, as he was sitting by himself, he resolved to take a tour that way and drop in upon Liberius about noon the next day. Pursuant to this resolution, he immediately sent for his groom and ordered him to saddle seven horses in the morning and let them stand until called for.

Having satisfied himself with this determination and devoutly recommended himself to the protection of Heaven, which he constantly did, at his usual hour he retired to bed, where, though he could not hinder a continual incursion of ideas for some time, yet they were such as proceeded only from an innate passion, from a natural tendency which is implanted in all mankind towards the objects they love and had nothing culpable in them. They proceeded from a chaste love, wholly guided by reason, and vastly distant from any tincture of lust, for where pure love dwells, no lust can find reception. Philaretus did not love Sylvia only because he had seen her, but because he imagined more than common virtues to be in her, and, what confirmed him more in that opinion, because he found she was a companion of Angelica's.

However, he had not been long in bed before he composed himself to sleep, when he was overtaken with a most pleasing dream. Philaretus thought himself surprised with a most melodious harmony of all kinds of music, sweetly playing in the air, when the firmament suddenly was opened, and a glorious chariot appeared in the midst of heaven, descending towards him. As it approached, he discerned three persons in it, two of which he supposed to be angels by the brightness of their countenance, their glorious wings, and shining garments; but what the other was he could not divine, whether it was an angel or any other, by reason of a white veil with which it was covered all over. In a little time the chariot was landed just by Philaretus. Then the two angels that appeared dismounted, and leading the third, that now seemed a female by the dress, down from her seat, they conducted her to Philaretus, and placing her before him, says the angel, that guarded her on the right hand, "Philaretus, this is the gift that is sent to you from heaven to crown your happiness on earth. Behold the jewel." Here the angels jointly lifted up the veil which was upon her, and who should appear but the representation of the lovely Sylvia, in her garments white as snow and clean as spotless innocence? Philaretus all in a rapture endeavoring to embrace her, the angels let down the veil and forbad him to attempt to touch her, saying, "Though she will be yours, she is not so yet." At this expression they all turned away and, the two angels reconducting Sylvia, they mounted the chariot again and returned the way they came, with the same harmony.[15]

As the heavens seemed to close upon Sylvia, Philaretus awoke in some concern for this visionary disappointment, but that soon vanished as he came to himself; and considering that it was but a dream and, if it portended anything, it portended a seeming good to him, he soon recomposed himself and went to sleep.

The night was now over and the sun began to appear when Philaretus, according to custom, arose and, having paid his morning devotions to Heaven, he began to think of his journey, though it was not above a dozen or fourteen miles, so that there needed no extraordinary haste.

And here, though Philaretus was not at all credulous of dreams, that which he had seen the night before would often crowd itself in upon his thoughts and force a way into his memory. Whenever he but just thought of the unknown lady, his dream was present with him; he fancied immediately he saw her standing between the two bright messengers of heaven, both with pleasing aspects and seeming willing to deliver her to him.

The impression this dream made upon him when awake had half-persuaded him of the truth of the common saying, *viz.*, that marriages are made in heaven; and that the lady he was going in quest of was designed him from thence. He was already become a platonic lover, and perfectly charmed with the ideal virtues he had conceived in her; and which afterwards proved to be substantial, not only in the notion, but real virtues.

With these and such like amusements he passed the time until near eleven of the clock, when he ordered his servants and horses to be in readiness, and dressing himself in his usual habit, in the space of about half an hour, he mounted and rid away with six attendants.

It was customary for Liberius and Angelica, when they had

[15] In *The Wandering Beauty*, Peregrina is prosaically presented to Sir Lucius by her mistress, Eleanora. Blackamore substitutes this Dantesque vision.

no great strangers, to admit Sylvia to dine at table with them, and so it happened that day.

It had been a standing rule in the family of Liberius for himself and his lady to go to dinner exactly at one, and they were now sat down when Philaretus arrived. The news was presently carried to Liberius who desired he would walk in. Sylvia was going to rise and depart, but Angelica bidding her not, she continued.

Liberius met Philaretus just at his entering into the parlor and, bidding him welcome, desired him to sit down and participate of their fare, when Philaretus answered that he came on purpose. Angelica also bade him welcome, and a chair being placed for him directly opposite to Sylvia, bowing to the ladies, he took his seat.

And here Philaretus enjoyed a double banquet, for his mind and body both together, the first of which he feasted more deliciously on the contemplation of the virtues that appeared in Sylvia than it was possible he could the latter with the greatest dainties, even at an imperial table. An appetite, even the most canine, may be glutted; the stomach may be charged with meats and drinks, but when are the eyes so filled with seeing a delightful object that they desire to see no more? Or when is the mind so filled with thought that it cannot find variety to think upon?

In a short time, after dinner was ended, Angelica and Sylvia retired, leaving the two gentlemen together to divert themselves as they should think fit. When the ladies were gone, Liberius and Philaretus betook themselves to a pipe and a bottle, which both of them allowed themselves in, though neither approved of excess. And now Philaretus had the wished-for opportunity to inquire who that lady was that dined with them, and Liberius answering that she was his lady's woman, Philaretus was pleased to say she was a beautiful person. "That she is," said Liberius, "and what is more valuable, she has a soul within her that abhors all ill."

Here Liberius entered into a large field in the commendation of Sylvia; he enumerated her particular virtues and expatiated very much upon them, concluding withal that in his opinion she deserved a better fate than that of a servant, and [he] himself had offered £700 which he would freely give to make her happy in a good husband, though at the same time she was a jewel in his family and such as he would never part with but for her own advantage.

Upon this, Philaretus, who had heard the character of Sylvia with the greatest attention and the utmost pleasure, discovered his affection to her and the design of his coming thither that day, which was only to hear what he now did and before believed concerning her.

Liberius was something surprised at this declaration of Philaretus and, taking it to be only the effect of a sudden passion, endeavored to dissuade him from it by recounting to him all the passages he knew that could prejudice him against such a match. He related how she came a beggar to his gate, was taken into his family, made scullion, afterwards his cook, and now his lady's gentlewoman; he could not but own indeed that she deserved better. He owned that her soul was fit to inhabit a body of the greatest quality, but then her extract was so mean, he could not but think it unadvisable for a gentleman of his rank to entertain any thoughts of her. But what he chiefly insisted upon was that it would be counted imprudence for a man of his estate to marry one with nothing.

To all that Liberius said Philaretus made this short reply, that in choosing a wife he should never regard pedigree so much as virtue, or disregard the latter for any deficiency of the former, that his own was sufficient, and that therefore he might marry one without a fortune; that he had settled his affections upon Sylvia and resolved to pursue his choice, if Liberius and Angelica would permit him the liberty of their house.

Liberius, finding his resolution fixed and that no arguments he used would make him recede, at last consented, assuring him that himself and his lady would serve him in what they could and that he should be welcome to their house.

Philaretus, having made this step with success, rested satisfied and diverted their discourse to some other topics. They protracted the time, until the evening drew on, when Philaretus desiring he might take his leave of the ladies, Liberius carried him to them, and having first saluted Angelica and afterwards Sylvia, he wished them a good night. Then, returning Liberius thanks for his past and promised favors, Liberius waiting upon him to see him take horse, he departed.

When Philaretus was gone, Liberius went into the room where his lady and Sylvia were and, directing his discourse to Angelica, he told her she must not wonder at the freedom Philaretus had taken with her, since it was only to borrow a kiss from Sylvia, and that she was now become the mistress of his affections and would hear more from him in a little time.

These words of Liberius put Sylvia into a blush like scarlet, while they raised a pleasant smile in Angelica, and made her a little more inquisitive. Liberius answered to all her questions and assured them it was really so, and that [he] himself had given Philaretus liberty to come and try his fortune. Sylvia's modesty was so great that she knew not what to say or how to behave herself; and what added to her confusion was this, her lady's pleasant banter upon this account.

"Very well, Sylvia," says Angelica, "I did not think you had been a person of such intrigue. I find you are like a mole; you can work under ground and can run away with gentlemen's hearts unsuspected. And could no less a person than Philaretus have served to be made your captive? Methinks you aim at no low game, when you hit such topping gentlemen as him. However, I hope, Sylvia, you will invite Liberius and myself to the wedding." "Indeed, madam," replied Sylvia, "I do not know what my master and your ladyship mean. I am perfectly ignorant of what you say, but, if it were so, I should not desire to leave your service to be mistress in his family; I know the satisfaction I have here, and I do not know what discontent may be there."

"You need not fear anything of that," said Liberius, "for Philaretus is a gentleman of a most excellent temper, always easy in himself, and has enough to make you so, if you do not stand in your own light and slight his addresses. For my part, if I had a daughter fit for him and could give her a million, I should think them well bestowed on Philaretus, for I do not know a better gentleman living." Here Liberius went on with all the fluency imaginable in the commendation of Philaretus, omitting nothing that could be said to the advancement of his character, and concluded that she was to blame if she neglected this opportunity.

Liberius, when he had ended, finding Sylvia to blush and pant exceedingly and unable to speake through an excess of modesty,[16] left her and his lady together to confer notes and deliberate upon what had been said.

When Liberius was departed, Angelica pursued the same subject with so many pressing arguments drawn from the happiness she might enjoy by consenting to the addresses of Philaretus that Sylvia could not but own it was a condescension in that gentleman too great for her to make such a proposal, to which Angelica replied she might depend upon it, that Philaretus was in earnest and that a few days would demonstrate it. For that reason she enjoined her never to absent her table for any company, assuring her that she heartily wished her advancement in the world and should rejoice to see this match proceed, though it was to her own detriment.

It was now supper time when Liberius returned and broke off their discourse, which was entirely at an end for that time, neither Liberius nor his lady desiring to put Sylvia's modesty to the blush any farther, though they hoped the excess of it would wear off as Philaretus became more acquainted with her.

After supper they took a walk and when bedtime came, Liberius and Angelica retired to their chamber, where Sylvia having helped her lady to undress and wished them a good night, she also retired to her own and slept soundly, having little regard or so much as thought of what had been told her by Liberius and Angelica.

---

[16] Peregrina only blushes once, and then "with Disdain" at Prayfast's slur on her background.

But the next day put her in mind of it again, for in the afternoon Phliaretus, resolving to lose no time, renewed his pretended visit to Liberius and dismounting at the gate, he immediately went into the house.

Liberius was at that time in his study, when Philaretus, inquiring for the ladies, was directed to them, and having first paid his respects to Angelica, he then saluted Sylvia, assuring her that this visit was designed to her in particular; that as Liberius and, he hoped, his good lady had indulged him the liberty of their house, he requested that she would not resent it if he made his addresses to her. And here, while a graceful blush adorned the cheeks of Sylvia and gave fresh luster to her silent beauty, Angelica told him he was welcome and, because she did suppose he might have something to impart to Sylvia, she pretended to call Liberius and left them together.

Being now alone with Sylvia, he reinforced what he had said before in somewhat plainer terms, *viz.*, that his coming to Liberius at that time was purely for the love of her, that he had been smitten with her at first sight, was proud to wear her chains, and should esteem it the greatest happiness could befall him to have a place in her favor.

By this time Sylvia, having recollected herself and mustered up some courage, made this reply. "A visit from Philaretus is too great an honor for Sylvia to expect; and I believe Philaretus more a gentleman than to act beneath himself, or do anything may reflect upon his reputation."

"Madam," said he, "I look upon it to be so far from a reflection, I think it my greatest honor to converse with you, and hope 'twill prove an equal happiness. What I profess is real, and that I love you is beyond dispute."

"I thank you, sir," replied Sylvia, "for your expression, but I hope you will excuse me that I do not return the compliment."

To which Philaretus answered, "My dear, you have your liberty, but give me leave to hope."

"What is it," said Sylvia, "a gentleman of your character ought to hope from a person of my circumstances? You say you love me, but the object is too mean. You do not know Sylvia." Here she recounted what she had been, dating her original from the begging trade, how she came to Liberius's gate, how she was taken in, and how she was advanced by degrees until she came to that post in which she now was.

If it had not been Sylvia's pleasure to relate this account, Philaretus would much rather she had forborne it. But as it was, the respect he bore to her obliged him to hear her out, though he very much dreaded one effect it might have upon her, *viz.*, lest her too-great sense of her own meanness should make her disbelieve the inclinations of a gentleman, especially of his estate, to be real towards her.

When Sylvia had ended, Philaretus took occasion from thence to run a panegyric in the commendation of virtue, extolled it beyond pedigree, riches, or any other sublunary enjoyment, and making it the only sterling nobility. "This, madam," said Philaretus, "is what will stand the touch, will bear any trial, and make one happy under pinching want, and in the midst of calamities. This is a noble mine, and more to be prized than those of Peru and Mexico, for they may be exhausted. This, Sylvia, is a treasure that dwells in you and, if your beauty was not exquisite, would be sufficient to attract and captivate the soul of Philaretus."

With these and such like discourses they had passed about an hour when Liberius and Angelica, willing to let Sylvia have a little breathing time, entered the room and Sylvia, taking that opportunity, departed, leaving them to entertain Philaretus for a time.

Here Sylvia retired to her chamber and, falling on her knees, she implored the direction of Heaven in this affair, which was of the greatest moment and on which her future happiness depended. And now, having ended her prayers, she began to consider what she had best to do. The person of Philaretus was so agreeable she had no objection to make against it. His estate was sufficient, in all probability, and without a more than ordinary infliction of Providence, to make them live in splendor. His disposition and virtues, she was abundantly satisfied from the character Liberius had given, she could depend on. In fine, there was no argument she could raise against the reasonableness of her compliance with Philaretus but this, that he might reflect upon her hereafter for the supposed meanness of her present condition. However, Sylvia soon got over that by considering she might then discover her parentage, the knowledge of which, she thought, might be more grateful to him when it was least expected.

By these considerations Sylvia had almost brought herself to a compliance, but common prudence and the law of reputation forbid too quick a surrender upon these accounts until some trial had been made of the constancy of the besieger; and therefore she resolved, for some time, to defer his satisfaction, and, as not wholly to discourage, so neither to give Philaretus so much encouragement as that he might think her overcome by the dazzling luster of his appearance.

And here the charming Sylvia returned to the company of the impatient Philaretus who desired nothing more than to live and die with her and thought every moment tedious until she came.

As she entered, Philaretus seemed delighted at her sight; and when she took her seat at a distance, Philaretus changed his and begged the favor he might sit down by her, and thus they spent the remainder of that afternoon in the company of Liberius and his lady with various and pleasant discourses. Liberius and Angelica were pleased in the conversation of Philaretus; Philaretus was transported with his Sylvia; and Sylvia was not displeased at Philaretus.

But the evening drew on, and it was time for Philaretus to return home if he designed that night. So, taking his leave of Liberius and Angelica, but especially of Sylvia (sealing it with a kiss and requesting her to remember and consider what he had proposed), he departed, promising to renew his visit the next day.

From this time for three weeks successively, Philaretus was a constant attendant upon Sylvia at the house of Liberius, ever behaving himself with that decorum and giving her such pregnant demonstrations of the sincerity of his affections that he perceived himself to grow in her esteem, and that Sylvia could not but own she began to love him.

Having extorted this confession from her one day, he continued to ply her closer than he had before with arguments, entreaties, presents, and the artifices that are used by lovers to obtain their mistresses. By the permission of Liberius he now made evening visits to Sylvia and kept her up whole nights upon the subject of love until, overcome by his importune addresses, she, at last, consented.

Had the empire of the world been offered to Philaretus, it could not have been more grateful to him than was this consent of Sylvia. He embraced her in his arms and imprinted a thousand kisses on her lips, thanking her for her compliance and sacredly engaging himself to repay her in conjugal affections. And here Philaretus put the question on what day she would be pleased to consummate his expected happiness? But she desiring that might be referred to Liberius and Angelica who, as they had been in stead of parents to her, she thought it highly reasonable that they should nominate.

The day began to dawn before these two lovers broke up at this time, when Sylvia went to hers, and Philaretus to the apartment that had been prepared for him; both agreed upon a happier meeting in a little time. Notwithstanding they went to bed so late, about nine Liberius ordered them to be called for breakfast, telling them that lovers ought to be like great counsellors of state: they ought not to sleep much for fear of an enemy.

When breakfast was over, Sylvia leaving him with Liberius and Angelica, Philaretus discovered to them the success of his last night's amour, and requested them in Sylvia's name and his own to appoint the day when they should be most at leisure to attend the nuptials. But Liberius and his lady both declined that office, desiring him to nominate, but withal, that the place might be at their house, Liberius offering to be at all the charge of the entertainment.

Philaretus would have excused Liberius from that trouble, but he would by no means hear of it. He told Philaretus that he designed himself to give her, and that he would give them the entertainment in token of his gratitude to Sylvia for the faithful service she had done in his family.

This was on the Tuesday morning, and among them they appointed the Tuesday following for the wedding, which Philaretus told Sylvia, and she acquiescing, they had nothing to do but to prepare for the celebration of it.

The next day Philaretus returned home to give the necessary orders for Sylvia's reception when the marriage should be over, while Liberius, his lady, and family were employed in preparation for it, at their own.

Philaretus had presented Sylvia with several pieces of the finest silks, laces, &c., which might have served for her wedding garments, but Angelica would provide her with all those things herself out of her own store; and accordingly she furnished her in as splendid a manner as herself was on the day of her espousals to Liberius.

During this time, Philaretus never failed to come or send every day to inquire after the welfare of Sylvia, but for the most part he came himself, though he made not so long stays as heretofore, his occasions not requiring, and his necessary avocations demanding his presence something more to direct what he would have done at his own house.

The day was now come, though no sooner than wished for by Philaretus, and about eight that morning he set out from home in as much state as if he had been going to marry a princess. He had not been sparing upon himself or equipage on this occasion, not esteeming Sylvia one whit the worse because she had no fortune. Philaretus was in his coach and six, with twelve servants in noble liveries on horseback, and attended with about forty gentlemen and ladies, who went to grace the nuptials.

A little before ten, Philaretus arrived at the house of Liberius, who met and welcomed them all at his gate and conducted them into his hall, while Philaretus went to pay his respects to his designed bride, that was nothing inferior to himself in her dress.

And here it is impossible to express the satisfaction Philaretus took in beholding Sylvia, while she, with a becoming modesty, was somewhat upon the reserve, not that she did not love and admire Philaretus or was going unwillingly to celebrate the marriage rites, but because of the many eyes would be fixed upon her and excite her virgin blushes, though they were in a fair way to be her last of that kind.

After the company, that came with Philaretus, were refreshed, and all other things disposed in order, something before twelve, Philaretus and the beautiful Sylvia were conducted in form by their respective bridemen and maids into Liberius's house, attended by that gentleman, the lady Angelica, and a numerous train of gentry besides, where Theophilus was appointed to perform the office, which he readily did; nor did he envy the bridegroom, but rather thought him a most imprudent gentleman to condescend to a bride of such mean extract.

The Gordian knot being thus tied, the bride and bridegroom returned into Liberius's hall, where they received the congratulations of all the company. When, dinner being ready, it was set upon the table, and Liberius bidding them welcome, after grace said, they sat down to a noble entertainment. It would be endless to describe the variety of meats, wines, and other liquors that appeared upon this occasion. Nothing to gratify the senses was wanting, nothing that might exhilarate and contribute to their satisfaction.

When dinner was over, and the table cleared, Liberius desired all the gentlemen and ladies there present to be free. He told them there was wine of all sorts, pipes, tobacco, &c. for those that liked; there was music the best that could be got; there was tables for cards and dice, with one for billiards, and a bowling green just at hand, that they might divert themselves according to their different inclinations, either with a bottle, dancing, or gaming, or his garden, if they pleased to walk. In a very little time the whole company were employed, some in one diversion, some in another, as their particular genius led them.

As for Philaretus and Sylvia they were generally among the dancers, though now and then he made his appearance among the gentlemen of the bottle to give and receive the usual compliments upon those occasions, while Sylvia continued among the ladies, and appeared like a diamond set in gold with them around her.

With these diversions they spent the hours until the tables were spread again, and supper was brought, which was alike becoming the generosity of Liberius; and from thence to bedtime the company were mostly employed in dancing. And now the bride was often taken out by the best of the gentry and danced to admiration, so far beyond what anyone, who had known her former circumstances, could expect that they thought her to exceed the best.

At last, for the most delightful pleasures will cloy, Sylvia was so tired, she began to be uneasy at the importunity of the young gentlemen that addressed her to dance, while every one of them was ambitious to obtain the last maiden dance she was ever likely to perform. But night going on apace, and Liberius measuring Philaretus by what himself had formerly been, he resolved to put an end to Sylvia's dancing himself and, taking her out, he assured her that should be the last desired of her that night.

When this dance was over, Liberius led her to the bridemaids and desired them to do their office, for that it was time; and accordingly, they conducted her to her chamber.

While the ladies were attending upon and undressing the bride, the bridemen were busily employed in unrigging Philaretus in another apartment and divested him of all, except that part in which he was to embrace the lovely Sylvia, besides a rich nightgown and slippers, convenient, especially upon such occasions.

When notice was given that Sylvia was in bed, they conducted him also to the place of his desire, and he went with greater pleasure than he would have done to be put in possession of a crown.

Philaretus and Sylvia were now got together, and the usual ceremonies at such solemnities having been performed, the curtains were closed and the company departed, leaving Sylvia to the sole disposal of her loved Philaretus and Philaretus to the rapturous enjoyment of his dearest Sylvia. What are the transports of two lovers meeting together in lawful manner is difficult to express, and perhaps cannot be done without breaking in upon modesty and transgressing the law of reputation. We shall therefore leave them to the experienced to recollect, while the unexperienced can only have a faint conception of them.

After this, the rest of the company returned to their dancing, which they protracted till three in the morning when, as it were by consent, they broke up and retired everyone to his rest, as he could find convenience, for which Liberius's house was now much straitened, apartments for the ladies only with some select gentlemen having been secured for that purpose.

After breakfast, to which Liberius engaged them, the major part of the company departed to their homes, leaving none but some relations and particular friends of Liberius and Philaretus's behind. These, through the solicitations of Liberius and Angelica, were prevailed upon for two days longer, when Philaretus carried his darling Sylvia home, accompanied by those who remained and particularly by Liberius and Angelica, who, good lady, could hardly tell how to part with Sylvia. Such is the effect of a long acquaintance; when two souls are, as it were, united by a long familiarity, they can hardly bear a separation; we can scarce bear to part with one we love, though it be to his advantage and with our own approbation.

Philaretus and his bride with their company were now arrived at his own house where he gave them a splendid entertainment and would have engaged them to tarry all night, but most of them resolved to take their leaves and did. However, they prevailed with Liberius and Angelica, who tarried with them a whole week with all the pleasure and enjoyment that heart could wish.

Though Sylvia was now become lady of that family, she could not forget she had once been plain Sylvia in Angelica's and, till Angelica forbade, she was as obsequious as when under her command. The sense of gratitude is so inherent in generous souls that no alterations of circumstances can make them overlook a benefactor, and there is no surer token of a good disposition than to be grateful.

Liberius was now resolved to return home with his lady, and the day was come. Accordingly, after many mutual good wishes on both sides for the health and happiness of both families, with many endearing expressions of love and friendship, but especially between the two ladies, and gifts to all their servants, they departed with their retinue.

All the hurry of their wedding being happily over, Philaretus and his lady began to be at ease, began to come to themselves, and have a little time for thinking, which had been so long interrupted; he in her, and she in him, being mutually happy, they enjoyed a continual scene of tranquility. No jars, no feuds, no ruffling clouds, were seen betwixt them, but all their days were a series of sunshine; unity was in all their actions, and a perfect harmony in both their affections. As their days were always pleasant, so their nights were without lectures, calm, and undisturbed, unless it was by their embraces.

In this happy condition, they had lived above a year and Philaretus, not knowing but it might be ungrateful to her, had never so much as asked Sylvia about her parentage; neither had she made any discovery of it to him. At last, one day as they were walking together, she requested of him a favor and assured him, as it was the first, so it would be the last of that kind she would ever ask. Philaretus, who was ever as ready to grant as she could be to ask, demanded what that was. Sylvia made answer that she had a mind to see some places in England and would be glad if he would spend a month or two in taking a tour with her round the country. It was no sooner mentioned by Sylvia but it was granted too by Philaretus, and the Monday following they appointed to set out which way she pleased and at her own discretion when to return.

On the day appointed Philaretus ordered his coach and six, with an equal number of horsemen to attend for this journey, which were accordingly got ready, together with their own neces-

saries, *viz.*, for Philaretus, Sylvia, and her woman that was to go
along with them.

Pursuant to their resolution, when all things were ready,
Philaretus, Sylvia, and her woman went into the coach, the servants mounted, and away they went for Worcestershire, Sylvia
having directed their first tour to the city of Worcester. However,
they made but very short stages because they visited several towns
and ancient seats of gentlemen that lay in their way, and they
would go a little out, sometimes, to see anything that was remarkable.

Eight days they were upon the road before they reached the
city they designed, where they made some stay, about three or
four days, and viewed all the parts of it with as much intentness
as if Sylvia had never seen the place before. From thence, as the
Vale of Esom is esteemed one of the gardens of England, it was
resolved they would pay a visit to it. Accordingly, they did, Sylvia
directing to the village just by her father's house and in sight of it.

The afternoon was far spent when Philaretus and his lady
entered this village, where Sylvia, knowing there was an handsome inn, designed to persuade Philaretus to tarry. Philaretus
wanted not any persuasion to anything that Sylvia liked; so the
coachman was ordered to drive to the inn directly. Philaretus and
his lady alighted, they were presently conducted into the best
room, according to their quality, and looking exactly towards
Sylvia's father's.

Here they ordered a supper for themselves and company, such
as the place would afford, and while that was getting ready,
Philaretus being willing to ask some questions about the country,
the landlord was sent for up to inform him. Sylvia, that had
already observed her father's house from the window, sat very
silent in expectation that Philaretus would inquire after it in his
discourse with the innkeeper; besides, she did not know but she
might discover herself sooner than she would, if she should inquire herself.

The innkeeper being come, Philaretus bade him sit, gave him
a glass of wine, and asked him several questions, such as what

towns were near, what remarkable places, what gentlemen's seats, and in particular, whose seat that was just before them.

Here the honest landlord, fetching a deep sigh, "O sir," said he, "that gentleman and his lady were once the happiest couple in all these parts but now are the most unhappy; for some years past they have been so melancholy, though they have a great estate, that nothing can be more. That gentleman's name is Sosander, and his lady's is Gratiana; it would pierce your heart to hear the story of them, and a great deal more to see them." "However," said Philaretus, "let us hear it."

At hearing this, Sylvia removed her seat a little farther from the light, that in case she should drop a tear, it might not be so easily discerned.

Hereupon the innkeeper went on. "Sir," said he, "that gentleman, Sosander, some years ago had one only daughter, the prettiest sweet good-natured creature living, and about fourteen years old; and her name was Sylvia."

Here Philaretus looking at his lady and smiling, said he, "So then, my dear, I find we are going to have a story of one of your namesakes."

"Yes, sir," said the innkeeper, "if my lady's name be Sylvia, and I protest to you, so very like her that nothing can be more, only that Mrs. Sylvia was not so tall nor so thick as this lady here. But, as I was saying before, she was pretty, and had a great many fine folks come a-courting to her, and among the rest, an old gentleman turned of sixty. Pox on him, I wish he had been far enough, for he spoiled the best gentleman in all our country by it."

Here the honest man stopped, being ready to cry, and Sylvia was so full she could hardly forbear to keep him company. But Philaretus asked him, "How so?"

"Why, I will tell you, sir," said he, "this old gentleman had gotten the length of her father's foot,[17] and he was resolved she should have him, but she was resolved he should not have her;

---

[17] To discover or know a person's weakness.

and you know, master, when women set themselves against any-body, they are strange things. Now, as I was telling you, her father would, and appointed the wedding day—nay, and had got the beef, pudding, and pies, and all things ready for it, but she would not and run away on the very day. Her father sent I don't know how many messengers to seek her, but they might as well look for a needle in a bottle of hay. She has never been seen or heard of since. Sosander and Gratiana never come out of doors since that time, but only into their walk before their gates about half an hour before dinner; and then if they meet with any stranger, perhaps they may invite him in. Before that accident, Sosander was the most generous man in the world to all his poor neigh-bors, and I am sure I feel the want of him."

Here the innkeeper ended his story which Philaretus said was a very melancholy one, as also did Sylvia, who was best acquainted with it, though she said nothing of that but only seemed to pity the gentleman and his lady very much.

This story of the innkeeper had stirred up the curiosity of Philaretus to observe the house a little more particularly, and taking notice of its situation, how it was seated upon a pleasant eminence, or rising ground, just by the side of the vale, from whence there was a prospect of all the country below, for several miles together, with a noble front and built after the modern fashion, and seemed to be accompanied with a great many out-houses and gardens that took in a vast quantity of ground, he inquired if it was not possible to see the house itself.

"Yes," said the landlord, "and I can assure you it is very well worth your seeing, for there is not a finer house in all these parts. There is a great deal of fine workmanship about it, noble paint-ings, good fish ponds, stately gardens; and if you should see the gentleman himself, he will show you his chamber of books, where he has a vast many rarities, old knick-knacks, of I don't know how many years standing, and which all gentlemen that have seen them are mightily taken with. And I cannot tell any better way for you to come at the old gentleman than by dropping upon him a little before twelve, when he is in the walk."

What the innkeeper said concerning Sosander's library and the curiosities in it was a spur to Philaretus's inclination, and he expressed his desire to see it, when Sylvia put in. "My dear," said she, "let us stay here tomorrow, and do you take the opportunity our landlord talked of. I could be glad you would see the gentleman and lady, and perhaps you may hear the whole story of their misfortunes from their own mouths."

At this the innkeeper began again. "O dear madam, I would not for the world that you should go along with the gentleman, for you are so like Mrs. Sylvia, their daughter, that it will revive their affliction; and I fear me she has destroyed herself long since, for else we should certainly have heard of her before now." The simplicity of the innkeeper and his observations made Sylvia both smile and blush at the same time, and Philaretus himself was something pleased at the fellow's notions.

Hereupon it was resolved that Philaretus, on the morrow, should go to Sosander's according to the innkeeper's directions, watch his coming out, and address him for permission to view his house, being a stranger in those parts.

By this time supper was ready and brought in, when the landlord and his wife were both called up and ordered to sit down with Philaretus and Sylvia. The landlady had been nurse to Sylvia in her infancy and knew her when she was grown up, even to the time she left her father's; and though she had not taken so much notice of her at her first coming, yet upon the observation her husband had made, she could not forbear staring at her now; and in this lady she found all the features of her former Sylvia. She imagined that she saw her eyes, nose, forehead, cheeks, lips, and even heard her speak when the lady in company opened her mouth, and could she have seen the back part of Sylvia's neck, where there was a mole that she remembered, her nurse had been confident of the person.

Sylvia knew her but endeavored to conceal herself, till she could make herself known to her parents first, but was willing to know beforehand how they had resented her leaving them and whether they would be glad to receive her.

When the supper was ended (which was something shorter than they used to have at home, though as good as travellers usually meet with upon the roads) they diverted themselves with various subjects of discourse until bedtime; and at their usual hour, Philaretus and his lady retired, giving the landlord orders that the servants should want for nothing.

Not to mention what passed in the morning at the inn, as being very little material, something before twelve, Philaretus walked towards Sosander's with only two footmen attending him; and he came to the place just in the nick of time. Sosander and Gratiana were there walking, hand in hand, in a very melancholy posture, with deep-fetched sighs and sad complaints of their hard fortune in the loss of Sylvia. This was the usual theme of their discourse; this was the continued cause of their mourning, and no wonder it was the constant subject of their condolence.

As soon as Philaretus entered the walk, Sosander and Gratiana espied him and, perceiving him to be a gentleman and a stranger, they stopped till he came up to them. After some usual compliments and some questions on both sides, Philaretus told Sosander that he had heard much of the commendation of his house, that it was worthy the notice of a traveller, and therefore he desired to be admitted to see it. "Oh! sir," said Sosander, "it is a melancholy one now, but, as it is, you are welcome to it."

Here Sosander and his lady desired him to walk in and, telling him now it was their dinner time, they requested that he would dine, and afterwards Sosander would gratify his curiosity. Philaretus was a complaisant gentleman and, accepting Sosander's offer, he eat with them.

After dinner, Sosander answered his desire by showing him the house and the conveniencies about it, with all which Philaretus was extremely delighted and made his observations so justly upon each particular that Sosander found him to be a man of sense, a gentleman and a scholar; and upon this last account, he told him he had one thing to show him he valued above all the rest, *viz.*, his library, which had formerly been his diversion and was now the greatest comfort he had in his afflictions.

Here Philaretus observed a noble collection of books, and Sosander showed him abundance of curiosities, pieces of antiquity, a great number of Greek and Latin medals, with several foreign rarities that were well fitting the closet of such a gentleman.

While Philaretus feasted his eyes with this delicious sight which was as grateful to him as any could be, he chanced to spy a picture in one corner of the library which surprised him. In it he thought he saw his own lady, just as she was when he first courted her and so very like her it could not have been more, had it been drawn for her. Here he called to mind what the innkeeper had said concerning Sosander's Sylvia and concluded that it was her portraiture; and being willing to be resolved, he took the liberty to ask him whose that picture was. To which Sosander, who could not forbear tears at that question, made this reply: "Sir, that is the picture of a daughter I was once happy in; her name was Sylvia and I myself forced her away from me. It was my own cruelty that did it, and I desire you to ask no more about her."

This recollection of Sylvia had put Sosander into such concern, had raised the passion of grief to such a degree in him, he could not endure to tarry where her picture was any longer; whereupon he desired Philaretus to walk with him to his parlor and take a glass of wine.

Here they entered upon several topics of discourse in which Philaretus so approved himself to Sosander that he was extremely pleased with his conversation and could have wished it longer. But it was now about five, and Philaretus began to excuse his departure by telling him he had left his lady at the village. Sosander expressed some concern that he had not brought her with him, would have engaged Philaretus to bring her the next day and to tarry what time they pleased, when Philaretus, being as much pleased with Sosander as Sosander with Philaretus, promised Sosander that he would on this condition that himself and lady, as it was now evening and pleasant walking, would condescend to walk with him to the inn and see his lady. Though another might, Philaretus found it no difficult matter to persuade Sosander, and accordingly it was resolved. The prevalence Philaretus had over him through his little conversation was greater than most of his intimate acquaintance could have had and who, indeed, having observed his discomposure and how uneasy company was to him, had seldom or never requested the favor of him.

When they came to the inn, Philaretus introduced them to his lady and, after mutual salutations, at the request of Philaretus they sat down. And here, what a struggle was there in the breast of Sylvia! Shame mingled with fear of surprising them into some inconvenience by a too sudden discovery of herself; and though she found that affection would overcome, she was willing, however, to keep it in till she could find how fairly matters stood.

They had not sat long when Gratiana, that beheld Sylvia with a great deal of intention [attention?], was seen to drop some tears, which Philaretus perceiving demanded if she was not well. Gratiana thanked him and excused herself by saying [that] the sight of that gentlewoman, his lady, brought her grief for the loss of a daughter she once had, and was most happy in, afresh to her remembrance; that she was so like her, nothing could be more.

"Oh! my dear," said Sosander, "that she was but here, I should think myself the happiest person living and would give my whole estate she was alive and well among us."

At these words Sylvia, unable to contain herself any longer, rose from her seat and going towards her father, she flung herself at his feet, though the tears of joy gushed out so fast that she could not speak a word for a short space.

This sudden motion of Sylvia's, as it amazed Sosander and Gratiana, so it greatly surprised Philaretus, till clasping her father about the knees, she said, "And can Sosander pardon Sylvia? I am Sylvia, the very same that was to have Stertorius."

As the excess of grief, so that of joy has the same effects; they equally strike people dumb until they can recover themselves and so it happened with Sosander. He looked very earnestly upon her, though he could not speak and scarcely believe his own eyes for above half a minute. At last raising her from the ground, he tenderly embraced her saying, "This is a happiness I never expected. Sylvia is not in fault; it was I, and only I, my dearest child."

Here the old gentleman wept like a child under correction, while he hugged and kissed her with the greatest passion and bedewed her cheeks with aged tears, while hers fell trickling down and joined them.

As soon as Sylvia was disengaged from her father's embraces, she addressed herself to her mother, Gratiana, imploring her pardon for all the trouble she had caused her in the like manner as she had done her father. Gratiana, having seen and heard all that had passed between Sosander and Sylvia and recovered pretty well from her surprise, was a little better prepared than Sosander. She received her with open arms, told her it was enough that she had seen her alive and well. She embraced her with all the affections of a parent and, kissing her, welcomed her return in the most endearing expressions.

These first joyful salutations being over, Sylvia directing herself to Philaretus, said thus, "My dear, these are my parents whom I have so long concealed, and now I hope my extract will prove no reflection to Philaretus."

Upon this Philaretus having embraced her with a tenderness that plainly discovered his love towards her and an exceeding satisfaction he took in the participation of their common joy, and leading her back to her father and mother, they jointly craved their blessing upon their knees, which being granted, Sosander and Gratiana both raising Philaretus and saluting him, they all resumed their seats.

And now Sosander and Gratiana that for some years had thought themselves childless unexpectedly were blessed with two. They who but a little before were perfectly oppressed with grief and almost sunk under the weight of affliction, were become alert, lively, and exceeding joyful. The scene was quite altered, and the conversation of Sosander had a new face.

The news of Sylvia's return was quickly noised throughout the village and occasioned an universal joy, because now they expected Sosander would appear among them as he used to do. The bells were all set on ringing and the people left their work, and flocked about the inn to see the new-come, long-desired Sylvia. Finding that the crowds thickened, Sosander ordered the inn-keeper to supply them with drink, while he with his lady, Philaretus, and Sylvia, went away in Philaretus's coach.

Being all at Sosander's, Gratiana was impatient to hear an account of her daughter's travels; how she got away from thence, which had been until then unknown; how, and where she lived all the time; what adventures she had met, and how she came to be so happy in a husband. Sylvia, willing to gratify her mother, gave her a large account of all that she required, only how she came by so good a husband she could not answer, unless by the particular direction of Providence.

At this point, Philaretus, who had been present all this while and heard her whole relation with Sosander, undertook to give an answer in which he told them that he never knew their daughter until she was gentlewoman to the Lady Angelica; that her beauty and other personal excellencies, joined with the best of characters which she ever had from all who ever knew her, were the charms that drew him to love and esteem her, which he did so entirely that he could not do it more upon the account of being daughter to Sosander and Gratiana.

Though it was late when they came from the inn, Sosander had ordered supper, which by this time was ready and set before them. While they were eating, Sosander took occasion to descant a little upon the last words of Philaretus and the entire affection he expressed himself to have for Sylvia. These, Sosander told him, he had heard with the greatest satisfaction and, before they parted, he would take an opportunity to make a grateful acknowledgment.

It would be endless to recount every minute circumstance that passed during their stay at Sosander's, which was a full month; and during that time, he kept open house, especially for the entertainment of the gentry that were pleased to pay their respects to Philaretus and Sylvia, excepting only on such days as themselves went abroad.

Sosander and Gratiana were now perfectly recovered of their melancholy and thought of nothing more than a journey with Philaretus and Sylvia, when they should return home. The time was now fixed for their departure and preparations were making for it, when, the second day before they set out, Sosander calling Philaretus aside, presented him with bills for ten thousand pounds, and gave him assurance of a far greater fortune to come.

Here Philaretus could not but bless his stars and commend his fortune that had given him a lady of the greatest endowments, beautiful, chaste, adorned with all manner of virtues, of the sweetest temper, well educated, and of extraordinary extract, though supposed to have sprung from the dunghill and to have had her original, at best, from a beggar. Philaretus was so pleased to find all these concurring in Sylvia that he thought himself the happiest of men.

The day was come on which they were to set out from Sosander's, who having engaged two nieces of Gratiana's to go with them, they were a company of two coaches. And thus on the morning appointed, Sosander took his leave of home with the rest of his company, attended by four of his own and the six servants of Philaretus on horses, besides the coachmen and postillions.

As they made no stay on the road, on the third day they arrived at the house of Philaretus, when the news of his return was quickly dispersed and of the company he had brought with him. As Philaretus was a gentleman universally beloved, so the discovery of Sylvia's parentage, especially being so extraordinary and far above what could be thought, was a satisfaction to all. Hereupon congratulations came from all sides and visits from every quarter. Among the rest, Liberius and Angelica were not the last to pay their respects. Only Angelica was a little displeased with Sylvia that she had not communicated her extraction to her before, that she might have treated her accordingly.

There was a continual succession of guests at Philaretus's house at that time, for which reason Liberius and Angelica returned home, though they were much importuned by Sosander and Gratiana, as well as the young ones with whom they were more acquainted. However, they promised to spend a week with them before their return and hoped Sosander would do the same with them.

Theophilus (chaplain to Liberius and between whom and Sylvia that gentleman had formerly proposed a match), as it happened, had not heard of Philaretus's return, much less of his success, before Liberius and Angelica came home. Then coming to wait on them, and Liberius asking him if he had heard that Philaretus was returned from his progress, he answered no.

"Then I suppose," says Liberius, "you have not heard the news. Philaretus has found out Sylvia's father, and he is a gentleman of a considerable estate in Worcestershire of some thousands; and that beggar which you despised so, not long since, is his only daughter. She left him upon a disgust, because he would have forced her to marry an old man of sixty, and I think the girl was in the right. However, he is reconciled to her now and has given Philaretus ten thousand pounds, with a promise of the greatest part of his estate in reversion. See what it is to stand upon punctilio. But I find you are like other men, and virtue in a threadbare coat is little set by."

"Sir," said Theophilus, "I believe it is only your pleasure to be jocose."

"Not so," said Liberius, "it is really so; it is fact. Her father is now at Liberius's [Philaretus's] house, and her mother too."

Theophilus was not a little nettled at what Liberius had said; however, he held his tongue and in a short time, paying his respects, he departed to get some farther intelligence among the servants, who all affirmed it and more, that they had heard among their fellows at Philaretus's. This confirmation of what Liberius had said and the jeers he had put upon him were such a weight upon the haughty spirit of Theophilus, who had the exact temper of some fellows of colleges, that it made him very chagrin and full of spleen, insomuch that he was obliged to retire to his chamber where he vented these expressions:

"Who could have divined that Sylvia was a gentlewoman? 'Tis seldom persons of fashion turn beggars. And who could have thought so young a creature could have been so great a dissembler and mistress of so much design? I believe I might have gained her affections at that time by the encouragement of Liberius and his lady, but I did not dream of such a fortune. Liberius, indeed, recommended her beauty and virtue, which are good qualifications in a wife, but they will not make the pot boil; and if he did offer £700 with her, what is that? But then, again, what had I? Nothing that I could secure to her. I wish I had taken up that offer. I might have kept my coach before this time and looked like other men. Liberius was in the right on't: see what comes of Pride. But I did not think of that. Because I was a fool, I was proud; and because I was proud, I have lost as lucky a hit to make my fortune as ever man had in my circumstances. I thought Philaretus very imprudent to marry such a person, but now I know myself a coxcomb for neglecting such an offer. This will teach me not to neglect a friend's advice for the future. But the steed is stolen, and it is too late to recall it. If it could be, I should act another part and not verify the saying, as I have, 'What mere scholars are.' However, since this mischief can't be cured, I must bear it with patience, and I resolve with myself never more to insist upon pedigree."

But leaving Theophilus to complain by himself, which he did until about midnight, when the image of Death, or a deep sleep, overtook him and lulled him into a soft repose, let us return to see how matters stood at Philaretus's house. For nine days together the concourse was not perceptibly lessened, but afterwards it began to decline; and the visitors were not so frequent, though there were constantly some of the best gentry who never failed to accompany Sosander and Gratiana while they were there, out of pure respect to Philaretus and his lady. And Philaretus was never better pleased than with the honor then conferred on his new-discovered father and mother. The respect given to them, he esteemed as given to himself, and whosoever was obliging to them, he ever respected.

Among those of the best rank and quality, Liberius and Angelica (accompanied by their son, whose eyes Sylvia had cured when she personated the beggar at Liberius's gate, which was the first step to her preferment) came according to promise to wait upon Sosander and Gratiana and tarried there a whole week. In which time Sosander and Liberius became particularly acquainted. The likeness of their parts, inclinations, studies, and tempers had rendered them so agreeable each to the other that they contracted a friendship, insomuch, that they wished their habitations joined, or rather that they might live together. But as that could not be, Sosander engaged Liberius to let his son go with him, when he should return home, assuring him that nothing should be wanting to accomplish his education during his stay with him, to which Liberius, being fully satisfied in Sosander, agreed.

Gratiana also and Angelica were become exceeding dear to each other, and both from the same principle. Gratiana loved Angelica for the kindness she had shown to Sylvia, and Angelica respected Gratiana, because she was Sylvia's mother, to whom she owed so many obligations. Upon this account they were always together during Angelica's continuance with Philaretus; and when they were by themselves, Sylvia's management in the time of her service was the common subject of their discourse, than the repetition of which, together with the account of her excellent behavior under her different circumstances, nothing could be more pleasing to Gratiana, and she often requested it. And here Sosander and Liberius could not be more closely linked together in friendship than were Gratiana and Angelica, insomuch that nothing grieved them more than the thoughts of parting. But they had all homes to go to, and those required the presence of their respective superiors, and having tarried a full week, Liberius and Angelica, with their son, returned to theirs, satisfied in a promise that Sosander and Gratiana would repay their visit, which accordingly they did in a little time.

And here Liberius, one day at table, was pleased to relate what had passed between himself and Theophilus concerning their daughter and how he had rejected her.

Theophilus was by when this was told and Sosander replied,

"I am glad the gentleman did not think her worthy, since she is now more happy than, probably, he could have made her, though I have such a respect for gentlemen of his coat, I should not have rejected him if he had come along with Sylvia to crave my blessing."

These expressions galled Theophilus so bitterly he sat with a great deal of impatience till dinner was over. That ended, he retired as quickly as he could, resolving, though he should disoblige Liberius by the bargain, never to appear again at his table so long as Sosander and Gratiana should tarry; who, when they had repaid their visit and continued at Liberius's as long as they thought convenient, returned to their son's.

Sosander and Gratiana had now been upwards of two months from home, and it was about time to think of returning. Accordingly, they resolved on the fourth day following to set out for Worcestershire, and they did so, taking with them the young Liberius, whom they valued as if he had been their own son.

Philaretus and Sylvia, Liberius and Angelica, and several others of the gentry attended them one day's journey on the road, when, taking their leaves with the kindest embraces and most endearing expressions of affection on all sides, Sosander proceeded on his journey, while Philaretus and his company returned to their respective homes.

And now, if it had been possible, Philaretus and his Sylvia lived more happily than they did before. This discovery of her parents had augmented the satisfaction of Philaretus in particular, having taken off the reflection and stopped the mouths of ignorant detractors that were willing, because they had nothing else, to object against the meanness of Sylvia's birth. That she was daughter to Sosander, and heiress to a great estate, were no new motives to his love. He loved her for her own sake and would have continued it, had her extraction been really what was supposed.

To a virtuous disposition there are no charms like the charms of virtue, no attractions like them; and when these are joined with beauty, when an angelic mind inhabits a body qualified with all these internal perfections as it did in Sylvia, no wonder that Philaretus loved her with the most ardent affection. Such a treasure is inestimable and cannot be prized enough. A love grounded upon such a basis can never miscarry; it is founded upon right reason; and the effect of wedlock concluded upon such a bottom is the most solid happiness this world can produce. And thus they passed their days in the profoundest tranquility, he all love, and she all over goodness.

And thus we have brought this relation to a conclusion, which though it was black enough and melancholy in the beginning, though it had not the least glimpse of light at first, but was set, as it were, in thick darkness, of the most hideous aspect, and promising nothing but a continued series of misfortunes, with a long and dismal chain of galling miseries attending it, at last broke forth into a dawn, and emerging itself into a glorious unexpected calm, the lovely sunshine of a cloudless serenity.

A great number of useful reflections might be raised from the various circumstances that attended Sylvia's fortune, but none more seasonable, or indeed beneficial, than this—that the whole may serve as an instructive lesson to parents how far they interpose their authority in such affairs and engage them to act with caution and not to be self-willed and peremptory in laying a restraint upon the affections of their children, lest, perhaps, they prove their own tormentors and repent at leisure what hasty resolution they sometimes too obstinately make upon the like occasions.

For, not to derogate from the authority of parents or to lessen their jurisdiction over their respective families, which in some case I must own to be unlimited and despotic, yet in others, I conceive it to be limited; and in such, they cannot transgress their bounds without incurring the censure of a breach of duty on their part. They are, indeed, the parents of our bodies and over our external actions they have a just prerogative, especially while we are immediately under their direction. But then the nobler part we are not beholden to them for; that is of an higher extract, and derives its pedigree from a freer original; the faculties of that are given for its own proper use and were never designed to have a restraint laid upon them unbecoming the freedom of their nature.

Love and aversion are innate principles of the soul, and when those are stopped in their proper channel, like a river, they will swell, overflow their banks, and very often run into loose extravagancies and wild disorders.

But this could not be said of Sylvia. Persecution is what nature has an aversion to, and to fly from that was never deemed a crime, especially in love. Tyranny, and usurpation, and a kind of lording it over our affections are things hard to be borne, and what could Sylvia do? She could not show her active obedience upon this account, and to be continually within the hearing of her parents' resentments, or what was more, in the embraces of the person she abhorred, was a burden too great for her tender years to support. She therefore took the wiser course. And sure, 'tis better to fly the tyrant's rage than stiffly stand, maintain one's ground a while, and after yield, when force compels one to surrender at discretion. The fate of this is seen too oft in such unequal matches, and if some of them seemed more calm and undisturbed than others, there still have been their secret stings, which ever render life and wedlock both uneasy.

FINIS

THE JAMAICA LADY

OR

The Life of Bavia

CONTAINING

An Account of her Intrigues, Cheats, Amours in England, Jamaica, and the Royal Navy.

A Pleasant Relation of the Amours of the Officers of a Fourth Rate Man of War with their Female Passengers, in a Voyage from Jamaica to England.

WITH

The Diverting Humors of Captain Fustian, Commander of the said Ship. And the Character of his Irish Surgeon; the Reason of his Preferment; and the Manner of obtaining his Warrant.

LONDON

Printed; and sold by Tho. Bickerton, at the Crown in Pater-noster-Row.   1720.

Price: Eighteen Pence

NOTE TO TITLE PAGE

According to Henry R. Plomer in his *Dictionary of the Printers and Booksellers who were at work in England, Scotland, and Ireland from 1668 to 1725*, Thomas Bickerton was active in London publishing circles from 1707 until 1720, moving successively from St. Paul's Churchyard to Little Britain and, finally, to Paternoster Row, from which this novel was issued. He was concerned with one semifictional work by Defoe, *The Dumb Philosopher* (1719), and was one of the publishers of Arthur Blackamore's first novel, *The Perfidious Brethren* (1720).

The Epistle Dedicatory.

To Mr. Tho. Cr – – – – ps, of Ha – – – – ls in Kent.[1]

SIR,

As it was you who encouraged me to write (though a treatise of another nature), this first fruit of my scribble is by right your due. Nor shall I make any apology for the dedication without leave, since I am so well acquainted with your goodness, as to be assured you'll not be offended at it.

I am sensible you employ your time in books of greater use, and apply your talent in those things which may not only be profitable to yourself but advantageous to posterity. Yet after you have fatigued yourself in the mathematics and are quite wearied with mechanics, this may serve to divert an hour.

I have received such signal favors from you, sir, that I embrace this occasion to make public acknowledgment. He only is a friend who is so in time of need. You I have tried, and found you bear the touch. Until opportunity offers to make a more suitable return, I desire you will accept this trifle from, sir, your obliged, humble servant.

W. P.[2]

[1] Probably Thomas Cripps. Musgrave's *Obituary* lists a "Tho. Cripps, Maidstone, Kent, 6 March 1685;" he may have been the father of the novelist's potential patron. "H – – – – ls" may be the name of a country estate near Maidstone. Circumstantial details in the novel indicate familiarity with the main Kentish highways.

[2] The author may be William Pittis (1674–1724), one of the wits at the Rose Tavern, a minor journalist in the reign of Queen Anne, and later a hack writer employed by Edmund Curll and others. This attribution, however, is very tentative. Pittis attended Oxford and published various Horatian imitations (W. P. quotes from Horace). He studied medicine (three of the characters are physicians) and later wrote a biography of Dr. John Radcliffe, to whom Steele had referred to in the *Tatler* as Aesculapius (the name of Bavia's husband). Pittis also produced an elegy on the death of Sir Clowdisley Shovell (mentioned in the novel) and, most important of all, he was a close friend

of Edward Ward, the author of *A Trip to Jamaica* (1698). Similarities between Ward's pamphlet and *The Jamaica Lady* are discussed in the Introduction. Pittis, who had never been to Jamaica, may have gotten other first-hand information and anecdotes from Ward. His last known publication was a criminal tract. John Dunton's epitome of him as "drunken Pittis" would seem to indicate that other aspects of the novel were congenial to Pittis. Theodore F. M. Newton's articles in *Modern Philology* (XXXII, 169–186; XXXIII, 279–302) are the most complete sources of information on Pittis.

The Preface

As it requires much more care and skill to draw the portraiture of some particular person and to make the copy exactly resemble the original than it does to paint a man in general, so is the task I have undertaken far more difficult than that of writing a novel only.

Novels are generally of two sorts. The author of one kind has commonly no more to do than to abridge the story of some larger history from which he picks and culls what he believes most apt to please the palate of the reader, and it is usually not much otherwise than a bare transcription. Or if there be an alteration, he is left at liberty to add or diminish, as his fancy dictates; and the language is such as is best adapted to his genius.

The other is a translation of some foreign piece, where the plot, humor, and discourse are ready made to his hand, and he has naught to do but to render it into English, which, if he performs in an elegant style, the reader's pleased and the author applauded.

But here are represented persons of different characters distinctly wide one from the other. And the story being true, an author, if he designs to have the picture known, without (like a bad painter) writing under it, is tied up close to the pattern, must suit his words not only to the reader's taste, but to the persons represented, both which I have endeavored and hope, in some measure, effected.

I have taken care to write with all the modesty the subject would permit, being very cautious of offending the fair sex, and, should there be an expression which may seem rough or harsh, I desire it may be imputed to the sea captain and not to the author. I have purposely avoided long discourses of insignificant courtship and tedious soliloquies, being of opinion they are neither pleasant nor profitable but serve only to increase the bulk and diminish the beauty of an history.

My design in publishing this story is, first, to divert and please the reader; and, secondly, to expose the vice of two notorious women, that others, whose inclinations direct 'em the same course, may (if not for fear of future punishment, yet) by the dread of present and of public shame, be restrained from their ill intentions. If I succeed in both, I have gained my end; if in either, I am satisfied.

Vale.

Bavia: or, The Jamaica Lady

Soon after the conclusion of the peace in 1713,[1] orders were dispatched to Jamaica to discharge all the officers then belonging to the victualling, stores, hospital, &c. and likewise to remand the ships that were then cruising on that station, which caused most of the discarded officers to have recourse to the admiral to procure his warrant for themselves and families to be received on board some of the men-of-war and to be victualled as the ship's company until their arrival in England, as is usually done in cases of the like nature. Pharmaceuticus, who had been an assistant in the infirmary, obtained an order to be taken on board a fourth-rate,[2] whereof Captain Fustian was then commander.[3]

The captain was a man of a morose, surly temper, one that generally gave unmannerly language without any manner of provocation and very often perfectly rude and abusive to those persons who, with the greatest civility and most profound respect, accosted him. He would frequently wrest the sense and put a forced construction on some part of their discourse and make his own applications, though never so foreign or affronting, and believed he showed his wit in being captious, though, poor man, he only exposed his ignorance. To be concise in his character, I need only acquaint you that he was a downright tar,[4] having

[1] The Treaty of Utrecht (1713) concluded the War of the Spanish Succession (1702–1713).

[2] Men-of-war were divided into "rates" according to the number of guns carried. There seems to be no precise or widely accepted system of categorization. However, a fourth-rate man-of-war is generally conceded to have carried between fifty and sixty-five guns in the early eighteenth century.

[3] Type-names (Pharmaceuticus, Phlebotomus, Fustian, Compass, Frutesius [blockhead?], Galenicus [cock?], and Cupidus) are intermingled with what seem to be thinly disguised proper names (Holmesia, Hemingius, Ebrardus), a procedure familiar in the works of Mrs. Mary Manley and other writers of key-novels. Bavia may have been suggested by Horace's Bavius, and Quomina is probably an actual Afro-Spanish slave name.

[4] Although a familiar term for a sailor, "tar" also meant a sea-bred superior officer, as contrasted with the military officers often appointed to command men-of-war.

had his whole education at sea, and his rise from a cabin boy under Sir Cloudesly Shovel.[5]

The best and surest way to gain his favor was by adulation, and when once you were entered into his good graces, he was as pliable as wax. You might mold him as you pleased, were his chief oracle without whose advice he'd scarce undertake anything, though of the least importance. Yet, though he appeared ridiculous and contemptible to others, he had a very good opinion of his own performances, would pretend to be master of the most gentleman-like accomplishments, and affirm he had gone through all the exercises at the academy; would talk of balls (though ignorant and wide of the matter) as familiarly as if he had been bred at court and often had dancing on board his ship, but never made one himself at a country dance, yet had vanity enough to attempt dancing a minuet before people of judgment, though a novice to both step and figure. He only hopped half a dozen times round the cabin, made an awkward honor, and so completed his minuet, affirming 'twas the same way that was used at St. James's, and that the other was only a new and unmannerly invention of the Americans, unknown to and not practiced by European countries. His two favorite tunes were "Pretty Poll" and "Dame of Honor," which he called by the names of the first and second minuet.[6] His shape was something of the grossest, and Nature had so adapted his proportion that had you seen him caper a French dance, he would have brought to your remembrance that preposterous animal called a dancing bear. And, really, had he been clothed with a skin of that creature, 'twould have been something difficult for a person of a nice apprehension to have distinguished any remarkable difference betwixt the rational and sensible performer.

[5] Sir Clowdisley Shovell (1650–1707) was famous for his naval victories over the Barbary pirates and the French. He became Admiral of the Fleet in 1705.

[6] Fustian's unstately "minuets" were danced to well-known English tunes. Sear's *Song Index* lists "Queen Bess's Dame of Honor" with words by Thomas D'Urfey, and John Gay used the tune of "Pretty Poll" for Air XIV of *The Beggar's Opera*.

He would sometimes pretend to politics, but was no party-man, for he believed a Whig to be a Presbyterian and a Tory to be a Papist, which were equally his aversion, and he'd swear they were both rogues, people of pernicious principles. 'Twas not their religion in itself he found fault with, for he was so far from inquiring into that of others that he could give no account of his own, neither did he trouble himself about a matter that much wiser heads than his could not agree on. Though he had a chaplain on board, 'twas with much reluctancy he permitted the hands to be called up to prayers, affirming that in good weather there was no occasion for them and in bad there was somewhat else to be done, which he thought was at that time of more concern than to stand still and cry "God help." But as to his politics, he would work you a traverse of two hours upon past transactions and villify both contriver and actor, then acquaint you with his own models, rail at the ministry, tell you that, if he had been consulted, our national affairs had been in a far better posture, for that those at helm minded nothing but their own private interests and valued not how the public suffered, so they could enrich themselves.

These were his failings. Now let us view his virtues to see if they will counterpoise. He was endued with courage equal to most, superior to some of the commanders his contemporaries. He was truly brave and (if commanded) thought no attempt too dangerous to undertake. He was so delighted at the thoughts of an engagement that did you then see him walk the deck, giving necessary orders, you would take him for another man. His cloudy look and surly language were changed immediately; you might now behold a serene aspect, a pleasant smiling countenance, and a cheerful, easy, unconcerned discourse. Nothing but fighting and dancing could work that metamorphosis. He was likewise a punctual observer of his superior's orders and a thorough sailor, very fit qualifications for a man in the post he was preferred to, but of conduct we can't expect the poor gentleman should have a great share, considering his misfortune.

'Twas his unhappy fate, when lieutenant of a bomb-ketch,

to be wounded in an engagement with a splinter of the ship, which made a large fracture in his skull; and the malicious surgeon under whose care he was, it seems, owed him a spite and stole some of his brains, so that the man might have been born with as much wit as his neighbors and, but for the roguish trick of the latronious empiric who, it's said, filled up the cavity with lead, might have been as well qualified for a flag as some of his tarpaulin brethren. But I leave the impartial reader to consider if that ponderosity was not of some service to him, for he would drink three times the quantity of strong liquor as would make another man light-headed. After the taking of half a dozen bottles of wine and two or three gallons of punch, he would be the same man as before, no more concerned than when he got out of bed in the morning. True indeed, he always kept a bottle of rum or brandy under his bolster to cheer his spirits, which made some who had no affection for him report he was never sober. The Commissioners of the Chest at Chatham,[7] to make some amends, ordered him one hundred pounds smart money— a small reparation, perhaps, it may be thought for so great a loss. But I am of a contrary opinion and do verily believe, could he have sold the remaining cargo after the same rate he did the sample, he would have no reason to complain of the market.

Pharmaceuticus, understanding the temper of the man, was puzzled to know in what manner he should address himself. He would willingly have had a convenient apartment but knew not how to obtain it. To lie public and let his wife be exposed to the view of every saucy Jack Tar went something against the grain. But at length he luckily hit on this project.

He was informed Holmesia designed for England in a merchantman, which was returning home under convoy of this squadron. To her he applied himself and acquainted her with the inconveniencies she must undergo in that ship which she designed to take passage in. He then gave her a short description of a man-of-war and told her all persons would allow that the

[7] Headquarters of the Royal Navy on the Medway near Rochester.

stateliness of her cabins, number of guns, complement of men, room betwixt decks, and the many other conveniences for accommodation, rendered her much preferable to any of our merchant ships, which were so fully freighted, each corner stowed with merchandise, that there was no space left free for a passenger, or scarce indeed for the ship's crew to get a tolerable berth to repose in. And he said he was then going on board Captain Fustian to have a convenient cabin built for his wife and self, that it would be both for the advantage of her health and ease to have a passage in the same ship where his wife and she might be serviceable to each other, that he had an interest with the captain and doubted not but for a good premium he could procure part of the great cabin. Holmesia consented, bid him use his endeavors with the commander, and money should not be wanting.

Pharmaceuticus took boat and went off to the ship, informed the captain that a prime lady of the island designed to make a trip to England, purely in curiosity to see the country and particularly that famous metropolis, London; to amuse herself with the divertissements of the court, park, and playhouse; to visit her husband's relations and lay out a considerable sum upon rich clothes, furniture, &c. That she, having had an extraordinary character of his courteous deportment and genteel behavior, was willing to take passage on board him, provided she could be accommodated with tolerable conveniences. That she would make him any gratification he thought reasonable, and (producing the admiral's order for himself, wife, and Negro boy) told the captain that if he would please to spare part of the great cabin, it would be sufficient for the lady and him, too, that they would lay in their own stock and mess by themselves. The captain adhered to the proposal. The price was agreed on, and he ordered a partition to be made to divide the cabin, and two bedsteads were fixed in one part for his passengers.

Pharmaceuticus and his wife came off in a wherry and acquainted the captain that Holmesia was ready to come on board if he would please to send his boat on shore for her. Accordingly the pinnace was manned, carpet and cloak spread, and orders given to make haste and bring the lady. Holmesia was at the seaside with only one Negro woman-slave, named Quomina, who was to attend her the voyage. She herself was a Creole and consequently of a pale yellow complexion, of stature tall and meager, very demure and precise in her carriage but haughty withal, and, when moved, of an implacable, revengeful temper, yet a great pretender to piety and virtue. Her language was a sort of jargon, being a dialect peculiar to the natives of that island, it being partly English and partly Negroish, so that unless a man had been some time in the country, he could not well understand their meaning.

In a short time the boat took her in and returned within ken of the ship; the side was manned, and the captain himself stood ready at the entrance to receive her. As soon as she was on board, he took her by the hand and led her down to the cabin prepared for her, musing all the way how he had best treat the lady and what compliments he should bestow on her. At length, according to his usual custom, he bid his boy fill a glass of rum and after he had drank to her, he expressed himself in this manner. "You see, mistress, I have taken as much care of you as of myself. I have let you have full half the cabin and have run a bulkhead betwixt us without leaving so much as a gangway, because I think 'twill be best for both our reputations, for the world is censorious and, as we both lie aft, perhaps the crew may say we are foul of one another." Holmesia was not overpleased either with her reception or with the harangue he made her, but being obliged to make a virtue of necessity, knowing he was king there and she under his government, returned thanks for his favors, and he moved his hat and left her.

The squadron was ordered to sail the next morning and just as they were going to unmoor ship, came a man off shore with a message to the captain, and told him there was a lady a small distance from Greenbank[8] who was very desirous of a passage

---

[8] The author in an appended "Table, Explaining the Sea, and other difficult Terms" defined sixty-six words and phrases. Definitions taken from

home, and she, understanding that he had already some ladies on board, was willing to go in his ship and that if he would take her in, he need only say what sum he expected and the lady would secure it to him, be it what it would. The captain acquainted him that he had already parted with half his cabin and could not spare any more of it. But if she would be contented with the cabin at the bulkhead of the steerage, which was now vacant by the absence of a lieutenant of marines who was ordered on duty in another ship, she should be welcome. But he inquired how she came into that cursed country, for he said none but mad people and fools, when possessed of a plentiful fortune or even of a moderate competency in England, in Paradise, would leave it to go to Jamaica, the sink of sin and receptacle of all manner of vices, a place so intolerably hot and suffocating that he swore there was only a brown paper[9] betwixt it and hell. The man answered, if the captain pleased to give him leave, he would relate not only how she came but who she was and the manner of her leaving England, as he had it from her own mouth; which being consented to and the man ordered to sit, he thus began:

"Bavia (for so is the lady called) is of a very ancient and wealthy family, the only child of a gentleman of great estate, who gave her education suitable to her birth. It pleased Providence to take away her mother, when she was about twelve years of age, so that the old gentleman, her father, had then no remaining consolation but what was reposed in his beloved daughter. She managed his family, took care of his domestic affairs, and acted with so much prudence that she increased (if possible) her father's love towards her, and so endeared his affections that he left his whole concerns purely to her management.

"A young lady of her beauty, virtue, and fortune could not

---

this glossary are indicated by quotation marks. *Greenbank*: "a Plot of Ground lying opposite to the *Port Royal* Keys, where Sailors are usually inter'd."

[9] Probably a medical term. In *The Rehearsal* Bayes, after falling on his face, reappears "with a paper on his nose" (III, i).

be long without many real as well as pretended admirers. But he who most prevailed on her affections was Cupidus, a neighboring gentleman who by rich presents, fair promises, and solemn protestations so far ingratiated himself into her favor as at length to obtain a promise of marriage. And having so far succeeded with the young lady, his next endeavor was to gain the father's approbation. He set his emissaries to work, made application to all her father's friends and companions to intercede for him. But he, alas, poor gentleman! being too, too willing to please his darling and finding 'twas her inclination, easily yielded to the match. A day was fixed and the wedding solemnized. I shall not be particular in relating the sumptuous entertainment or the many jewels and precious moveables her father bestowed on her, for without them, the large portion he gave her merited a far more deserving person than Cupidus.

"However, they for some time lived in perfect happiness, so endearing to each other that it was difficult to discern which was most fond or more obliging. But this was only honeymoon. The tables soon turned. Cupidus grew uneasy at home without cause; sought diversion abroad, frequented plays, balls, masquerades, and all public places of resort, especially where the ladies used; affected a more nice and costly dress; grew more airy and more complaisant abroad, though more reserved and rigid to his wife at home. So that he had engaged himself so far in the favor of the fair that he was praised by one, caressed by another, sent to by a third, and. . . ."

The captain, being weary of such a piece of impertinence, interrupted him, saying, "You shoot too much at random, friend, to make a good gunner. Pray level your piece at the mark."

The man proceeded: "In short, sir, the young lady bore it patiently, still received him at his return with complaisance and affection. But he grew worse and worse, fell from folly into vice, chose him a mistress, maintained her in fine lodgings and a genteel equipage, and, not content with that, he brought her home and kept her under his wife's nose. As this was too great an injury to be silently suffered, Bavia endeavored mildly to persuade him to refrain these courses. He, barbarous, returned her nothing but reproaches. She told him that though she only bore the weight and underwent the torment now, 'twould prove his ruin in the end. But he, so far from taking good advice, replied. . . ."

The captain again broke in upon him thus: "Nay, friend, don't lengthen the engagement, but let me have them board and board."[10] The man promised to be brief and went on:

"Cupidus so highly resented this discourse that he locked her up in a garret, kept her there for two months, and suffered no person but an old woman (his creature) to come near her. He grew more fond of his mistress and consequently more averse to his wife and thought if he could by any means get rid of her, he should be happy. And after several contrivances which seemed to him ineffectual, he fixed upon this project.

"Bavia's father was possessor of a lordship on the Isle of Wight, where he had built a small hunting seat, kept a pack of harriers, and at certain seasons retired thither to divert himself. Cupidus addressed himself to his spouse in a more affable manner than of late was customary, told her he was sensible of his faults, and, if she had goodness enough remaining to forgive his follies, he, for the future, would endeavor to be the best of husbands to her, who was the best of wives. The poor lady was all tenderness; she wept for joy, took him in her arms, and uttered all the kind and endearing expressions her passion prompted, when he, Janus-like, acquainted her that he was informed her father had got a fall in hunting, and though the hurt received was not great, yet, if she thought fit, they would take a ride not only to visit him but to divert her after her confinement. She readily agreed and accordingly they mounted and proceeded on their journey, came to Southampton, and after some refreshment, took boat for the island, as she thought. But the waterman, instead of carrying them to Newport, put them on board a vessel lying in the road.

---

[10] "Close together, or side by side."

"The young lady at first did not dream of their design, but when she saw her husband going and did not take her with him, she threw herself on her knees and begged he would not leave her there to the hazard of a merciless element and, she feared, to a crew of more merciless men. Let him but carry her home and use her as he pleased, again confine her, keep her with bread and water, do anything but leave her and she'd not repine. But prayers and tears were of no prevalency with the obdurate husband. He went off and ordered the watermen to row back as fast as they could. Pleased with the thought of being freed from his chain and resolved now to give a loose to liberty, he went to [South]hampton, took horse, and posted away home, where we shall leave him wallowing in wickedness and triumphing in his guilt, and return to Bavia.

"The poor lady wept, prayed, beat her breasts, tore her hair, and committed a thousand extravagancies peculiar to a person in despair, but to no effect. The master had a heart of flint; he was inexorable, immediately weighed anchor, stood out to sea, and crowded all the sail he could. Six days thus passed before the master would have any discourse with her; but after he had lost sight of land, he seemed more humane, went to her cabin, and endeavored to comfort her. (Small comfort, alas, had she known whither he designed to carry her!) He pretended he was sorry for her misfortune, but was obliged to undertake the business and that he had orders to put her on shore where she would be as well treated in every respect as if she were at home.

"Perfidious crocodile," (the man went on) "to weep o'er the prey thou art just going to devour!" The captain stopped him and said, "Prithee, fellow, don't part thy story. There is more trouble to splice it than the tale is worth. I will have thee steer thy direct course: there is no occasion to work upon a traverse when the wind is aft."

The man, promising to observe his direction and make no paraphrase, continued his relation: "In a short time the affable behavior, courteous and virtuous disposition of the disconsolate yet charming Bavia so wrought upon the stubborn temper of the mariner that he began to mollify, relented his undertaking, and with pity and sorrow unriddled the whole plot to her. He told her that Cupidus had agreed with his owner for a large sum of money to transport her into Turkey and there sell her for a slave, but that a lady of her beauty need not doubt a good reception and the best of usage, for whoever bought her would make advantage of his bargain and, to ingratiate himself with the Grand Seignior, would certainly make him a present of her, and that in the Seraglio she would have all the satisfaction she could desire.

"The recital of this detestable contrivance confounded the poor innocent creature. The loss of her country, loss of friends, but more than all, the apprehension of losing her chastity so dispirited her that her pure crimson blood, which might be seen through her transparent azure veins, returned to its center, left her limbs cold and useless, hastening to cherish her drooping heart; but it would not do, 'twas so surprised and overwhelmed with sudden transport at the violence was like to be offered to its delicate and beloved mansion and swelled at such prodigious rate that it could scarcely be contained in the fair breast that bore it. This vehement emotion threw the poor lady into a swoon, but what with sprinkling cold water, smell of strong spirits, chafing her temples, and by the application of such other restoratives as the master's knowledge dictated, she regained her senses.

"And after some pause she thus addressed herself to him: 'Captain, what advantage can accrue to you by the ruin of an unfortunate woman? Rather throw me into the sea or bury me alive in the earth as soon as you reach land; do anything but expose me to be a prostitute. Consider the action in itself; 'tis contrary to the laws of God and man; and whenever the fact shall be discovered (as doubtless it will come to light, how close soever carried), if you escape prosecution, you will be shunned by all that know you. Your credit is gone. Nay, even the person that has employed you will fear to trust you, for it is natural to imagine that he who will be guilty of such a horrid crime will not stick at anything for his benefit. But if you will return to England and deliver me to my father, you shall have what gratuity you'll ask.'

"The master answered: 'Madam, I am too well acquainted with the disposition of my owner to transgress his orders, for should I hearken to your proposal and agree to your request, I should not only lose the command of the ship, but he would not rest until he had my life as the forfeiture of my fidelity, and what you desire cannot be effected without his knowledge.' She (believing it was best to soothe him in his own way) replied, 'Sir, I acquiesce with your opinion and shall no more press a return to England. But though it does not consist with your conveniency wholly to desist, yet you may alter the measures, carry me to the West Indies, sell me for a servant there. 'Twill be some ease to me to live amongst Christians, and a greater happiness to preserve myself inviolate. And I here promise, nay, on my knees I swear not to write home or by any means divulge the true cause of my exportation, but do you all the service that lies in my power.'

"The master, who began to be sensible of Bavia's charms and imagined this was a fit occasion to press his wicked purpose, acquainted her with his brutal passion and said, if she refused to grant him his desire, she could not expect he should comply with hers; but let her begin and when she had obliged him, he would put her request in execution. Bavia, being mistress of as much prudence as beauty, calmly told him it was in vain to urge his suit, that her honor was dearer to her than her life, for, that once gone, her life would become odious; but after life was gone, her honor would remain and be a means to keep her name alive forever. She acquainted him that what she had liberty to bestow, she would freely give him, and said she had one rich jewel of a very great value, which she brought with her by accident, but had hid it so secretly in the ship that if he ripped up every plank he could not find it; and this she assured him, if he would either send or carry her to any island in the West Indies, should be his own. The master, weighing the matter and being greedy of lucre, accepted the offer, tacked about and stood directly towards the channel, where he cruised for some days in expectation of the Jamaica fleet.

"At length he espied a sail, and coming up with her, understood she was bound for this island. He went on board the Jamaica-man. What agreement was made, I know not; but at his return Bavia gave him the promised jewel and was put on board the other ship, which brought her to Jamaica. And the master sold her to Colonel Hemingius, living on the north side of the island, where she behaved herself so discreetly that she soon gained the affections of the whole family and was treated as a friend or near relation, not like a servant, always sat at table, and gave and received visits with the colonel's lady. She has resided there for seven years past, but his lady being lately dead, she is willing to return to England, and to that end, sir, has sent met with the message I have before delivered to you."

Captain Fustian lent an attentive ear to the narration but really imagined she had been no better than a domestic servant, nothwithstanding the varnish with which the man covered it, and was inquisitive to know how he should be paid for her passage. The messenger told him he need only signify his demand and she would draw a bill on her father, that it would not only be discharged at sight, but his returning him his only daughter, after so many years absence, would likewise be rewarded with a handsome present. That, moreover, the old gentleman had good interest at court, and it might be a means of advancing him to a flag, or at least to gain a commission for his son, who, he was informed, was now only a midshipman under him. The captain, partly in good nature and partly in hopes of reward and preferment, condescended to the request, ordered the man to return with all expedition to give her notice that she might prepare herself and his boat should follow to fetch her off, which was accordingly performed, and the boat's crew found her waiting for their coming.

The cockswain, at first sight of her, doubted whether he had best take her into the boat; he thought he never saw such a piece of deformity. She was of a dead wainscot complexion with large, pobble[11] walleyes, bottle-nose, very wide mouth with great blubber-lips, her teeth broad, long and yellow, with space enough betwixt each to fix one of a moderate size, and one of her legs was much shorter than the other. She certainly was the most disagreeable woman that ever eyes beheld, and the fellow had certainly refused her, had not the dread of punishment for disobeying orders altered his resolution. They got on board when the men were heaving at the capstan and the captain standing by on the maindeck. But when he saw her, Heavens! what a surprise he was in! He was so astonished that he (a thing very unusual with him) blessed himself, heartily repented he ever sent for her, wished he had her intelligencer on board to give him the civility of the ship for the story he had forged, for, seeing her so different from the person that the fellow had represented, he believed it (as he afterwards found it) all a romance, and contrived purely to gain a passage, and would have sent her back, but that he saw the admiral had hoisted sail, so could not wait the return of his boat. He thought her the picture of ill luck and feared her appearance, just at the beginning of the voyage, portended some dreadful disaster, which made him once more lift up his eyes and pray Heaven to avert the omen. Bavia still continued on deck, expecting the captain's approach to give her welcome. He, seeing she moved not, turned towards her with a frowning aspect, and (pointing to the cabin) said, "That's your kennel, woman. You had best turn in, for you do more hurt than good here." Away she hopped in a fright, shut herself up directly, and there continued for two days and two nights without speaking to or being spoke to by anyone, nor had she so much as a bit of biscuit during the whole time.

The ship made sail with the rest of the squadron and continued her voyage. But I shall produce no journal of her way nor take notice of anything but what relates to our present history.

[11] Dialectal variant of *pebble*.

There were two lieutenants (as is always allowed to a fourth-rate) belonging to the ship, the first of which, named Frutesius, was a man of much cupidity, a great admirer not only of the fair but of the female sex, as will appear by the sequel. He verified the old proverb, [and] "would play at small game, rather than stand out," and has often said he never saw that woman, how indifferent soever, that could not afford him some diversion until a fairer object offered. He was the only knight that endeavored to rescue Bavia from her enchantment, and he succeeded in the attempt. He prevailed with the captain to take her into the mess; she was called out to dinner, the captain reconciled, and she treated with respect.

The wind being fair and blowing a fresh gale gave general content, and each person strove to shorten the voyage with diversions. The ship's crew stormed the forecastle, the petty officers went to cards, the warrant officers to backgammon, and the captain, lieutenants, and passengers to "Questions and Commands," "Cross-Purposes," and such like pleasing pastimes. After which Frutesius invited the ladies to his cabin to drink tea and complimented them with the use of it for a drawing room during the voyage, it being much more pleasant and airy than any other part of the ship. Bavia soon accepted the offer and usually continued there the chief part of her time.

There happening to be a squall about the middle of Frutesius's watch, he run to his cabin for shelter, where, finding Bavia alone, for want of other recreation, he made his addresses to her, counterfeited a sort of passion for her, and was importunate for the last favor. She soon condescended and yielded on the first summons; there was no occasion of a storm. But (as the Devil would have it) the quartermaster at the conn[12] asked the mate how he should steer his course. The mate, not willing to give directions without orders from the commander of the watch, hastened to the cabin, where, pulling open the door, [he] perceived what modesty forbids me to repeat. Frutesius, though

---

[12] "the directing of the Person at Helm how to steer."

pretty well furnished with assurance, was much more surprised than Bavia. She rather (shame to her sex) gloried in her guilt and was proud to have it known that she had acquired so complete a gentleman for her gallant. This, though whispered in the ship, was no public discourse for fear of the lieutenant's resentment and, notwithstanding they made use of several opportunities, it reached not the captain's ear, so that hitherto all was quiet. But frequent repetition soon cloyed the spark. He grew weary of his amour and had a mind to change his mistress.

He had a design upon Holmesia but how to accomplish it was the difficulty. She (as before related) was of a reserved behavior, which served only as a whet to our amoroso's appetite. Seldom a day passed without her coming to his cabin, but she was never there alone; either Bavia or Pharmaceuticus's wife always accompanied her, so that he could only speak in praise of her perfections and utter compliments of course. At length he undertook a stratagem which, though something new, yet he believed 'twas feasible. He resolved to acquaint Bavia with his purpose and persuade her to be his procuress. He imagined she would be startled at his first proposal but thought it was the action, not the person, that delighted her, and therefore purposed to return the favor by engaging Compass, the captain's son, to supply his place with her. He discovered himself to Bavia and promised that Compass, whose hammock hung in the steerage near her cabin, should visit her that night. The captain's son made good the engagement, and the next morning she applied herself to Holmesia in behalf of Frutesius.

But before that business could be brought to bear, a strange alteration happened in her own affairs. Some prying sycophant, either in good will to the captain or ill will to his son, discovered the intrigue to old Fustian, who was much perplexed at the relation. And as he was revolving in his mind how he had best act in this affair, Bavia entered to make him a visit. The sight of her so enraged him that he could not contain himself and, had it not been for the persuasion of Frutesius, he had certainly beat her. But he ordered her to her cabin and told her if she designed to see England, she had best continue there and behave herself as she ought, for if ever she had the impudence to come again to his apartment, he protested he would throw her out of the gallery window. Away posted Bavia, and the old gentleman followed with a design to chastise his son, whom he met with in the steerage. He first belabored him with such ill language as was peculiar to him, called him spawn of hell, seed of the devil, &c., and then ordered the corporal to put him in irons.

Compass was about eighteen years of age, had a handsome face, but shaped something like his father. He had very good natural parts, which want of education rendered useless; and having been always bred under his father, who was too fond of him, he seemed to be a chip of the old block. The old gentleman had so great an opinion of his discretion that he generally followed his instruction, so that the son was commander-in-chief, and Fustian only acted under him. And indeed, he was in some measure obliged to it, for the lad, still encroaching on the privilege his father first allowed him, arrived at such a height of impudence and disobedience that he would contradict him in the public face of the whole ship's company. He had a notable spirit and was usually very saucy, especially on board ship or to those under his jurisdiction, would frequently give his father the lie, and use such opprobrious terms to him as are shocking to name. He was sometimes so willing to receive correction that, when the old gentleman has threatened him with irons, he would of himself call the corporal and command him to put on the shackles. But the captain was sure to suffer for it, who, being uneasy to see his darling in duress, would immediately order him to be released; but the stubborn youth would not permit it until old Fustian had submitted, begged pardon, desired "Compy-boy" to forgive him, and promised to be a very dutiful father for the future.

This has been for small offenses, when he thought his father in more fault than himself. But now being sensible of his crime and knowing the old gentleman had reason to resent it, [he] believed, should he permit himself to be ironed, 'twould be some time before his father's choler would abate and consequently that he himself, and not the captain, would undergo the punishment. So [he] resolved to bid defiance to him and preserve his liberty. In order thereto, he reached down a cutlass and protested that whoever offered to come near him to execute the order should feel the effects of his resentment. The captain commanded the corporal to call more hands to his assistance and do his duty; the corporal put himself in posture of defense; but the fellows knew, should they obey their orders, they themselves would suffer for it. They were sensible the captain acted purely by his son's direction, who would not fail, without a real fault, to accuse them and have them punished, so that though they made a seeming offer to approach him at the captain's menaces, yet in reality, they came not very near him.

The captain's fury increased to see his orders condemned. He run into the cabin, brought out a pistol, cocked it, and swore he would shoot him through the head (though neither ball or powder in it), if he did not presently submit, and threatened the fellows with the geers[13] if they did not lay hold on him. But both parties knew him too well to take any manner of notice of it. The captain then made an assault himself, pistol in hand, and Compass traversed his ground and flourished his cutlass, but still gave way and retreated faster than the old gentleman could follow. After half a score breathings round the steerage table, Compass perceived his father begin to flag, being almost weary of the pursuit; and he, believing he had now pretty well cooled his courage though heated his corpse, made to the gangway, mounted the ladder, and took a turn on deck, but threw down the cutlass as he quitted the steerage, which the captain reached up, and seeing he could not easily take a further revenge, threatened (at his coming home) to tell his mother of it, and remained satisfied that he was master not only of the field but of his enemy's weapon, too. So he retired to his cabin and whipped off a whole bottle of rum as a refreshment after the engagement. Bavia was

[13] rigging.

all the while in her own cabin, beheld the combat, and was not a little pleased that her knight, though he had lost his honor, had escaped a scouring and kept his liberty, being of opinion they might now find opportunities to continue their amour.

Frutesius, during this combustion, was contriving means how to accomplish the design he had on Holmesia; he could not now expect much assistance from Bavia, who was very cautious how she appeared out of her cabin, for fear of exasperating the captain, for she really believed should she encounter him before his passion was appeased it was very likely he would make his words good and set her a-swimming, and, as light a housewife as she was, she did not care to venture the experiment. So Frutesius, having nothing but his own management to rely on, knew not what measures he had best take. What most chagrined him was that he had no opportunity to speak with her alone. Pharmaceuticus or his wife being always in the cabin with her. Could he think of any way to single her from their company he did not much distrust but that his addresses would have the desired effect; yet that being very improbable, if not impossible, he saw no likelihood of succeeding. But as the difficulty of the enterprise made him more eager in the pursuit of it, and Bavia having assured him that Holmesia had heard her discourse without showing signs of any great reluctance, he determined to make use of the first conveniency that offered and did not doubt, though yet ignorant of a method but that he should think of some device agreeable to his intentions. He had been hammering his brains all day without any sensible satisfaction when he fixed on a project. 'Twas a very dangerous one, *sed omnia vincit amor* (not to give it a harder denomination) he resolved to attempt it, though with the hazard of his life, and, having the second watch, designed that night to put it in execution.

Accordingly about one o'clock he mounted the roundhouse, got over the taffrail, and descended to the gallery window. Had his foot slipped and his hands lost hold, the ship having fresh way, he must inevitably have perished; but the Devil was not willing to lose a gamester. He entered the gallery safe and went into Holmesia's bed. No noise was made; all was hush and silent; she lay as quiet as if fast asleep and did not dream anything of the matter. But whether she was as willing to receive as he to offer his service I know not, or whether she imagined loss of honor consisted only in the discovery and that 'twas more shame to let the world know the opinion Frutesius had of her and the rudeness offered than privately to permit him to take his own liberty; but there he continued some hours and frequently afterwards repeated his nocturnal visits at the usual time.

As the pitcher never goes so often to the well, but it returns broke at last, so fared it with our amorist. For one night Pharmaceuticus had been taking a cheerful glass with his brother Phlebotomus, who was surgeon of the ship, and stayed so late that he returned to his cabin just after Frutesius had come in at the window and before he had time to get into bed. It was so dark that neither of them could see the other, and Pharmaceuticus, having some necessary occasion to visit the gallery before he went to rest, run against Frutesius and by chance took hold of one of the buttons of his coat sleeve, which much surprised them both, and Pharmaceuticus in a sort of fright called out to the sentinel of the steerage to bring him a candle. The fellow, either not hearing or at least not minding, came not near him, so that he quitted his hold and went to fetch a light himself. In the meantime the bird was flown. Frutesius was returned by the same way he came; yet, though Pharmaceuticus had been taking a hearty bottle, he was not so far gone in liquor to lose his senses, but was positive there was a man in the apartment and gave a shrewd guess both at the person and his business.

The next morning he went upon deck and related his discovery, which was well enough known before to those who had the watch, though some news and private diversion to the other part of the warrant and petty officers, but none dared mention it to Frutesius, or if they had, would he have made more than a jest of it. However, Holmesia was under terrible apprehensions, and her greatest fear was of its coming to the captain's knowledge. She was in great want of Bavia, not only for advice but to be a messenger to Frutesius to take instructions from him how to behave herself in case the captain taxed her with it. She sent Quomina to call her and after some consultation, Bavia, though a very unfit piece of stuff to make a Mercury, hopped forwards and backwards several times in a great hurry, but at last brought the good tidings that she should not be concerned but leave all to him, for he had thought of a way to clear both her and himself, let the captain begin as soon as he pleased.

It was not long before the captain was informed of the business which broiled so much on his stomach that he was forced to take a large dram to qualify it and then went up on deck. He appeared something moody but did not speak a word till he had taken half a dozen turns to consider what to say. Then turning towards Frutesius, he thus expressed himself: "I thought, Lieutenant, you had been a man of better principles than to make a brothel of the Queen's ship, though you went every night on shore to your loose woman at Jamaica. I passed it by without notice, but this is such an affront to her Majesty that I am obliged to resent it."

Frutesius, who well knew how to soothe him, answered: "I am sorry, sir, you have so ill an opinion of me to believe I would be guilty of such a crime. If not my allegiance as a subject, yet my duty as an officer would restrain me from attempting to defile that which under you, sir, I am commissioned to take care of. But I have heard of the intrigue and of the judgment that has been passed on it. For which reason, partly to discharge the trust reposed in me and partly to free myself from a false accusation, but more especially to clear the reputation of Madam Holmesia, whom I believe to be a lady of an unspotted character and would not willingly have the innocent suffer for the guilty, I have searched to the bottom of it and found out the real truth of the adventure. It seems, sir, the actors of this farce did not make their beginning here. They have often practiced and performed the same at Kingston in Jamaica and have now only changed the stage. There has been a long and vicious correspondence betwixt Forestaff, sir, one of your midshipmen, and

Pharmaceuticus's wife, and she, knowing her husband would be engaged in the surgeon's cabin last night, gave him notice of it and prevailed with him to make use of that opportunity to supply his room."

Pharmaceuticus, who was walking on deck, heard the charge and, not being willing to have the odium due to Holmesia cast upon his wife, said this was a story feigned only to excuse the one and accuse the other, and unless Forestaff himself would justify it, he should give no credit to so unlikely an aspersion.

Forestaff was a man of prodigious impudence and so great an observer of Frutesius's direction that he would not stick at a greater matter to please him. The captain sent for him. He presently appeared and, being prepossessed by the lieutenant, without any hesitation repeated the same tale which had been before related and to make it the more credited, confirmed it with an oath, to the diversion of the quarter-deck and the satisfaction of the captain, who believed his lieutenant was innocent and did not much concern himself with the aggression of a petty officer.

Pharmaceuticus was now the only dissatisfied person. He walked the deck in great uneasiness, ruminating on the invention he had heard. He first considered the improbability of it, for that his being in the surgeon's cabin was an accident unforeseen both to his wife and self, so that that part of the story relating to the invitation must be false and he would fain persuade himself upon his wife's integrity. It's true, indeed, he had caught her tripping at Jamaica, but that he thought was not so much the fault of the woman as of the climate, believing that cursed malevolent planet which predominates in that island and so changes the constitution of its inhabitants that if a woman land there as chaste as a vestal, she becomes in forty-eight hours a perfect Messalina, and that 'tis as impossible for a woman to live at Jamaica and preserve her virtue as for a man to make a journey to Ireland and bring back his honesty. Then he considered she was never guilty in England. He had always found her to be a loving, faithful, and obedient wife. That somewhat comforted him, but it did not last, for he imagined she might play the same game there, only used more caution and cunning and so concealed it from his knowledge; or if she did not, that her now having lived five years in Jamaica was time long enough not only to tincture but to change her whole mass of blood and totally alter her nature, and that a disease so long growing was not to be presently eradicated. Then he thought of the old adage, *Quo semel est imbuta recens servabit odorem testa diu.*[14] This made him think his wife would never claw it off, which so troubled his anteled [antlered?] head that he posted down to the cabin, first upbraided his wife, and then, notwithstanding her tears and protestations, pinched, beat, and kicked her, and with all expedition hasted to his brother doctor that, by complaining of his sufferings, he might give some ease to his mind.

Captain Fustian had walked so long that his appetite began to remind him of the rum bottle, and, as he was going down the ladder in order to take a sip, he spied the sentinel coming out of Holmesia's apartment and presently imagining he had been with the Negro wench, thus saluted him: "What do you there, you rascal? Have you been caterwauling too? If you must have a scout,[15] stay till you come to England. Go to hell in the common road and be damned. Don't make a cuckold of the Devil, you dog. But I'll reward you for leaving your post. Here, call the boatswain's mate. Seize this fellow to the geers and give him the Levitical law, forty lashes save one."[16] The sentinel on his knees entreated mercy, said the girl called him in to give him a dram, that he did not stay three minutes, begged to be excused, and promised that he would never be guilty of the like offense. The man could not have entered a better plea; the very word "dram" had something cordial in it. He thought if a needy sailor had been guilty of a greater omission to obtain a dram, 'twas pardon-

---

[14] "The vessel, once it has been stained, retains the odor for a long time" (Horace, *Epistles*, I, 2, lines 69–70).

[15] "an Expression us'd by the Captain for a lewd Woman."

[16] The captain is mistaken in his count. See *Deuteronomy* XV: 30 ("forty lashes and no more").

able. That word "dram" so mollified his temper that he immediately forgave him.

But what the fellow was indebted, poor Quomina was forced to pay. It seems she had made bold with her mistress's citron-water bottle,[17] had drank and given away above a pint, which so enraged Holmesia that she flew at her, threw her down, cuffed and kicked her unmercifully, then laid her on to that degree with a manatee skin,[18] that she fetched near the same quantity of blood from the wench's sides which she missed from her citron-water. But that not replenishing the bottle, neither the girl's entreaties or her sufferings could assuage her rage, but still swelled full of choler, she hurried to the captain and told him he ought to make an example of that impudent rogue who had assisted the wench in the theft. The captain very gravely replied, "I have heard talk of Furies with whips of steel and hair of serpents, and if it be true that the Devil does employ such instruments, a Negro had better live in Hell than with a Jamaica termagant. Look you, mistress, I did not concern myself with the correction of your slave. Neither shall I take your instructions how to govern myself in relation to the punishment of my own ship's company. I see you are at best but a makebate,[19] so desire you will keep in your own apartment."

Pharmaceuticus (as is before mentioned) went down to the surgeon of the ship to ease his mind by relating his misfortunes and give an account how he had chastised his wife. Phlebotomus (who was a Teague-lander)[20] having patiently heard the whole discourse, thus answered: "Aragh bee mee shoul, dou beesht very mush to blaum to abuse de good woman for wat she cannot help, and dou beesht in a very great deal more faut to put de beat

---

[17] Brandy flavored with citron peel.

[18] "the Skin of a Fish resembling a Cow, the Flesh of which is very good Food; and the Skin being cut into Thongs, twisted and dried, makes a sort of Whips or Switches, with which they flog their Negroes. But the Punishment being look'd on to be too severe, there is an Act of the Country, which prohibits the use of them in the Correction of Slaves."

[19] One who stirs up strife.

[20] Nickname for an Irishman.

upon dee wife den she to lie wid de man. As I will tell dee, bee mee fait, I did once upon a time, broder, catch my wife upon de same sport. Indeed lade [*sic*] man had a sword at his tail, sho dat I did say nothing till he was gone, but den I did fall upon my wife and did all to be-break her faash, in trot. But de woman did give me good words and did desire me to put up my pashon and to hear what she could shay for herself. And she did tell me in trute dat de man did follow her a long time wid his sollicitations, and dat she did strive and strive wid all her might to resist de great temptations, but did still find dat de man did gain more and more upon her inclinations, which did sore trouble de woman, and sho she did resolve to go to de conjurer to take his counsel upon de matter, and in good fait when she did come to de cunning-man, he did shay, dat all de happiness or misery which did befall us in dis world was preordained by Providence before ever we were born, and dat it was not in our power to alter de fate dat was allotted for us, but dat he would erect a scheme and give her his best advice.

"And after he had drawn his trangums,[21] he did tell my wife dat at her husband's birth Jupiter was predominate in Taurus, a cardinal sign, and Mars posited in Capricorn in sextile to dat malevolent planet Saturn, which did denote dat I was born as well to be a cuckold as a cuckold-maker, and dat what de stars had decreed, de Devil himself could not prevent, and therefore bid her be easy, for if she did consent, it must be imputed to her husband's fortune, and not to her faut. De woman, seeing de man's great knowledge and understandings in astrology, did pray him to calculate my nativity and, by my fait and trot, de man was so cunning to do it, though neider my wife nor I can tell when I was born, and he did shay dat Mercury being lord of the ascendant, posited in Aries, and in conjunction wid Venus, did signify dat I was a pimp, and should rise to preferment by de procuring some pretty lady for de great lord and, bee mee shoul,

[21] An odd or intricate contrivance, a puzzle.

broder, de man's words be come to pass. I will tell dee in what, but do desire dat dou wilt be secret in de matter.

"My fader was a barber in Dublin and did teach me to shave, but his trade was so small dat it did hardly afford us meat for our bellies and much less clothes for our backs, and I did hear dat my countrymen who went to England did get into very good plaashes and live very braave, sho dat I did run away from my fader and went to London. I did not stay dere long before I did get into a very braave plaash. A very great lord did taak me into his house and did maak me his footman, and in a little time my lord did trust me wid his loves. And because he did find me faitful and diligent to fetch de lady, he did maak me his valet and did promish to maak me a man. And he, having interest in de navy, did afterwards get me a warrant to be surgeon of dis ship and now, joy, I have told dee de whole trute of de matter."

Pharmaceuticus asked him if his wife had made this relation of the conjurer whilst he was a footman or after he was warranted, but found 'twas after he obtained his warrant, which confirmed him that the story was made by the wife only to amuse the husband. He then asked him how he passed his examination at Surgeon's Hall; who answered, "Oh! bee mee fait, broder, I had a trick for dat. De Irishman is not so great a fool but he can sheat the English, for when de time was fixed for Phlebotomus to be asked de hard questions, I did hire a gentleman who understood de ting, and he did go in my naam, and when he did answer all deir questions, dey did give him a certificate dat Phlebotomus had pass de examination for de fourt-rate ship, and he did deliver it to me in good fait." Pharmaceuticus acknowledged it was a lucky contrivance to get a fool made a physician but could not be of his opinion as to absolute predestination, for then said he, "What must become of free-will?" He had scarce uttered the words, when the captain's servant came and told him his company was desired in the great cabin, which obliged them to leave their discourse, and he went up to wait on the captain.

Pharmaceuticus's wife, taking it mightily to heart that she should be not only scandalized by the lieutenant and midshipman but beat by her husband without cause, applied herself to the captain, who at her first appearance gave her a very cold reception. But what with her tears, protestations, and reflections on Holmesia, the old gentleman began to be of opinion that she was wronged and, understanding by her that her husband was no stranger to the whole series of Holmesia's life, had sent for him purposely to relate it. And when the captain had satisfied Pharmaceuticus of his wife's innocency and on what design he was called, he readily obeyed the captain's command and began as follows:

"Holmesia's mother was a shoplifter in London and followed that course of life till the law pursued and overtook her. She was arraigned at the Old Bailey, convicted, and condemned, but pleading hard for transportation, 'twas allowed her. And in order thereto, she was put on board a Jamaica-man then lying in the river and was observed, during the passage, to hold too much familiarity with a mulatto belonging to the ship and, as appeared afterwards, was with child by him of this very woman that is now the subject of this discourse, so that Holmesia is at best but a mustee.[22]

"At the ship's arrival in the island, she was assigned to a planter on the other side the Blue Mountains. But he, finding her to be of a very turbulent spirit and a very idle baggage, gave her the country correction,[23] but to no purpose. It made no amendment; she grew rather worse than better. And at length perceiving that she was with kid, [he] was willing to get rid of her at any rate and proposed to give her her liberty, which she refused, saying she was now near her time and not in condition to shift, but if her master would entertain her till she was delivered, she would willingly accept his offer, though ignorant of the country or what course to take for a livelihood. He kept her

---

[22] Technically, the offspring of a white and a quadroon; loosely, a half-caste.

[23] "being stript to the Waste, and whip'd with a Cat-of-nine-tails, Horse-whip, or *Mannatee*-skin, till they leave their Back and Sides raw.

there till she was brought to bed, and within a short time after, the day was fixed for her departure.

"The appointed morning being come, she left the plantation and trudged with her bairn at her back till she came to Kingston, and the first place she happened into was the Brewsters, with which because, sir, you may not be acquainted, I will give you an account of them. The Brewsters are a covey of small houses, or rather hovels, adjacent to the Common, a little on the left hand of the road which leads to Liganee[24] and are inhabited by the most scandalous and infamous people belonging to either sex. One of these houses the woman with her brat entered, and 'twas the fittest receptacle she could have met with, for, as she was a new face though owner of a very indifferent one, she was presently entertained, and in a short time insinuated herself so much into favor of the rakehelly customers, out of whom she cajoled a small sum of money, that she scorned to be a plier any longer but took a little hut, set up for herself, and had her house the most frequented of any in the whole seraglio, by which means she procured for herself and daughter a competent, though a vicious maintenance.

"And as the girl grew in years, she trod in her mother's footsteps and, being young, was a great favorite with the buccaneers, who then swarmed in the island and are the most extravagant sort of people can possibly be met with. She brought much custom to her mother and much money to herself, all which she bestowed in fine clothes, and those drew more admirers, so that the more her finery, the more her followers, and the greater her extravagance, the greater her gains. She outshined the greatest merchant or planter's wife or daughter of the whole country, and became as famous amongst the women for her rich gowns and petticoats as infamous for her manner of obtaining them."

The captain said he could see no reason why that vice, which was natural to all the inhabitants, should be reckoned a greater crime in her than in the rest of her sex, and that those persons

[24] The Liguanea plain on the south coast of Jamaica.

should pretend to find fault who followed the same business. Pharmaceuticus answered that the observation was just, but, according to the old saying, "Two of a trade can never agree." And besides, though their calling was the same, they had a quite different method of practice; and that that woman is of greatest reputation in Jamaica who manages her intrigues with the most prudence and not she who has the greatest share of modesty; for that the scandal does not lie in the action but in the discovery, and that they are as great enemies to virute as to public vice. And said, that should such a prodigy happen, as a virtuous woman to land and reside in the island, she is sure to be the subject of the whole sex, shall have amours and meetings made for her and reported in all companies, and the more her innocence, the more scandal shall be heaped on her, till they have brought her to be like themselves, and then she may sin on as quiet and as undisturbed as the rest of the frail, frippery fry of Satan's emissaries. But to return to the story.

"Holmesia thus continued in her glory (as it was there called) for several years, but then fell very ill. She was so much out of order that she was obliged to keep her chamber and none of her gallants permitted to see her. I, being then newly arrived, was sent for and undertook the cure. Her mother indeed gave it out that she had overheat herself in walking and got a surfeit. But her real distemper was *Morbus Neapolitanus*[25] and had been so long increasing that she was in a very miserable condition, which obliged me to use the extremity of my art and experience to overcome it. At length, with long application and much difficulty, I set her in *statu quo,* and the contagion had been so industriously dispersed that I had abundance of patients, which was the only welcome I met with in the island.

"Holmesia appeared abroad again in all her splendor, looked so fresh and gay that she made new conquests and secured her old ones. Just about that time Galenicus came to Jamaica and was so taken with the charms of the new-furbished lady that

[25] Venereal disease.

he hired a very spacious house, took her home under the pretense of being his housekeeper and, falling into good practice, maintained her handsomely. Holmesia, now she had a color for her crime, obtained a reputation, had a fair character, and was as much esteemed as anyone in Kingston. For most people imagined Galenicus would make her his wife, she being in their thoughts (as she seemed constant to him only) as fit, if not a fitter match for him than any in the country, and the remembrance of her public infamy was soon buried in oblivion.

"Two years had not fully passed before Holmesia thought herself with child, at which she was extremely pleased, believing now was her time to draw him into matrimony. She communicated this news to Galenicus and seemed much concerned at the censure she should be exposed to, if he did not prevent it by marriage, and told him that not only she, but he himself would suffer under the same scandal. Galenicus had no intent to snap at the proposal but was heartily vexed it should happen at that juncture, because he had a more alluring bait in view, a merchant's daughter of good fortune, to whom he was then going to make his first addresses, and thought when this was known, 'twould put a stop to his proceedings.

"Whilst he was perplexing his brains to find some shelter to avoid this storm, a ship came to Kingston with several servants from England. Galenicus went on board her, and seeing a lusty young fellow, who was a carpenter by trade, agreed for him, had him assigned over for the usual time, and took him home with him. After a few days Galenicus applied himself to Holmesia, told her it was requisite she should have a husband, more to cover his disgrace than hers, and that he had bought that man for that purpose. That if she consented to his design, he would not only enfranchise him immediately but likewise, in kindness to her, would buy them such utensils as were necessary to furnish a house and supply him with money to carry on the business he had been bred to, and that, by this means, they should have a conveniency to continue their amours with greater freedom and less suspicion. He, perceiving she was no way inclined to embrace his contrivance, told her that her future welfare depended on her acceptance or refusal for, if she would not be advised, he would turn her out of doors, and the worst that could happen to him would be to keep the bantling and let her shift for herself.

"Holmesia, having no inclination to re-enter upon her old calling, thought best of two evils to choose the least. So making a virtue of necessity, agreed to take the husband, and the matter was proposed to the fellow, who very joyfully embraced it. So they were married, a house taken and furnished at Port Royal, and a good stock of timber laid in to set him to work. The man proved a very good workman and has been so careful and diligent in his business that he has considerably improved the fund he was first entrusted with. He has bought several slaves, trained them up to his employ, gets money apace, and is now reckoned one of the most substantial carpenters in the island. The two old friends still continued their correspondence. And Galenicus, having affairs which required his presence in England, so far prevailed on the good husband's easy nature as to permit his wife to go over to see the country and visit his relations. Galenicus is now on board a ship under convoy of this squadron; and as you know, sir, I prevailed with her to come on board of you."

Pharmaceuticus having thus finished his relation, his wife added: "If, sir, notwithstanding this account, you are diffident of the lieutenant's being the person that my husband surprised in the apartment, I must inform you that seldom a day passes but, according to the Jamaica custom, they take a nap after dinner upon her bed for refreshment. I left him there when I came to you and doubt not, sir, if you please to give yourself the trouble of looking into the cabin but you may find them still together."

The captain, though well enough satisfied of the verity, was willing to have a further confirmation from his own view, and hastened away to the steerage where, seeing the door was not open, he stole softly thither and thrust it gently from him, putting his head in to try what he could discover. But it so unluckily fell out that Frutesius was gone and Holmesia was just at that time putting on a clean shift. The captain, seeing that, would willingly have withdrawn, but was prevented by Quomina, who, happening to cast her eyes toward the door, espied him and thought he had been coming into the cabin. The girl, knowing 'twas no convenient time for her mistress to receive a visit and taking more care of her mistress's concerns than she did herself, run in great haste and clapped the door to with all her strength, catching the captain by the neck before he was well apprehensive of her being near him. He drew back and strove to disengage himself, which pulled the door the closer and held him the faster. The wench too lent him her assistance to squeeze as hard as possible, till her mistress called her off and so released him.

The blow the girl had given him and his own struggling put him into some agony, but nothing so much as the apprehension of the disaster being known. He imagined the ship's company would think that he, who a little before had been documenting his lieutenant, was now endeavoring to follow his example, and that what he condemned in others, he was attempting to put in practice himself. Then the thoughts of it being known in the squadron terrified him, for he believed, were it once published in the fleet, he should be as bad harassed by his brother captains as Acteon was by his hounds after his metamorphosis for casting a sheep's eye at the forbidden fruit of Diana: neither knew he on the sudden where to bestow himself. He was ashamed to go upon deck, and Pharmaceuticus's wife was in his cabin, who he believed had contrived this plot purely to abuse him, for which affront he could not presently brook the sight of her. But after some consideration, since he had a precedent for his misfortune (one of the chief admirals having been caught in the same sort of trap when he peeped into his maid's garret), he resolved to venture upon deck. But the story was there before him.

The first person he spied when he came up was Bavia, who sat fronting the gangway. The sight of her added to his gloomy temper, so that he shifted sides and took a sullen walk without uttering a word to anyone. But he had not been there long before his son came up and very pertly thus accosted him: "You threatened t'other day to tell my mother. Who shall tell now, pray? Begin as soon as you will, I care not. I have enough to tell of you, I think." This reproach galled the old gentleman grievously, though he made no answer, and obliged him to have recourse to his old remedy, a dram.

In going down to take which, just as he came to the first step of the ladder, he cast a malicious look towards Bavia, which occasioned him to miss his footing, and down he came. He fell from the quarter-deck quite down to the steerage, and sorely bruised his shoulder. The surgeon was sent for, to whom the captain showed his hurt and told him it was his looking on that ill-favored carrion was the cause of it, and that he really believed she was a witch. The surgeon told him that his second mate was her countryman and could give him some account of her. The captain, having his shoulder well fomented with spirits of turpentine and somewhat revived his drooping spirits with half a dozen hearty pulls at the rum bottle, sent for the mate and, giving him a dram to encourage him, bid him declare what he knew concerning Bavia and not any way mince the matter or palliate the circumstances, but tell him the whole truth of what he knew concerning her. The mate said he knew her and her relations very well, having been born within few miles of them, and that the recital which had before been given of her was fictitious and wholly false, but he would relate everything exactly.

"Bavia, sir, was born at Maldunum, a large boroughtown in Wiltshire,[26] which has a very good market, more especially famous for the vast quantities of cheese it sends to London, and lies on the main road betwixt our two chief trading cities, London and Bristol. Her father is a Scotchman, who marrying a woman of that neighborhood, turned pedagogue and fixed the mansion of his instruction at this place, which succeeded to his wish. He had the care and tuition of most of the young gentlemen of that country, gained a good reputation in his profession, and was believed to gather riches apace. I shall not trouble you, sir,

[26] Marlborough.

with Bavia's juvenile years but acquaint you that she was the only child, and pass to her years of maturity.

"She never was tolerably handsome, or indeed passable, which, though the West-India climate has something altered her for the worse, may easily be discerned by her features. And to add more to her natural deformity, she received a fall when she was a child and broke her leg. The fracture was both transverse and oblique, which, for want of a skilful artist, was never rightly reduced and the sinews permitted to contract in such a manner that (as it is very facile to be observed in her gait) there is as much disproportion in her supporters as betwixt a giant and a pigmy. This defect of corporeal perfections was not the only fault appeared in her, for she had as great a carity[27] of virtuous fundamentals, as she had of formosity, her vicious inclinations being visible to the minutest observer without the help of a microscope."

Frutesius, who had been called to hear the story, checked him and said the captain expected a true and plain history of the woman's adventures and transactions and not a parcel of nonsensical bombast, which was not only ridiculous in itself but unintelligible to others. He would have him speak in a phrase that might be understood and not cant like a mountebank, for that, by endeavoring to appear an able practitioner in making use of terms not applicable to the business nor rightly apprehended by himself, though it might be applauded by an illiterate coxcomb, 'twould only make him censured by men of judgment to be an ostentatious quack and bid him avoid such affected expressions. The young fellow blushed, made a bow, and went on.

"Bavia, sir, was a liar from her cradle, and so great a sower of dissension that there was scarce a family in the whole town in which she was admitted as a frequent visitor or intimate acquaintance but she raised a dissension. So that in short time her company was as much avoided as a person infected with the pestilence. She remained a long while without having any man

[27] Dearness, scarcity.

so much as dissemble a respect for her, notwithtstanding her father used all the cunning of his country to ensnare some of his young students. But it would not do. It required a far greater skill to make that bitter potion palatable to a nice stomach, which made him endeavor to gild it with the plausible pretense of giving her a great fortune. At length a very deserving gentleman, named Aesculapius, made some pretensions, but whether induced thereto by the hope of riches or the father's soothing persuasions is uncertain. There was small application requisite, or made use of, to gain her consent. Her father promised sixteen hundred pounds, but never made it good.

"However, the match was concluded on. She married, Aesculapius settled at Ackmanchester[28] and had all the chief business of the place, being in very great repute with all the nobility that frequented it. But Bavia, as was soon after discovered, had for several years before her marriage held a criminal correspondence with some of her father's boarders; and though she then acted privately under a visor, she now pulled it off and trod the stage in public, making herself notorious to the whole world by the scandalous and infamous course of life she followed in a town which has the greatest resort of nobility and gentry, not only of our own, but of all foreign nations.

"Aesculapius and she had some small difference in relation to her behavior. She could not bear advice nor suffer herself to be controlled, but took pet and left him, returning to her father, whose business at Maldunum was so much decreased that it did not bring in wherewithal to maintain him, for which reason he had adjourned to Ingleford,[29] in expectation of better employment. Thither 'twas Bavia went to him, and that she might not be a burden to the old man, who had hardly wherewithal to keep himself, her husband allowed her a small annuity of thirty pounds, which was but a poor stipend to support her extravagances. And though she had some assistance from a gentleman living within two miles of the place, with whom she then kept

[28] Bath.
[29] "now called Hungerford."

company, it did not hold long. He soon grew weary of his mistress and consequently of supplying her with money.

"Her father, being in debt, was forced to leave the country but left her to dispose of his household implements and went for London. When she had converted his antiquated lumber into a more portable and necessary commodity, she followed—to London, I mean, but did not come near her father. For since Fortune had forsaken him, he lost her favor likewise, so keeping his money, [she] left him to starve, and the poor business he has now undertaken is writing petitionary epistles to charitably disposed gentleman, to whom only he is beholden for his daily bread.

"Bavia, by her residence at Ackmanchester, had acquired the knowledge, though not the favor, of the principal families of England, was conversant in their genealogies and acquainted with most of their intermarriages, by which means she imagined she had an opportunity at her first appearance in town to make some advantage. She took good lodgings and set up for a place-monger and matchmaker, pretending by her great interest at court and intimacy amongst rich people to help persons, for a moderate premium, to such posts of preferment as their inclinations and abilities led them, and persons of either sex, who wanted money, to such fortunes as their occasions required. She bubbled several of their money, but of one amongst the many she deceived I shall inform you, because 'twas the last she was concerned in, and that which sent her out of England.

"An old almost-broken beau, who wanted wherewith to repair the circumstances which his folly and expensive manner of living had reduced him to, made application to Bavia for redress. She told him he was too well known to obtain any eminent post, and an indifferent one would not suit his necessities; that the only way to raise his sinking station was matrimony, and that too would be difficult because his poverty was as universally known as his person, and his calamity as much derided as his character; that what was to be effected must be on some country beauty, and if he would give her two days consideration, she should be better able to inform him how far she was capable of serving him. The beau took leave, with many protestations of acknowledgment, and at his going slipped half a piece into the maid's hand, which was the same thing as if given to herself, for all profits which accrued by virtue of the office were returned into her exchequer.

"The time mentioned being expired, the spark came, and Bavia had provided for his reception. She informed him that nothing could appear with a more promising aspect than an accident which had intervened since the last time she saw him, for Clotilda, who was a lady of considerable fortune, as well in present specie as in lands and demesnes, had been a widow about three months, was her particular friend. And as she was informed that morning by her steward, was newly come to town; that she designed to make her a visit and give her an invitation to her lodgings where he, calling in his chariot, might have the opportunity of seeing her, but that she expected he should supply her with money, not only for coach hire and other incident expenses to attend and receive the lady suitable to her quality, but [also] to furnish herself in all respects as was necessary to carry on the design. For, though there had been a mutual kindness for many years cultivated and carried on betwixt them, yet want of fine clothes and utensils to make a good appearance might weaken the enterprise, nothing being a greater strengthener and continuer of friendship than prosperity and no probable prospect of any occasion to want each other's assistance.

"She said that she proposed this only for his advantage, she having already wherewith to gratify her own inclinations but that she would be a good housewife and be contented with fifty guineas in hand, neither did she desire him to hazard that till he was satisfied as to the lady's fortune, and wished he would go immediately to Doctors-Commons and read the will, told him her husband's name was Honorius, a gentleman of Suffolk and she would take care that the steward (who must be bribed to be of their party, because he had a great influence on his lady) should meet him at her lodgings the next day and show him the rent-roll of the particulars of her estate. This was agreed on, and the beau posted away to the Commons, where he found everything answerable to his expectation.

"Bavia maintained two or three Irishmen as her gallants so that, paying dear for her pleasure, her ill-got wealth was but of short duration. One of these she had prepared to represent the steward, and contrived sham writings to deceive the unwary bubble, who at his next coming was so satisfied of the sincerity (as he imagined) of her intentions toward him that he strained hard and with some difficulty raised the fifty guineas and made Bavia a present of them, and promised a further reward at the consummation of the marriage, with a grateful acknowledgment to the pretended steward, not doubting (being a very opiniona- tive spark) of his good success with the lady. Few days passed before he had notice when Clotilda would be there. He accord- ingly prepared for the encounter. There was no want of oils, essences, or pomatums to smooth and sweeten his declining carcass.

"The time appointed being come, he repaired to Bavia's lodgings, found a lady there in mourning, fell desperately in love at sight, and was not backward to let his mistress know it by all the foppish actions and extravagant expressions he was master of. The lady carried herself with much modesty and a seeming air of indifference, not appearing to receive or repulse his addresses, but told him she took it as a piece of gallantry, and that it was customary for accomplished gentlemen to show their wit by bantering poor silly women, and though it was not yet a seasonable time to make her the subject of his diversion, yet as it did not affect her, neither should it affront her. A great deal of such discourse was bandied from one to t'other, till the lady going was pressed for another meeting, but she would not con- sent to it, so took coach and left him.

"It was agreed that Bavia should go the day after to feel the lady's pulse and report her temperament to the gentleman. She went and returned with an account that Clotilda had a great esteem for his person but surmised she should expose herself to the censure of the town if she yet received addresses of that nature, though she could not perceive that Clotilda of herself was averse to it, and she was of opinion the best way would be for her to give the lady an invitation to supper, at which he should surprise them, renew his pretentions, and not part with her without being married the same night, and said she had seen a handsome set of plate in his apartment, which would be necessary to be sent to her lodgings, because in the more grandeur she herself appeared, the less distrust of fraud would remain in Clotilda. The beau was ravished with the thoughts of his approaching happiness, and sent his plate.

"To be brief, sir, the lady was invited, came accordingly, and the spark was punctual in his attendance. Supper being ended and the cloth removed, he plied her with his passion and, not to mention the arguments pro and con, he would not slip so fair an occasion, lest to defer might be a means to make him lose the bliss on which he said his life so much depended that 'twas impossible for him to survive, unless she consented to that his present felicity. Bavia seconded his importunity, and in the end the lady was overcome. A priest was sent for from the ambassador's, and they were married, after which, by Bavia's persuasions, they adjourned to his lodgings, where she saw them in bed and then returned to her own.

"The next morning the gentleman urged his bride to move what family she had in town to his apartment, or take him and his to her own. She gave him several reasons to the contrary, but none convincing enough to satisfy him. He wanted present possession of her wealth and ordered his chariot to be got ready with design to accompany her home. She, seeing there was no other way, fell on her knees, begged he would forgive her, and promised to declare the whole truth to him. This put him in a great consternation, but however he raised her from the floor and gave attention. She told him he was imposed on, that she was not the person she represented, that she had for several years had a violent affection for him, and was willing to embrace this offer made her by Bavia to gratify her passion and mend her fortune, that since he would in time come to the knowledge of all her miscarriages, she would herself reveal them. She said her necessities and not her inclinations had obliged her to take an ill course of life, but now she was fully resolved to reclaim and would prove the best of wives to him.

"The new husband appeared like one thunderstruck. He for some time had no more motion than a statue, but soon after recovered his faculties, beat his wife, turned her out of doors, run to his chariot, and hastened away to Bavia's to finish his revenge on her for imposing a beggar and a strumpet on him. But when he came, she was gone and had moved all her effects. Her landlord could give no account of her, for she not only went to seek better cover for herself but to secure his plate likewise. The bubbled spark thought a woman of her business could not be long concealed and swore he'd be her death as soon as he could find her.

"This match and the beau's resentment was quickly spread and became the diversion of the town. Bavia was not the last that understood the danger that attended her and thought if she should contrive means to appease his fury, she was now become too notorious to continue the employ; and the money and plate being soon confounded betwixt her and her gallants in riotous and disorderly living put her to a nonplus. She durst not appear in public, and if she stayed at home, she starved. She was informed of a rich planter's wife who was then going to Jamaica and resolved to attempt getting into her service. Accordingly she went, pretended to be very expert at her needle, and was received. The planter's wife hired her and took her along with her into the country. I have been informed likewise of her behavior after her arrival, but know not whether you are willing to hear it. If you please to signify your commands, sir, I shall readily obey them." The captain ordered him to go on with the history, and Frutesius bid him avoid prolixity and not use tautologies or unnecessary repetitions. He promised to be concise and thus proceeded:

"Bavia had not been long at the plantation before, by false suggestions she whispered into her master's and mistress's ears, she made each jealous of the other's having too familiar a converse with the slaves, which caused such a disturbance in the family that, instead of peace and quietness, as usual, there was nothing but fighting and scratching amongst them. The master whipped the men, and the mistress the women, and then went to't themselves. But this did not hold. They came to a right understanding and sent her who had been the cause of their difference to shift. She, being now again put to her trumps, went away towards Spanish Town.[30] But, calling at a plantation by the way to beg refreshment, telling the owner she wanted a service and was a complete mistress of her needle, the planter, who was a widower and had one only daughter, entertained her, where she continued several years.

"Her master's daughter was very young at her coming, and though not overburdened with wit, was very pretty for a native of that country and increased in beauty as she did in years, which a neighboring gentleman observing, had a great inclination to debauch her. He met with Bavia in the field, sounded her on the matter, and finding her answer his design, he promised her a large reward, and she him her assistance. After she came home, she pretended to the young gentlewoman that she had great skill in geomancy and would needs tell her fortune. After she had scribbled a few unintelligible characters, she acquainted her that there was a very strong appearance of her having Colonel Ebrardus for a husband, and that she did not doubt by her art to bring the business about, provided the girl would be ruled and follow her directions.

"Dacia (for that was her young mistress's name) promised obedience but questioned the truth, because the colonel was then married. Bavia told her that was of small moment: the wife would shortly die and for proof of her science in soothsaying, she would have her walk in the plantation the next Sunday evening, for she foresaw that something would happen to convince her of her knowledge. Dacia, being very willing to gain the affections of

---

[30] Villa de la Vega, the Spanish and later English capital of the island, which was originally called Sant'Iago.

Colonel Ebrardus, who was a handsome gentleman and possessor of several good plantations, agreed to the proposal, of which Bavia gave the colonel notice. Sunday came, Dacia took her walk, and Bavia hopped after to attend her. By that time they had passed two fields, they spied the colonel coming towards them. He accosted Dacia with much ceremony and many compliments, extolled her beauty to the skies, discovered his passion, and said that, unless he could persuade her to sympathize and compassionate his affections, he was forever miserable. But the old gentleman, Dacia's father, walking towards them, prevented any further discourse of that nature. The good man, seeing the colonel so near his pen,[31] gave him an invitation to walk in and take a bottle, which he, excusing, took leave.

"Dacia was so overjoyed at the colonel's addresses that she could scarce contain herself from uttering it in her father's presence. She now really believed the stars and Bavia to be cater-cousins and resolved to do whatever she ordered her. Within a few weeks after, the Assembly (of which our colonel was one) was to meet at St. Jago de la Vega, commonly (as you know, sir) called Spanish Town. Bavia persuaded her to get leave of her father to go thither to see the appearance, as was usual with most of the chief traders of the island, but to prevent, if possible, the old gentleman's going with her. The father gave consent and, as it happened, had business that he could not accompany her himself, but ordered Bavia to take care of her and two or three Negroes to wait on her.

"In that little journey Bavia did not fail to instruct her pupil. She advised her to comply to everything that Colonel Ebrardus should desire of her, even though he pressed for favors not consistent with her virtue, that she should not refuse him, for (she said) she foresaw by her art (having that morning consulted her occult science on purpose) that if she denied any of his requests, their whole design was frustrated; but, on the other hand, if she complied with his importunities, she gained an entire conquest. It was not long before they reached the town, where the colonel

[31] "a Place where they keep their Stock of Cattle, Sheep, Fowls, &c."

(who before had notice) soon perceived them, had them to his lodgings, and made them an handsome entertainment, after which Bavia pretended business for a moment and left Dacia with him, who endeavored to put his design into practice.

"The fort, being betrayed, made no great resistance. He gained an easy conquest, and robbed the young girl of her honor, had frequent meetings with her afterwards, but gave Bavia only fair promises and puts-off, instead of the desired premium. This correspondence did not continue long before Dacia perceived she was with child and knew not what measures to take to conceal it from her father. She acquainted Bavia, who was more terrified at the apprehension of the father's resentments than Dacia, but still comforted the foolish girl and told her all would end according to her prognostication. She packed away to the colonel and informed him of the disaster, that her life lay liable to the old gentleman's passion as soon as 'twas discovered, so desired he give her the gratification he had before assured her of, that she might be gone from her service before the murder broke out. But all in vain; no money was to be got, and at her return, she found Dacia had confessed all to her father, and was no sooner entered the house but was laid hold on by the old gentleman's command, bound hand and foot, and for three days fed by an old Negro with nothing but cassava bread and water, then stripped bare to the waist, and tightly lashed by the overseer with a horsewhip, and this continued for a whole month—the same provisions and every third day the same correction, and then turned off to seek better food for herself.

"But Dacia, who still had faith in her predictions, conveyed a paper to her which, when she opened, appeared to be a recommendation to a friend of hers at Passage Fort,[32] with a request to accommodate the bearer with lodging and necessaries till she should hear further from her.

"The news of Dacia's being with child by Ebrardus was soon known, which so much grieved his wife that, either by placing

[32] "a small Village by the Sea-side, where People may be provided with Horses for *Spanish Town,* from which it's distant about 7 miles."

that misfortune too near her heart or by the relapse of a former distemper, she soon after died. And the colonel, not being willing to live long a widower, whether touched with remorse of conscience for having ruined an innocent young creature or that he really loved her or whether he believed most of the women in the island were under the same predicament and that it was better to take one of his own than of another man's making, but so it happened that he married Dacia, who did not fail in all companies to applaud the skill and cunning of Bavia, by whose art alone she thought she gained her husband, so that Bavia was presently had in great esteem. Multitudes resorted to her to know their fortune and, as her reputation, so her wealth increased. But as in England, so in Jamaica, she could not be without her gallant, who took care to keep her poor enough, for I believe when she came on board she had not three bits[33] left of all her ill-got treasure."

The captain asked him if he could give any further account of that scurvy baggage and her tricks. He answered he had been informed how she passed her time till the moment she left the island, and the captain desiring to hear it out, the mate went on with his relation.

"There was a young merchant at Port Royal who had a very great affection for a Jew's wife at Kingston and she being young and buxom, her husband old and decrepit, had as great an inclination to him. Though they knew each other's mind by letters and messages, yet one of the merchant's billets falling into the husband's hands, they could find no opportunity of meeting, for the old Jew, being acquainted with their amours, was as watchful as Argus. The golden fruit in the garden of Hesperides was as easy to be come at as the charming Jewess; she was so strictly guarded by this old dragon that he never suffered her to go over the threshold unless he was with her. The merchant set all his wits at work, tried many experiments but all to no purpose;

---

[33] "*Ryal* [also *real*, *rial*], a *Spanish* coin, of the Value of 6*d.* Sterling, and goes for Seven Pence Half-penny, being the smallest Money passable in that Island.

the husband was too cunning to be deceived. This restraint of the wife and disappointment of the lover made them both more desirous to enjoy each other's company.

"The merchant, having heard of Bavia's profound science and that by charms and incantations (as a tale never loses by carrying) she could make great proficiency in love affairs, and though they were attended with the greatest difficulty and opposition, that she by magic could accomplish his desires, applied to her for assistance. She gave him encouragement and finding him to be a good client, undertook the business. She told him that by her art she could so far blind the old husband as to secure them a meeting, but 'twould not last. If he designed to enjoy her to himself, 'twere best to take her off the island. The merchant said he should be very well pleased with the advice, could he see any probability in it, but 'twas not possible to effect it, for, in the first place, there was no getting her from her husband and, in the next, no master of a vessel durst take her on board, under penalty of five hundred pounds, without a certificate from the secretary, or posting her name at the three chief towns of the island, both which were equally destructive to the design.

"She bid him take no care about that but prepare a vessel and leave the rest to her management. He told her there was a sloop belonging to New York now taking goods at Kingston, which would sail in three or four days. She ordered him to get all his effects on board except his sugars, but let them lie on the wharf till the morning they were to sail, and when all things else were taken in that he should give her notice. He followed her instructions and let her know that the vessel would be going in two days.

"She took boat for Kingston, where her character was very well known but, as it happened, not her person. She went to the old Jew with a pretense of buying cocoanuts[34] and, having a billet ready prepared, slipped it into the wife's hand unperceived by the husband, containing an account of the merchant's design to

[34] "the Nut of which Chocolate is made."

transport her and himself to New York, that she should provide all things, she designed to take with her in readiness against the next night, and withal, the method how she intended to take her from her husband and ship her off. So making no positive bargain for the nuts, but taking a sample, promised if she found their goodness answer their looks, to be his chapwoman for the whole cargo. She took a lodging at a house very near to that of the Jew, the mistress of which was ready to lie in, and having informed the merchant of the whole design, prepared him to be ready to help carry it on.

"About one or two o'clock the same morning that the sloop was to sail, Bavia came thundering at the Jew's door, said her landlady was then in labor, and desired she would come presently to her assistance. The old man would not prevent such a necessitous piece of friendship, but ordered his wife to make haste to her relief. She dressed and took what she had before prepared, being the best of her clothes and some of her husband's money, plate, and a few emeralds, and went out to Bavia who, as she had already got all she could worm out of the merchant, was not willing to part with his mistress without giving her likewise a taste of her skill. So, taking the bundle from her, [she] bid her hasten to the wharf to the merchant, and said before she could get on board she would bring the things after her; but as soon as the woman was out of sight she made off another way with her booty, well knowing their business was of too great importance to be delayed or to permit them to pursue her.

"The Jewess went down to the waterside, where the merchant with one Negro only attended her coming, and having provided an empty sugar cask ready for the design, put her in, and headed her up. The Jew, at his uprising, finding his wife was not returned, went to his neighbor to inquire how the good woman in the straw fared but understanding there had been no symptoms of a labor and that the lodger was absented, presently imagined that it was a trick to get his wife from him and that she was going to New York with the merchant. He flew with all the wings of jealousy to an officer, and took him with him to search the sloop.

They came just as the sugars were taking in. The merchant (though he dreaded the consequence) forced a smile at their approach and told them they were free to search not only the vessel but even his portmanteau if they thought convenient, he having affairs of greater moment in his intentions than to run away with a silly woman. Notwithstanding, the officer with the old Jew at his elbow searched the hold thoroughly and did not leave so much as a chest of any tolerable size unpeeped into. But having no distrust of the sugar casks, did not discover anything. So the sloop hoisted sail, stood out to sea, and proceeded on her voyage.

"The Jew at his return, being informed that his pretended chapwoman was the conjuress (as people called her) who concerned in Ebrardus's match, did not then doubt but she had posted his wife away before upon a broomstaff, but was resolved to have his full revenge on her, so took horse immediately and rode away to Spanish Town to get a warrant from the governor and was fully bent to try her for sorcery. But Bavia had intelligence of his design and thinking it best to be as retired as she could, by the advantage of her plate, money, and jewels, made interest with the man that she used as a messenger to you, sir, who sent her to his pen, and there she has continued private till she had this opportunity of a passage for England."

After Captain Fustian had ruminated on the second part of this relation—how the death of Ebrardus's wife and his marriage with Dacia had truly answered her predictions—he really believed that she likewise made use of some diabolical art to deceive the old Jew and convey away his wife, which confirmed him in his opinion that she was a sorceress, and, calling to mind that she was partly of Sclavonian extract,[35] did not doubt but she was a witch of the first rate, if not a limb of the Devil. And since she might as well have transported herself to England in an egg shell, he thought 'twas pure spite and malice brought her on board him, purposely to do mischief, and that she had been the principal promoter of all the disturbances and misapprehensions they

[35] Slavic. Apparently this is an invention of Fustian's fancy. On page 121 she is described as having a Scottish father and an English mother.

had been perplexed with. Then he considered her person and was of opinion that it was impossible for anyone to have a natural inclination for such a piece of ugliness, which was rather an antidote against than a provocative to sensuality, and that she never could have seduced his son, unless by the help of her old friend, Satan; thought she had given "Compy-boy" a philtrum; and made a resolution that, as soon as the bruise on his shoulder would give him leave, he would heave her overboard.

The very thoughts of revenge only mitigated the pain of his shoulder but also diminished the torment of his mind. But his unlucky stars would not permit him to be long easy. His unhappy memory soon altered this serenity of temper by suggesting this story to him which he had heard when a schoolboy:

That a certain conjurer had so great a command over the Devil that he often obliged him (in the shape of a horse) to carry him journeys. And being once upon the road with him, the Devil-rider spied a man with a burden of straw under him, upon a topping gelding which he had a great inclination to have. He fell to bartering with the owner about a swap. They agreed and changed; the cunning-man took the horse he had a fancy to and gave the man his *cacodaemon*. The fellow in his return home had a rapid river to ride through, which was likewise very deep except just at the ford where the man was to pass. He had no sooner entered into the current but his Devilship vanished, leaving the man nothing but the straw to support him, which by the swiftness of the stream was soon carried into the depth, and the straw by degrees growing wet could no longer keep its rider above water but put the jockey to shift for himself, who was taken up by a boat that crossed the river by accident, otherwise the fellow had been drowned.

So that the captain thought, since the Devil, catlike, did not care to wet his feet, should he set her a-swimming and her sooty friend not come to her assistance, it must inevitably cost her her life. And perhaps he himself, at his return to England, [must] pay the price for it, by being convicted and trussed up on her account, which was a compliment he did not design to any of her generation. But then the thought of her deluding his dear "Compy-boy" returning fresh into his noddle so transported him that he could not be easy without inflicting some punishment on her. He had heard that when witches were imprisoned, they lost their diabolical power, for which reason he forthwith commanded the carpenter's mate to nail her up in her cabin and ordered his servants to give her victuals and drink through the scuttle; and this being done, it gave him some small satisfaction.

The captain, seeing 'twas a clear, pleasant evening, determined to take a bowl of punch with his officers on deck, and ordered his steward to prepare a large dose. The cup went round merrily and their discourse, being interlarded with forecastle jests and tarpaulin phrases, was as diverting as the liquor pleasant. But before they had finished their nectar, the wind freshened and increased to that degree that it blew a perfect hurricane. The sky before was clear, but the clouds then gathered into a heap and o'ershadowed the preceding light, and the darkness did not come alone but was accompanied with thunder, lightning, and a great shower of rain, and all the thoughtful crew expected a dreadful storm at hand. All hands being immediately called up, yards were lowered, sails furled, and all necessary measure taken to stem the approaching tempest.

But Captain Fustian began to think all their endeavors would be fruitless. For notwithstanding he had confined Bavia, she, having more than common interest in Hell, was undoubtedly the cause of this michief and would not give over till she had sunk the frigate and pickled the whole ship's company. That there was no danger of her being drowned with the rest, because, though her Grand-master would not venture into the sea to save her, yet before she was come to that pass, he might convey her home upon a hand-spike. Then he considered what a number of lives would be cast away, for if his crew could all swim like Tritons, yet being so many hundred leagues from land, they must perish for want of food unless they could partake of their nature too and live upon salt water and such excrements as the sea cast up; or should each one provide himself with necessaries, jump astride a dolphin's back and make as much melody as Arion did with his harp, yet still the Queen's ship would be lost. That was his greatest trouble. And should it be known (as without doubt it would) at his arrival in England that the disaster was occasioned by his affronting Bavia, the sea-captains, when he came to his trial at a court-martial, might be so malicious to impute the ship's loss to his ill-management; and then, though he escaped drowning, he was sure of being hanged. This much perplexed him, not that he valued his life but was unwilling to lose it in that dishonorable manner. He knew not what to do to extricate himself from this labyrinth of trouble and asked his lieutenants what measures they thought best to be taken.

Frutesius took this to be a happy juncture to bring the women (if not into favor) at least to an enjoyment of their former liberty; for as each of them had displeased him, they all shunned his sight, and Pharmaceuticus's wife being continually in the cabin with Holmesia, he was deprived of his usual freedom. For which reason he thus opened himself to the captain: "I believe, sir, the women are all in a confederacy, and though none but Bavia held conference with the Infernal Gentleman at their coming on board, yet it's possible it may be otherwise now. For as they have all suffered in their reputations (and, as I am of opinion, without any just occasion), it is enough to exasperate them. And what will not a malicious woman do to have revenge? I will not pretend to direct you, sir, who are my commander and best know how to act, but I really think if you would seem to stifle your resentment, all things might be yet made easy.

"I could wish, sir, Bavia was released from her confinement and an excuse made, not only to her, but to the others likewise for the unjust aspersion they have been traduced with; and if you think convenient, I myself will be the messenger. And to take the odium off from you, sir, I will place it upon some busybody in the ship and promise them that for the first fault I can perceive him guilty of, he shall receive severe correction. I think likewise, sir, if you gave them an invitation to dinner tomorrow, or, as their stock of provisions is very near exhausted, should you take them into the mess, it will be no great charge to us, and a sure way to please them. And as you know, sir, according to the old proverb, 'The Devil is good when he is pleased.' I assure you, sir, I do not speak this out of any self-interest for, let what will happen, I do not fear shifting as well as others. Neither is death so terrible to me to make me fawn on or flatter them for preservation of my life alone, were nothing more at stake. But as I have the honor to bear commission under you, sir, I am obliged in duty to use all methods for the safety of the Queen's ship."

The captain answered: "Lieutenant, you have hit the nail on the head. There is nothing else puzzles me. Were it not for that, it were all a case to me, sink or swim, but, as you say, the ship must be taken care of. And though 'tis a crime to have to do with such wicked people, yet of two evils, the least is to be chosen. And since we must hold a candle to the Devil, the sooner 'tis done the better. I desire you will undertake it and act as you think good."

Frutesius, not a little pleased he had overreached him, went presently and proclaimed a gaol-delivery, had Bavia's door unnailed, and took her with him to Holmesia's, where they diverted themselves with the captain's apprehensions. And the women were very well satisfied that they were to eat at the old gentleman's table, being assured of good living to the end of their voyage.

The storm had pretty well spent itself before day appeared. Its fury was all lost, and when the sun came in view, the clouds dispersed, the sky grew clear, and no symptoms of bad weather were to be seen. This was all attributed to the women. It was conjectured that their agent, being Prince of the Air, ordered storms or calms just as they frowned or smiled, which made everyone avoid displeasing them. So meeting with no more uneasiness, they passed their time with pleasure, and having a brisk steady gale, the ship arrived safe in the Downs.

Before they could come to an anchor, the women pressed for a boat to put them on shore. But the captain, now he was got safe into harbor, resumed his natural temper and told them he had something else to do than to wait their motions, that the world was come to a fine pass if her Majesty's boat must be at the command of every scurvy scout. Let them get ashore in some of the Deal yawls that come off, for the Queen's boat should not attend them. But the wind, blowing hard and shifting to another point of the compass, ran the ship foul of a merchantman, carried away her bowsprit and very much damaged her rigging. The captain believed this misfortune was owing to the good wishes of his passengers and being willing to get rid of 'em at any rate, ordered the pinnace to be manned for himself to go on board the admiral, and that the yawl should be hoisted out to put the women ashore.

After the captain had paid his respects to the admiral, he bid his cockswain steer for Deal and approached shore just as the ladies were landed. They, seeing the captain coming out of the boat, stayed to take their leaves of him. There run a very great surf (as usually does in that place) which made it a difficult landing; but two of the boat's crew took him betwixt them in order to carry him out. A swelling sea came rolling in and tripped up the fellows' heels, so that down came they and the captain together and were heartily drenched, which much pleased his well-wishing spectators, more especially Bavia, who was so overjoyed that she could not contain from laughing at that immoderate rate that she could scarcely keep on her legs. The captain got up and observing that he had spoiled his best coat, was assured 'twas Bavia's malice, and thought unless he could draw blood from her, she would always retain that power over him.

At her he flew and scratched with so good a will (he not being the nicest man in keeping his nails in decorum) that he furrowed her face most lamentably, leaving her ill-favored phyz covered over with blood to supply the defect of that skin which he had raked off with his tenters. Bavia cried out fearfully, which brought the mob down to that part of the strand where they stood. She was very fluent of her tongue and, being now got out of his territories, failed not to give him all the ill language she was mistress of, and he being pretty good at such sort of repartee, returned it as home to her and her accomplices. The mob, seeing the captain in a dripping condition, imagined the women had abused him and ought to suffer for it; but whether they had or had not, he was captain of a man-of-war (a demi-god with them) so must be in the right, and resolving to be of his side, let fly a whole volley of foul-mouthed expression at them and had left words and proceeded to action, but that the malignants foresaw the danger and scoured into the next house for shelter. And the captain marched off likewise to prune his feathers and qualify himself to appear amongst the rest of his fraternity.

As we have brought our ladies safe to England, it may not perhaps be thought improper to trace them to London and examine what sort of lives they lead there, whether they repent and amend, or continue their wickedness till punishment overtake them. In order to which, we must for some time leave Bavia at Deal to take care of her scratched countenance, and set out with Holmesia, who, after two or three days divertissement with her beloved Frutesius (who came ashore to her), began to think of her journey. She spoke to her landlord for a horse, but was very curious in her choice. For it seems she had never been on horseback, so did not dare to venture upon one of any height or courage. At length one was found for her turn, it being such a poor, little dull scrag as everybody else had refused. The sidesaddle was put on, but that was a gimcrack beyond Madam's apprehension, so it was taken off again and a good old woman's panel procured, by which she might hold with both hands. This fitted, and being so equipped, she mounted and left Deal, Quomina walking after with an instrument of correction, being a middle-sized faggot-stick, which served for two uses, to be a support to herself and drive her mistress's kessil.[36]

The first day they passed on quietly without meeting with any adventure worth taking notice of. Neither could they make a good stage of it, because the horse, who was used to carry sailors, run his head in at every alehouse door, and when Quomina beat

[36] Possibly from the pejorative application of "kestrel."

him, made bold to enter the habitation, her mistress not knowing what use to make of the reins; so that the girl was obliged to
lead him by every house and through every town, then turn him
adrift and drive him.

On the second day of their journey, a little before they
reached Rochester[37] they saw a pedlar passing by, driving a
laden ass before him. Holmesia, being willing to be satisfied if
she were in her right road to London, thus after her manner
asked the man, "You, Baccararaman,[38] which is de way to grandee
town?" The fellow, looking on her, thought by her appearance
and her cant that she was a gypsy, so drove on and made no
answer. Holmesia was so very angry at the fellow's neglect that
she ordered the girl to punish him and thus gave her directions:
"Quomina, fumfum yon Baccarara, fumfum him grandee." Away
run the wench, crying out, "Boonsam yamyam the Baccarara, can
he no savé speak to somebody?" The man did not perceive the
Negro till he heard her at his heels, when turning and seeing her
black face, he thought certainly the gypsy had sent the Devil
for him. The fellow was in a terrible fright and prepared to make
off, designing to leave them his pack to excuse his carcass, for
he believed it was his goods only that the supposed stroller
wanted. But just as he was going to set up a run, what with fear
and too much haste, he stumbled at the cart route and fell.
Quomina, who was just behind him, took that advantage and
belabored him soundly with her supporting corrector, her mistress all the time encouraging her. The man cried out vehemently
for help, but never offered to rise, for fear of being carried
off bodily.

[37] Holmesia takes the main highway to London, through Canterbury,
Chatham, Rochester, and Dartford. Bavia, after her escapade in Deal, goes
first to Maidstone to elude possible pursuers.

[38] According to the author's glossary, this and the following remarks of
Holmesia and Quomina are in "the *Negroish* Tongue": *Baccarara*—white;
grandee town—"the great Town, or London"; *fumfum*—beat; *Boonsam*—the
Devil; *yamyam*—eat; *savé*—"know, or can tell; but it's a Word improperly
thrust into most of their Discourse."

At length two countrymen, who had been hedging hard by, came to the poor pedlar's assistance and asked the meaning of this usage. He told them that those strolling vagabonds had an intention not only to rob but to murder him and would surely have executed their design, had not they been so kind to come to his rescue. The man first laid hold on Quomina and then went to unhorse her ladyship, who (being afraid they designed to beat her) said: "Me no savé touch de bundle, me be de Creole tramping to grandee town." But one of the fellows pulling her off the horse, she cried: "Boonsam yamyam de Baccarara, can he no savé be quiet and let somebody alone?" The man replied, "Don't think your gibberish shall save you! We know you are a pack of counterfeits and stroll about only to cheat the country under pretense of telling fortunes. You watch your opportunity and strip all the hedges and hen roosts you meet with. It was but t'other day some of your gang made a fool of our vicar, for all he's a scholar. His maid called them into the house to tell her fortune and made them eat and drink, but in requital one of them slipped upstairs and stole the sheets off from her bed. I suppose you pass for queen amongst them, but we'll take care of your queenship. You shall have a taste of the whipping-post before you go, and glad if you come off so."

And away they hurried them towards Rochester, in order to carry them before a justice. But just as they were entering Chatham, a gentleman overtook them, which, as good luck would have it, proved to be Galenicus, who (as is before mentioned) came over in the same fleet; but the ship, not being so good a sailer, did not come so soon into harbor, which caused him to be so much behind in his journey to London. He, seeing Holmesia guarded and led as a criminal, inquired into the cause; which when he understood, he acquainted the fellows with their mistake, telling them what she was, from whence she came, and whither she was going; but all he could say would not satisfy them, till he had put his hand in his pocket and paid her ransom, by which means the prisoner was discharged and he took her along with him.

They hastened forward as fast as Quomina could follow, intending, if possible, to reach Dartford, that they might have an easy stage the next day. But night overtaking them, when they had got something more than half way, made them put up at an inn in a small village on the road, which made a tolerable appearance without, though but indifferently furnished within. And since they there met with ill usage, it may not be amiss to give some account of the landlord.

He was a fellow much more noted for bulk than brains, and had a far greater share of knavery than knowledge. He was in short, a designing, tricking blockhead, one that would cheat his father to enrich himself. He thought there was no good but gain, nor greater hurt than honesty. By the help of good neighbors who lent him money, he purchased the goods and placed himself in that house, but bit his benefactors and abused his best friends, was as proud as poor and as impudent as ignorant. He took such particular care of what was brought into his house that if a silver-hilted sword or such trifle happened to be left in a room by forgetfulness, he would lay it up so safe that the owner should be sure never to see it again.

To this hopeful mansion our travellers betook themselves. Whilst supper was preparing, Galenicus ordered good beds to be provided and went himself to take care of it, not so much for the sake of having good lodgings, as to know the direct way to Holmesia's chamber, for he was unwilling to pretend that she was his wife, because he saw a man at his first entrance that he believed knew him and did not know but he might declare the contrary to the innkeepers. But he need not have used that caution, for the landlord, rather than not keep a bawdy-house, would make it one himself. He maintained a little brazen-faced dirty whoozel that served both as mistress and servant, though somewhat different from the common method, for she was mistress all day, would huff, curse, and force the fellow to be observant of her humors, but at night grew humble and was subservient to her master, letting him have his will in all respects.

Supper being ended, each one hastened to their appointed

bed, and when Galenicus, who lay in a ground room, thought all were fast asleep, he got out of bed and tripped upstairs with nothing on but his shirt. The landlord was equipped in the same manner, and, at the same time, making a sally down to his trull, who lay below at the contrary end of the house to that of Galenicus. The innkeeper spied him, but he saw not his landlord. This was too fair a temptation to be withstood. The fellow entered the room that his lodger had just quitted, took his breeches from under the pillow, cleared the pockets, returned the breeches to the same place, and then repaired to his wench, where looking on the booty, [he] perceived a gold watch and betwixt forty and fifty pistoles. This was too great a prize to be parted with, but there being no more guests then in the house, how to keep it without making himself suspected was the question.

The girl, having a quicker wit than her master, bid him go back to the same room, break a pane of glass out of the casement, then open it, and make all the haste he could to his own bed and not rise, whatever he heard, till she called him, for she said she had thought of a way to bring all off without any manner of suspicion. The fellow did as she directed, and by that time the wench thought she had given him sufficient time to execute her orders, she put her head out of her own window and bawled, "Thieves, thieves!" which alarmed the hostler, who got up and came to her rescue. She pretended she heard a noise in the street and, looking out, saw two men making off from that end of the house, and, as she imagined, one of them came out of the little parlor window, but said the gentleman that came in that night lay in the room and bid him go with her to see if it was safe.

Galenicus, during the time of their discourse, had quitted Holmesia and retired to his own apartment, so that at their coming in, they found him in bed and wholly ignorant of any misfortune, except the being deprived of passing the night with his mistress. The girl viewed the window, showed the hostler the hole by which the thief, as she said, had opened the casement to come in, and that they were in such haste to be gone that they did not stay to shut it, for it was open still.

Galenicus, hearing this, examined his breeches and in great consternation acquainted them with his loss. The wench seemed much concerned and flew upstairs to her master's chamber in a pretended heat, and thus greeted him so loud that it might be heard all the house over. "You are a special stick of wood for business indeed, to lie snorting and snoring here whilst your house is robbed. But you won't be advised. You can never go to bed without your paunch full of guzzle. Here's the gentleman has lost God knows what and 'twas a mercy we had not all our throats cut. They might have stole the teeth out of your joulter head, for anything you mind, you drunken beast, and if somebody did not take more care than you do, you might e'en continue as shabby a rascal as you were before you took this house."

The fellow was not very well pleased with the last part of this harangue. He thought she a little overacted her part but made no answer. He made haste down and showed much seeming concern that such an accident should befall the gentleman in his house and said he would use his utmost endeavor to recover the loss, so bid his hostler take a horse, ride towards Stroud, and if he saw any suspicious persons on the road to get them secured, whilst he went the other way on the same design.

By that time the seekers returned, 'twas time for our travellers to set out. They call a reckoning and, notwithstanding the fellow had so well paid himself beforehand, yet he brought in an unconscionable bill, which Holmesia paid, and away they went with a heavy heart and got safe to London. But the last night proving so expensive, Galenicus (as the best and cheapest way) thought it convenient that Holmesia should forthwith repair to her husband's brother, who received her with all imaginable kindness and took care for his brother's sake to treat her far beyond her desert or his own ability. But she had been there no long time before he and his wife perceived their sister's follies. Their house was seldom free from a visitor, either Galenicus or Frutesius (who was now likewise come to town) being daily with her, and she by her imprudent management so exposed herself that the brother would entertain her no longer. He only gave her time till the next week to provide herself.

Holmesia was very much concerned at this unexpected calamity, to be turned out of doors in a strange country, without any manner of acquaintance except her two gallants, and had no money but what came through her brother-in-law's hands, who she was assured would now keep her short enough unless she relinquished their society, which was a penance she was unwilling to submit to. And complaining to Frutesius, she was sensible, would be to very little purpose, for he had not travelled in vain, was too well acquainted with the world to part with his money foolishly. He loved to indulge himself with pleasures so long as he could have them gratis, but would be at no expense for the purchase of them. And Galenicus had lately taken pet; he was grown distrustful of the lieutenant's being too much in favor and had not been near her for three or four days, so that she thought it was in vain to seek relief from him, unless she could contrive means to cure him of his jealousy, which was beyond her skill. She imagined in this extremity she had no recourse left but to make application to Frutesius for advice, for that, as it cost nothing, she knew he would be liberal enough to dispose of. She writ him word how her affairs stood, as well in relation to Galenicus as her brother and desired his assistance.

Frutesius, after a small consideration, scribbled three or four sham epistles, as from himself directed to Holmesia, stuffed partly with large encomiums of her beauty and his own passion, and partly with complaints of her own insensibility and rigorous usage, with his own sufferings, and that since he perceived her uneasiness at his addresses, concluded with a promise to desist giving her any further trouble, but rather bear the whole burden of his sufferings with silence, than cause the least disturbance to a person for whom he had so great a value. He antedated some of those letters, but dated one on the same day it was wrote, then subscribed them, and persuaded her to show them Galenicus, as a convincing evidence of her integrity to the one and refusal of the other.

She followed his directions, and it had so good an effect that her old lover was fully satisfied, hired a larger lodging than he was before provided with, and maintained her in the same apartment. But in a few months, either his money grew short or his affections cool, for he informed her that he could no longer continue that expense, advised her to return to Jamaica and assured her, as soon as he had completed his business, he would follow her and, in order to her going, a passage was taken.

She went on shipboard and arrived safe in the island, but found things in a far different posture than she expected, for her brother-in-law had been beforehand with her. He had sent her husband an account of all her transactions, that she was a scandal to her sex, and he was forced to get rid of her, for fear of bringing an ignominy on his own family in the neighborhood. The husband, on receipt of this letter, made some inquiry into her former behavior and soon heard enough to fix him in the following resolution. He sold off all his stock, Negroes, household goods, &c., and took ship for the continent of America, saying at his departure from the island that his design was to transport himself from thence, in the first ship he could meet with, to any place where he might be sure his wife should not hear of him. So that Holmesia had a cold reception, though into a hot country, and was forced to undertake the meanest drudgery to acquire a miserable livelihood, which, how bad soever, was rather too good for a person that had been so infamously scandalous.

It will now be convenient to seek after our other lady, whom we left at Deal, to mend (if possible) her ill-favored captain-clawed face.

Bavia had a relation in London, into whose hands Aesculapius paid the yearly stipend we have before mentioned to be allowed her, who took care to remit it to her in Jamaica. But there being some small sum now remaining in his custody, it gave her an opportunity of making an advantage to herself, though to the prejudice of the Dealians. She pretended to be owner of several large plantations in the West Indies, but, having been much lefrauded by her agents, had been over to do herself justice, that she had completed her business to her full satisfaction, settled her estates according to her mind, and brought home effects of a very great value, and designed, as soon as she received moneys, which she had ordered to be returned her from London and recovered from the fatigue of the voyage to go up to town herself to take care of her business. She, by inquiry, understood that there were some people at Deal who had considerable quantities of India goods, which they durst not run the hazard of sending up to make the best market of them because they were prohibited,[39] for which reason they were to be bought a great pennyworth.

Bavia imagined this, with good management, might turn to some account. She prevailed with the gentlewoman where she lodged to go with her to two of these clandestine dealers, lest she, being a stranger, might not readily be admitted to a sight of their commodities. She there likewise took occasion to magnify her riches in Jamaica and to make a plausible pretense for being no better clad, said she had disposed of all her rich habiliments to a very great advantage in that country, well knowing she was coming to a place where she might supply herself better cheap, and that she designed, if they would sell at a reasonable price, not only to equip herself but to lay out a considerable sum with them to enable her to pleasure her friends at her arrival in London, but at that time she would only buy for her own present occasions. She agreed for a piece of chintz at each place and drew bills on her kinsman, payable to the persons or order at sight. But, though the people offered her to take the goods with her, she would not receive them till they were assured the money was paid, which being in a few days certified, she sent for the chintz. Her chapfolks, seeing the payment of her bills presently complied with, in hope of further benefit, having before sold at more than common advantage, each gave her an invitation

[39] To protect the English woolen trade, in 1701 a law was passed forbidding the importation of any cloth from India, except plain calico, which could be brought in to be printed for export.

to dinner. She on two successive days went to both, bought betwixt sixty and seventy pounds worth of chintz and atlases[40] at each place, drew bills as before, and pretended she had then an opportunity to send part of them safe to town, but that she herself should continue some weeks longer amongst them. The people were very forward to be deceived, and she took the goods with her. She had before bargained with a chaise and six to carry her to Maidstone and ordered them to be at her lodgings exactly at seven o'clock that evening, because she had a fancy to travel in the cool.

The chaise came at the appointed hour, and she (having sent her landlady on an April-day errand) placed her cargo and self therein, and drove Jehu-like to Maidstone, where she immediately hired another fresh conveniency and posted to London, leaving the Deal merchants on the advice of the non-acceptance of her bills to curse their own credulity and the mischievous contrivance of their customer.

Bavia had not been long in town before she played the same game over again, taking up large quantities of goods of several shopkeepers, which I shall forbear to particularize, because the frauds having some sympathy with that committed in Kent, I would avoid tautology. But the Londoners, inquiring more diligently, discovered who she was and sent their bills down to Aesculapius, who, to avoid trouble (knowing the law would compel him) paid them off and inserted her name in the public newspaper (a common practice, though of no legal validity) to prevent her being trusted for the future.

This, in some measure, had its desired effect, for her credit was not now so current as before, which made her endeavor a revenge on her husband. She found out a proctor fit for her occasion, a noted undertaker of such scandalous causes as were refused by

[40] Chintz was originally the painted calico imported from India. According to Pope (*Moral Essays*, Epistle I, 248), the celebrated actress, Mrs. Anne Oldfield, with her dying breath asked to be buried in "a charming Chintz" rather than in the woolen shroud required by law. Atlas was a silk-satin made in the East.

fair practitioners and men of reputable characters. It may not be impertinent shortly to touch on a small part of a story relating to his practice.

He had been very intimate with the wife of one of his neighbors, who in a little time after died, leaving a considerable quantity of assets, but in quality a larger proportion of debts. The proctor, not willing his mistress should be left destitute, which must have been if each creditor had received a *quantum meruit*,[41] and not designing to part with any of the substance, for a color to plead *plene administravit*,[42] provided a match for her, that he might secure the effects to the wife and charge the debt on the husband. He procured a woman to be dressed up in man's clothes, gave her a new name in which he took out a license, and had her married to his mistress, to whom he himself stood father. But the trick did not answer expectation. The cheat was discovered, and at a trial proved against them in open court.

This, by way of digression to show you what a hopeful agent Bavia had made choice of. He cited Aesculapius into the Commons for non-performance of conjugal duties, but the husband took care to have such strong depositions of her cohabitation with Compass that after a long and expensive contest, he got the better of the cause.

Bavia, being now put to harder shifts for support of her extravagances, took to that which generally is the last with such infamous wretches. She broke open a chest of drawers belonging to the people where she lodged, made bold to convey away and dispose of several things she found therein, for which she was arraigned at the Old Bailey. But more for the credit of her rela-

---

[41] Literally, as much as he has deserved. When there is no formal agreement about compensation for services, the law implies a promise on the part of the employer to pay a just amount. In the case of a *quantum valebat*, the purchaser must pay the just or full value of goods received.

[42] Literally, he has fully administered. This is a plea in bar entered by an executor or administrator by which he affirms that he had not in his possession at the time of the commencement of the suit, nor has had, at any time since, any goods of the deceased to be administered.

tions than in regard to herself, interest was made with the prose-
cutor and witnesses, by which means she was acquitted, and, as
soon as discharged, she was put on board a vessel and transported
to Ireland, that she might no longer be a disgrace to her friends,
or a subject for us to continue any further remarks on.

PHILIDORE AND PLACENTIA

OR

L'Amour trop Delicat

By Mrs. Haywood

Each is himself disposer of his State.
'Tis our own Faults, or Virtues, mold our Fate.
DRYDEN.

LONDON

Printed for Tho. Green, near the corner of Spring Gardens,
Charing-Cross; and Sold by J. Roberts, at the Oxford-Arms
in Warwick-Lane.   MDCCXXVII.

(Price One Shilling)

NOTE TO TITLE PAGE

Thomas Green was associated with three other works by Mrs. Haywood between 1724 and 1732. James Roberts was even more closely connected with her phenomenal career as novelist, and with the publication of prose fiction in general. Between 1710 and 1736 he was involved in at least sixty-five fictional publications. He was Master of the Stationers' Company from 1729 to 1731 and died in 1754.

Dedication

To the Right Honourable the Lady Abergavenny.[1]

MADAM,

The greatest happiness as well as glory of an author being the privilege we have of imploring the protection of the great and good, the eminence of your Ladyship's character in both these capacities, while it justifies my choice to the world, will also induce you to excuse my presumption for laying at your feet an offering not otherwise worthy of acceptance than by the motives which prompted me to present it.

To go about to make any just description of those excellencies which render your Ladyship the pride and emulation of our sex and the admiration of the other is a task which, as conscious of my inability, I dare not undertake. So I am certain there is no omission I should be so readily forgiven, because there is nothing more true than that those who most deserve praise are the least pleased with receiving it. 'Tis the pretenders to merit who delight to hear their imaginary virtues the theme of flattering panegyric, but true perfection stands in need of no light but its own luster to make itself conspicuous.

It remains then only to congratulate your Ladyship on the many blessings you so deservedly enjoy, to wish you to live long the ornament and example of the age and the happiness of your illustrious consort; and that, when both shall depart this world to take possession of a more sublime and permanent degree of grandeur, you may leave behind you many inheritors of their parents' virtues, who may, till Time shall be no more, perpetuate your name.

I humbly entreat your Ladyship's acceptance of the following pages, which alone can assure me the presumption of so mean an offering is not a crime too great to be forgiven in,

> Madam,
>> Your Ladyship's most devoted, most faithful,
>> and most obedient servant,

ELIZA. HAYWOOD

¹ Catherine Tatton, daughter of Lt. General William Tatton and wife of Edward Nevill, 13th Baron Abergavenny and Premier Baron of England. A year after his death in 1724, she married his successor and cousin, William Nevill, the 14th Baron Abergavenny. According to Sir Walter Besant (*London in the Eighteenth Century* [London, 1925], p. 267), the first match was a "Fleet marriage," performed at the notorious chapel in Mayfair, near Hyde Park Corner. Mrs. Haywood may have dedicated her novel, which deals with overpowering love and implied *mésalliance* with more point than tact.

A final irony is that Lady Abergavenny was caught in the act of adultery by her second husband in 1729. Although she died before the trial of her partner in 1730, Lord Abergavenny was awarded £10,000 damages for "great Loss, Disappointment, and Uneasiness." Highly circumstantial depositions of various servants who discovered the affair are reported in *An Account of the Tryal of Richard Lydell, Esq....for Carrying on a Criminal Conversation with the late Lady Abergavenny*...(Printed for A. Moore, 1730). I am indebted to Professor Lois G. Morrison for this information.

[156]

PART I

Philidore was descended from a very ancient and noble family, but the indolence or unfashionable honesty of his predecessors had left him little but their virtue to inherit. He had qualifications, however, which might have raised his fortune in some employment worthy of his birth and genius; nor did he want friends whose recommendation would have been of service to him had he been inclined to apply to them, but alas! he labored under the pangs of an unhappy passion which was not only infinitely more grievous to him than all he had to fear from a narrow fortune, but also entirely took from him the power of attempting anything for himself or in the least answering the expectations the world had of him.

It was his fate to meet a lady, in a visit he made at the house of a distant relation, with whom he fell so desperately in love that from the first moment of his seeing her, one may date the last of his repose or capacity of acting in a manner any way becoming either his circumstances or education. All those thrilling pleasures, those sweet softnesses with which the dawn of love is generally accompanied were strangers to his heart, and in their room, despair, with all its black attendants, racked him with unceasing anguish.

Love, when by hope supported, invigorates the mind and makes it fit for noble undertakings. Nothing appears too difficult or dangerous which affords a prospect of rendering the lover worthy his desires. But the unhappy Philidore, wanting that prop, sunk into the deepest melancholy; a kind of lethargic dullness seized on his spirits. His once gay air was changed into the most sluggish heaviness, his sprightly wit and enlivening conversation into a sullen silence; or if he spoke, it was rather to contradict than oblige those to whom he directed his discourse.

The alteration was soon taken notice of by all that knew him, as indeed it was too visible to be concealed from those of the least discernment, though the cause of it was from those who had pretenses to the most. And from hence it may be inferred that the passion with which he was possessed is most fatal to the breast that harbors it. When most it is endeavored to be suppressed, the struggling flame grows stronger by opposition and, by being kept close from the air, gathers more force and burns with greater violence.

Our enamoured youth thought he should be looked on as ridiculous if he had discovered his desires, so very much superior in point of fortune was the object of them. Nor was that the only obstacle to his encouragement. She was also of a humor so reserved, so haughty, and so averse to love that those who had solicited her for marriage, though possessed of all the advantages he wanted, had been repulsed by her with the extremest disdain. 'Tis certain that he so far judged rightly, that whoever he had made the confidant of his passion would have endeavored to divert him from it by the impossibility there appeared of ever obtaining his wishes. To add also to the real disproportion between them, his fond imagination found greater yet. His fancy pictured her so divine a creature that not only himself, but all mankind beside were unworthy to be styled her servants. It was with the most enthusiastic adoration only he regarded her; and angel-like Placentia, would he say to himself, was formed only for the wonder of the inferior world. But to think of aiming at her possession is sacrilege beyond that of robbing the altar, and the presuming wretch should be struck dead with the lightning of her eyes. Scarce could he think her mortal, so high an esteem had he conceived of her.

Never after that time already mentioned had he the opportunity of being in her company, but the sight of her at a distance he seldom failed of enjoying every day, either at chapel, at public shows, or at her window; for not a day, scarce an hour passed without his attending about the door of her house, watching the happy moment of her appearing.

In this manner did many months pass on, he suffering himself to be wholly buried in his hopeless passion and neglecting all the means of improving the little estate left him by his father or acquiring any post by which he might support himself in a fashion becoming his birth or those endowments he was master of before this unhappy flame had degenerated his nobler faculties. But love, which is of an encroaching nature, be it never so timid or bashful, would not always suffer him to content himself with those transient views he had hitherto enjoyed of this idol of his soul. He longed to be near her, to gaze upon her always, to hear her speak, to breathe in the same air, and sleep under the same roof; and to compass this desire, he formed a contrivance which one had need be very deeply influenced by the passion he was to excuse him for.

Never did nature adorn a head with more lovely hair than was his, all which he cut off and in the room of it wore a little periwig of a dark color. His fine and delicate complexion he disguised with the peel of walnuts insomuch that he appeared of the Egyptian breed. His gay apparel was converted into homely russet, all the fine gentleman into a country boor; and thus transformed, he went to the house of his adored Placentia, having been informed she wanted a servant, and offered himself in quality of one. With great difficulty he was admitted by the housekeeper as coming without any recommendations, but protesting he was the son of a farmer, who, being ill-treated by a stepmother, had quitted the country in hope of getting a better livelihood in service; and mingling some sighs with his melancholy narration, she took pity on his misfortunes and ordered he should be received.

It was, however, a great while before he was put into any place of trust, his office being only to go on errands, whet knives for the butler, draw water, and such like servile employments. Yet did he submit to this with a patience which would have argued the most abject meanness of spirit to have borne even to have preserved life. So much will love humble the proudest mind. So little in competition with the gratification of that passion are all other considerations. He had the blessing of beholding the lovely Placentia every day as he went into the rooms, bringing coals, lighting up candles, or some other office suitable to his post. He had the boundless happiness of stealing to the coach-house and embracing the cushions on which she sat, kissing the step on which she trod; and by chance, when none of the higher rank of servants were in the way, of being honored with her commands of fetching something she wanted, and these were the joys the world could not afford him any equal with, absent from her.

For a whole year did he live in this manner while all his friends lamented his loss, not doubting but the misfortunes to which they found his small estate was reduced had drove him to some desperate remedy for the ills of fate. Placentia was all this while wholly ignorant of the conquest she had made, nor certainly had never suspected him for other than he seemed had not an accident awaked her penetration to take notice of him.

She was walking one evening alone in an alley of her garden which led to a walk, commonly called the Valley of Grots because there were many fine little close arbors, where one might lie, and in the noon of day enjoy a midnight's shade. She had not passed many paces from the house before her ears were saluted with the accents of the most harmonious voice she had ever heard. The more she advanced, the more distinct were the notes; and she, who had a great genius to music herself, presently perceived that the person that sung had received his instructions from the best masters. She stopped and listened for some moments; but, curiosity prevailing above the pleasure she took in hearing, [she] proceeded to discover to whom she was indebted for it. The sound, still continuing, directed her which way to go, and being come pretty near, just as one stanza was ended, heard another made up of these words:

> All regards of Fame and Fortune leave me,
> Ambition no more charms me,
> 'Tis Love alone now warms me,
> And in sweet slavery true joys can give me.

As much charmed as she was with the voice, her eyes were too impatient to attend any longer on the ears; and finding the person who sung was in one of those grots already mentioned, she put back the branches of the trees which darkened the alcove and to her inexpressible amazement perceived her man Jacobin concealed in that place, for by that name the enamoured Philidore was now distinguished.

"Jacobin," cried she, "how came you by that heavenly voice? How could a youth of your low breeding acquire such judgment in music?"

Never was confusion equal to his at this demand and the sudden presence of her who made it; but recollecting himself as well as he was able and rising from the posture he was in, "Excellent lady," replied he, "if there be anything like art in the accents you have heard, I profess myself a stranger to it and rather think it is owing to your own harmonious soul, which turns to concord everything it hears, than any real melody in the sound."

"A courtier, too!" resumed she. "I knew not that I had such gallantry in my family. Prithee, tell me who didst thou serve before me?"

"None, madam," said he. "You are my first, and will be my last mistress."

"That is more than you know," cried she, laughing. "I may discharge you immediately, perhaps, and I suppose you have not gained an estate in my service to support you for life."

"I have gained that, I am certain, madam," answered he, "will never let me want one thing, which is a pride too great to become an attendant on any other, having already been so to you."

"Well," said she, throwing him a small purse, "there is something, however, to make that pride more easy; and since you are so well pleased with your service, be assured I will never turn you away till you behave yourself worse than yet I have heard of you."

He took up the favor she bestowed on him and retired with a low bow, glad now to be released lest in the present hurry of his spirits he should say or do anything which might render him liable to suspicion or offend the goddess of his desires.

She, who thought to have asked him some further questions concerning his birth and education, was once or twice about to call him back; but something, which at that time she could not account for, stopped the utterance of her words. Nor till he was quite out of sight could she recover herself; but when she did and the power of consideration was returned, the adventure appeared more strange than it had done even at the first. The sweetness of the voice and the skill by which it was directed making her imagine it proceeded from some person of condition who had, unknown to her, concealed himself in her garden, opened her eyes to discern something in Jacobin which till then she had never regarded.

In spite of his mean habit, she perceived he was the finest and most just proportioned man in the world; that his eyes had in them an uncommon share of wit and vivacity; that his hands which now, as well as his face, began to resume their native whiteness were far from that rusticity which one should expect in a person of his rank. But when she reflected on the answers he made to what she said, the graceful bow with which he rose from his seat as soon as she approached him, and the whole air of his deportment afterwards, she cried out in a kind of transport, "It cannot be but that he must be of a birth superior to what he pretends or else that he is a miracle inspired by Heaven and Nature with all perfections in the scorn of Art." And then again would she say, "If this man be in reality a peasant, how mean are birth or titles or education? The lovely Jacobin, without these aids, is all o'er excellence! He speaks and looks and moves and sings a pattern for the less accomplished great ones happily to imitate."

In fine, she was charmed with him without knowing she was so and, insensible of the danger, suffered herself to become a prey to it without the least endeavors for defense. She threw herself down on the grassy turf on which he had been sitting and indulged reflection till she became quite lost and swallowed up in thought. Already was she entered far into the mazy labyrinth of passion and ignorant of the road or the consequences which attend such wanderings of fancy. Reason grew intoxicated with the sweet enchantment and had no more the power to give her aid.

Some company being come to visit her, one of her women roused her from that delightful daydream of the mind, but little was she capable of entertaining them. Her head run continually on the merits of her servant; and so little was she sensible herself how much she was affected with them that she related to her guests the whole story of her surprise, extolling the fine voice and graceful behavior of Jacobin in terms so feeling and so warm that everybody had a curiosity of seeing and hearing him. He was immediately called for; but having been searched for all over the house was not to be found, and they were obliged to defer being witnesses of the truth of what Placentia had told them till another opportunity.

But they had no sooner taken leave and left this enamoured lady again to the freedom of her thoughts than she began to be uneasy that the object of them was not to be found. The music of his voice was still in her ears; she longed to hear the ravishing melody repeated, and though yet she was not sensible of that wish, she also longed to see the man from whom it proceeded. She caused him to be sought the second time; but word being brought that he was not within call, she went out into a field behind her garden, where she wandered a considerable time. And though night was now so far advanced that there was not the least remains of light but what the moon afforded, giving loose to contemplation, she thought not of returning nor of the dangers to which she was exposed by such a ramble.

Thus alone and unguarded, on a sudden two men rushed out of a thicket and lay violent hands on her, bade her deliver her jewels and what money she had about her. Frighted and trembling, she prepared herself to do as they would have her, entreating them the while she was searching her pockets to sheath their swords, which both of them held pointed to her throat.

Jacobin, who had retired to that field on purpose to ruminate on the adventure which had befallen him in the grot, heard the voice of his adorable, and by her speeches to the ruffians was sensible of her distress. He was unarmed, but had he been certain of being cut to pieces by these remorseless villains, he could not have refrained attempting her relief. Being a man of very great strength, he tore a bough from a tree and with that leafy shield run to the place where they were just at the moment as she was giving up what treasure she had about her.

"Turn, monsters!" cried he, "nor sacrilegiously presume to approach the shrine of that divinity with unhallowed hands."

With these words he thrust the bough between them and the lady, and so artfully defended himself against their swords that, after having suffered them to make many unavailing passes against it, which did no other harm than to disrobe it of its leaves and some little twigs, he pushed [the] spiry end directly in the eye of one of them, and, perceiving how well he had aimed, ran in that moment and, closing, disarmed him. But the other villain, coming behind him in the meantime, had certainly run him through the back if Placentia, agitated with a more than ordinary concern for her valiant defender, who by this time she knew, had not catched up that serviceable bough and with it run between Jacobin and the assassin and, beating down with her utmost force his murdering sword, prevented the blow from falling with what weight it was designed, and glanced only with a slight wound on the hip of Jacobin, who, being now provided with a weapon, flew on his antagonist with so much violence that he was glad to quit the place and follow his companion, who, distracted with the anguish of his eye and incapable of revenge, had fled before.

Jacobin thought it not prudence to pursue him, and, rejoicing that he had relieved the lady, entreated her to make what speed she could to the house while he followed, looking round about him everywhere lest any more of the disturbing gang should be lurking near that place and rush upon them to retrieve the disgrace of their companions.

But not all the terror Placentia had been in nor the danger from which she was not yet wholly freed could make her neglect giving her faithful Jacobin those praises his valor and dexterity merited from her and had probably delayed her removal from that place till it had been fatal to her had not his devoted soul, more taken up with the care of her safety than delighted with the notice she took of him and what he had done, made him in a manner force her to depart.

But when she came home, the joy to see herself safe and to have been delivered by him made her utter such things in his commendation as surprised all who heard them. The rapture she was in at first made her not presently discern that he was wounded but, happening to turn her eyes and observing some drops of blood on the floor and at the same instant recollecting whence they proceeded, she sent forth a great shriek and immediately dispatched a servant to bring a surgeon, while with her own arms she supported him to a couch, he being pretty faint with loss of blood together with that excessive agitation of spirit which the adventures of this night had involved him in.

"Make haste!" cried she. "Fly! The valiant, the faithful, the accomplished Jacobin perhaps now bleeds to death of the wounds he has received in my defense!"

The earnestness with which she spoke, the confusion in her countenance rendered it apparent that no concern was ever more deep than that she was possessed with. Her domestics, though better acquainted with their duty and too much awed by the grandeur of her state to take any notice of what they observed in her, could not forbear laughing in their sleeves, and while they wondered at the sudden alteration, envied the happiness of their fellow servant.

The surgeon being come, Placentia was presently eased of the pain she had been in by his assuring her it was no more than a slight wound which in a few days would be cured. He was conveyed to a bed on the low floor because she would not suffer him to be carried upstairs for fear the motion might be prejudicial to him. The hurry of the evening being thus happily over, all but the person ordered to attend Jacobin retired to their respective apartments to ruminate on this affair, according as the circumstance of it or their different inclinations led them.

Placentia, as most interested, passed the night in the greatest perplexities. She was no sooner at liberty to reflect than she grew amazed at herself for having expressed and still feeling so uncommon a concern for the service she had received from Jacobin.

"He did no more," said she, "than was his duty. Nay, any man would have done as much for a woman to whom he had not the least obligation" if distressed and assaulted in the manner she had been. "Why, then," continued she, "does the action appear so charming, so meritorious from him? 'Tis certainly the surprise to find so much gallantry and courage in a man of his mean birth that has caused this disorder in my soul. Were he my equal, I should think it was love had seized me. But, oh! far be it from me to debase myself so far. Yet again," would she retort, "what can I wish in man that is not to be found in this too lovely slave? Has he not every qualification that should endear him to me? Has he not youth? Has he not valor? Is not his person every way graceful, easy, and fine proportioned? Would he not become grandeur who can so well set off rusticity and shame the noblest youths who vainly boast the advantages of education, birth, and titles? Besides, who knows but that his descent may be otherwise than he pretends? I have heard of princes who have wandered in strange disguises. He may be, in reality, as far above me as he seems beneath. It cannot be that he is the son of a peasant; a boor could never produce so angel-like a form, nor could a homely cottage inspire him with a behavior so elegant, a courage so undaunted, and a mien and voice so languishing and delicate. Some accident has happened which obliges him to shroud himself in this mean shape. Perhaps," added she, with a sigh which proceeded more from pleasure than pain, "Placentia may not have seemed indifferent to his eyes, and 'tis this method he takes to obtain the presence of one who never yet afforded it willingly to the man who had declared himself her lover."

The thought that there was a possibility for such a thing to be had no sooner entered into her head than she indulged it with an infinity of rapture. She painted him in imagination the most desperate, dying lover that ever was, represented the transports she should be in when the blesséd discovery should be made, held long discourses with him, and formed answers such as she supposed he would make on such an occasion.

Thus, for some hours did she beguile her cares; but love, who takes delight sometimes to torment his votaries, would not permit her to enjoy this satisfaction. She must have her vicissitudes of pleasure and pain; and having indulged the one, the other now claimed equal share in her disordered soul. Reason, with stern remonstrances, checked the romantic turn of her late thoughts and showed her the improbability of the hope she had entertained.

"Were he," cried she, with an agony proportioned to her former transports, "of any degree which could encourage his pretensions to my love, he could not for so long a time have endured the servile offices to which he has been put. Some way his ingenious passion would have found out to have revealed itself. No, no; he is neither a lover nor a gentleman, and I but raise chimeras to distract myself. What, then, are his charms to me? How have I been exposed today by my inadvertent admiration? How could I descend so low as to think any perfection in a slave worthy of regard? But I'll retrieve it all yet; I'll discharge him from my house and service. He is an enchanter and has bewitched me from my reason, and never, never more shall he behold my face."

Thus would she rave when the cold fits of her aguish distemper were upon her; but whoever has been the least acquainted with it themselves or seen the symptoms of it in others need not be told of how short a continuance all resolutions are which tend to a cure. There is something so pleasing even in the pains of love that none can be wished to be freed from. The most desponding wretch hugs his despair and prides himself in dying a martyr to the sweet destruction.

Not all the pride and state of this lady, not all the disparity which appeared between her and the meanest servant in her family could defend her for any long time against the delight she took in loving him. She no sooner thought that she would think of him no more than all those graces which had so much charmed her returned with added luster to the eyes of fancy, and instead of repenting she had taken notice of him, looked on it as her greatest merit that she had done so. In this position of mind, let us leave her for a while and see in what state his was who had wrought so wonderful a transformation in her.

'Tis easy for anyone who considers what a love he was inspired with, which could enable him to go through fatigues he was so little accustomed to [to] submit to employments so unsuitable to his birth and genius, to conceive how much he was transported at the condescensions he had received. Her seeking him in the grot, the pleasure she took in hearing him sing, the discourse she held with him, and the familiarity with which he had been treated by her put his whole soul into a tumult of disordered joy. He knew not how to contain himself. He was almost bereft of reason, and the only proof he gave that he had remains of it was to get out of the house and seek a place where he might, with less danger of being observed, vent that extravagancy of ecstasy so unhoped a blessing had filled him with.

The field he made choice on to indulge his meditations was that in which she afterwards was attacked by the thieves, and where he had an opportunity so happily to relieve her. The praise she bestowed on that action, the tender concern she expressed at perceiving he was wounded, all her behavior to him since she had heard him sing in the grot was such as might have ravished a lover less passionately devoted than he was. Yet did he not impute the kindness she had shown him to any incitement of that passion from which, in reality, it sprung, but to an excess of goodness, a divine compassion on his meanness, and a peculiar beneficence of nature.

"Some men," said he, "might perhaps be vain enough to interpret the care she expressed to me as the effect of love, but far from me be any such gross ideas. She looks on me as I truly am, so infinitely beneath her that she can lose no fame by blessing me with her favor. How wonderfully sometimes does Heaven descend to grace abject mortality! Angels have frequently descended to hold conversation with us earth-born wretches; why then may not the excellent Placentia look down with pity on the adoring Jacobin?"

The truth is, he saw not that she loved him because he wished not she should do so. With so pure and disinterested a zeal did he worship this goddess of his soul that he desired not to inspire her with a passion which, as their circumstances were, could not but be uneasy to her. The height of his ambition was to remain always in her presence, to be blessed with her commands, and in fine to be regarded by her as he seemed to be at present.

How few of those who call themselves lovers shall we find of this description? They swear, indeed, that nothing is so dear to them as the satisfaction of the beloved object; but if we look into their hearts, we shall easily discover that a blind gratification of their wishes is all they aim at, and to obtain that, no matter what becomes of the fortune, fame, and reputation, nay, the very life of the woman they pretend with so much ardency to adore. But if most men are agitated by too gross a passion, Philidore was certainly by one as much too nice. He never reflected that there was a possibility for Placentia to think he had merits which might overbalance his other deficiencies; but he trembled at the apprehensions of her entertaining an opinion so prejudicial to her peace of mind and the interest of her fortune. But these suggestions no sooner took birth within his mind than he immediately checked them as too aspiring, as a sin to the divine excellence of Placentia, and a vain imagination of a fault she could not be guilty of.

Her behavior all the time of his being confined to his chamber strengthened him in this opinion, she never coming in to ask how he did, though she inquired every day. Hard was it indeed for her, indeed to put this restraint on herself; yet did the fears of being censured for the extraordinary kindness she had discovered on the first knowledge of his wound prevail on her to effect a coldness afterwards which was in reality a stranger to her soul. She now was sensible of the passion with which she was inspired; and though at times, on the consideration of his merits, she could absolve herself for it, at others did she endure severe struggles with her pride and, indeed, her reason which represented to her how unworthy such sentiments were of her.

'Tis probable, however, that the inclination she had to see him would have furnished her with some pretense to visit him had he been absent much longer; but the violence of his passion not permitting him to tarry from her presence a moment after he had recovered strength enough to bear him to her, he went into the room where she was sitting and, falling on his knees, thanked her for the charitable care she had taken of his health in terms so humble, so submissive, and withal so tender and gallant that if she was charmed with him before, she now became infinitely more so.

But stifling her disorders as well as she was able, "As you received your hurts," said she, "in my service and defense, I should have been strangely unworthy of finding any further proofs of your fidelity had I neglected anything which might contribute to the cure of them."

She then proceeded to inquire if he were fully recovered, and being told he was, "I have observed," resumed she, "some qualifications in you which makes me think you deserving a better post than you have hitherto held in my family; and that you have not before now been preferred is owing only to your own modesty, which has made you sit down contented in the meanest offices while you saw others of less merit exalted above you. You shall from this day forwards be the groom of my chambers. I will order the director of my domestics to set you down as such and give you a salary accordingly, and would have you believe my gratitude looks on this as a mean recompense for the service you have done me and will study something more hereafter."

Though Philidore could not but be transported at this offer, which testified how greatly he was in her favor and would also have given him an opportunity of seeing her in a more familiar manner than he could do while he continued as he was, yet durst he not accept it. He considered that if he did, he must be obliged to dress like a gentleman and must be seen by all company who came to visit her, and consequently run an eminent hazard of being discovered, it being scarce possible but that among so great a number of guests as frequented her house, some must know him as Philidore when his disguise and the meanness of his employment no longer screened him from their observation. After a pause, therefore, of three or four minutes, he entreated she would give him leave to attend her in the same manner he had done, excusing himself from entering into an office which, he said, he had not advantages enough of education to go through with any reputation, either to himself or those who should confer it on him.

The surprise she was in at his refusal was more than can be well expressed. He complained on the want of breeding with too much good breeding not to make her sensible that was far from being the true reason of his rejecting her offer and was wholly at a loss what he meant by it. She said no more to him at that time, however, being fearful, in the present disposition of her soul, that she should say too much if she gave herself the liberty of discoursing with him any longer. She therefore dismissed him from her presence, bidding him take care of himself and not to venture out too soon, and telling him she would talk with him on this head at more leisure and when he had better considered on the advantages of the post she would wish to put him in.

After this, for some days he avoided her sight, not knowing what to think on the offer she had made him, nor she of his refusing it. But as women, especially in the affairs of love, are ordinarily more impatient than men, she could no longer support his absence; and being alone one day in her closet, the door happening to be open, she saw him cross the gallery at a good distance, on which she rose hastily from her seat and called him to her. As soon as he entered, "Well, Jacobin," said she, "have you thought on the affair I talked on the last time I spoke to you? Are you yet convinced how well I wish you, or are you resolved to disappoint my gratitude and leave me still your debtor?"

"Oh, madam!" answered he, bowing down to the ground, "it is not in the power of my whole poor life to do you the thou-

sandeth part of that service which might deserve acknowledgments such as your excessive goodness showers upon me. Had I
done more than fancy can invent to testify my duty and my zeal,
your acceptance of the deed would overpay it all. But if I needs
must be requited, I beg it may be your permission to continue
as I am. I know myself unqualified, unfit for any higher post,
nor have I ambition to desire it."

"Want of ambition is sometimes a fault," interrupted she
hastily, "and I know not if you could be guilty of any I should
be less inclined to pardon. Nor are you a judge of your own
worth while thus you suffer it to be buried beneath a modesty
which, like other virtues, degenerate[s] to a vice when it exceeds
the bounds of reason and moderation. It is enough I think you
fit for a more exalted station than this I would place you in. Nor
am I without regard to my own interest when I would remove
you to a sphere where I might hold discourse with you without
exciting the wonder of all who see me do so. I believe you to be
prudent, faithful, and a sincere well-wisher of my interest; your
advice might often be of service to me, were you in condition
such as might embolden you to give it me."

Here she ceased, and the pretended Jacobin, in the utmost
perplexity between the pleasure he took in hearing her and the
uncertainty in what manner he should reply, stood speechless for
some time, but in his lovely eyes was so much of his soul
deciphered that from that moment she assured herself of what
most she wished, that he was not only of a birth superior to what
he said, but also that it was her charms which had caused this
transformation in him.

New and the most pleasing hopes now rose within her breast
that he would no longer defer declaring himself for what he was
and was already preparing an answer to what she was expecting
he would say, when, to her most cruel disappointment, he
answered in these terms.

"Overwhelm me not, I beseech you, madam," cried he, "by
an excess of goodness I am so far from meriting that I am
ashamed and in pain to receive it. Nor farther press me to accept

of honors which would but be disgraced by my wearing. Rather, dismiss me from your service, though such a doom were far more terrible than death. Banish me forever from your house and presence; 'twill be less severe than forcing me to live in a station which by my ignorance how to behave in as I ought will give the world but too much room to tax your prudence for bestowing."

All the presence of mind, the fortitude, and courage of Placentia was wholly overthrown with these words; so unexpected a shock to her high-raised expectations entirely destroyed all caution, all reserve, and, guided only by the first emotions of her passion, "Obstinate, ungrateful man!" said she. "Is it thus you requite favors the noblest of your sex would hazard life to purchase? Know I am not to be deceived. I am well assured your birth and education is not such as you have pretended. I see the gentleman through the disguise of rusticity and, sir, I take you at your word and this moment will order your discharge. I will have none among my family who think me unworthy of their confidence. Keep still your secret and your humor, and for once I will have mine."

She spoke no more, but flew out of the room, agitated with emotions which were too violent for restraint, leaving the amazed and despairing lover in agonies which were very near depriving him of his senses. He went out of the closet and run to his own chamber where, shutting the door upon him, he gave a loose to tears and to complainings. Though he had his own reasons to avoid the preferment offered him by Placentia, he could not have believed she would have parted with him on account of the service he had done and but mentioned being dismissed to put her off from any further attempts to remove him from the place he was in. He knew not well how to interpret her anger and was sometimes, in spite of the respect he had for her, tempted to believe it sprung from the cause it really did, especially when he reflected that she had entertained an opinion that he was of a birth superior to that which he pretended.

"If it be so," cried he, "I must submit to the misfortune of being banished from her sight. Better a thousand such as I should perish by despair and absence than, by their fatal presence, occasion so great an ill to her."

Thus did he argue with his passion, no consideration of self-interest or gratification being able to lessen his concern for her welfare or to make him entertain a wish which might be to the disadvantage of her peace of mind or reputation. This must be said of him, that while he suffered all that a hopeless passion could inflict, he had one reflection to console him, which was, that by dying a martyr to it, he proved a generosity which 'tis to be doubted if ever man before him could boast in so eminent a degree.

The disconsolate Placentia had, in the meantime, no interval of ease; love, despair, disdain, and rage racked her with unceasing torments.

"Heavens!" cried she in the impatience of her soul, "have I refused the noblest and the bravest men to die for one who seems so far beneath me? Nay, it must indeed be so; for were he not, have I not made sufficient advances to oblige him to declare himself? But suppose he is in reality what he pretends. His spirit is as mean and groveling as his birth, else would he have had courage to have told me that he loved me? I even begged the question, threw off all modesty, forgot all pride to force him to a confession. For what unknown crime am I thus punished? To be rejected—rejected by my slave! Oh, that I could die and end my miseries at once! They are too great to bear! But I'll retrieve my peace; I'll banish the deceiver, the imposter, the curséd destroyer of my peace and fame. He shall go hence this moment."

But alas, it was but for a moment she retained this resolution. The woman's softness immediately returned; and that desire of indulging the fond fire, which few who feel it can overcome, would not suffer her to be so cruel to herself as to drive him from her out of whose presence she could know no joy.

For three or four days, however, did she continue undetermined what to do. At last, love getting the better of all other considerations, she pitched on a desperate remedy for a desperate disease; and, having summoned all her charms into her eyes [and] passed the best part of the day in consulting what look and what habit would become her best, she put on one of the most languishing and tender that her instructive passion could direct her to assume and, clothing her delicate body in the richest undress, threw herself on a couch with a studied but most engaging carelessness. Then ordering Jacobin should attend her, [she] received him in that manner. As soon as she perceived him entering, she bade him shut the door.

"What I have to speak," said she, "needs no witnesses; nor will I have, if my commands are of any force with you, that displeasing distance which you have too religiously observed be held any longer between us. You must sit down," continued she, "and forget you have been my servant or that there is any difference in our circumstances."

Philidore who, on being told she wanted to speak with him, imagined now the fatal hour was arrived in which he was to be discharged, approached with so trembling an air that scarce had he the power of obeying her. Having, however, executed the first part of his commission, that of locking the door, she again repeated the other, on which, "No more of this unnecessary homage," resumed she, perceiving he stood aloof and bowing. "If I had not told you so, 'tis, alas, too easy for you to observe the pain it gives me. I charge you, therefore, to sit down, and near me, too, because I know not but there may be eavesdroppers of our private conference."

"I shall obey you, madam," replied he, "in all things in which I can do without forfeiting that respect which it is not even in your power to banish from my soul. Thus will I attend your commands."

With these words he drew near the couch and stooped down his head in the posture of a bow that he might the more easily hear what she had to say without obliging her to speak loud.

"Must I then make use of force to draw you to me?" said she, catching suddenly one of his hands and pulling him to a chair close to the couch. "I once more tell you," pursued she, "that I am assured you were not born for offices such as I have received from you. Reveal to me the secret which has engaged you to undertake them, and I swear to you by everything that we esteem great and sacred there is nothing you can ask I will refuse you."

"I am certain, madam," answered he, "that no consideration of myself will ever oblige me to ask anything you may not grant with honor. But, madam, pardon me when I again declare 'tis only the excess of goodness you have towards me deceives you into an opinion of my birth, which is no other than I have said."

"Then be it so; I will no more inquire," resumed she, "but since, as you confess, I am inclined to think so well of you, does not the favor require some grateful sentiments from you?"

"All that I am is yours," cried he hastily. "I wish to live but to do you all the services that are in my poor power. My whole soul is devoted to you, nor does one wish rise in my breast but for your happiness and peace of mind."

"Yet you alone have robbed me of it," sighed she out; and at that instant the violence she did her modesty in acting in this manner deprived her of the power of proceeding, and she sunk motionless and fainting.

Now was Philidore in the utmost perplexity that ever lover was involved in. He dare not call her women to her assistance, fearing her being found so and in the room shut up with him should make them with more boldness talk what already they began to whisper, and was wholly at a loss what means to apply for her recovery. He took her head and laid it gently on his arm and, with the other hand, endeavored to unfasten some ribbons which seemed to confine her breath too much. While thus employed, 'tis easy to judge with what wild emotions a heart so young and so enamoured as was his must swell; yet did his respect and the awe he had of her prevail above them. He offered not to touch her lips nor satisfy his longing passion with the smallest bliss.

Her senses soon returned, and with them a double portion of shame. She was ready to die away a second time when she reflected on her last words and the sight of her own naked bosom which, by his untying the ribbons, she found was all exposed to his view.

"Leave me, Jacobin!" cried she. "I can at present say no more. Anon you shall hear farther from me."

He stayed not now for a second command but withdrew with the extremest reverence, though an inward confusion which is not to be described. It was now past doubt if she loved him and with a passion which could not be exceeded, and sure he was the first lover that ever regretted such a discovery. But so much above his own did he regard her happiness that he even cursed himself for being the occasion of her disorder, resolving rather to die and by that means put an end to the disquiets he had caused, than by becoming her husband give the world an opportunity to censure her conduct in marrying a man who had no other jointure than his love to endow her with.

He sat some hours, giving a loose to thought and meditation, and 'tis probable had indulged it longer had he not a second time been sent for by Placentia. She was still in the same room but in a different posture, and as soon as she saw him, "Read that," said she, throwing him a letter, "but spare my eyes the shame of seeing you do so. And whatever doom you shall decree for me, give it me in writing."

She turned hastily away when she had done speaking and retired, leaving him at liberty to peruse the paper which he found contained these lines:

"To the too charming Jacobin,

"What shame denied my tongue the privilege of declaring, receive from my pen. I love you with a passion which will suffer itself no longer to be concealed. All my endeavors to vanquish it have been ineffectual; and if my person and fortune are not disagreeable to your eyes, [I] desire no other blessing of Heaven than to give you to me for a husband.

"I will no more inquire into your birth. Whoever you are, 'tis only you to whom I can devote myself, and only in your breast it is to decide the fate of
                                        "The passionate,
                                        "and almost dying,
                                                "Placentia"

This was no more than he expected before he opened it; and having already determined what to do, he took pen and paper and answered her letter in these words:

"To the most adorable of her sex, the beautiful and divine Placentia,

"A discovery such as you have made in my favor would to any man but me afford a bliss too great to be endured; yet such is my unhappy fate that to me it brings only grief of heart and the most bitter anguish. Could I be brought to think of you as lovers ordinarily do of the women they adore, how much beyond the reach of words would be the happiness of my state. But oh, I can never consent that you should do an act the world might justly blame. How greatly would your reputation and your prudence suffer when it should be known that you had disposed of yourself merely to gratify a blind passion. I love you with a tenderness as undescribable as the charms which inspired it; and to restore you to that peace of mind my fatal presence has deprived you of, I inflict a voluntary banishment on myself.

"Yes, I will go forever from those eyes which but to gaze on at an humble distance filled me with more joy than Heaven before ever vouchsafed to man. Forget me, then, I beseech you. Drive from your breast all memory of a passion that is rendered fruitless by the demerits of its object.

"And to reconcile you the more to yourself for having entertained it, I will now unfold [that] which before not even your commands, all sacred as they are in all things else, could not prevail me to reveal. I am what your belief represented me, a gentleman, but of a fortune too mean to justify your choice.

"Long have I been an adorer of your perfections, but with so pure and disinterested a zeal that I take Heaven to witness, I never had a wish but such as your guardian angel might inspire. All the indulgence I allowed my passion was to be near you; and to that end, disguised and under a borrowed name, gained admittance to your house.

"You know the rest. Oh, that I had died ere [I] entered it, since the occasion of so much disquiet to you. All I can do now to repair the injury I have unwarily committed is to take from your sight a person you can no longer look on without prejudice to your fame.

"May you, oh most lovely, most excellent of all created beings, live long and happily, whatever shall become of the
"despairing and
"most wretched
"Philidore"

This, having sealed up and directed, he gave to her woman to deliver, telling her it had been left for her lady by a stranger who came on horseback to the gate and rode away as soon as he had left it. He used this precaution, fearing that if he should give it with his own hands, she would have leisure to examine the contents before he could be out of reach of the pursuit her passion might induce her to cause being made after him. The moment he had given the letter, he went out of the house and, hiring a horse at the next inn, made all imaginable speed to his own little habitation, which was about twenty miles distant. Thus industrious was he to destroy his own happiness in the imagination that he established that of the woman he adored.

But with what words shall I represent the wild distraction of Placentia's soul when she received his letter! Here the reader's imagination must help me out; nor can any imagination but that of a woman who loves as she did and has been, like her, deprived of all her soul holds dear, do justice to the agonies with which she was possessed. She called immediately for Jacobin, but word being brought that he was nowhere to be found.

"He must be found," she cried. "Fly! Take horses; ride some one way, some another. Let none return without him! Search the whole kingdom; inquire of all you meet. Who brings him obtains my favor and an ample recompense!"

The servants, hearing her express herself thus impatiently, knew not what to think and stood staring one on the other, uncertain whether they should obey or not.

"What, are you stupid," cried she, "or deaf to my commands? Begone! Let me not see a soul of you remain behind." And then presently reflecting on the interpretations [which] might be put on the disorders she appeared in and willing to disguise the truth as much as possible, "He has robbed me," pursued she, "stole from me what is dearer to me than my life. If, when found, he refuses to come willingly, get officers; let him be forced back."

Having thus repeated her commands, everyone endeavored to be the first in the pursuit of this fugitive; and in a short time there were none but the maids left with her in the house. Never were anxieties greater than those she felt, at some times enlivened by a dawn of hope, at others pressed down almost to death by her despair. In vain her favorite made use of her utmost endeavors to give her comfort. Though trusted by her in all other affairs of life, she had not been made a confidante in this; and though she guessed her lady's disease, not daring to mention it, could afford no balsam to heal the wounds of her tormented soul.

All night, sleep was a stranger to her eyes, and the morning found her in inquietudes not to be conceived, so terrible is it for a person not accustomed to disappointments to endure the first approaches of them. But as severe as she then thought them, she soon found how greatly they can be increased and how much more dreadful is the certainty of a misfortune than the apprehensions of it when, the next evening, her people all returned without being able to bring the least intelligence of Jacobin. The most raving frenzy was then mean to that which she suffered; and no longer regarding what the world said of her, she uttered such things as made all who heard her sensible it was of no other treasure than her heart of which Jacobin had deprived her. But giving herself no more pain to conceal her sentiment, she repented nothing but that she had not given his real name to those who went in search of him because it was much more probable he might have been discovered by that rather than by the one which there was no doubt but he would throw off with his disguise as soon as he had left her house.

"It was not Jacobin my servant, but Philidore, the fine, the accomplished gentleman for whom I should have ordered them to inquire." None but her woman being in the room when she spoke these words, she took the liberty of repeating them, adding, "Is Jacobin then, madam, a man of rank and called Philidore?"

Placentia, having betrayed thus much, no longer made a secret to her of the whole, and having related the history of her amour as succinctly as her present disorders would give her leave to do, showed her the letter he had left for her at his departure.

Emanthe, for so she was called, expressed prodigious amazement at the recital of so uncommon a proof of generous affection and, willing to ingratiate herself more than she already was in the favor of her lady, offered to take coach and go in search of him herself.

"There is no doubt, madam," said she, "but he may be found. Comfort yourself, therefore, and depend on certain intelligence at my return."

Placentia embraced her, and as drowning men catch hold of every little twig in hope of safety, so did she readily suck in her words and built strange expectations on her care and diligence. Nor did she fail in the performance of her promise. She went that moment and succeeded so well in her endeavors that in a few hours she returned with the knowledge of his family, the misfortunes of it, and the place where the small remains of his paternal inheritance were situate, on which it was agreed between them that Emanthe should go there the next day and carry a letter from her lady, to which she was to add whatever she thought fit herself in order to persuade him from a nicety so much to the ruin of his passion and that of the woman he so tenderly loved.

Never did any soul long with more impatience than did that of the enamoured Placentia for the approach of morn. Soon as the dawn appeared, the coach was got ready; and the faithful Emanthe, being got into it, proceeded on her errand, the coachman being ordered to make his best speed. She was no sooner gone than her expecting mistress began to languish for her return. She counted the minutes and rejoiced to see them fly, welcoming the approach of night because she hoped that with it her griefs would end, and early the next day she should behold her dear fugitive, brought by Emanthe to a just sense in what manner he should return the tenderness of a lady who loved him in the manner she did.

But alas, her misfortunes were not so soon to know a period. It was ordained for her to know more and greater ills than as yet she had any notion of or was able to conceive. Emanthe returned indeed, and as early as she could expect her, but alone, and with so sad an air as before she spoke let the afflicted Placentia know there was nothing more for her to hope. She durst not for some moments inquire the success of her journey; and the other, knowing the impatience of her temper, was fearful to inform her.

Awhile they both stood speechless, but at last, "I see," said Placentia, "that I am undone. But tell me in what manner does the ungrateful refuse to come? Or has not thy search been effectual to find the place of his abode?"

"I would not have returned," replied Emanthe, "either with his denial or the uncertainty of what I took to find out. I have been at the house which was lately his but which he has sold to a neighboring gentleman. And but yesterday, some hours before I came, he took post for the first seaport, 'tis thought with a design to embark for Persia where, I am told, he has an uncle of great credit. Endeavor therefore, madam," pursued she, "to forget a man so much his own enemy and think that, as he was unworthy of you, Heaven has inspired him with this uncommon delicacy to prevent his taking any advantage of your partial love."

But it was not with such kind of reflections the distressed Placentia was to be consoled, nor indeed were any other Emanthe could make use of in the least effectual. She raged and lamented by turns, according as the different passions agitated her mind. Extremity of grief, of indignation, and a still unquenchable desire threw her at length into a burning fever. Her life was despaired of and when, in the sad looks of all about her, she read what were their expectations, she seemed rather pleased than the contrary, telling Emanthe she wished for nothing so much as death since deprived of all hope of ever seeing the charming Philidore again.

But in this she was also disappointed and found by experience what she had often heard, that love and death fly the pursuer and that the most certain way to avoid either is to court it. In fine, she recovered of her distemper, but was so altered by it that she scarcely to be known. Detesting all society, she quitted her fine house and, with only her faithful confidante Emanthe, retired to a remote part of the country where she indulged a melancholy which knew no intervals of pleasure. All day she sought some lonely, unfrequented shade where, undisturbed, she might enjoy her griefs; and all her nights were passed in burning sighs and unavailing languishments.

Fourteen moons were passed in this manner, which affording no variety, we skip over; but at the end of that time, she received letters from her brother who, having been sent young to travel for improvement and was absent twelve years without any news arriving of him, was supposed by everybody to be no longer in the regions of the living. It was his supposed death that made Placentia mistress of that vast fortune that had made all beneath the first rank of nobility despair of obtaining her and which had raised her so high above the hope of Philidore and consequently was the original of that over-humility and niceness in his passion which had made them both unhappy. This gentleman, who must be distinguished by the name of Bellamont, now wrote word that after many misfortunes and almost incredible adventures, he was at last in a condition such as might promise him a certain expectation of returning home in a few weeks; and his letters being dated some time before the receipt of them, every day afforded a probability of bringing him.

Had not the mind of Placentia been entirely overwhelmed between her love and her despair, she must have received this news either with pain or pleasure; the certainty of being deprived of that grandeur she had hitherto enjoyed in his right would have alarmed her pride or the thoughts of beholding a long-lost brother have awakened her tenderness. But neither the one nor the other had any effect on her. A settled and impenetrable gloom, a lethargy of soul had seized on her, and nothing that related not to Philidore was capable of moving her.

But because 'tis probable my reader may by this time begin to think a little on Philidore, let us take our leave of her for a while and see what became of that voluntary, though unhappy exile.

The intelligence which Emanthe had received concerning him was truth: he was in reality embarked for Persia, not out of any hope of making his fortune with an uncle, who could easily have put him in the way of doing it; for he, alas! was dead to all considerations of interest. He had no other wish than to remove himself forever from Placentia, hoping that time and absence might restore her to that tranquillity his presence had deprived her of. As for anything that might befall himself, he was wholly unconcerned. He took indeed his little effects with him; but in what manner he should employ them, had never been at the pains to reflect.

As it happened, 'twould have been unnecessary, for when they were within two days' sail of their intended port, the ship he was in was attacked by a pirate who, after a small dispute, boarded them, took possession of the ship and cargo, and clapped all from whom they feared any resistance under hatches. Of all who were made prisoners in this fight, none bore their misfortune with so much patience and disregard as the disconsolate Philidore. Life or death, slavery or freedom were things so indifferent to him that he seemed neither to fear nor hope which of them might be his chance.

The captain of the pirates, however, delighting less in blood than men of his profession ordinarily do, they had tolerable good usage while in their captivity and in about ten days' time found they had cast anchor, on which, the long boat being ordered out, they were set ashore on a desert coast which afforded only a prospect of desolation. The captain, pitying the lamentations which some of them made, gave everyone a sword and a gun to defend them from the wild beasts, and some biscuits to sustain them till they could reach the inland part of the country, which he told them was inhabited by people not altogether barbarous.

Five of this unhappy company, which were twelve in number when set on shore, died in this desert strand. The remaining seven travelled by weary journeys till they saw, to their great comfort, some little huts; from which the smoke ascending, they concluded it to be inhabited by humanity. They made use of their best expedition to come up to them and found some poor people who, on sight of these strangers, ran frighted into the country, making a most terrible noise all the way they went. Our unhappy wanderers pursued them, though making signs that they came not to hurt them but implore their compassion.

At length they followed them till they beheld a town, out of which a great number of men armed with bows and arrows coming out against them, they fell on their knees in token of submission; and by putting their fingers to their mouths and showing them some crumbs of the biscuit the captain had given them, signified they craved succor and that they were almost famished.

On this the others signed to them to lay down their arms, which having done, they were conducted into the town; and word being conveyed to the governor of their arrival, a place was ordered for them to be lodged in and provision allowed them.

Two more, however, died in a few days; and the rest labored under a severe disease occasioned by the extraordinary heat of the climate, the change of eating, and the calamity of their condition. Nor indeed could anything be more unhappy; they were in a place they were entirely ignorant of, as of the language, of the people, their manners, and what would be ordained for them if they recovered.

Philidore, as least concerned what might befall him, was the first that regained his strength; and walking out one day into a fine field near the place where they lodged, he fell into discourse by signs with a man who was digging up the ground. He made him understand what he meant by east and west, north and south. And pulling out of his pocket a book which had in it a small map of Persia, he made him sensible, by pointing to that and directing him by his finger the way he had come, that he wanted to know how far distant they were from that kingdom, and felt as much satisfaction as the forlorn condition of his mind would permit at perceiving they were at a very small distance from it.

He returned to his companions with these joyful tidings, but fatal did they prove to be to one of them who, having a wife and several children there, whom he had never expected more to see, the sudden thoughts that there was a possibility he should return to them filled him with so vast a transport that it overwhelmed those small remains of strength and spirit which the disease had left him, and he expired that moment.

There were now but three, besides Philidore, who survived, and one of them in a condition as could give them no hope of his life. The other two, therefore, having consulted with Philidore what they should do, went to the governor's palace where, waiting till he appeared, they all fell prostrate on their faces, as is the custom in all the Eastern parts to do before the ruler. And having paid their homage, Philidore presented him the map and, pointing to Persia, made signs that it was to that kingdom they were bound if they might be permitted to depart. They made themselves so intelligible that the governor easily understood them, and not only granted them his leave, but ordered they should be furnished out of the storehouse with things necessary for their journey.

Philidore, however, had too much generosity to leave their sick companion, and therefore deferred it till he should be in a condition to accompany them, if ordained for life. But death soon eased them of the pain of suspense; and having taken care to see him put into the ground in as decent a manner as the place would admit, Christianity not being professed there, they all three set forward for Persia.

Philidore, having an excellent capacity, had by this time acquired enough of the language to be able to inquire for the towns and cities which he was to pass; and though the misfortunes of his passion had very much dulled the nobler faculties of his soul, yet was it to his care and conduct chiefly that his companions were indebted for many escapes from the dangers to which they were exposed in those wild and desert places through which they passed. But though they had miraculously preserved themselves hitherto, a fatal day arrived which took two of them away and left the unhappy Philidore to wander wholly alone.

A furious tiger, rushing out of the woods, seized on one of these unfortunate pilgrims and with one grip deprived him of life, tearing the flesh from off the bare bones. Philidore and the other survivor drew their swords and ran against the beast, hoping to revenge the death of their companion; but alas! while Philidore ran him through the body, he had catched hold of the other and given him a mortal crush, both dying together.

With aching heart did he quit that sad sight, but had not gone from it many paces before a new adventure met him. It was a young man of a most beautiful aspect, though disguised in blood and dust, who, with his back against the trunk of a large tree, was defending himself against three that attacked him. Philidore no sooner came in sight than he cried out to him for help.

"If you are a man of honor and a European, as your habit makes me hope you are, assist an unfortunate Christian oppressed by these barbarians."

The condition in which he was exposed had been sufficient without his adjuration to have engaged our noble-minded lover to have engaged in his defense. But much more was he prompted to it when he found he was a Christian and an Englishman. He drew his sword immediately and, bidding him be of courage, placed himself by his side and charged his adversaries with so much force that they soon began to lose hopes of accomplishing their intent.

Awhile the fight continued doubtful, but victory at length inclined to the weaker side, one of the other party being killed on the spot. And those who survived, becoming faint through loss of blood yet continuing their attempts still on the beautiful stranger's life, both neglecting Philidore or any future care of their own safety from him, made at the same time a full pass at that intended victim. One of them pierced his side, but his fellow was disappointed of his aim by the conquering sword of Philidore, which he received quite through his body. It was in vain for the only now remaining assassin to make any further attacks; besides, having compassed his design first, as he imagined, against the person he fought with, he thought it best to escape, if possible, from the fury of him who had come to his assistance and was making what speed he could from the place when Philidore, pursuing his conquest, called to him to turn back, which he refusing, was run through the back. He fell immediately after the blow and followed his accomplices into another world.

On which Philidore returned to the person whom his assistance had obliged, beginning to burn for the knowledge [of] who he was and by what means reduced to such distress, with a greater impatience than he had ever done for anything since the time he had quitted the presence of his adorable Placentia. But that gentleman, who had alone and for a long time sustained the fury of the now dead assassins and had received many great wounds, was now fallen as motionless and to all appearances as incapable of ever rising more as they were.

The grief of Philidore to see him thus was wonderful from a stranger. He had never seen him before, was wholly ignorant of his name, his circumstances; he could not be sure that he had not been guilty of some base action which had drawn him into this misfortune and that, instead of a brave and worthy man he had defended, he had not been hazarding his own life for the sake of the worst criminal: a man who, though he called himself a Christian and by that powerful plea entreated his assistance, might yet be banished from his country for some shameful and wicked action. Yet was he attached to him by an impulse which he could not at that time account for. Though this was the first moment of their meeting, already did he love him with a brother's tenderness. He had hoped to hear the story of his misfortunes, to have condoled with him on them, to have had the opportunity of being serviceable to him, and to have testified by every humane, friendly office what an interest his heart took in everything relating to him, and to see these expectations frustrated gave a disappointment more touching than he could have imagined he could have been sensible of after the loss of the dear-loved Placentia.

He threw himself by him on the ground, hung over him, bathed his face in tears, uttered a thousand incoherent and extravagant exclamations. In fine, whoever had been witness of his behavior would have believed he lamented the death of a person bred with him from his infancy and who, by some uncommon obligations and proofs of love, had been rendered of more value to him than his own life.

But long had he not been employed in this manner before, to his great surprise as well as joy, he felt some motion in the seeming-dead body and, presently after, saw him open his eyes with a heavy faintness which soon after obliged the lids to close again. Being now convinced that he was still alive and presently imagining that his late swoon proceeded as much from loss of blood as any other motive, he tore his own linen to bind up his wounds, and that being not sufficient, made use of that which the lovely stranger had on his head in a turban, he being in everything habited like a Persian, though his speech as well as his words declaring he was a Christian made him not doubt but that he had been bred in England.

The little skill he had in surgery would have rendered his endeavors fruitless to do him service if, as he was attempting it, an unexpected relief had not arrived for his preservation. A litter, near which several noble persons rode attended by a great number of servants, passed close by the place where Philidore was employed in the manner already mentioned.

He no sooner saw them than he fell on his knees, entreating them by the most pity-moving gestures imaginable, to have compassion on the wounded youth. He which seemed the head of this company made a halt and, beholding the posture and having given orders to some of his people, they took the stranger and carried him to the litter, where they laid him by a person who, by his habit, appeared to be of great account. Philidore accompanied them on foot, blessing their charitable compassion on the unknown. Though what he said was in a language they understood not, yet they seemed to take great notice of the affection he expressed for the wounded man and talked to each other of it with great admiration, as he was afterwards informed.

They travelled until about the close of evening, at which time they arrived at a magnificent castle, a pleasing sight to Philidore not only because he hoped now to taste that repose he had for a long time wanted and that his new friend would doubtless here receive the assistance he stood in need of, but also because he beheld there a French renegado[1] who served as an interpreter to the owner of that palace. From him he soon learned that they were now under the protection of one of the most noble and hospitable of all the Persian lords, that he was in great favor with the present Sophy[2] and, having an esteem for the Europeans, frequently made use of his interest at court in their behalf.

Having given Philidore this pleasing intelligence, he let him know that he was commanded by his lord to inquire who they were and by what means his companion had been reduced to so lamentable a condition. On which our traveller made no scruple of relating to him his name, his country, and the motives which induced him to leave England; his being taken by pirates, the hardships he had since endured, and the design he had of repairing to his uncle, satisfying him at full in everything relating to himself. But as for the other person concerning whom he was asked, he said they must wait till he should be in a condition to tell his own story, he being as ignorant of it as they who desired to know it, and then repeated in how much danger he had found him engaged, the help he had given him, and the

---

[1] An apostate from any form of religious faith, especially a Christian who becomes a Mohammedan. Renegades appear frequently in early eighteenth-century fiction and are often villains.

[2] Surname of the ruling dynasty of Persia until 1736.

whole proceedings of the fight in the same manner as it happened.

Scarce could he gain belief when he affirmed that he was so much a stranger and at the same time expressed so extraordinary a tenderness for him. But Chamusi, for so their present protector was called, believing there might be some reasons for concealing the history of that young man, forbade that Philidore should be pressed any farther concerning it.

The two guests were lodged in the same chamber on different sofas; and the surgeons, having searched the wounds of the unknown, soon let Philidore know by the interpreter that he had none that were mortal and that, if there was any danger of his life, it was only occasioned by having lain so long in the open air. They seemed, however, not to despair of his recovery, and that in a short time, provided he were kept extremely private and free from noise and had no inward disorders of mind to retard his cure.

Philidore, who watched continually over him and overlooked those who were appointed to attend him, took care that the orders of the physicians should be punctually observed but was in fear that the exception they made concerning his innate tranquillity might in reality be prejudicial to him for, his clothes being plucked hastily off on his first being brought into the room, there fell from his breast a little picture which Philidore, taking hastily up and examining, found the representative of a lady in whose face there were so many charms that for some moments he doubted if it were possible for it to be drawn from life. It seemed a beauty even exceeding that of Placentia, and he assured himself that if it were indeed so dazzling a form, his new friend must certainly be an adorer of it. And this belief, more uniting him to him by a kind of sympathy of soul, he longed with more ardency than ever for the discovery of his affairs.

But how strangely was he surprised when the surgeons, being busy in examining his wounds and finding he had one in the upper part of his thigh, seemed to look on one another with a kind of surprise. Philidore, who happened that moment to have turned his eyes that way, observed that alteration in their countenances and, trembling for fear they had found something which they were sensible was beyond their skill to cure, ran to them immediately and, having a full view of the body of the unknown, soon perceived what it was that had alarmed them.

This beautiful person had been deprived of his manhood, not in the manner as those are whose parents, designing them for the seraglio, in early infancy qualify them for it; but this seemed to have been lately done by the yet recent scar, and consequently the effect of malice. This misfortune, joined with the sight of the picture, made Philidore half-assured that love had been the cause of his disgrace but, not doubting but that there must be something very remarkable in the story, had his curiosity doubled for the knowledge of it.

In a few days the unknown was able to lift up his eyes and speak, which he no sooner had the power of doing than, looking earnestly on Philidore and remembering the service he had received from him, "Oh, generous man!" cried he. "How is it possible to thank as it deserves the wonders you performed in my defense?"

He was about to add something more when the surgeon, who happened to be in the room at that time, would not suffer him to proceed, telling him that all his art could not avail to save his life if he contributed not to it himself by his silence and, as much as possible, avoiding all violent emotions.

Never did Philidore more prove the mastery he had over himself than on this occasion, though he so passionately desired to hold discourse with this stranger, to learn his adventures, and to let him know the interest he took in everything relating to him; yet from this time forward did he avoid giving him any opportunity of speech. Whenever he saw him beginning to say anything which tended not to common affairs, such as calling for what he wanted and the like, which he always did in the Persian language, he would stop his mouth with these or the like words.

"I beg you will defer all expressions of your gratitude for the little I have done to serve you till you shall be established to command me more greater testimonies of my zeal to do you service."

Notwithstanding the constraint he did himself all this while and the real disquiets of his soul occasioned by his never-to-be-extinguished passion for Placentia, he behaved himself before this stranger with a serenity of countenance which, when he afterwards heard the history of his misfortunes, was amazing to him.

Day by day still bringing him increase of strength on his desire to be informed, Philidore related to him, concealing only the name of the lady for whom he had suffered so much rather than make himself the most happy of mankind by an act which he thought might be a prejudice to her. The unknown held up his hands and eyes in token of astonishment.

"I thought," said he, "that love had been a passion of so encroaching a nature that it suffered no other consideration to take place. But yours is of so delicate a kind that were it delivered by any mouth but your own, I know not if I should give credit to the possibility of such a thing. When those who have the care of me will permit me to speak much, I will entertain you with an adventure no less extraordinary than yours, but methinks more conformable to nature and that notion which is commonly had of love."

Philidore told him that, though he longed for the account he now promised, he would be far from pressing him till he could do it with safety.

A little time, however, satisfied his desires; the stranger grew not only out of all danger from his wounds, but also had strength enough to sit up and talk with a great deal of ease and freedom to all who were about him, which the other observing with an infinity of satisfaction, reminded him of his promise. But the performance of it must be deferred by me till another opportunity, when in a second Part shall be fully discovered who this unknown person was, the strange adventures which had befallen him, as also the misfortunes, perplexities, and dangers to which the despairing passion of the enamoured Placentia occasioned her to reduce herself, and the catastrophe of Philidore's surprising fate.

The End of the First Part.

PART II

The beautiful unknown having recovered his strength, Philidore could no longer contain his impatience for the discovery of adventures which promised to have something in them very extraordinary. And expressing the desire he had to be informed of them, the other hesitated not to gratify it in these or the like terms:

The History of the Christian Eunuch

"My misfortunes," said he, "being of such a nature that, though innocent of any crime to draw them on, inflict a lasting disgrace on me, I entreat you will permit me to conceal my name and that of my family. It shall suffice to let you know I was born in England, descended from an ancient and honorable house of which I am the last surviving male heir.

"Being left very young in possession of a large estate, I fell into the common error of the age, that 'tis impossible to be an accomplished gentleman without the improvements of travelling. To which end, with a train and equipage proportionable to my vanity, I made the tour of Europe, took a pride in collecting the choicest rarities of every country I passed through, and forgot nothing of their fashions. But as I was on my way home from Constantinople, the last of my intended progress, a sudden storm arising obliged us to shift our sails and make towards the Oguzio[3], all the wind blowing full that way.

"We were driven much farther out of our way than we at first believed. For four and twenty hours did we sail on, in spite

[3] Presumably a section of the Mediterranean coast occupied by the Oghouz Turks, original founders of the Ottoman Empire. A check of the bashaws during the sultanate of Achmet III (1703–1730) reveals no Bashaw of Liperda. Mrs. Haywood's lascivious and cruel Turk was, however, a familiar romantic and novelistic stereotype. Baravat, where Placentia is sold into slavery, must be in "the dominions of the Grand Sultan," though it appears to be the novelist's invention.

of our teeth, and then, the wind ceasing, so great a calm ensued that all we could do was to tow the vessel back. But why should I delay your attention with fruitless particulars? As great a trouble as the calm was to us, what followed gave us yet more pain. A second tempest overtook us and with such violence that our ship, before very much impaired, could not sustain the shock; and after combatting, as it were, with the waves for almost a whole day, sank with the weight of water which from all sides burst in upon us.

"Our captain, seeing the danger before it came upon us, threw out the long boat, and he and I and as many as could get into it endeavored to save ourselves that way, having the melancholy cry of those we left behind us in our ears till eased from it by the sad prospect it gave our eyes to see them all swallowed in the relentless ocean. We had little reason to think there was any possibility of avoiding the same fate. We were far from shore, and he must have been possessed of a stronger faith than any of us to believe that poor boat could live long on so rough a sea. The terror of our expected fate gave us, without dying, the pangs of death; all our misdeeds came flagrant to remembrance, and the thoughts that we were allowed no time for penitence took away the power of making use of what we had. Judge of the horror of our state, encompassed round with all that can be shocking to the sense or staggering to the reason.

"At last the tempest ceased but not our danger, for, distant from any shore and altogether unable to guess where we were or, had we known, without means to steer our course either one way or the other, with aching hearts we cast our longing eyes as far as sight would reach, but nothing appeared in view but skies and waves. In this terrible dilemma did we continue floating some six hours and the night coming on heightened our fears and our confusion, when all at once we spied a gallant ship making her way directly after us. Joy to behold relief so near us and the terror of being run foul on, by having nothing wherewith we could avoid her, divided every soul. We cried to Heaven for deliverance and at the same time to the men whom we saw on deck, but sure it can be ascribed to nothing less than a miracle that we were preserved.

"Having lost our oars, we paddled with our arms as well as we could to shun the quick approach of that overpowering sail. And rowing in that manner towards the west to escape one danger, we ran on another, which, however, was not only our own safety but that also of the ship. A huge rock lying out of the sea, our inadvertency ran on it and the boat was staved in many pieces. Having all pretty good skill in swimming, by that means we were saved. Those in the vessel, being instructed by our damage, steered off and sent the long boat to take us in.

"Having escaped so great a peril, 'tis not to be doubted but that the first thing we did was to render thanks to Heaven and its instruments of our deliverance. But soon, alas, our joys were damped when we found by some Christians whom they had taken prisoners that those people in whose power we were were Persian privateers, who made it their business to scour the seas and bring all whom they subdued slaves not to be redeemed for any ransom whatsoever. Death now appeared a lesser evil than that to which we were reduced; and, for my part, I stood in need of all the religion as well as philosophy I was master of to keep myself from throwing myself into the sea.

"The weather continued prosperous. In a small time we cast anchor at Liperda, where, being set on shore, all who were captives were chained and conducted to a house appointed for the purpose. Whence, after taking some refreshment, we were carried to the market place, there to be disposed of to the best bidder. It being nothing material to the history of my adventures to relate the fate of my companions, I shall only say that mine was to attend to the Bashaw of Liperda, who, it seems, taking a fancy to my person, bought me at an extraordinary price.

"When in his palace, I was treated with a kindness which left me nothing but the name of slave. All the others he was master of were ordered to serve and obey me. All the employment allotted me was to attend in his chamber, more for state than service, and sometimes entertain him with singing and playing on the lute, which I had learned in Italy and had been accounted to have tolerable skill in. The liking he had to me, making him desirous of talking with me concerning my country and those I had travelled in, with more ease than he could do by an interpreter, he ordered masters to instruct me in the language of the Persians, which, when I was perfect in, never did two intimate friends, equal in birth and fortune, hold discourse together with less constraint.

"Such a slavery had been a glorious fortune for some men, but the remembrance of my friends and country rendered vain all the bashaw's endeavors to make me happy. And though I appeared before him with as much serenity as possible in my countenance, yet did he see through my disguise and complained of my want of gratitude for the favors he bestowed on me. The kindness with which he treated me made me sometimes resolve to ask my freedom of him, but having revealed my intentions to a fellow slave, who had been a long time with him, he deterred me from it by these arguments.

" 'You are not acquainted,' said he, 'with the disposition of the persons of this country. If they show you any favor, 'tis to please themselves. The bashaw loves your company, because you are capable of diverting him. Think you, therefore, he will part with you? No, you may as well imagine he would give away a fine garden, a palace, a rich jewel, or any other thing which affords him delight. He thinks on those whom ill fortune has reduced to be his slaves but as part of the furniture of his house, something he has bought for his use, and the more necessary to his contentment, the more improbable he should quit.'

"The haughty disposition of the Persians in general and the little consideration I perceived they had of anything but self-satisfaction made me approve the reasons my companion had given me for not urging a request which, 'twas likely, would not only be denied me but also deprive me of all those freedoms which at present softened my bondage. But soon, alas, had I more prevailing motives to neglect all means of regaining my liberty.

"The pleasure the bashaw took in hearing me play and sing made him keep me so eternally about him that I could not avoid the opportunity of seeing Arithea, the most loved and beautiful of all the numerous train which crowded his seraglio. Taking delight to do everything which he thought might be obliging to her, he would needs have me frequently entertain her with my voice and lute. And though whenever I was brought into the room where she was, she immediately pulled her veil over her face, yet it being made only of a fine thin silk crepe, I easily discerned charms through it, which it was impossible to behold without being devoted to them. Oh, Philidore! Such eyes, such a mouth, so many thousand loves and graces! But why should I attempt to describe what language cannot speak. You have seen the shadow of that adorable substance, and, though the painter's art but faintly represents the wonders of her beauty, yet may it give you a better idea of it than anything I am able to say.

"Never was a heart more overwhelmed with passion than was mine. And though the utter impossibility there appeared of ever possessing her or indeed of declaring what I felt might have served to check such desires in their beginning in any reasonable man, yet did the new transport afford so much delight as even despair had not the power to quell. I attempted not to overcome it. I took pleasure in indulging it. Methought it was a blessing to adore such excellence. In fine, my infatuation was beyond all bounds, as it was beyond all excuse. Wishing still to see her more and to be more her slave, I ran hazards which madness only could have led me into.

"Everyone knows 'tis death inevitable for any man who enters the seraglio walls. And though, as I have already told you, the bashaw made me frequently attend him there to entertain Arithea, yet had I been detected in an endeavor to have visited either her or any other of his wives or concubines without his license, the worst of tortures must have been my doom. I knew all this, but I regarded it not, and by some presents making a friend of one of the eunuchs who waited in that forbidden quarter of the palace, I was admitted in a mute's disguise. There, oh Philidore, did I behold the charmer, behold her in a manner such as I think must have inspired the coldest heart with love and adoration! But because it may serve to give you some idea of the luxury of those people you are going to live among, as well as in some measure to justify the wildness of my flame for Arithea, I will describe to you as near the truth as I can.

"The heat of the sun in this climate not permitting any refreshment from the air the whole day, the fondness of the bashaw had contrived a place for Arithea to enjoy the benefit of the freshest breezes at the noon of day. A huge mound being cast up at one end of the garden, an alcove was built upon it, all composed of the most beautiful shells the ocean could afford. From a thousand different springs the water was carried up by aqueducts, which falling down again into a large basin made of mother-of-pearl edged round with coral seemed to form a little kind of sea encompassing the throne on which the charmer sat. Vast fans played by mutes, who unseen stood behind the alcove, wafted a pleasing gale like that which Zephyrus breathes through the groves.

"Negligent of her beauties and all unsuspicious of any observing eyes, she came with robes ungirt and loosely flowing, her panting breast exposed, unshaded even by the lawn which hung in careless folds down to her slender fine-proportioned waist. The extreme heat of the day added to her natural freshness and the rosy tincture of her cheeks set off to vast advantage the matchless whiteness of those parts of her face and neck which blushes never paint. To speak of her eyes were to describe lightning; such and so quick the shining darts flashed forth their beamy fires. Imagination cannot reach the dazzling beauties which played about her. She seemed the Queen of Love just rising from the sea to charm the wondering heavens and diffuse immortal pleasures.

It was her custom to sit in this place and posture some hours together every day. By the assistance of the same friendly eunuch

I missed no opportunity of beholding her and, having acquired while I was in Italy some little skill in painting, I provided myself with materials and, sitting close under the covert of a large orange tree, drew her picture as near the life as colors could bring it. Pygmalion-like, I now doted on an image of my own formation, and could kisses have inspired breath into the inanimate plate, mine must certainly have warmed it into life.

"My time was now wholly taken up between the shadow and the substance. When she quit the garden, I did so too, and throwing off my disguise, either shut myself in to my chamber or retired to some unfrequented shade and, gazing on my dear picture, gave a loose to transports which were little different from frenzy. In fine, I was no longer master of my reasons; all power of reflection and consideration quite forsook me; I neglected everything. When the bashaw called me, I was not to be found; or if I was, appeared before him with so wild and so confused an air, made answers to what he said which were so little to the purpose and behaved in everything so unlike myself, or as I ought to have done, that he imagined my brain was in good earnest disordered. Not suspecting that there could be any other cause for it than the impatience I had to return to my country, he one day questioned me concerning it, adding something which made me think it would be no difficult matter for me to obtain my liberty, if I desired it.

"But I had now abandoned all thoughts of my religion, kindred, friends, country, and freedom; and lost in the sweet infatuation of Arithea's charms, placed all my heaven in gazing on them. Rather terrified than pleased at the overture made me by the bashaw, I threw myself at his feet and conjured him not to discharge me from his service, assuring him that I thought it greater honor to be his slave than to command in any other place. He seemed to take this testimony of my fidelity extremely kind: yet had I retained any portion of common sense, I might have perceived he was not perfectly satisfied with the earnestness I had expressed. 'Tis certain that from that moment I had a diligent watch put upon my actions.

"Frequent escapes making me grow secure, easy was it for me to be betrayed the third day after that in which I had this discourse with the bashaw. I was seized coming out of the seraglio garden by a guard of eunuchs who, having searched my pockets and taken thence my picture, conveyed me to close prison, where I was kept with no other sustenance than bread and water for a whole month. After which I was brought into a large yard and lashed with iron whips a hundred strokes on my naked back. It was looked on as a particular grace that my life was preserved, though sure such a punishment was more terrible than death, nor could it be accounted less than miraculous that I survived, so cruelly had the steel torn my flesh and such a vast effusion of blood had followed every blow. After this I was carried back to the dungeon with no other support than before and at the expiration of another month, the same disgraceful, painful doom inflicted on me. In fine, it was three times repeated, which, with my manner of living, brought me into such a condition that my death was hourly expected.

"Intelligence of it being carried to the bashaw, he sent orders that I should be carefully attended, saying that he intended not my death but humiliation. It was, however, a long time before I recovered enough to be able to walk. But as soon as I was, the master of the eunuchs had command to bring me before him and having repeated my crime and represented to me the heinousness of such a presumption, extolled the goodness of the bashaw in sparing my life with such extravagant hyperboles that I could scarce acknowledge, as I was required to do, the truth of them without blushing.

"After this penance I received his pardon and was restored to my former office, though infinitely short of that respect and favor with which I had before been treated. Nothing could be more deplorable than the state of my thoughts in this juncture. I was now without hope of ever seeing the adorable Arithea more. I had lost that dear picture on which to gaze kept me from the greatest part of the tortures which attend despair. The kind eunuch who had admitted me to the seraglio had been put to death for the favor he had done me. I had nothing to reflect upon but what gave me the most excessive disquiet, and not one dawn of hope to comfort me in the midst of so many calamities.

"Strange will you think it that I should still be fond of misery. Had I been the master of the least share of soul or spirit, or had been possessed of any part of that fortitude and resolution which every man ought to have, I should have exerted all the remains of interest I had with the bashaw to have prevailed on him to have suffered me to depart, or not succeeding in my request, have ventured everything for my escape rather than have tarried in a place where I was doubly a slave. But so strangely had the witchcraft of Arithea's charms wrought on me that I had no power to form one wish to leave her. Though hopeless of ever seeing her more, to breath in the same air, to hear her name repeated, to behold those who had the privilege of beholding her, and tread sometimes in the dear path her feet had blessed, all these shadowy joys were to be felicities preferable to the real ones of liberty and every laudable desire of life.

"My very torments seemed a happiness nor would I have parted from them for an empire. So much I prized my pains that, having not the least notion of a possibility of being eased of them, I desired nothing but to die a martyr to them, and had folly enough to think I could not make a more glorious exit from the world. I indulged the most unaccountable chimeras sure that ever were. 'When I find I am dying,' said I to myself, 'I will choose out the most commiserating and gentle of all who are witnesses of my fate and, relating to him the melancholy history of my passion, will entreat to have prefixed on my tombstone that I died for love and Arithea.' It pleased me to think how many unhappy lovers would lament my misfortune and praise my constancy. 'Even Arithea herself,' thought I, 'cannot but pity my unhappy fate and how glorious would be my doom,' resumed I, 'to draw a sigh or tear from her.'

"I was one day soothing my lovesick fancy with these day-dreams when a slave whom I very well knew belonged to Arithea put into my hand a sealed paper which when I had broke open I found contained these lines:

'To the charming slave,

'That I no sooner sent you a consolation for the ill usage you received on my account was owing not to my want of gratitude but power of doing as I would. The faithful slave who brings you this will find the means to conduct you to my bed and arms, if absence and the severity of my cruel husband have not effaced that image in your breast which cost you so dear to make present to your eyes. I will not, however, so far affront my own charms as to believe you would not readily undergo greater tortures, if possible, than any you have yet sustained, to obtain the recompense I now offer. But I intend at a proper season to chide the coldness of you Europeans, who can content yourselves with so little when you so much merit all. It was only the want of a necessary boldness which brought you into any misfortune, since it had been more easy as well as more safe to have had the real substance than the shadow of Arithea.'

"Ah, Philidore!" said he, "it is impossible for you to conceive what 'twas I felt, even though, as you say, you have known what 'tis to love and to despair. Had all the curtains of the sky been drawn and every wonder of futurity revealed, my astonishment could not have been more, or more my ecstasy, had I beheld my name the foremost in the rank of the immortal blessed. The slave to whom she had imparted her whole mind told me that she was pleased with my person the first moment she beheld me and had often wished in secret there were a possibility for her to entertain me without the knowledge of the bashaw whose wife she was not by choice but constraint; that when she heard of the sufferings I had endured on her account, she had been like to die with grief; and that it was only on her request that my life had been preserved. Many other particulars he related to me which made me think myself the happiest of mankind. But it being dangerous to be seen to hold any long discourse together, he took his leave after having appointed the time and place where I should meet him in order to be conducted to my expected heaven.

'The moment, which I then thought blessed, being arrived, I posted with a more than common lover's haste to the dear rendezvous, where the punctual eunuch immediately appearing, we went together into the seraglio by a back gate of which he had the key. He had taken care to dispose the greatest part of the guard at distant waiting, and those who kept that quarter, being introduced by him, took no care to examine me, not doubting if I was any other than I seemed—a mute.

"Having safely passed the avenues, I was conducted into the most magnificent room I had ever seen, where my guide taking leave of me, the all-dazzling Arithea immediately entered. As soon as I saw her, I threw myself at her feet and was beginning to express my passion in the most humble terms, but she would not suffer me to proceed, and, raising me with a smile, told me I had already suffered too much for my humility; it was now time for me to demand that reward my sufferings deserved. With these words she led me to an alcove and, making me sit down by her, by a thousand tender words and looks encouraged my submissive passion to proceed to the greatest liberties with her. I was just on the point of being as happy as the utmost qualification of my desires could make me when suddenly from behind the arras rushed out the bashaw attended by five or six armed slaves.

"Not all the respect I had for Arithea nor the favors she had bestowed on me could hinder me in the first emotions of my surprise from believing I had been betrayed by her and that she had laid this snare for me only to punish the presumption of loving her. But she giving a great shriek as they forced me from her arms and afterwards falling into a swoon, as well as the reproaches made her by the bashaw, soon convinced me of my mistake, and that I had only my own misfortune in this discovery to lament.

"The bashaw, who had before resolved what to do with me, spoke but little to me, but, giving a furious look, ordered I should be taken from his sight and the doom he had acquainted them with be immediately executed on me. He had no sooner spoken the word than the slaves, seizing all at once upon me, dragged me from the room and bore me to prison where, having bound me, with instruments proper for the purpose, they deprived me of all power of ever injuring their lord or any other person in the manner I was about to do and left me nothing but the name of man. Thus wretched, thus become the scorn of both sexes and incapable of being owned by either, there was now nothing to wish for but death, and 'tis certain that I opposed all the means made use of to the cure of my wound as much as the principles of my religion would suffer me to do.

"I recovered, however, and for my greater mortification was ordered to attend the beauties I was now deprived of all possibility of ever possessing. Being qualified for the seraglio, I was compelled to attend there under the direction of that treacherous eunuch who had been entrusted by Arithea to bring me to her and had, as I afterwards learned, betrayed us both to the bashaw. When first I saw Arithea, after my misfortune, shame and grief overwhelmed us both. In her expressive looks I read her pity for my fate, but the fears of falling herself under the displeasure of the bashaw or bringing on me yet more ill usage prevented her from speaking to me. My post being among the most inferior of the slaves that waited on her, I had seldom any opportunity of seeing her, nor did I now much endeavor it.

"My sentiments were changed with my condition and, as I had no longer the power of enjoying, had very little of the wish remaining. Slavery also seemed a less misfortune to me that it had been. I quit all thoughts of ever returning to my country. Obscurity was now my only desire and I chose rather that my friends should believe me to have perished by some accident rather than enjoy their society with this disgrace upon me.

"Involved in a kind of stupid melancholy did I linger on about six years. At the expiration of which time, happening to be walking alone in the seraglio garden, near the apartment of Arithea, she threw out of the window a small bundle which, retiring to a remoter part to open, I found contained a sum of money which in our country coin amounted to about a thousand guineas, her picture set round with diamonds, and a letter in which she wrote these lines:

'To the most injured but most dear of all mankind:
'Tis not enough to say I pity your misfortune without I give you some further proof of the sense I have of it. Would to God that the best part of my blood, nay, all of it, could make you what you were before my fatal love brought on you this irreparable mischief. Gladly would I yield my throat to the remorseless axe or bowstring—but, alas, it is not in the power of even Heaven itself to restore to you what the cruel bashaw and his cursed instruments have taken from you. But because it must certainly be an addition to your misfortunes to continue in the place where they befell you and where everything but serves to remind you of them and render your disgrace still flagrant, I send you the means of quitting Persia forever. Fly this barbarous place, O thou once most charming of thy sex, and still valued, though an eunuch. Remember Arithea, but lay not the blame of thy ill fate to her. Trust nobody with your intentions to escape. There's not a creature depending on the seraglio who has a grain of honor. We have experienced the treachery of those who professed most fidelity, else had not I suffered in the total disappointment of my wishes, and thou in so severe a manner. If you yet have any remains of tenderness for me, my picture will deserve your notice. I send it you as a proof of mine, and with it what I hope will be sufficient to bear your expenses from this inhumane court, which I shall never cease to curse while I am Arithea.'

"How transporting would such an opportunity of returning home have been to me at my first arrival in Persia and how little did I now relish it. I had no inducements, indeed, to tarry in a place where I had suffered so much. Yet was I so sensible of my disgrace, which I doubted not but would be soon discovered, that I could not think of supporting the ridicule which I thought would be made of it, with any tolerable share of patience. And I can truly aver that no other reason in the world but the desire I had of being in a place where I could have the free exercise of my religion won me at last to make use of Arithea's bounty.

"Having determined to quit the service of the bashaw, I

stole one night, when all his numerous train but those who were employed as his bodyguard were drowned in sleep. Knowing the watchword, I passed the gates without any difficulty, and before break of day lost sight of that detested city. I thought myself now secure and began to slacken my pace and travel by easy journeys. I had indeed most certainly escaped all pursuit, had I had foresight enough to have changed my habit, but in the eunuch's garb, the badge of servitude, had I not been infatuated I could not have hoped to have gone on without being remarked. Morning was no sooner come, as I afterwards heard, than the bashaw, being a little indisposed, called for me to play on the flute. I was immediately missed and after some hours of fruitless search, several Janissaries were dispatched, some one way and some another with orders to bring me back dead or alive. Those whose fortune it was to overtake me would have performed the most favorable part of his injunction but I refusing to yield, they fell upon me altogether and reduced me to that condition from which your courage and generosity relieved me."

The lovely stranger here ended the story of his misfortunes, and Philidore, truly touched with them, omitted no arguments which he thought might afford him consolation. And as his friendship was perfectly sincere, what he said had a force in it which not all the studied compliments of the unaffected can boast. The charming youth was so much delighted with the society of Philidore that it seemed a great addition to his other woes that they were obliged to part. Fain would he have persuaded him to return with him for England, assuring him that if he would do so, he should not only be let into the secret of his name and birth but also share with him in all the goods of fortune which, he acknowledged to him, were sufficient to glut the ambition of any two reasonable men.

But this, alas, was no temptation to the love-sick Philidore. He could not be prevailed on to do a thing which he thought might be a prejudice to the peace of his dear Placentia. Nor would he trust himself a second time with her charms, lest the force of them should compel him to do her an injury, for such he still looked on becoming her husband would be, without some greater recommendation to her bed than mere affection. In fine, he would suffer no consideration to surmount the niceness of his passion. And though he had the extremest tenderness for this Christian eunuch that one man can possibly have for another, yet he found it no difficulty to part with him, in all probability, forever, when the interest of Placentia was in dispute.

The generous Chamusi continued his kindness to them till they left his house, nor when they did, did he suffer either of them to depart without guides to conduct them on their way and prevent any further adventures of the like nature which brought them there. The now-enfranchised slave threw off his Persian habit and, putting on one more agreeable to his country and religion, was in less danger of being known than he had been. He had, however, four or five slaves to accompany him to the seaport. And Philidore, though he had but a small journey now to take, was not suffered to depart without two to serve him as attendants. I will not trouble my reader with any repetition of the mutual testimonies of affection which passed between these friends at taking leave of each other. I shall only say that nothing could be more tender or more sincere, each vowing that if ever Fortune permitted them to meet again it would be his greatest happiness to have some opportunity of proving that affection he had possessed.

This farewell being over and the most solemn and grateful leave taken of the obliging Chamusi, each proceeded on their different roads, but that of the beautiful eunuch being not my business to relate in this place, I shall for the present confine myself to the history of Philidore who, with no cross accidents in his way, safely arrived at Ispahan, where he was received by his uncle with all imaginable kindness. And the old gentleman by long sojourning among the Persians having learned a good deal of their luxury, there was an eternal round of pleasures about his house which might have banished melancholy in any heart where it had taken a less deep foundation than in that of

Philidore. But love, of all the passions, is least capable of being diverted. Everything serves but to remind the person possessed of it of the darling object, and the more he seeks for ease, the less he is able to find.

About a year did Philidore continue in Persia, with the same disposition with which he entered it. But his uncle dying at the expiration of that time, a vast alteration ensued both in his circumstances and humor. He found himself left the heir of such immense treasures as he could not have imagined the industry of one man could have heaped together. He was now not only in a condition which might entitle him to marry Placentia but a woman of the first quality in the kingdom, excepting the blood-royal. A kind of an assured hope now succeeded the place of despair and smiles now dissipated all the gloom which had heretofore o'erspread his face. He had no sooner celebrated his uncle's funeral with that solemnity it required than he began to call his effects out of those hands in which they had been lodged and, having completed all his affairs, embarked with the first fair wind for England.

But though he set out with the most prosperous gale that could be, they had not been out at sea above four days before it veered as much the contrary and growing very high and at last coming about full in their teeth, they were obliged to alter their compass and steer towards Baravat, a part of the dominions of the Grand Sultan. They continued sailing for some days, but having no design to touch at that or any other of those ports near which they were compelled to go, the pilot kept out at sea as much as possible. A storm, however, arising, they were glad at last to cast anchor at Baravat, which being an excellent harbor, they lay secure till the fury of the tempest was over.

The winds still kept in the same point, and there being no possibility while it lasted so to hoist sail, some of the passengers had a curiosity to go on shore. They did so, but at their return related so melancholy a story to Philidore as he could not hear without being moved in the most sensible manner.

"The market place," said one of them, "being pretty near

the sea side, my companions expressed a desire to see it. We went all together to it, being directed by the vast crowds who were going there. It seems a prize has been lately brought in here by an Algerine corsair, and a great number of unhappy passengers being taken in it were this day brought to be disposed of. Several who appeared worthy gentlemen and young and beautiful ladies were partakers of the same sad fate, with others of a more inferior and less pity-moving appearance. But among the number there was one whose air bespeaks a woman of superior birth as her eyes demonstrate her of inimitable beauty. She was set up at a great price but, nothwithstanding, became the purchase of a merchant, one of the most churlish, as appears by his character, of all who frequent the market. Everyone pitied the severe fate of so beautiful a creature, while she herself seemed unmoved and unconcerned till her new master taking her by the hand in order to lead her away, she suddenly snatched his scimitar from his side and was about to plunge it into her breast. But the press of people which was very thick about her to gaze upon her charms not permitting her to draw her arm out to a length sufficient to command the point, she was prevented from perpetrating the execution she designed. She was carried away," continued he, "but a young woman, who by her habit seemed a native of the same place, followed her with cries, till she was out of sight and hearing and afterwards expressed such tokens of grief and desperation as drew the pity of all who beheld it. I must confess I never saw a scene which touched me more, though frequently a witness of the sale of slaves."

The Persian here ended his little narration, and Philidore, being by nature of the most tender and compassionate disposition imaginable, could not help believing that it must be indeed something extraordinary which could so deeply influence the soul of a barbarian and immediately took a resolution to ease the distress of this unknown lady, if possible. For that purpose he ordered the long boat to be got ready and sent the person who had expressed so much concern with a commission to make a purchase of her, if the merchant who had bought her would be prevailed on to part with her on any terms.

The fellow employed in this message went about it with so good a will that he could not fail of accomplishing his intent, though it had been in a matter of more difficulty than this was. But the truth was that the fair slave appeared so desperately bent to die rather than submit to the fate intended for her that her new master already repented him of his bargain and was glad to dispose of her again lest he should lose all the money he had laid down to purchase her. In a very short time the messenger returned with the lady, who seemed little better satisfied with this slavery than she had been with the other, and it was as much as all the mariners who manned the boat could do to prevent her from throwing herself overboard.

Philidore observed her from the deck and in spite of the distraction she was in imagined he saw something in her air which he was not unacquainted with. But, O God! when she approached more near and he could have a full view of her face, what were his emotions when he found the woman whom his charity alone had induced him to redeem was no other than the goddess of his wishes, the still loved, still most adored Placentia. He sent forth a cry of joy and wonder which echoed to the skies. Scarce could he withhold himself from leaping into the waves to meet her. The sailors stood amazed, but though he was asked several times if he knew the lady, he had no truce from transport to hear or make any reply to what was said. The charmer was at length lifted on deck, and joy now gave him boldness to seize what before he shunned out of too great a respect. He caught her in his arms and repeating a thousand times in a breath her dear loved name, made her, in spite of his Persian habit, know him for that Philidore she had despaired of ever seeing any more.

"Oh, Philidore," cried she, no less transported than himself, "what dangers have I dared to seek you! What terrors undergone! And how unhoped do I now meet you!"

"With what a profusion of bliss does Heaven surcharge me," rejoined he. "Can it be possible I see you here and know you came thus far merely for the sake of Philidore! Oh, where shall I find words to give a vent to that excess of ecstasy with which I am overwhelmed! Placentia! Oh, most divine Placentia! Miracle of goodness, of constancy and love!"

Kisses, embraces, and all the fond endearments of rewarded passion made up for want of speech. In their expressive looks and eager graspings, the violence of their mutual flame was more plainly demonstrated than it could have been by the greatest elegance of language. Those of the Persians that stood by, who understood not English, easily perceived not only that they were lovers, but also that they were so to the most unbounded height of tender passion.

But the first emotions of that glad surprise which their unexpected meeting had occasioned being a little abated, Philidore took his charmer by the hand and led her to the cabin where, after giving a second time a loose to transport, he entreated she would relate to him the history of her adventures since the time he left her and by what means she had been reduced to the misfortunes from which he was so happy to deliver her. She, who desired nothing but to oblige him and give testimonies of her affection, readily complied with his request in these terms.

A Continuance of the History of Placentia

"I will not," said she, "detain your attention with any particulars of that despair which you know too much of, my soul, not to be sensible I was involved in at your cruel departure. It shall suffice to tell you that madness was inferior to what I felt and that, without dying, I endured a thousand times a day all the pangs of death. All the principles of Christianity were scarce of force to withhold me from laying violent hands on my own life. And had not that faithful girl, whom I alone made the confidante of my passion, kept a continual watch about me, I had certainly in some abandoned moments put an end to the miseries I had sustained, by the most unwarrantable means.

"Disappointed even in my desires to die and hopeless of any joy in life, that spirit which had fed my rage being evaporated, I sunk into a stupid calm, a numbness of soul; a cessation of thought came over me; no longer was I capable of pain or pleasure, no more knew what it was to wish or to repine. They tell me that I sighed and frequently the silent tears would steal down my cheeks; but I protest I was wholly insensible of them. Every faculty of my mind was deprived of its force, and I was in effect no more than a piece of imagery wrought by some skilful hand which walks and seems to look, yet knows not its own motions.

"In this condition, which I have since heard was judged by the physicians to be more difficult to cure than my former raging grief, I continued till the news arrived that my brother, the Baron Bellamont, who had been many years abroad and thought dead, was on his return home. When the letters were read to me, I felt a sudden spring within me, like the first start of life. The power of thought returned and, being now able to recollect the scattered memory of past events, I felt a pleasure which no words can speak. The vast possessions I was mistress of in the right of my brother being the greatest motive that had made me wretched in my love, never woman rejoiced more at acquiring an estate than did I in the loss of mine.

" 'I shall now,' cried I to myself, 'be equal with my dear Philidore, nor can his scrupulous passion now refuse me.' The change that was in me surprised all that knew me. Some thought it only a turn in my distemper and that my melancholy would now be converted into a raving frenzy. Others, more judicious, believed me cured and imagined the joy at the recovery of a long-lost brother had burst the cloud of grief which hung about my heart. And some were malicious enough to impute it to a quite contrary cause and insinuated that the cheerfulness I expressed was no more than counterfeited to conceal the inward vexation I was in at the loss of so great a fortune. But none there were who hit on the truth.

"At length he came, and he took the pleasure I received him with so kindly that he offered to share with me that estate I had wholly possessed in his right. But I would accept of no more than what was left me by my parents, and as soon as I had put into his hands the writings and accounts of what had been received and laid out, I took my leave, pretending to go on a small journey in order to visit a relation in the country, taking nobody with me but Emanthe and one footman. I took shipping at Gravesend, and from thence went to Holland, whence I heard there were continually vessels going out for Persia. But I was obliged to wait some months before I could find the opportunity I desired.

"Fortune, however, at last grew favorable, and with a fair wind I set out on my wished-for voyage, and I may truly say that 'tis impossible for my heart to be more taken up than mine was with pleasure at the enterprise I had engaged in. Next to receiving proofs of the lover's affection, nothing affords a more sincere delight than to give them. I thought the long and dangerous voyage I had undertaken to see you and the relinquishing all the favors my brother's kindness would have bestowed on me such demonstrations of my passion as could not fail of inspiring you with the utmost tenderness. I represented to myself the surprise in which my first appearance would involve you, the fondness which would ensue, formed long discourses between us. In fine, I made you such as [I] would wish to find you, and such as you indeed now prove yourself—all gratitude, all constancy and love. In these, the common daydreams of a love-sick fancy, did I pass my time, till a dreadful interruption put a stop to them and was very near depriving me of even the wish ever to look on Philidore again.

"The captain of the vessel, who from my first coming on board had treated me with an extraordinary civility, though I then regarded it as no other than on the account of my sex, came one day into my cabin and, after some discourse on ordinary affairs, began to entertain me with a most passionate declaration of love. And perceiving I turned away my head in token of disdain, 'I confess, madam,' said he, 'that you are an utter stranger to me. But whatever is your birth and fortune, my love will find the means to equal us. If above me, my courage and my industry shall raise me to the same; if inferior in the goods of chance, your charms make up for that deficiency, and 'twill be my pride as well as pleasure to exalt the woman I adore.'

"I remember not the reply I made him at that time, but I know it was far from being any encouragement to his hopes, and the more pressing he grew that I would accept of his devoirs, the more I rejected them and flattered myself with a belief that a continued scorn would cure so unavailing a passion or at least oblige him to give over persecuting me any farther with it. But alas! the desires he was inflamed with were of a different nature from all I had ever experienced in myself or been acquainted with in others. He loved me not for my sake, but his own, and believing it in my power to gratify a brutal passion, had little regard by what means he obtained me or the miseries such an action might draw upon me. Enjoyment any way was what he aimed at and he soon let me know he would not much longer attend the consent he had so often asked and that, if I still persisted to refuse making him happy by an honorable marriage, he was not of a humor to despair and would be master of his wishes on terms which would perhaps oblige me hereafter to repent the ill treatment I had given him.

"Judge how much I must be terrified with such a menace from a man in whose power I so entirely was that, should he resolve to do as he said, nothing less than a miracle could preserve me. Fear, which of all the passions I had till this moment been least acquainted with, now filled up all my soul. I grew pale; I trembled; I discovered all the marks of cowardice, which he perceived with satisfaction, imagining he had found the way to make me yield to be his wife rather than suffer that greater evil which was threatened. To confirm me, therefore, in a belief so favorable to his desires, he persisted still in talking to me in the manner he had begun and swearing the most unheard-of oaths that I should be his, either by the one or by the other means, gave a loose to his presuming passion in familiarities which left no room to doubt if he would stop at anything.

"Frightened and shocked at his behavior, beyond what is in the power of words to express, I begged he would permit me but three days of consideration, at the end of which time I flattered him with the belief that there was a possibility I might be brought to consent to his first proposal. He complied with this request but let me know it was a great favor and that I must not hope he would afford a longer reprieve. I need not tell you my confusion nor my grief in such a perplexity. You must be sensible I suffered all that both could inflict. I was angry with myself for what I had said when the three days were almost expired and I was still as far from any visible means of being delivered from as when I petitioned for a delay of the mischiefs he had threatened, and which I now looked on as unavoidable but by death, and to that it was the final determination of my soul to have recourse if he persisted in his design.

"The fatal period of time was now arrived in which I was to give my answer and he sent orders to have the cabin cleared of all but myself. To hear the message, though it was no more than I expected, gave me such a shock that I resolved to stick a penknife in my throat before his entrance, but Emanthe, perceiving my intent, ran to me and snatched it from my hand; then, falling on her knees with a flood of tears, conjured me to give over such intents. 'You know not,' said she, 'how far you may prevail on him to grant you yet a longer time. Or, if you fail to move his brutish soul, Heaven will certainly disappoint his wicked aim by some other means. Forfeit not your hopes of its protection by a deed so much the reverse of its decrees. . . .'

"She would have added something more, but the messenger returning told us he had orders to force her from me, on which she suffered him to lead her out, leaving me in a horror which is not to be conceived. The author of my terrors immediately appeared, and in his eyes, though he had put on a forced complaisance, I read the confirmation of my fate.

" 'Well, madam,' said he, 'are you yet prepared to be my wife? Have you considered on the deference I pay you, and how much you are obliged to my obsequious passion? [I] who having you in my power, choose to make you mine only by such means as virtue will permit?'

" 'Yes,' answered I, summoning all the remains of courage I was mistress of to my aid, 'I have considered that if you were, in reality, possessed of that passion you pretend, you would not attempt to force but wait with patience the result of my inclination. Humility is the truest mark of love, nor can I think your heart at all devoted to me when you make use of menaces to obtain your wishes. Were you indeed my lover, I should have greater power over your actions than my ill fate has given you over my person.'

" 'We will hereafter,' resumed he, smiling, 'dispute on the niceties of that passion. My present business is the gratification of it, and you must strangely differ from your sex, if I hear you not some time hence confess that the fury of my impatience is a more agreeable testimony of love than that cowardly submission and resignation you seem to praise at present. But come,' continued he, 'this is the happy night which is to prove how well I love. A priest attends my call. Speak—are you determined?'

" 'Oh, no,' cried I, 'never can I consent to give my hand where the affections of the heart are wanting. Allow me time to know your worth and to fashion my soul to regard you in the way you wish.'

"At these words his face grew all enflamed and his eyes sparkled with lust and rage. A thousand oaths, if possible, he uttered in a moment that Heaven itself should not prevent him from enjoying me that night. 'Nay,' cried he, 'this hour, this minute,' and immediately proceeded to actions which let me know he was not to be prevailed on to desist. In vain I wept, I knelt, I begged, I threatened; my anger and my grief were equally ineffectual. What would I not now have given for that little weapon the caution of Emanthe had deprived me of. Had I been mistress of it, I certainly had plunged it in my own breast or that of the villain who attempted to dishonor me.

"But Heaven provided better for me and when I thought myself most abandoned of it, care was nearest to me. Just as my strength forsook me and I was on the point of being made the most wretched of my sex, a sudden, great and dreadful shout sent forth by the ship's crew, and at the same time, three or four of the mariners bursting at once into the room cried out, "An Algerine corsair is making full sail against us!" This intelligence obliged him to let go the grasp he had taken of me and run hastily on deck. For two hours I heard nothing but the roar of guns and the cries of dying men, in which time I remained in the most cruel surprise. Either way I looked on myself as lost to everything this world calls dear: if we overcome, my honor must infallibly become a prey to the base lust of our captain; if the Algerine was conqueror, I could hope for no other than an eternal slavery.

A shout of victory at last assured me that one side had gained an entire conquest and presently after several armed men, who by their habits I knew to be Turks, came into the cabin and took from me all that I had valuable about me. By some of our men, whom I saw afterwards chained in rows, I learned that the captain and the other officers were carried on board their vessel in order to be disposed of as slaves, as we were all, as soon as we came on shore. Great as this evil was, I thought it less than that other I had by this means avoided. I will not trouble you with the particulars of our voyage in which nothing happened remarkable.

"A fair wind conducting us to Baravat, we landed there and in a few days were carried to the market, where it was my fortune, as you know, to be the purchase of a Persian merchant. Hitherto had I submitted to my fate with a tolerable share of patience, but I no sooner found whom it was I was to serve than I beheld in his train the lustful captain who, it seems, was bought by the same master before I came into the market. He came up to me, just as the merchant was about to lead me away. 'I shall now,' said he, 'have full opportunity to compass that which the Algerines deprived me of before. Our present master will gladly give you to my embraces for the propagation of slaves. I doubt not but to present him with two every year in recompense of his bestowing on me so sweet a partner in my toil.'

"This insult and the probability that indeed I should be

able to find no defense from his persecutions entirely overthrew all the resolutions with which I had endeavored to fortify myself and wholly swayed by my despair and rage, I snatched a scimitar from my new master's side and had that moment deprived him of his slave if some people who stood behind me had not been quick enough to prevent me. When I was brought home, I appeared so bent on death that the merchant had reason to repent of his bargain and was willing to get rid of me on any terms. The person you employed to purchase me found it so. I thought no other than an exchange of one master for another but was pleased to be delivered from a place where I was in continual fear of that brutish captain.

"When I perceived myself carried to the seaside, my discontents and my terrors revived. I was in apprehension that the captain had by some means regained his liberty and that it was on board his vessel I was about to be conducted, which made me in that distraction you were witness of. The dear surprise I was in at the sight of you I need not go about to describe; you saw it. You knew before, my soul, each secret avenue was laid open to you. You were but too sensible that not a fiber which held my trembling heart but was filled with gentle thrillings for the dear, the charming Philidore. The ecstasy of my soul to find I am not yet lost to his remembrance is more than words can speak. Oh, guess it therefore and spare my tongue the pains of attempting what is impossible to be represented."

The charming slave here ended her narration, and let any reader of the male sex at least guess if the enamoured Philidore suffered her to conclude it without endeavoring to convince her that he was the most happy person in this interview. After a thousand demonstrations of the most tender affection on both sides, Emanthe happened to be mentioned and the consideration of what that poor girl might endure in her slavery made Philidore immediately send back the person who had been so successful in his negotiations for Placentia in order to redeem that faithful maid.

Now did these equally passionate lovers endeavor which

should most tenderly express theirselves. But Placentia being desirous of hearing what had befallen Philidore since the time he left her, he gave her a faithful account of every particular. She listened to him all the time he was speaking with a pleased attention, but at the conclusion grew so extremely pensive that he could not avoid perceiving the alteration and being very much surprised at it. He sat with his eyes fixed on her for some moments, but she continuing silent and looking steadfastly on the ground, he took her in his arms and tenderly embracing her, entreated her she would let him know in what part of his conduct he had so greatly erred as to occasion that sudden displeasure he saw in her. "You have been to blame in nothing that I know of," answered she with a dejected air, "but Fate is our common foe. Inquire no farther at the present. If the heavens permit us to land safe in England, you shall then be satisfied."

The messenger employed to redeem Emanthe from slavery that moment coming into the cabin with her and another person who was a stranger put an end to their conversation at this time. Placentia, having embraced Emanthe, turned her eyes on the person who accompanied her and finding those of Philidore intently fixed on him, demanded of him who he was. "I know not," said he, "and am as desirous of being informed as you can be. I read something in his face which seems, methinks, to merit some regard." Having answered Placentia in this manner, he commanded the person who had brought him there to relate what he knew of him and by what means he was becoming a passenger.

"The little that I am capable of informing you of," said he, "concerning this stranger I shall immediately speak, but hope you will from himself have some account which may justify the charity I have shown him and engage your pardon for my having exceeded the commission I had from you. As I was discoursing," continued he, "with the merchant concerning the ransom of Emanthe, this young slave who was waiting in the room, perceiving we were like to agree, fell on his knees to me, conjuring me to redeem him, protesting he had friends in England who would gladly repay the cost I should be at. He expected, he said, soon to hear from them and to regain his liberty, but having seen Emanthe he had conceived so violent a passion for her that he could not live deprived of the blessing of beholding her.

"I told him that I could do nothing of myself, that I was but employed by another person and could not dispose of any part of his money without his permission. 'But,' said I, 'when I return to him I will acquaint him with your desire and if you can make it appear that he will be no loser in laying down the price of your liberty, I doubt not but he will comply with your request.' 'Oh,' replied he, 'a thousand accidents may prevent what you design. The winds or that gentleman's wishes to be at home may hurry away the ship and in it the charming Emanthe. Oh, therefore, if you are really as charitable as you seem, assure me that I shall be the partner of your voyage by taking me with you now or leave that precious pledge in token of your return.' A flood of tears accompanied his words and that inexpressive grief which appeared in his voice and gesture. I resolved to do what I could for him and, having purchased Emanthe for a less sum than I expected, I laid out the remainder of your money for this stranger." Philidore was of too generous and compassionate a disposition not to be very well pleased with this action and, instead of discommending what he had done, assured him that nothing could have obliged him more.

Placentia looked earnestly on the lately redeemed slave at this discourse of the Persian and, finding nothing in his face she had ever been acquainted with, was surprised to hear of his passion for Emanthe. That young maid expressed no less surprise than her lady to find herself so much the object of love in the heart of a person who, though she had remembered she had somewhere seen, she could not recollect when or where. And being asked both by Philidore and Placentia if she knew him, she answered in the negative but was preparing to say something more when the person who had occasioned this consternation in all who were witness of it, addressing himself to Philidore in a very graceful manner:

"The obligations I owe you, sir," said he, "are of so high a nature that till my actions may in some measure attest my gratitude, my tongue would find no other theme, did not the surprise in which my presence has involved you require that I who alone am capable of unfolding this seeming riddle should do it immediately. I am," said he, "the only son of Mr. Tradewell, an eminent merchant, who, having gained himself considerable advantages by the sea, was unwilling, however, to trust my fortune on that uncertain bottom, and therefore, laying apart for me what was sufficient to support me like a gentleman, that I might the better become that title, sent me to the university of Oxford.

"I had been there about two years when this lady," continued he, bowing to Placentia, "came into that city to visit some relations. She was then attended by the sweet Emanthe, with whom at first sight I became infinitely charmed. She was so continually employed about your ladyship that I never could get an opportunity of speaking to her and I perceive she regarded not the distant homage I paid her whenever I had the happiness of seeing her in the walks, the church, and public shows. But why should I detain your attention with a long detail of particulars which I doubt not but are common to every heart in love? In fine, you left the place and me the most wretched of created beings in the loss of all I coveted on earth, the lovely Emanthe.

"Impossible to live in a place where there was no probability of ever seeing more that charmer of my soul, I departed from Oxford without leave and came to London where my reception from my father was such as indeed my disobedience to his commands would have merited had it been caused by any other motive than what it was. He was extremely incensed against me for having quitted the college and assured me that I must expect no favor if I did not return to my studies by the first return of the coach. I made innumerable excuses for tarrying but he was not to be prevailed on.

"Distracted in my thoughts I wrote a letter to Emanthe containing a full discovery of my wishes, but the person whom

I entrusted with it betrayed me to my father and gave the billet into his hands. On which he was so much enraged that, a ship of his being ready to sail for Lisbon, he ordered I should be put on board, writing at the same time to a correspondent he had in that city to detain me there till I should be entirely cured of a passion which he could make no objections against but that it was not for an object altogether so rich in the goods of fortune as he expected.

"All the resistance I could make was in vain. With streaming eyes and bleeding heart, I forsook my country and more dear mistress, resolving in my mind, however, to disappoint my cruel father's aim and return the first opportunity, whatever should be the consequence, but Heaven opposed the designs of both. Our vessel was boarded by a Turkish galley who, falling on us with superior force, soon took it and made us all prisoners. We were carried to Baravat where I became the purchase of the same merchant to whom it was afterwards the fate of the admirable Placentia and Emanthe to be sold.

"What transports did I not feel to behold her in a place where I so little expected her. I hoped now to have a full opportunity of relating what 'twas she had inspired me with and flattered myself that the consideration of what I had suffered for her would induce her to have some little pity for me. But, above all, it charmed me to think that when my father should send my ransom as I doubted not but he soon would, I having by letter informed him of my condition, it would be in my power to prove how much beyond myself I prized her happiness by restoring her to liberty and remaining myself a slave. But before I had time to perfect any one of these desires, you sent to purchase her freedom. What followed you are already informed of, and by giving me the blessing of attending that everlasting mistress of my soul have given me more than life or liberty."

Young Tradewell here ceased to speak, but his history had so much endeared him to the minds of our illustrious lovers that they seemed to outvie each other which should most applaud a love so disinterested, a constancy so unshaken. Emanthe, blushing, confessed the obligation she had to him and testified by her countenance that her heart would be no farther than the modesty of her sex obliged reluctant to the impression he wished to make.

Some time was taken up in these discourses, after which Philidore took the first opportunity to pray and press his adored Placentia that she would unfold the mystery of those words she spoke when they had been interrupted by the arrival of Emanthe and her lover. But that lady was resolute to conceal her meaning. And though it was many weeks before they reached England, yet did she not either by design or chance let fall a word which gave him the least light into her meaning, nor could he prevail on Emanthe who, he supposed, was no stranger to the secret, to let him into any part of it.

At length they all arrived in England, and Philidore having conducted Placentia and Emanthe to a house where they might refresh themselves after the fatigue of their long voyage, he pressed the former for the performance of her promise, which she assured him she would perform but not till an answer arrived to a letter which she had written and was about to send by the post to her brother, the Baron Bellamont. He appeared more amazed than ever at this proceeding and told her he hoped to have had the honor of conducting her to that brother and entreating his consent for the celebration of their nuptials. But all he could say was ineffectual to remove her from a certain resolution she had taken. Nor would she consent to leave that place till she should receive an answer to her letter. Philidore was obliged to content himself as well as he could with the assurance she gave him that at the return of the post he should be informed at full of everything he desired to know.

In about three days after, as they were sitting together, a gentleman inquired for Placentia, who, being presently admitted, she knew to be her brother's steward. He told her that his lord, who was extremely impatient to embrace her, was detained only by a small hurt he had received from a fall from his horse and begged that she would make all imaginable speed to London where he then was. She replied that nothing should prevent her from beginning her journey that day and, presenting Philidore, told him he was the person to whom the baron had been obliged for the restoration of his sister. The steward on this made him many compliments from his lord and then put into his hands some bills of exchange for the expenses he had been at for her ransom and that of Emanthe.

The amazement of Philidore at this behavior may more easily be imagined than expressed. Scarce was he capable of making any reply but giving Placentia a look of as much reproach as the respect he had for her would permit him to do convinced that lady what his thoughts were. She therefore desired all who were present to quit the room for a few moments and leave them together, which command being obeyed, "I perceive your surprise, Philidore," said she, "but as my love is not inferior to yours, will prove that my generosity is also as great. The regard you had for my interest would not suffer you to accept of the offering I made you of my person and estate, because you were at that time incapable of making me a jointure suitable to the latter. Fortune has changed the die. The advantage is wholly on your side. You are master of very great riches; I am entirely portionless and I should ill return the obligations I have received from you to become your wife."

She would have proceeded, but Philidore, who could no longer contain himself, interrupted her by crying out, "Oh, madam, what is it that you mean? For Heaven's sake, torment not thus a heart that adores you. Can wealth be any purchase for perfection such as yours? The treasures of the Indies could not make me worthy of you. 'Tis by my love alone that I can hope to merit the glory of being yours." He said many other things of the like nature, but she remained fixed in her determination, telling him that were they on an equality she could have submitted to the meanest way of life with him but never would be brought to be obliged by him who would not be obliged by her.

She had no sooner given him this final answer than she called the steward and Emanthe to come in and, as soon as they were, desired the former to lead her to the chariot which her brother had sent for her, which she and Emanthe entering, Philidore, who would not stay behind her, mounted horses which they got immediately saddled and accompanied the steward. They reached the house of the Baron Bellamont the same night, and Philidore, with Tradewell (though uninvited), made himself a guest there, entreating by the mouth of the steward to be admitted to his presence.

That young nobleman, who wondered the person who had redeemed his sister should stand in need of any other to introduce him, immediately ordered he should be brought into his chamber, which, as soon as he was, never was surprise equal to that which filled the breasts of both. They stood and gazed a while as if to assure themselves that they were not deceived in their conjectures, then ran into each other's arms with all the eagerness of impatient friendship. "Do I again behold the preserver of my life," said the baron, "and is it to him I also owe the recovery of my sister?" I believe 'tis almost needless to say that Philidore in the Baron Bellamont found the beautiful Christian eunuch with whom he had commenced so tender a friendship, and also that the baron, having been long since informed by him of the passion he had for a lady whose name he concealed, no sooner knew it was Placentia than that he assured him he would make use of his authority to oblige her to break the resolve she had made.

That lady therefore (who, while they were talking, suspecting her brother's intentions, slipped out of the room) was immediately called for. But the servants answered that she had taken coach with Emanthe and had left no word when she would return. This intelligence was enough to alarm the new-raised hopes of Philidore, but the baron comforted him by saying there was no doubt but she would come back and, renewing his promises of giving her to him. "You shall not quit my sight," said he, "till in full possession of all you wish."

They waited some hours in an impatient suspense but

Philidore, growing unable to endure the pangs of uncertainty any longer, was about to go in search of her, nor was it in the power of all Bellamont could say to prevent him, when a messenger arrived from her with a letter to Philidore containing these lines:

"To the most generous and deserving of his sex, the accomplished Philidore: Impute not my retirement as the effect of ingratitude. I am sufficiently sensible of what I owe you and [you] may judge of the good will I have to pay when you remember that I once would have thought it my greatest happiness to have given you all. But, oh, Philidore, I cannot consent to become yours when by being so I am the party obliged! I still love you with the same unbounded tenderness as when I threw off all my sex's pride and shame to offer myself and imagined fortune to your refusing arms. But the same reason which made you then forsake me drives me now from you. I hope my brother has honor enough to make it the business of his life to retaliate in what he can those obligations you have conferred on his sister, and which I perceive by your discourse he has also received from you on his part. I have no other way to do it than in my prayers and good wishes for your prosperity, the first step to which is your forgetting me and placing your affections on some happier maid than the every way unfortunate Placentia.

"P.S. Attempt not to dissuade me from the resolution I have taken of seeing you no more. 'Twill be but in vain and render us both more unhappy. Our mutual ease must be in forgetfulness of each other, which I earnestly entreat you will endeavor on your part, and I may then perhaps be enabled by degrees to do so too. Farewell forever! Commend me to my brother, to whom I am in too much confusion at the present to write."

The distraction of the faithful and ever-passionate Philidore may easily be imagined at reading lines so contrary to what he had lately hoped. Being desired by the baron, he made no scruple of letting him peruse this cruel mandate, and it was as much as all that tender friend could do to prevent him from laying violent hands on his own life in the first emotions of his rage. He that for so many years had borne the pain of hopeless love had not now fortitude to sustain the present disappointment. So much more terrible is it to fall from expectation than to languish in the want of it.

Bellamont, however, resolving to bring his sister to more just considerations, if possible, ordered his chariot to be got ready and, making Philidore go with him, he vowed in his presence never to return home till he had heard some intelligence of Placentia. "And if we find her," added he, "I have that in my head to do for her which will entirely destroy all those scruples her over-curious passion has raised against your mutual happiness." Philidore thanked him as well as his despair would give him leave, but never man appeared so truly dejected and forlorn. All that he had suffered in captivity, in his wanderings in the deserts of Persia, or in his former grief for his voluntary banishment from Placentia was mean to what he now endured.

But I will not detain the attention of my reader with a fruitless detail of particulars which 'tis easy for him to imagine. After a long inquiry at every house where they could hope to find her, they at last had the good fortune to spy Emanthe at a window. Philidore was the first who saw her and in a transport of joy cried out to the coachman to stop, which being done, the baron leaped out and desiring to speak with that maid, the person to whom he spoke denied he knew anything of her, on which they both affirmed they had seen her and would not depart till they had discoursed her. Bellamont exerted his authority in so forcible a manner than Emanthe came running down and entreated his pardon, telling him what he very well knew that she but obeyed the commands of her lady in what she had done. He easily forgave her but insisted on seeing his sister, who, he said, he knew was in that house. Emanthe denied it so faintly that they were confirmed in what from the sight of her they before believed and the baron, growing impatient, burst open a door which he perceived was shut.

Just as he came into the entry, he found Placentia lying on a couch half-drowned in tears. She rose on the entrance of Bellamont and Philidore and, turning to the former, "Why,

Brother," said she, "do you endeavor to prevent me from seeking that repose which is not permitted me but in solitude and a retirement from all who have known me in a happier state? And you, Philidore," added she, looking on him with as much haughtiness as she could assume, "is it the business of a lover to disobey his mistress? Think you I will be compelled to entertain you as such? What cause have you to complain? I but imitate the pattern you set me. 'Twas your turn once to refuse and fly me. 'Tis now mine to do the same."

'Tis not to be doubted but that he here fell on his knees and omitted nothing that the most desperate dying love could suggest to bring her to another temper. But Bellamont, perceiving that she was still inexorable and, to oblige him to give over his prosecutions, had in both their hearings made a solemn vow rather to die than consent to be his wife, unless some accident should happen which should render her not under any obligation to him in being so, put an end to the dispute by telling her she was no longer on an equality, for that he had resolved to make her mistress of one-third of the estate immediately, which he said, with the advantage of birth, would not only render her a fortune on the level with Philidore but somewhat exceeding what he could hope were his aim in marriage interest.

Thus was the mighty scruple over, and this fair lady's delicacy no longer an enemy to her inclinations. She no longer hesitated if she should comply but met the embraces of the soul-ravished Philidore with equal rapture. The first emotions of tumultous joy being over, they both paid to Bellamont those acknowledgments his indulgence merited.

Nor was this all the obligations they received from that generous brother and faithful friend. He settled the remainder of his vast estate on them and their heirs after his decease, being well assured he should have no children of his own to inherit it. But that was a secret which even Placentia was ignorant of, nor did Philidore ever reveal it.

Thus did these equally enamoured, equally deserving pair

bring inquietudes to themselves by an excess of that which is too much wanting in the generality of other lovers. Yet did their happy meeting in marriage at last fully recompense their former cares. Being thus blessed, they forgot not the faithful Emanthe and her generous lover, but presenting that young gentleman to his father, the joy of seeing him again, together with a handsome sum of money which Placentia gave Emanthe, easily reconciled him to the marriage, which was performed the same day with that of her lady to the accomplished and generous Philidore.

Nothing could be more splendid than the celebration of their nuptials. And of their future bliss the reader may better judge by their almost unexampled love, their constancy, their generosity and nobleness of soul, than by any description I am able to give of it.

FINIS

THE ACCOMPLISHED RAKE

OR

Modern Fine Gentleman

BEING

An Exact Description of the
Conduct and Behavior of a
Person of Distinction

When Conqu'ring Vice Triumphant takes the Field,
Virtue Dethron'd must to its Pow'r yield;
And when Good Characters are all at stake,
The Best of Bad Ones is, th' Accomplish'd Rake.

Printed in the Year MDCCXXVII, and Sold by the
Booksellers of London and Westminster.

NOTE TO TITLE PAGE

By Mrs. Mary Davys. In March, 1727, John Wilford's *Monthly Catalogue* listed the novel as printed for the author and sold by J. Stephens at the price of 2*s.* 6*d.* This information is probably correct; Stephens was the bookseller for Mrs. Davys's *Reform'd Coquet* (1724) and her collected *Works* (1725), both of which were printed by Henry Woodfall for the author.

The Preface [1]

'Tis now for some time that those sort of writings called *novels* have been a great deal out of use and fashion and that the ladies (for whose service they were chiefly designed) have been taken up with amusements of more use and improvement— I mean history and travels, with which the relation of probable feigned stories can by no means stand in competition. However, these are not without their advantages, and those considerable, too. And it is very likely the chief reason that put them out of vogue was the world's being surfeited with such as were either flat or insipid, or offensive to modesty and good manners, or that they found them only a circle or repetition of the same adventures.

The French, who have dealt most in this kind, have, I think, chiefly contributed to put them out of countenance, who, though upon all occasions and where they pretend to write true history, give themselves the utmost liberty of feigning, are too tedious and dry in their matter, and so impertinent in their harangues that the readers can hardly keep themselves awake over them. I have read a French novel of four hundred pages without the least variety of events, or any issue in the conclusion either to please or amuse the reader, yet all fiction and romance, and the commonest matters of fact, truly told, would have been much more entertaining.

Now this is to lose the only advantage of invention, which gives us room to order accidents better than Fortune will be at the pains to do, so to work upon the reader's passions, sometimes keep him in suspense between fear and hope, and at the last send him satisfied away. This I have endeavored to do in the following sheets. I have in every novel proposed one entire scheme or plot, and the other adventures are only incidental or collateral to it, which is the great rule prescribed by the critics,

---

[1] Taken from *The Works of Mrs. Davys ... in Two Volumes* (Printed by H. Woodfall, for the author, and sold by J. Stevens [*sic*], 1725).

not only in tragedy and other heroic poems but in comedy too. The adventures, as far as I could order them, are wonderful and probable; and I have with the utmost justice rewarded virtue and punished vice.

The *Lady's Tale*[2] was writ in the year 1700 and was the effect of my first flight to the Muses. It was sent about the world as naked as it came into it, having not so much as one page of preface to keep it in countenance. What success it met with I never knew, for, as some unnatural parents sell their offspring to beggars in order to see them no more, I took three guineas for the brat of my brain and then went a hundred and fifty miles northward, to which place it was not very likely its fame should follow. But meeting with it some time ago, I found it in a sad ragged condition and had so much pity for it as to take it home and get it into better clothes that, when it made a second sally, it might with more assurance appear before its betters.

My whole design, both in that and the *Cousins*[3], is to endeavor to restore the purity and empire of love, and correct the vile abuses of it, which, could I do, it would be an important service to the public. For, since passions will ever have a place in the actions of men and love a principal one, what cannot be removed or subdued ought at least to be regulated. And if the reformation would once begin from our sex, the men would follow it in spite of their hearts, for it is we have given up our empire, betrayed by rebels among ourselves.

The two plays[4] I leave to fight their own battles; and I shall say no more than that I never was so vain as to think they deserved a place in the first rank, or so humble as to resign them to the last.

[2] *The Amours of Alcippus and Lucippe. A Novel. Written by a Lady,* was printed for James Round in 1704. The dedication was signed "M. Davys." In her 1725 revision, Lucippe becomes Abaliza.

[3] This imitation of the Continental *nouvelle* is set in Spain and is wildly melodramatic in plot. It is indicative of contemporary reading tastes that it was pirated in 1732 as *The False Friend: Or the Treacherous Portugueze.*

[4] *The Northern Heiress* was presented three times at the New Theater in Lincoln's Inn Fields in April, 1716. *The Self Rival* was never staged.

I have been so anxious for the credit of my *Modern Poet* that I showed it to several of my friends and earnestly begged their impartial opinion of it. Everyone separately told me his objection, but not two among them agreed in any one particular. So I found to remove all the faults would be to leave nothing behind, and I could not help thinking my case parallel with the man in the fable whose two wives disliking, one, his gray hairs, and the other, his black, picked both out, till they left him nothing but a bald pate.

Perhaps it may be objected against me, by some more ready to give reproach than relief, that, as I am the relict of a clergyman and in years, I ought not to publish plays, &c. But I beg of such to suspend their uncharitable opinions till they have read what I have writ, and, if they find anything there offensive either to God or man, anything either to shock their morals or their modesty, 'tis then time enough to blame. And let them farther consider that a woman left to her own endeavors for twenty-seven years together may well be allowed to catch at any opportunity for that bread which they that condemn her would very probably deny to give her.

Dedication:

To the Beaux of Great Britain.

Gentlemen:

There is a certain ingredient in the compound of a dedication called *Adulation* or *Flattery,* which is a weed grown so rank of age that I am afraid it may offend your nice noses. And for that reason, I am resolved to pull it up by the roots, though it is very possible some of you may believe there is no such thing, since to men of so much merit all is due that can be said. But as I am now in a vein of writing something new to please you, I intend to throw in a scruple to the contrary scale and for once let truth and justice hold the balance. I know if I should tell you of a thousand fine qualities to which you can never make title, it would be no more than a weak imitation of my predecessors. But as I now set up for an original, my words and thoughts are to be entirely my own, and I alone accountable for them.

It is very likely you may be a little surprised that I should draw the character of a rake, and then lay it under the protection of a beau. But I must tell you I had a very advantageous view, when I pitched upon you for my patrons, for I thought you were much more likely to stand by me than the worthy gentlemen deciphered in the following sheets. There is certainly a good deal of difference betwixt the two characters, for though the one may not altogether preserve the strictest morals, yet in many cases, he is careful to avoid any material reflection on his honor. For example, he may have bravery enough to leave his country in defense of it, whilst the other stays at home to guard his own dear person and the ladies. And I must own myself better pleased with the courage and conduct of a real engagement with the Spaniards[1] than in any protestations of stabbing yourselves for love.

[1] If this satirical dedication was written immediately before publication, the reference was to the virtual state of war with Spain which had resulted from Townshend's alliance of England with France and Prussia by the Treaty of Hanover in September, 1725.

But gunpowder and perfume is a very odd mixture, and why should I talk of battles to such a peaceable part of the species. No, I shall confine myself entirely to your nicer qualities and particularly enlarge upon the elegance of drawing gold snuff boxes instead of daggers, and writing billets-doux instead of challenges. And everyone must give into this way of thinking who compares the prudence of the one with the rashness of the other. I could repeat a thousand things, wherein our pretty fellows excel the unpoliter part of mankind, and most will agree it better to drink barley-water for a smooth complexion than Burgundy for a red face. Oh, how preferable is the charming nonsense of our *gentilshommes des amours* to those profane oaths which make so great a part of the conversation of blustering Britons. It must be owing to the bad taste of that age that a great deal of powder and white hands should be called foppery and effeminacy, or that the gentle, easy study of women and dress should be thought inferior to that of men and letters, and, sure, they must mistake the literal sense of *beau*, who don't call it a Fine Gentleman.

To conclude: that your fine faces may receive no freckles, your embroideries no tarnish, nor your fortunes any shock are the unfeigned wishes of,

Gentlemen,

Yours, &c.

The Modern Fine Gentleman

Young Galliard, who is to be the subject of the following leaves, will (with his own inclinations, and a little of my additional discipline) be a very exact copy of the title page. For, though I shall be very punctual in delivering nothing but plain fact in the fundamental part of his story, it is not impossible but by way of episode I may intermix now and then a pretty little lie, and since it is to be both little and pretty, I hope my reader will excuse me if he finds me out, and let him convict me if he can.

The above-named gentleman was born in one of the largest counties in England. His mother was a woman of distinction and claimed a share in some of the best blood of the nation. Her education, perhaps not very regular, an airy, roving temper, unconfined and free, would know no bounds nor bear the least restraint. Pleasure was her idol, at whose altar she became a constant votary, but the veriest trifle in domestic affairs gave her insupportable pain. Two days spent in the same diversion was abominable pleasure, but fresh delights were worth continued notice. His father was a person of a very different character, wise and prudent, yet had the utmost tenderness for his lady and looked on her weak behavior as one would on a sick child—with pity, not with anger or reproach. He had served his country in many reputable capacities and was just chosen knight of the shire when the smallpox too fatally seized him, of which in ten days he died, during which time he seemed exceeding anxious for his children, having, beside his son, one daughter, and both too young to be left to the care of a negligent unmindful eye.

An affair of this importance required more time than he now had to spare, and how to manage for their good jointly, with the satisfaction of his lady, he knew not. To leave them to her care and management (her temper considered) was throwing them into the mouth of ruin, and to substitute another, at least while they were so very young, was showing those faults too plainly to the world which his good nature would fain have hidden even from himself. Many of his poor restless hours were made infinitely more so by those sad reflections, yet the tender regard he had for his lady took place, and he at last determined to do nothing with his latest breath that should give her the least indifference for his loss. He considered his children were hers as well as his and hoped when he was gone she would then consider that there was none left either to indulge or wink at her follies, would wisely remember herself a double parent, and show her true concern for his loss by a more than common care of them.

He therefore, ere his dying moments came too near him, called her and his children to his bedside and thus addressed them:

"I have now before me all that I hold dear on earth and it is no easy task to go forever from your eyes. But I am now arrested by a cruel hand which will take no ransom, but insists upon a speedy payment of that debt I owe to nature, nor will by any means let go his hold till my freed soul shall take her flight and find a rest on some unknown shore. Since then I must go, all that remains for me is to recommend those tender pledges of our love to the utmost care of you, the dearest partner of my bed, and as a dying request beg their education may be such as may give them a true and early notion of virtue and honor.

"As for you, my beloved son, you are now turned of fourteen. You are blessed with a promising genius and, though you are yet but young, you may remember the words of a father, whose last request to you is that while you travel through this life, you will learn to keep your footsteps steady so that they may neither sink you on the one side to the heavy dull pedant or raise you on the other to the light flashy coxcomb. Let a strict virtue regulate all your actions, despise and shun those libertines who may strive to poison your morals, be dutiful to your mother, love your sister, and marry a woman of virtue. I leave you sole heir to a very flourishing estate, which has for two centuries been in your family. I beg you will never lessen your ancestors by a misapplication of those talents Heaven has blessed you with. I would say more but my spirits grow faint and I have now no more to do but die in peace and close my eyes forever."

He had hardly done speaking when a convulsion seized him and catched his latest breath, and in him died a worthy patriot, a tender husband, and a careful father, in the thirty-sixth year of his age, and had his dying words been of any force with those he left behind, his children might have made as good a figure in life as their predecessors had done before them. But Lady Galliard was left tolerably young, a good face, a better jointure, and dried up her tears so soon that decency, ashamed of such light proceedings, with a blush cried, "Fie," and left her.

Sure unjustly are we called the weaker vessels, when we have strength to subdue that which conquers the lords of the creation, for their reason ties them down to rules, while we, like Samson, break the trifling twine and laugh at every obstacle that would oppose our pleasure. Lady Galliard had too much resolution and courage to struggle with grief but, like an expert fencer, gave it one home thrust and silenced it forever, hardly allowing so much as the common decorum of a month's confinement to a dark room, though her wild behavior told the world she was but too well qualified for such an apartment forever.

But I now give up my observations to time, who will probably alternately bury and raise her shame. To him I leave her for a while and call upon young Galliard, her son, who is now arrived at one step of honor, being the third baronet successively of his family. Sir John, therefore, for the future we call him, and if he behaves below his manhood and dignity, we must beg the mother to answer for the son, since the father left no example behind him but what was worthy of the strictest imitation and had not the too hasty hand of death snatched him hence so soon, his indefatigable care had made his son what he really was himself—a perfect *fine gentleman*.

It is a common saying that "manners make the man," but that word, like "friendship," includes much more than is vulgarly understood by it, and a false education, like false wit, only serves to varnish over the defects of our scene and behavior which, when tried by a true touchstone, lays us open and shows the deformities of both. But if a wrong discipline in youth be so pernicious, what becomes of those who have none at all? How many young gentlemen have we among the better sort of men that are in a manner wholly neglected and left to branch into numberless follies, like a rich field uncultivated that abounds in nothing but tall weeds and gaudy scentless flowers. This is doubtless the reason why the town is so stocked with rakes and coxcombs who wisely imagine all merit is wrapped up in fine clothes and blasphemy. A laced coat, gold-clocked stockings, and a toupee qualify a man for a *modern fine gentleman,* and if he can but whore, swear, and renounce his Maker, he is a modern fine gentleman indeed.

Too much like this it fared with our young baronet, who is now left to think and act as he pleases himself, and he that is his own teacher has too often a fool for his schoolmaster. Though young Galliard did not want sense, but on the contrary had more than could be expected from one of his years, yet alas, for want of due measures, it grew up rank and sprouted nothing but excrescences. He now saw himself with the eyes of vanity, which was daily increased by the flattery of the servants, a thing he liked so well that his whole time was spent among the grooms in the stables or the wenches in the house, and doubtless his natural good sense and acquired good manners met with all the improvement that such refined conversation could furnish him with. Two whole years slipped away in a careless lethargy, which lost time was of much more value than the annual rents of the estate, considering one revolves but the other is lost forever. We generally expect a man complete at one-and-twenty, and two years out of seven is too considerable to be trifled away, besides the sad disadvantage of imbibing ill customs which, like the king's evil, is seldom or never removed.

The neglect of this young gentleman alarmed all that loved his father, which was just as many as knew his worth. But in a near part of the neighborhood lived one Mr. Friendly, who was always conversant with and loved by the deceased. He in a very particular manner lamented the misfortune of the almost ruined Sir John, but knew not where to apply for a remedy. The knight was too young, too thoughtless, and too fond of his own will to harken to any advice that did not concur with it. And for Lady Galliard, she was too positive, too proud, and too careless, either to be persuaded by her friends or to join in concert with reason for the good of her child. However, he had a stratagem in his head, which kind chance furnished him with and which he hoped might be of some service to his design. In order to put it in practice, he made an invitation to some of his nearest neighbors, among which Lady Galliard and her son were bidden. While they were at dinner, among the rest of the attendants was a spruce, clean footman who had something in his air that looked as if he was not born one. Mr. Friendly seemed to use him with some deference and said, "Pray, Tom, do so and so." Tom seemed very diligent but a little awkward, and some of the company observed a tear often starting in his eyes, which gave them a curiosity to inquire who he was, and that gave a good lift to Mr. Friendly's design. Dinner was no sooner over than he took the opportunity and gave the company the following account:

"This young fellow, whom you all seem to inquire after and whom I received but three days ago into my family, was the son of a private gentleman who had a very easy fortune in life but by an ugly accident broke his leg, which threw him into a fever and killed him. This poor young man, who was then about twelve years of age, is too sad an example of the want of care in a parent, for his mother, though a very modest and good sort of woman, was extremely covetous, which prevented all that care which should have been taken towards making her son a man. She fancied time and nature would do as much for nothing, as if she should put herself to a deal of charge, which perhaps at last would turn to no account. Tom, on the other hand, loved play and idleness, hated school and learning, said he would never have anything to do with crabbed Greek that stuck in his throat and was ready to choke him, though now and then for variety he vouchsafed to make his master a visit and handle a grammar, though he was never rightly acquainted with its rules.

"Time, however, would not wait till reason thought fit to show him his folly. So, spurred on by his boyish inclinations and nobody to restrain them, he run on from one diversion to another, grown perfectly headstrong and spoiled till he was twenty years of age, at which time his mother fell sick (some say, brokenhearted at his proceedings, which she might thank herself for). But be that as it will, she then died, and he was left for the other year to the care of an uncle, who managed so well as to cheat him of part of his estate, and the rest, as soon as he came to age, he squandered away on game cocks and race horses. So that for want of due discipline while he was a boy, he was utterly ruined, as too many of his betters have been before him, and is now grown up to man as you all see under the honorable circumstances of a footman."

In all probability, Lady Galliard and her son took the application as it was designed to themselves, for they both colored at the end of it, which Mr. Friendly perceived and was resolved to go on. "We have the advice of a wise man," proceeded he, "to train up youth as we would have them act when riper years take place.[1] Learning we all know is the first step towards the improvement of our sense, as good conversation is towards that of our manners, and it is so hard a matter to bring a man to an exact behavior in life that he ought not to lose one minute in the pursuit of it."

"But, madam," continued he, addressing Lady Galliard, "now we are upon this topic, may I with the freedom of a friend ask your ladyship how Sir John is to spend his time till he writes man. Methinks I long to see him in the road his worthy father travelled, to draw whose character requires too many master strokes for my shallow capacity, nor would I attempt to delineate a picture where the original was so well known. Your fancies can form a better judgment of his perfections than a dull description from an unable tongue—in short, he was worthy of the name

[1] Solomon. See *Proverbs* XXII:6.

of man, which all who stand erect cannot make a just title to. It requires a pretty deal of pains to distinguish ourselves from brutes. We must have a share of probity, honor, gratitude, good sense, and a complacency for our species in general to render us worthy of that name, so that all who are designed for men are not rightly called so till acquired advantages confirm their title."

"Sir," said a gentleman present, "methinks you arraign the care of the Almighty or His judgment in making man, if you say they are not born complete. Beside, Mr. Friendly, good sense is not an acquired quality."

"To say I arraign Providence," returned Mr. Friendly, "when I affirm man is not born perfect is the same as to say, when I have a thousand a year given me, it is no present unless the kind donor sits down every day to tell me how to spend it. When the bountiful hand of Heaven was opened to man with the noble gift of reason, it left that very reason to improve itself, and there it is we join with beasts when we neglect to listen to it. I own good sense is not an acquired quality, but it is so very capable of the highest improvement that, with a small latitude of expression, it may be called so. For he that takes it in its natural simplicity and lets it lie fallow may be justly said to bury his talent, and it dwindles by degrees till it degenerates into downright folly; and we may as well expect a boy to speak Greek and Hebrew without being taught, as good sense to keep its ground without some care to improve it."

During this discourse Sir John sat very attentive, making his own private reflections upon the design of it. He was very conscious he wanted improvement rather than a talent to improve, and soon guessed the point of the darted arrow was aimed at himself or his mother, which was equally piercing, because she had thus far indulged his negligence. But, as he had sucked in a careless indolent way of life, he was now resolved to persist in it and made the following answer:

"I am too much a boy, Mr. Friendly, to enter into dispute with one of your solid judgment, nor is it in my power to baffle your assertions, but I think. . . ."

"Stay, child," said Lady Galliard, interrupting Sir John, "you are not the person concerned in the oblique affront. It is at me the sidelong glance is cast, and the reproach reaches my conduct, which possibly I could clear if I thought it worth my trouble. But as I am resolved to be always mistress of my own actions, I shall never think myself obliged to account for them to anybody."

"Madam," returned Mr. Friendly, "I blush to think your ladyship can have such an humble opinion of my good manners as to imagine I could say anything to you in my own house with a design to affront you. I wish you would put a kinder construction upon my words and believe they were spoke with a very different view. Sir John Galliard succeeds [to] the estate and honor of one of the finest men in England, and can you, madam, who are a party near concerned, blame those who loved his father, if they wish to see the son inherit the virtues too?"

"I own, Mr. Friendly," replied Sir John, "you have glossed your affront with the best sort of varnish, because it has the shining appearance of friendship, and I must likewise own I believe it is real. But while you make my father (whose memory I revere) a shining brilliant, you seem to call his son a worthless pebble. I am not yet seventeen years of age and if I have lost a year or two of improvement, I may possibly make it up in my future life. But if I never do, I shall not miss it."

"A man of fortune and a fool may be highly content with what he has," [said Mr. Friendly] "but where there is the additional blessing of a fine genius to accompany that estate, it will act like a prudent merchant who when he has acquired one thousand pounds goes on and improves till he has got another. Even you yourself, not seventeen, would call that person's conduct in question who, having but a hundred pounds, should daily spend it and starve when it is gone. Everything ought to be improved or else we do not carry on the system of life as it was by Providence designed we should. And if our money ought to be increased, sure our sense should be so, which is infinitely more preferable. But I find all I can say meets with an unkind reception, so let us drown the ungrateful subject in his Majesty's health."

Which when ended the ladies withdrew, and after Sir John had a little recovered his temper, he asked Mr. Friendly if he had a mind to part with his new footman, Thomas. To which Mr. Friendly answered, with his wonted good nature, he had a mind to do anything that could oblige Sir John Galliard and hoped, if he did part with him, he would believe that was the only motive. Upon which Tom was called in and Mr. Friendly asked him if he had a mind to change his new master for a better. The young man answered very handsomely that he had no reason to believe there could be a better, but as he had a new fortune to raise in life, he thought himself obliged to do his best in order to it. "Then," said Mr. Friendly, "wait upon Sir John Galliard tomorrow morning, and receive his commands."

"But, Sir John," continued he, "if I resign my footman to you, will you oblige me in another point? There is a young gentleman of my acquaintance who would make an extraordinary companion for you. He is a man of worth and learning, and his example and instruction would, I am sure, be of use to you if you are inclined to something in the nature of a tutor. Inform Lady Galliard and let me know your result. He is a man of the best sense and if you go no farther than his good conversation, it will help to keep up the spirit of your own."

Sir John told him he desired nothing more than to oblige him and he was very sure Lady Galliard would not oppose it. So he desired the young gentleman, whose name was Teachwell, might come to him the next morning, which he did, attended by Tom. Things were immediately concluded and he was fixed in the family under two capacities, one as chaplain to my lady and the other as tutor to her son. He was of a sober mild behavior, affable to all but very industrious to bring his new charge to a sense of those rudiments which neglect had made him a stranger to. And had so much good fortune attended Sir John as to have sent Mr. Teachwell two or three years sooner, it might have been of the first consequence to him but, alas, he was now grown headstrong and past advice.

Tom behaved very well in the family and gained the love of everybody in it. But after he had lived two years with Sir John, he came one afternoon into the dining room where his master and Lady Galliard were set at the tea table and desired to be dismissed, for he heard his uncle was dead and was impatient to know how matters went in his family, but said if Sir John desired it, he would wait upon him again in a few days.

"I do not see," replied Sir John, "any business you have to go at all, or what expectations there can be from the death of an uncle who has left children of his own. You may be sure when he cheated you as fast as he could it was not with a design to do you justice at his death."

"No, sir," returned Tom, "I never expected any from him either dead or alive, but he has left but two daughters and one of them I think myself pretty sure of, though absence perhaps may have made some alteration and that is what, with your leave, sir, I would be satisfied in."

"Your most humble servant," cried Sir John. "I find then you are going to complete your happy circumstances in that mighty blessing called a wife. I wish you joy, sir, but hope you are not in such violent haste but you can stay till I have filled up your vacancy."

"For that matter, Sir John," said Lady Galliard, "you may take Dick or Will, 'Tis pity to hinder the poor man, for there is nothing like a close application to keep a woman's inclinations ready. Come, Sir John, at my request, dismiss him for a while, and when he has secured his beloved Dulcinea, he will wait upon you again, at least till you can provide yourself to your liking." Sir John gave a consenting nod, and Tom vanished.

"I always fancied," said Lady Galliard, "that Tom grew weary of his livery and would have had you some time ago to have found a better place for him. It is not unlikely but that is the reason why he is gone."

"When you urged it, madam," returned Sir John, "your

reasons were all wrong. Had he been born a footman, promotion might have made him thankful, because so much above his expectations, but to turn him into a gentleman again would never do, for he would doubtless have thought all due to his own merit and have grown so cursed proud upon it that I should only have spoiled a very good footman to make a very ill valet."

While they were thus discoursing, Mr. Teachwell came to them and after some little introduction to what he was going to say, he went on thus: "I am a little surprised, madam, that neither your ladyship or Sir John seems inclined to his spending a year or two at the university or making a tour into France or Italy. I have been his daily attendant these two years and have often lamented to see his time elapse without that great improvement his fine genius is capable of. I entreat you, madam, to join your commands to my request and let us prevail with him to see the world and know something more than killing a fox or hare, than leaping a gate or setting a partridge. For Heaven's sake, sir, rouse yourself from this careless lethargy which has so long benumbed your senses. Exert your reason and give it leave to act for your own advantage. I am ready and willing to wait upon you anywhere and hope I have not behaved so ill as to make you weary of my company."

"You are come," answered Lady Galliard, "in a very critical juncture, for the very next thing I intended to say to Sir John was to persuade him to spend a little time at Cambridge,[2] where I know his father designed he should go, and it is what I as earnestly desire. You are now in your nineteenth year, and if you ever design to improve yourself, it is high time to begin. I was never so earnest for your going before, though I fear you are but indifferently qualified for any examination."

"Sure, madam," replied Sir John, "you do not imagine that men of fortune go there for learning or anything else but to amuse time and spend it agreeably among the best companions. It is turning porter to carry a load on our backs, and learning

---

[2] The author lived in Cambridge, where she was proprietress of a coffeehouse, from 1718 until her death in 1732.

is certainly the worst sort of luggage, under which we founder before we get halfway on our journey. Let those tug at learning's oar that are destined to live by it. For my part, I am well provided for and will be no beast of burden, though to oblige you, madam, I do not care if I trifle away some months there. And if I bring away no Greek or Latin, I shall be sure to meet with the best conversation in the world."

"Sir John," said Mr. Teachwell, "whatever your inducements are for going to Cambridge, I am very much rejoiced to hear you resolve upon it, and doubt not but when you come there, you will think very differently from what you do now and will see a great many worthy gentlemen of the first rank tugging with pleasure at that very oar you have so lately mentioned, though few of them are unprovided for. But, madam," continued he, addressing Lady Galliard, "will your ladyship be pleased to take Sir John in the mind and forward his departure with the utmost expedition?"

Lady Galliard accordingly gave order to have all things got ready and in a week's time he was to go. But the morning before he was to begin his journey, whether it ran in his head a little more than ordinary or that he had any other disturbance I know not, but he was up some hours before his usual time and, after a walk in the garden, ran up to Mr. Teachwell's chamber, whom he found in a very thoughtful melancholy posture.

Sir John, after the morning compliment, asked him if he was thinking of his next day's journey. He said no, his thoughts were employed on a more important affair. "What, I warrant," returned Sir John, "you were thinking on your last journey and after what manner you shall get to Heaven."

"You are out again, sir," said Teachwell, "it was of less importance than that too. But ask no farther, I entreat you, sir. Knowledge is what we often seek after, but ignorance gives us the most ease."

"Then what the devil are we going to Cambridge for?" replied the knight. "I always told you knowledge was a damned troublesome thing, and yet methinks your last words have raised my curiosity. They seem to have something ambiguous in them and sound as if I were a party concerned. I am, however, too well assured of your veracity to believe you would know and yet conceal anything to my disadvantage. I therefore insist on a clear explanation of what you have said and, as you value my future friendship, be brief without reserve."

"Sir John," returned Teachwell, "none breathes that wishes your happiness more than I do, and it is to preserve it I would keep this secret to myself, but as we all lie under an indispensable duty of preventing evil if in our power, I think it mine to acquaint you with this affair that you may endeavor to put a stop to a very pernicious one which at present rages in your family. Know then (but arm yourself with patience to hear it) your mother is the criminal."

"My mother!" cried Sir John, with the utmost surprise, "my mother a criminal! How, when, where, what is her crime? Who her accuser? Who dare accuse her? Speak, distracter, or ——."

"Be calm, Sir John," interrupted the good man, "lest your too furious vindication of her honor should expose it more. The family, I believe, is at present unapprised of the matter and unless her woman be privy to it, as sure she must, I think myself the only person who has found it out, which I by the greatest accident did this very night. When I came up to bed, I cast my eye upon Molière, which lay upon my table, and got so deeply engaged in it that I read till almost two o'clock. There is a little wooden window yonder at my bed's head, which looks into the great hall and which I never opened in my life till this night, because I always took it for a cupboard which I had no use for. Before I had a mind to part with the companion in my hand, the candle burned out and when I had thrown the snuff in the chimney and was getting to bed in the dark, I thought I saw a gleam of light in the cupboard, as I took it to be. I went immediately to it, perhaps a little startled at a thing so unexpected, and, trying to open it, found it very ready to comply. Not so willing were my eyes to consent to the sight they met with, which was Lady Galliard hanging upon the arm of a man.

The light shaded so that I could not command a full view of his face but fancied he resembled Tom. I ran immediately to my chamber door, which I opened before they came within hearing and flew to the end of the gallery, which you know faces my lady's lodgings. And there I saw Tom so plain that I was soon convinced I was not at first mistaken. They both went in together and left me in a state so restless that I have never either warmed my bed or closed my eyes this night. Oh, Sir John, I grieve for your distress, nor am I less at a loss how to advise you on this sad occasion."

Sir John, who till now had never been touched to the quick, flung himself on Mr. Teachwell's bed, where his eyes gave vent to a heaving passion. He indulged it for some time and then got up crying out with transport, "Tell me, Mr. Teachwell, for you know the world, tell me, I say, are all women such? O, say they are, and give my mind some ease."

"Hum, Sir John," said Teachwell, "you may with the same reason ask when you see a malefactor executed whether all men deserve the gallows. No, virtue forbid one single faulter should infect the whole species. Women no doubt are made of the very same stuff we are and have the very same passions and inclinations which, when let loose without a curb, grow wild and untameable, defy all laws and rules, and can be subdued by nothing but what they are seldom mistresses of."

"What shall I do?" cried the enraged Sir John. "Shall I ever more behold the face of her that gave me being? Can I survive the infamy she has brought upon her family, or be so much an accomplice in her lewd proceedings as to suffer her paramour to live? No! I'll first make that dog a victim to my just resentment and then leave the kingdom where I must share the scandal, though I am innocent of the crime. Death! I now can penetrate into all and fairly see the whole design—first to secure the gallant and then to banish her son, whom she would never hear of parting with till now. Confusion seize him! How I long to drench a poniard in his lustful heart!"

"Ah, Sir John," returned Teachwell, "how nature mixes itself with your displeasure. I see you would fain lay a mother's crime to the charge of one whose humble thoughts were depressed too low for such aspiring hopes had not something more than bare encouragement raised them. But as I have been the unhappy discoverer of this intrigue, I would by all means divert you from a cruel and dangerous revenge. Murder is certainly a greater crime than fornication, and while you would wash out your mother's stain, you blot your own character. Without success in your endeavor, again, to kill the man would only serve to fill fame's trumpet, and that which is but whispered now in your own house would in a few days be sounded all the nation over. Besides, women of a warm constitution, if they lose one lover, will soon provide themselves of another. So that what I would advise you to is this. Defer your intended journey tomorrow and find an opportunity to catch them together. Reproach her (as you justly may) with stigmatizing her family, get her promise of banishing the fellow, and then persuade her to marry."

"As for my designed journey," returned the knight, "I have already laid it by and am resolved to leave the kingdom, but first I must lay a charge at a mother's door, and in such bitter invectives as cannot fail to shock my very soul even while the words are yet upon my tongue. Yes, this night I will surprise them together, which I can easily do, for last week I found in my father's study a key which commands all the doors in the house. Lady Galliard's chamber is within the little dining room, the door of which is always open for the advantage of the air, so that I can convey myself into her very bedchamber without the least noise, and my key will let me into the dining room. But how, dear Teachwell, tell me how to govern my exasperated spirit, to chain up the wild emotions of my just resentments. Say, is it possible for me to see that dog in my father's bed with temper? Can I behold a guilty mother's shame and stand unmoved at such a vile accomplice? O Teachwell, my reason leaves me and I grow distracted at the thought. Say, then, if the bare thought can rack my tortured soul, what shocking horror will attend the sight?"

"I know, Sir John," replied Mr. Teachwell, "your anger, pride, shame, and confusion are altogether up in arms, hurrying you on to dire revenge. But I have already said all I can to divert your hand from blood, and have no more to do than to beg you will put it out of your own power to do an action which may bring you many days of repentance as well as the hazard of your own life, by going armed with nothing but your patience. That weapon can do no harm and a very little time will cool your blood and set your reason in its proper place. Come, sir, if you please, we will go down and try to dispel those angry vapors which crowd your understanding and strive to eclipse your natural good nature. I advise you to feign an indisposition to retard your designed journey, and a little time will too certainly convince you."

Our young knight had no occasion to feign an indisposition. The real agitations of his mind had made him exceedingly restless and disordered, which Lady Galliard at dinner took notice of and said, "I fear, Sir John, you are not well today, for you neither eat nor talk as usual."

"I believe, Mamma," said Miss Dolly, his sister of whom we have hardly yet spoken, "my brother is in love with our Jane, for I saw him kiss her one day when she was making my bed, and she has been so proud ever since that I can never get my tea in a morning till she has done."

This made a little mirth quite round the table and forced a smile even from the disturbed Sir John, to hear the young telltale. But the rest of the day went off with the utmost impatience for night, and no tranported lover, who was to sink into the arms of his yielding mistress, ever wished for it more. At eleven of the clock Sir John proposed going to bed, as having not rested well the night before. Lady Galliard seemed sleepy and was ready to comply. All dispersed separately to their several apartments; only Sir John got privately into Teachwell's chamber, where he placed himself in the dark at the little window to watch whether Tom was conveyed the same way as the night before. The house was now grown quite still, when Sir John

liscovered a light in the hall, and, in short, everything contri-
)uted so much towards his expectation that he was extremely
nortified with the cutting sight. He gave them time to get to
)ed and then prepared with trembling steps to visit them in
:heir retirement.

He got by the assistance of his key in the dining room with-
)ut any noise and, coming to the chamber door, he heard his
mother in the height of passion say as follows:

"And is it thus you reward all the tender sentiments I have
had for you? Can it be possible that what you say is real? And
can you barbarously snatch yourself from my arms when I so
fondly gave myself to yours? Have I not sacrificed my honor to
the irresistible love I had for you, and in a manner banished my
only son, whom I could never think of parting with before, that
so no interruption might break in upon our happy hours? Did I
not invent a way to disengage you from your master's service,
because I could not bear the thought of cruel separation, and
do you, after all, tell me you must be gone? O monster of ingratitude, unsay that word and save a heart that breaks whene'er you
leave it!"

"Madam," said Tom, "I do acknowledge you have loaded me
with unexpected as well as undeserved and unsought favors, but
I entreat your ladyship to remember that when you first discovered your passion in a letter you gave me one day, the first
private interview I had with you I laid before you the inconveniences that must inevitably attend what you proposed. Yet
nevertheless I have been subservient to your will, even to the
hazard of my life and the disturbing of a quiet mind."

"Then," replied Lady Galliard, "to put you out of danger
and remove your inward disorder but, above all, to convince
you of my utmost esteem, take one promise more and that a
superior to all I have ever yet made you: I'll marry you the hour
Sir John leaves me."

"O, madam," answered Tom, "those misfortunes which before
hung loose upon my shoulders are now, by so kind an order,
firmly rivetted, and that secret must come to light which has

so long been hid in obscurity. Know, therefore, to my eternal uneasiness, I am married already and to the very person my abused master thinks I am gone to. This I had told you at first but that I hoped your passion would have worn out with a few nights' enjoyment, and I found an inward check when I first complied. But if we once come to consult with flesh and blood, they certainly get the better and the most forcible arguments are on their side."

The impatient Sir John, no longer able to hear, entered at these last words and, snatching up a taper which stood upon the table, he ran to the bedside with as much temper as he could possibly command, just when Lady Galliard was going to swoon. But one surprise beat back another, and the fresh concern of her son being so near recalled her sinking spirits, though poor Sir John lost his. For the blasting sight had such an effect upon him that his tongue faltered, his hand trembled, and his legs not able to support his weight, laid him speechless on the floor. The guilty couple in bed took the advantage of his retired reason and ere he could recover it had gotten on their clothes and left the room.

Tom made the best of his way from a house he had now grown weary of and consequently never desired to see again. But Lady Galliard, who had always been subservient to nature, was now touched with it in behalf of her only son, and no sooner saw her favorite footman gone than she returned to her chamber, where she found Sir John as she left him, in a happy state of ignorance. She then called for help which, with the assistance of time, brought him to himself. But the return of his senses were accompanied with such reproaches as let Lady Galliard into the secret of her own character; but, as she was a woman of the most consummate assurance, it gave her the least disturbance in nature.

"And is it thus, madam," said the recovered Sir John, "that you treat the memory of the deceased and the remaining part of him, his children? Do you imagine while your honor suffers shipwreck that ours can escape the storm, or even his that is no more? Do you not rake up his ashes to disgrace and infamy, calling his fondness folly, that could doat on so much ingratitude and believe a woman could be faithful? Good Heaven! Was there nothing in the race of mankind to please a depraved appetite but a worthless footman? Pardon me, madam," continued the knight, "I now recollect you are my mother, but beg you will likewise remember I am your son and you the first aggressor. And if a criminal behavior should alienate the duty and affection of your children from you, say to yourself but say it softly, 'I deserve it all.' "

While Sir John was going on with his just invectives, Lady Galliard was studying an evasion and thought, as the fellow was gone clean off and her son had for some time been senseless, it would be no hard matter to persuade him all he saw and heard was delusion or a dream, and answered as follows:

"I own, Sir John, your words are extremely shocking to me, because I plainly see your brain is turned, nor dare I so much as ask you the meaning of them, lest it should throw you into a farther delirium. But I beg you will give me leave to call up some of the servants again that they may help me to convey you to your bed. I was afraid of some growing distemper when I saw you indisposed at dinner yesterday."

"I confess," returned Sir John, "such proceedings where a man is so nearly concerned may well be thought to turn his brain, and my confusion, grief, and shame is too great to bear many witnesses. No, madam, I can go to my bed without assistance, but remember you have destroyed the sweet repose that should attend me there. And do you, after all, to excuse yourself, persuade me I am deaf and blind? Would I could wipe away those faults which busy time is laying up in store and will at last produce to your confusion. O, would I could blot them out, though even at the expense of eyes and ears, which are at present of no use to me but to confirm the ill opinion you have too justly given me of your conduct. And I am now so far let into women's frailty, that the whole race of mankind should cease ere I would endeavor to increase my own species. Heaven! That it were in my power to believe myself deceived, but, madam, you may be assured this unhappy son of yours is not the only witness to your weakness. I will leave you, though with much concern, and hope you will make some home reflections on your past actions. How far my tottering principles may suffer by such examples I cannot yet determine, but if you never see me more, do not rack your invention for the cause."

At those words Sir John with some precipitation left the room, where Lady Galliard continued in much confusion, and spent the rest of the night in tears, perhaps more for the loss of the lover gone than the son going. But that which touched her most sensibly was telling her he was not the only witness to her faults. That nettled her exceedingly and she would fain have been informed who it was that shared the secret with her son but feared to ask any questions, lest they should be answered with new reproaches. But, being impatient of spies about her, she resolved to rid herself of every mortal in the house except her woman, who was privy to all her affairs. Sir John, she thought, would soon steer his course towards Cambridge, and then she might make what revolutions in the family she had a mind to.

Accordingly, in two days he took his leave, attended only by Mr. Teachwell and one servant. The latter, after three or four miles riding, Sir John ordered to keep at some distance and then applied himself after the following manner to his tutor:

"I believe, Mr. Teachwell, I shall a little surprise you when I tell you I am absolutely bent against the journey you think I am going to take. The seat of learning is no place for me. I now begin to have a taste for pleasure and am resolved to spend my days where I may glut myself at the fountainhead. London, therefore, is the way. The very road which I intend to travel leads to that glorious city so much extolled by all that have a taste for true delight. Thither I mean to go and try to wear away those disagreeable thoughts which gnaw and interrupt my ease and peace. You will, I doubt not, disapprove of my design for double reasons. I know you will be anxious for my welfare and perhaps a little dubious about your own. But I will certainly see you well provided for before we part and, for my own actions, I am fully determined to let them take their swing."

Mr. Teachwell, who had been forming many schemes in his own breast for the advantage of his young charge, listened to his resolutions with the extremest concern and told him he very greatly feared the success of his unadvised design. "And pardon me, Sir John," continued he, "if I say you are in the height of danger and may very possibly list yourself under the banner of knaves and fools. For know, Sir John, to the great discredit of humanity, there is a superior number of that sort to those of a different character. You are young, raw, and unpracticed in the artifices of those men, and when you have bought experience at too high a price, you will have more time for repentance than perhaps you will care to bestow upon it. I wish my words were of any force with you. I should then with pleasure multiply them, but to my very great trouble I find you resolute and past all advice but what you give yourself. Would but that great share of reason which Heaven has bestowed upon you interpose betwixt you and ruin. It would advise you to seek out some improvement and, if you dislike learning, spend a year or two abroad, make a tour into France and Italy. And, since you love not books, read men, study your own species through every stage and scene of life, then try whether it be possible for one of your early sense to give into the grosser part of mankind and join their guilty actions with ease and approbation."

"Mr. Teachwell," replied Sir John, "I cannot but own the justness of your remarks and will always acknowledge they are greatly worth my notice. But I am young, as you yourself observe, and pleasure must be had, whatever it cost."

"Pleasure, Sir John," said Teachwell, "is in strictness no longer so than while, like an easy meal, it goes lightly on the stomach, without loading or loathing. And what we vulgarly call pleasure too often includes a great many criminal actions. Could I by strength of argument be so happy as to instill an innocent notion of pleasure into your breast, I should gain a very considerable point, but you are now going to a place where religion, virtue, sobriety, and, in short, every action worthy praise is by the gay and young exploded. To carry you through the course of the town, you must learn the following axioms:

"You are to kill your man before you can be reckoned brave. You must destroy your constitution with diseases ere you are allowed a man of gallantry; unman yourself by immoderate drinking, to qualify you for a boon companion; blaspheme your Maker by execrable oaths and curses to avoid all show of sneaking religion. And if fortune forgets to be your friend, while the dice are in your hand, you must fling away your estate to some winning bully, lest you should pass for a man of prudence and thought—which brings you to the last degree of misery, and you are a beggar before you know your danger. And thus, Sir John, I have described the modern man of honor, which in my opinion is the most dishonorable man upon earth, from which character, as from the plague, may Heaven always keep you."

"But why a man of honor?" returned Sir John. "Is honor concerned in any of the crimes you have named?"

"Yes," replied Teachwell, "in the major part of them, as the world goes. For, if you received a challenge and refuse to answer it, your honor bleeds to save your carcass. If you have an intrigue with a fine woman, though another man's wife, you will readily tell her you have too much honor either to disappoint her or tell again. When you have lost a thousand pounds at play, though you have not a hundred to answer it with, you cry ' 'Tis a debt of honor and though my family at home should starve, it must and shall be paid.' Indeed, as to drinking and swearing, I think there is not much pretense to honor, nor did I ever hear anybody lay a claim to it on those occasions. But, alas, it is very falsely placed where it is laid, and honor, like a virgin's virtue, is too nice to be fingered by every dirty hand that knows not the value of what they sully. No, Sir John, a man of true honor will avoid every action that cannot be answered for by it. Remember what your favorite *Hudibras* has said upon that topic:

Honor is like that glassy bubble
Which give philosophers such trouble,
Whose least part cracked, the whole does fly, &c.[3]

Now if a breach in honor be like one in the Commandments, how careful should we be to make a just title to every branch of it. Believe me, sir, the word honor is no more than a strict observance of that duty we owe to God and nature. And when we fail in any part, the smallest breach extends itself till it becomes a dreadful chasm, gaping with pleasure to devour every action that virtue and reason commend. It is commonly said, example goes beyond precept, and we are certainly too apt to follow a multitude in doing evil. Fashion (both in dress and action) is what we all imitate, though never so ridiculous, and when our faults are once in vogue, it is then a crime to think them such, because what everybody does, nobody thinks wrong, or at least nobody will own they do."

"How often," returned the knight, "have I told Mr. Teachwell he is an excellent preacher, and what a pity 'tis he has not now a fuller audience, though there are some critics that would have charged you with too hasty a transition from honor to fashion, which I pass over because I know your zeal. Come, Mr. Teachwell, I believe you are my friend and as such I will always use you, but I now beg we may have no more of this grave stuff. It is Fortune only that divides our opinions. She has confined your notions of pleasure by a scanty pattern, while mine is dilated by a more affluent turn of her precarious wheel, and when we get to London, perhaps I may do better than you imagine."

"I hope, sir," answered Teachwell, "you do not take Heaven's favors as a toleration for misusing them. They were designed for blessings, which they will never prove if wrong applied, and you are extremely out when you imagine that plenty makes the rake, because I have known many of that character reduced to

[3] *Hudibras*, Part II, Canto II, lines 385–387. Teachwell's memory is faulty or he is quoting from a corrupt text; the second line should read: "That finds philosophers such trouble."

the lowest ebb, who have yet pursued what you call pleasure with as strong a gust as Sir John Galliard can possibly do in the midst of a fine estate. Again, I have seen a man whose lavish fortune has defied extravagancy, yet reduced to the want of necessaries because he wanted a heart to enjoy his wealth. So that it is here very plain that neither poverty nor riches make the happy or the wretched, but the want of a due application has many proselytes of the latter sort, and it is depravity of inclination that must answer for the failure. But I find this sort of conversation is perfectly disagreeable and, though I know myself obliged to urge it farther, the despair which attends my hope of success puts my good designs to silence. Yet I have one question to ask, which I hope will be neither improper nor impertinent: how do you expect to be supplied with money at London? I doubt Lady Galliard will be so exasperated at your willful journey that she will be a little backward in answering your expensive demands. For London, Sir John, is no place of pleasure if a man pulls out an empty purse in it."

"Those, Mr. Teachwell," answered Sir John, "who make false steps themselves will never be surprised to see another stumble. Lady Galliard will certainly give liberty as well as take it, and while she considers her own conduct, will never be angry with mine. But if she should happen to like her own faults better than other people's (as I believe most folks do) and should deny to answer a few extraordinary expenses, I have been told there are scriveners in London, and it is but taking up upon the reversion at last.[4] You know I am now pretty well advanced in my nineteenth year and shall ere long command what I am now forced to sue for."

Mr. Teachwell was just going to enter his protest against that unhappy project of taking up on the reversion when they were overtaken by a coach and four which enclosed Mr. Friendly,

[4] Galliard intends to borrow money from a broker, using as security the estate which he will inherit when he is of age. Presumably Lady Galliard has rights to the usufruct of the estate until it "reverts" to her son upon his majority.

his lady, and daughter, going to London. He was full of astonishment to see Sir John Galliard on that road, because he thought him gone to Cambridge and had accordingly taken leave of him a few days before. Sir John was surprised as well as Mr. Friendly and not in a very good condition to excuse himself. He knew some questions would come from the coach which he could not very readily answer, but being resolved to pursue his eager desires after pleasure, he thought it best to look easy and seem pleased that fortune had favored him with such good company.

Then, turning his horse's head towards the coach, he saluted the ladies with an air of profound civility and expressed the greatest satisfaction at a prospect of such entertaining company in London. "For thither I am going, Mr. Friendly, and I beg you will not lecture me, because Mr. Teachwell here has done it so very home that if my will, like the laws of the Medes and Persians,[5] were not unalterable, I should ere now, by dint of argument, have been beaten out of this road. But resolution added another spur to my heel and has kept my horse's head forward. I daresay, Mr. Friendly, you can remember since you thought it hard young men should not indulge."

"Sir John," said the modest Mr. Friendly, "when the beginning of our days are called to account by the middle part of them, we generally answer with a blush. I must own, though I was never headstrong or past advice, I can call a great many inadvertent actions to mind, which I am now ashamed of. I know that youth, like a wild horse, is ungovernable and loves no reins or bit, till years and experience cure the folly. But for your part, Sir John, you are a man of so much good sense that I shall leave you wholly to the dictates of it, without the least admonition, though never so kindly designed or received. I fancy you have no acquaintance at London and wish, when you have, they may all prove sterling. In the meantime, if you please to command a bed at my house, both that and my table are at your service as long as you will honor me with your company."

[5] *Daniel* VI:8.

Sir John seemed very sensible at so kind an offer and when they got to London accepted of it, to which place three days more conveyed them. Where I shall for a while leave Sir John and cast an eye back to Lady Galliard, whose story would end very abruptly, unless a little further pursued. I left her somewhat uneasy in her mind with a design of turning away her whole set of servants, because her son had assured her there was some in the family privy to her mismanagement. And since she knew not where to fix the knowledge of her failing, she was resolved to turn out all at once (her woman excepted, as I said before), not considering that had any of them been in the secret, her proceedings was the only way to publish her faults all over the country. But she consulted nothing further than getting rid of her spies, and the poor innocent servants, who knew nothing of the matter, were turned off with no satisfaction but their wages, full of wonder at so sudden a revolution.

Miss Dolly, her daughter, was now grown a great romping girl and, lest she should turn observator too, was sent to a boarding school to confirm that character. For, as the poor young creature had always been left to her own will, running about the house like a tame rabbit, or rather a wild one, she had no notion of anything but play and impertinence, which turned her instructions into the most ridiculous imitations. So that Mr. Hop, her dancing master, only fixed the hobble in her pace, and Mr. Quaver made her squall worse than Graymalkin making love. All music in general was her aversion and every sort of work she abhorred. The French tongue she chewed and mumbled till it banished her English without taking its place, and she gabbled so many incoherences that her master in a passion left her and said he should teach her a new language till she knew none at all. However, there she was placed, if not to improve, at least to waste her time. She was neither ugly nor a fool but had a sprouting pride and a full-grown ill nature which blasted the blossoms of her wit and beauty. In short, she had more of the mother than the father, and here I leave her for some time to get ahead, then catch her again, when she thinks herself out of my clutches.

Lady Galliard, having thus cleared her house of every inspecting eye, entertained a new set of servants, but not so much to the advantage of either fortune or credit as she expected. For Tom, the occasion of the general remove, was now to be recalled, though at the expense of both, and the following invitation was accordingly sent him from his lady's own hand:

"It is now but a few days since I had some reasons for parting with all my servants. The vacancies which the steward and housekeeper made are yet to be filled up. And if your wife and you think them worth your acceptance, they shall be yours, with all encouragement from

B. GALLIARD"

This letter was written for the view of the wife, though the first that was ever sent with that design, which she no sooner read than she seemed transported, because she knew nothing of the previous intrigue betwixt the lady and her husband. But Tom, not quite so ignorant, was filled with very different sentiments from those his wife indulged upon such a happy occasion (as she, poor fool, thought it). He foreknew what accounts would be expected from his stewardship and plainly saw that while his wife kept the house, she must give up her right to his affections, which he thought within himself was a little hard. But the offer being so very advantageous, and his innocent wife amazed at the full stop he made, after some minutes' silence, he considered it was impossible to refuse it without discovering the whole affair, since no other objection could be made, and therefore sent her ladyship word they would both wait upon her as soon as they could put their own small concerns into a little order.

This made Lady Galliard perfectly easy as to that point. But then a dissatisfied blast blew fresh upon her hopes, when she considered what the sentiments of her enraged and absent son would be when he once came to see or hear the defiler of his mother's bed was again returned. But her sanguine temper soon dispelled the mist that would have clouded her warm imagination and she resolved to hope Sir John would like a college life so well that some years would drop before he came again. But while she was pleasing herself with thoughts of this kind, the postman knocked with a letter for her. The hand she knew was Mr. Teachwell's and, making a ready passage to the inside, she read these words:

"MADAM: The concern which attends my hand while I send your ladyship this account makes me almost unable to write at all. It proceeds from a double cause. First, I dread the impending ruin which may attend Sir John in this new world of temptation; and next, I fear you will blame my care and conduct that has not diverted his design in coming here. But may his misfortunes be as far from him as my endeavors and persuasions were near at hand when he first assured me he would go to London. Yet let this bring you some consolation—he is now under Mr. Friendly's roof and care, with whom I shall always join in giving the best advice I am able, as he does now with me, in sending our most profound respects to your ladyship. London, Oct. 20."

Lady Galliard read this letter with a vast deal of surprise because she never knew Sir John seem to be the least desirous of going to London. And it was very likely such a resolute action would have given her a considerable share of uneasiness had not a prospect of her own satisfaction banished the present concern. She was now unapprehensive of any interruption in her own faulty pleasures and with reason believed those of the town would so firmly engage her son that she might with the greatest safety indulge herself in the criminal company she best liked. But whatever her private sentiments were on this occasion, she thought it very proper to show some resentment, which she did in a letter to her son filled with reproaches, both for his want of respect and duty to her and for going to London with so much obstinate folly before he had spent a year or two at a place more proper for him. However, she expressed her satisfaction that he was under Mr. Friendly's care and begged him to continue with him as he valued either his own good or her favor.

Sir John received the epistle, read the rebukes with perfect indifference, and took the advice as far as he thought fit. Yet it must be owned in his favor that while Mr. Friendly continued in town he kept to pretty good decorum, which was some months. And since I have nothing to say of the knight at present, rather than lose so much time, I think fit to return into the country and see how things are transacted at Galliard Hall, where I no sooner entered than I saw Tom and his wife arrive, one to take possession of a new place and the other of his old one.

To say much upon this head would swell my episode to a bulk too large, but, though I would avoid irregularity, I cannot but fancy the reader will be a little curious to know how Lady Galliard goes on with her new steward. The wife indeed was a woeful obstacle betwixt her and her proposed enjoyment and often stood in the way while as often wished out on't; but the incumbrance was a force upon Lady Galliard because without the wife the husband was inaccessible. The poor man had certainly an honest value for her and one faultless moment spent with her was more preferred than all those guilty hours which ended with remorse. But interest is no single devil; it is a legion attended with as many ills. His fortunes were now sunk too low to be raised again without a wretched disagreeable compliance, and every other day (under pretense of being sent board) confined him in his old apartment. But the wife, who had no notion of those frequent excursions from home and at night, too, began to ask herself the meaning of those nocturnal sallies, for the night succeeding those days he always shared his lady's bed. She had had many disputes with her own thought about this occasion but had never opened the grievance to her husband, for fear he should think her jealous.

But a little while after, in the middle of one of his absent nights, she awoke out of a frightful dream which told her she was in a great deal of danger, that her husband was in bed with her lady, and if she did not suddenly leave the house, she would never leave it alive. All this, though she believed it no more than the effect of her troubled fancy, lay upon her spirits for some hours, and tears instead of sleep now filled her eyes. She heard the clock strike four, then left her restless bed, expostulating with herself in favor of a husband whom she would fain believe she had wronged by an unjust suspicion of him. Her roving fancy carried her from the chamber, though she knew not where she went or why she left it, when after a wandering half-hour spent she knew not how, she cast her eye towards a window that looked into the backyard where the stables were. She heard a door unlock but could not see the person that unlocked it.

Fear, rage, despair and jealousy had all taken their seats in her breast, but a bare suspicion with certainty of her fate was more intolerable than all the rest. She therefore resolved, while she shuddered with the dread on't, to venture out and see whether it was her husband, as fancy had suggested to her. And when she got into the kitchen she saw a dark lantern stand on one of the dressers with a lighted candle in it which was, as she supposed, left there by the person that had just entered the stables. She was well pleased at so ready a provision for her discovery and, taking it up, shaded the light till she heard a horse come out. She then raised it to the face of the rider which proved to be one she was pretty well acquainted with, but she concealed herself and got in undiscovered though not unsuspected. Tom rode off as usual, and his wife, now satisfied of her ill usage, returned to her bed where no interruption disturbed her racking thoughts, but gloomy despair gave a helping hand and added to the pressures of a wounded heart. She lay till daylight called her to her business in the family but her swollen eyes and dejected countenance told the inward troubles of her mind.

She was now but too sure that some intrigue was privately carried on but was still a stranger to the sharer in her husband's iniquity, though she had little room for doubt when she considered Lady Galliard the very individual person who always sent her husband on those pretended errands. The usual hour brought him home and the wife, resolving upon a more complete discovery, received him with her wonted cheerfulness, disguising her chagrin with all the art that true dissimulation could assist her with.

The night came on which carried Tom to the lawful embraces of a wife he loved, and, though all her art was summoned to conceal her cold indifference, it was plain, from all her slight embraces, that every one was forced. Tom perceived it and as soon guessed at the cause. He had all day fancied his wife was the person that clapped the dark lantern to his phyz in the morning and, if so, had good reason to believe it would cost him some pains to clear up the matter. But, as he knew his wife a woman of some penetration, he was very sure a thousand lies would never satisfy her doubts. And being weary of the engagement upon his hands, he e'en resolved it, if she charged him with his crime, to own it all and join their endeavors to extricate themselves as soon as possible.

Tom then asked his wife (and desired her answer without hesitation or reserve) whether she had seen his face any time that day before ten o'clock. She told him with tears she had but hoped he had not known her. "But since you are upon inquiry," continued she, "may I not ask in my turn where you were going at such an odd hour and where you had been all night? I confess your dark proceedings has given me a great deal of pain, because I always made myself very sure of that heart which I now have cause to fear is lodged in another breast. Heavens knows I always prized it at too high a rate to part with it while I had power to keep it, but now that power is gone and it is mine no more."

"Think not so cruelly," replied Tom. "My heart is now as firmly yours as it was the first moment I gave it to you, though I will briefly own I have wronged your bed. And it was to prevent those wrongs that I so unwillingly consented to my lady's proposals, which nothing but your own eager persuasions should have forced me to comply with. But I had no objection to make against such an advantageous offer, unless I had confessed my fault to you, which I now wish I had done, since I am forced to it at last, after many repetitions of my crime."

"If I have been the cause of my own injuries," replied the wife, "it was because I was ignorant of your private dealings. But now that I am let into the secret, I will resolutely starve rather than stay another day within these cursed walls. Oh, infamy, infamy, who can bear it!"

"Nay, hold, Cousin Margaret" (as he often called her), said Tom, "and believe me when I tell you I am full as weary of those walls as you can be. But since I have been a rogue so long, I will have my reward before I leave them and beg you will stifle this rising anger, which yet I do not blame you for, till a very short time has finished my design. My lady's bed I will never more approach, but I'll be paid, and very roundly too, for all the guilty time I have spent there."

His villainy was rather persuasive than natural, and ill advice from our superiors is too often swallowed with greediness. And it is almost impossible for a man to see his danger before he falls a victim to the temptation. This was at first Tom's case. He thought it a fine thing to be liked by a fine woman, and one so much above him too. But what feasted him then glutted him soon after, and he is now resolved to put an end to all. In order to which, he told his wife he would acquaint his lady that she had found out the intrigue, and bid her if any questions were asked by Mrs. Busy, the lady's woman, to say she watched him more than once into her lady's apartment.

The next day Tom was to go from home as usual on his sham errand and was at the wonted hour conveyed by Busy into her lady's bedchamber, where she left him and went to her own. He no sooner saw himself alone with Lady Galliard than he affected a melancholy silence and waited to be asked the cause, but instead of that, the lady herself put on a gloomy air, and some minutes succeeded one another before either spoke. This made Tom think his lady understood *Mekachefa*[6] and had like

[6] "A Word in the *Persian Tales* for knowing Peoples thoughts" (author's note). The reference is to the translation by William King and others of François Petis de la Croix's *Les Mille et un jours, contes persans,* and *Histoire de la sultane de Perse et des vizirs, contes turcs,* which appeared in 1714 as

to have balked his design. But being fully determined to keep the word he had given his wife of coming near his lady's bed no more, he thus began:

"I know not, madam, nor can I so much as guess at the reason of your silence, unless you know the cause of mine, which is easily justified when once it is explained. But the story is so ungrateful it hangs upon my faltering tongue, nor can it force a passage, hence you. . . ."

"Peace, dissembler," interrupted Lady Galliard, "I know thy base, thy treacherous, thy black and mercenary soul, better than thou dost thyself! 'Believe me when I tell you I am as weary of those walls as you can be. But since I have been a rogue so long, I will have my reward before I leave them.' "

Tom was under some astonishment when he heard his own words repeated and was going to reply when Lady Galliard thus went on: "Most justly hast thou styled thyself a rogue, and it is pity the reward thou art grasping for is not answerable to thy character. 'But I will be paid, and very roundly too for all.' "

"Pray, madam," said Tom, interrupting her, "do you think it an easy matter to account for sending spies to watch a man's words and actions in private with his own wife?"

"No villain," returned Lady Galliard, "I sent no spies. It was I that left the dark lantern in the kitchen, the errand to which place was too kind for thy ungrateful ears to hear. I perceived somebody coming and absconded till your wife had taken it up and went out with it. I then foresaw a discovery and my curiosity carried me last night to your chamber door."

"Then, madam," returned Tom, "that very action has let you into my design, and I may save myself all future trouble."

"Very well sir," replied Lady Galliard, "and pray, may I know how high this round payment runs which you expect? It is pity, methinks, to balk your reasonable demands."

The Persian and the Turkish Tales, Compleat. This particular term actually appears in the story of Chec Cahabeddin, *Turkish Tales* (II, 30), where it is glossed as "a Science by which the *Santons* [holy men] pretend to discover the most Secret Thoughts of Men."

"Madam," answered Tom very pertly, "my demands run high in proportion to the lowness of my fortunes, which you well know are below my raising. Three hundred pounds will pay off a mortgage of part of my estate. That sum you can spare and it is that only that can set me above want and you safe from scandal."

"I understand you, sir," said Lady Galliard, "and if you can preserve my credit at three hundred pounds expense, I shall think it no dear purchase. Would you could give me up my honor too for such another sum."

"Not a farthing more, madam," replied Tom, "I intend to throw in your ladyship's honor to the bargain, and as I never desired the keeping of it, I can with less regret give it up again."

Lady Galliard was so provoked at this saucy treatment, which joined itself to her own inward accusations that, though her pride forbade her tears, her passion with her irritated blood burst out at her nose.

"Villain," said she, "am I become thy sport? Leave me this moment and expose me the next to all mankind. I had much rather write my faults in my own forehead than stand obliged to thee for thy concealment, though bought at a price that should not be worth thy thanks. Begone, and know thou art already wounded in a part it seems I never had a share of."

Tom found he had gone a little too far and would fain have recalled his words, but Lady Galliard, too much incensed to listen to any excuse, got up and left the room, telling him he had liberty to go whenever he pleased. And, as for his reward, part on't he was like to take with him, though he knew it not; the rest she hoped Fortune at some time or other would pay for her. When Tom saw himself alone and his bullying project come to nothing, he returned to his wife and gave her an account of his successless proceedings. She told him she was not very well and begged, whatever came of it, he would begone, for poverty with innocence was in her breast of much more value than affluence purchased by guilt. He promised to give up his accounts the next day and desired she would be easy till then.

What other discourse they had I know not, because I was called away to lend an ear to Lady Galliard and Busy. "I see, madam, by your eyes," said the latter, "you have had some unpleasing contest with Tom. I wish it were in your power to withdraw your affections from that ungrateful whelp, who has always returned your love with contempt or, at least, indifference. Everything, madam, partakes of its origin, and the sordid fool is better pleased with the trifle, his wife, than with the shining jewel you put into his undeserving hands. Snatch it from him, madam, and see the brute no more."

"Ah, Busy!" replied Lady Galliard, "what friendly advice would this have been had it come when first I made you privy to the reigning folly in my breast. Remember your own faulty words: 'Why, madam, are you uneasy, while you can redress your own grievance? If Heaven has given us appetites, can it be angry that we indulge them? And when we have a choice of being either happy or wretched, who would not choose the former? If you like Tom, let Tom be the man. I think it is now fit you should cater for yourself.' This (base as thou art) was the pernicious counsel which I, unhappy I, with a too voracious appetite most greedily swallowed till the poison infected my whole mass of blood and has turned me from thy mistress to thy slave, obliged to buy your secrecy at the expense of my own liberty. And instead of commanding, as usual, [I] must now act the servile part and be subservient both to him and you. Why did I not consider this before I involved myself in a link of faults, before I gave a loose to my own desires, and ere I resigned my virtue to its cursed opposite, vice. But what's to be done? Say what measures I must take to disengage myself from this labyrinth of destruction which on all sides surrounds me? But, alas, thy talent lies towards nought but mischief. Thou art dumb and mute, where good advice is wanting."

"The misfortune of servitude, madam," answered Busy, "never shows itself in fuller colors than when our chiefs humble themselves so low as to ask the advice of one they know dare give none but what they are satisfied will concur with the inclination of those who ask it. And had my late advice run counter to your ladyship's wishes, the consequence on my side would have been to lie under a lasting grudge and on yours, to act as you thought fit without it. You may be assured, madam, when I first observed your affections growing so fast towards a man in every respect so unfit for you, I likewise saw the innumerable inconveniences that would attend it. And as you have been pleased to remember my words, give me leave to repeat a few of yours: 'I tell thee, Busy, it is the hardest thing in life to subdue our passions, and I have one for Tom so very powerful that all my attempts are fruitless and I can no way bring it under. Have him I must, nay will, though I marry him.' Now, madam, after such a declaration, what could my weak persuasions avail? Why then am I blamed for consenting to what I could no way hinder or prevent?"

"It is now in vain," said Lady Galliard, "to talk any more of what is past. I am now to consider of what is still to come. Three hundred pounds is Tom's demand with which he would disengage his encumbered estate. I do own I have done him an injury which a greater sum cannot atone for and which I now lament. But it is past as many more of my crimes are, and the remaining part of my life shall be spent in contrition for them. Go you to him in the morning and carry what I shall then give you to his wife, tell her I beg her pardon for all I have done to her and desire them to be gone immediately. Her wrongs indeed are great and so is my concern for them. But no more—I will now to bed and try if kindly sleep will lull me to a dream of quiet, for waking I shall ne'er be so."

The morning no sooner appeared than Lady Galliard rang for her woman, by whose assistance she got up and, going to her closet, fetched thence a bag and bid her give it to Tom's wife with her last desire of going away as soon as possible. The poor woman was no less transported with the order to be gone than she was with the present, sent her thanks to her lady, and a few hours carried them away. Tom made a right use of the money and redeemed part of his estate, but his poor wife had a short enjoyment of it, for in less than three months she died of sweating illness which wore her to nothing, not without violent suspicion of foul play.

Tom was inconsolable for the loss of her and looked upon her as a martyr to his villainy and his lady's malice, whose words he often called to mind—when she told him he was already wounded in a part she never had a share of. He knew his wife a woman of virtue and thought it hard she should be sacrificed to one of a different character. Each very new minute filled his mind with tender sentiments succeeded by grief, till at last revenge took place, of which more hereafter, for I am this minute going to take coach for London again, where I left my young knight in the careful hands of Mr. Friendly and Mr. Teachwell. But at my return, I heard the latter had fallen ill of a consumption and went to the Bath, where he died, and Mr. Friendly, after seven months' stay at London, was now preparing to go again into the country, to which place he would fain have persuaded Sir John to accompany him, but the town was now grown dearer to him than any other place and not to be parted with on any terms. In three days Mr. Friendly and his lady went home, leaving his daughter, a lovely young girl, to the care of his own sister.

Sir John is now left at London, sole master of his own actions, and Mr. Friendly was no sooner gone than he took lodgings at the Court end of the town and began to frequent all the public places more than ever, by which means he soon became acquainted with all sorts of people, but unluckily pitched upon a wrong set for his constant companions. He was a man of a very exact form and made as much for admiration as any young beau about the town. He had a pleasing sweetness in his looks, an easy regular shape, a gentle rakish air, but a temper so very affable that it complied too readily with every temptation. The first progress he made in modern gallantry was to get into the unimproving conversation of the women of the town, who often took care to drink him up to a pitch of stupidity, the better to qualify him for having his pockets picked. And a frequent repetition of this sort of usage forced him to write home for more money, as he had often done since Mr. Friendly left the city, whose purse as well as house was always at Sir John's service.

But Lady Galliard, whose adventure with Tom was quite ended and who now resolved to leave off intriguing, had the greatest desire in life to get her son home again. She knew feeding his growing extravagances with more money than a minor ought to spend would be no politic scheme for getting him from those pleasures he was now grown too fond of, and to bridle his follies when they were grown headstrong would only serve to give him an opportunity of breaking the reins and hating the hand that laid them on. She therefore thought it best to interlard her letter with a layer of wheedle and a layer of severity. She first told him how agreeable his company would be at Galliard Hall, that she had now given up all pleasures but those that centered in him, that if he valued the true repose of a mother he would endeavor to contribute towards it by consenting to her wishes. But if he wanted that love and duty he owed her, she was resolved to return it by retrenching his allowance and bringing it into narrower circumstances.

It is certain good words do not mollify so soon as threats exasperate, and the latter part of the letter roused the lion in the knight, which provoked him to the following answer:

"MADAM, Since the reception of your last I have considered your project which I find is to starve my pleasures. But as I love them too well to see them want, I am this minute come from the scrivener's, where I have taken up a brace of hundreds on the reversion of my estate. I hope, madam, you remembered last Thursday was my birthday and that entered me into that year, which ended, will give me a power separate from that you now use with some tyranny. As for Galliard Hall, it is a country seat and, till I am tired of London, shall hardly see it, though my respects and duty are always there to attend you and assure your ladyship, I will always be your most obedient son and humble servant, J. GALLIARD."

How Lady Galliard digested this return from her son I

never heard, because I never inquired, but my knight went on in the beaten road of modern gallantry and, as he thought his own stock of wit sufficient for a whole company, his set of companions were a disagreeable mixture of fool, knave, and coxcomb. The last was a full-grown baronet got to years of discretion, though he never had any, whom I shall call Sir Combish Clutter; the first, a country esquire called Clownish Cockahoop,[7] an excellent companion when a man aims at nothing but sport; the other (and by much the worse) a stooking[8] gamester, who generally took care of the loose corns the pretty ladies left in Sir John's pockets, though sometimes he got the start of them and left them only the gleanings.

O men of merit, say what avails good sense when left in the hands of a careless libertine who had much rather tie it down with links of iron than listen to the friendly admonition it kindly offers? Sir John Galliard had so good a share of that fine quality that, had he given it room to play, it would have made him a shining companion for the finest genius in the nation, but vanity, pride, folly, and every other opposite to it were let loose in a wide room, while it was confined to a narrow closet, starving and rusting for want of food and exercise.

A night or two after carried Sir John (with a set of his choice companions) to the play, where he saw Miss Friendly conducted to a front box by a gentleman he had never seen at her father's. The advantage of her dress added to her natural charms and showed her much more amiable than he ever thought her before. That minute created a criminal admiration in him and he made himself large and pleasing promises of her ruin. It is true his

[7] In the 1756 edition, *Galliard* is changed to *Gaylove*, Sir Combish Clutter to *Sir Trifling Flutter*, *Squire Clownish Cockahoop* to *Toby Wimble, Esq.*, of *Wimble-Hall*, and *Bousie* to *Freelove*. It is difficult to see what was gained by these alterations. *Galliard* (Fr. *gaillard*) more clearly represents Mrs. Davys's concept of her hero.

[8] *Stook* was thieves' cant for a handkerchief, hence *stook-hauler*, a pickpocket. This gamester may be Bousie (*bouse*: drink, liquor, a carouse), who reappears on page 364 and is responsible for Galliard's final London misadventure which causes his return to the country.

barbarous design against her shocked him a little when he called to mind her father's disinterested friendship towards him, but men of pleasure find little room for reflection, at least till they have gratified their own unreasonable desires.

The lady was young, brisk, airy, and something of the coquette, which made her aunt very watchful over her, and the gentleman with whom she had entrusted her was her own son, come just from Italy. Sir John paid a distant respect to her and ogled her the whole time the play lasted. He grew impatient for the ensuing day, the afternoon of which carried him to visit her, which was but the second time since her papa left her. He approached her with more respect than usual. She, on the other hand, was not pleased he came so seldom, told him he was a very slow visitor, gave her fan a flirt, and said she did not care *that* for him. "But, Sir John," continued she, "I think I saw you at the play last night. How did you like the scene betwixt ——?"

"Madam," interrupted Sir John, "every scene was alike to me, because I minded none. I had too lovely an object from the box you sat in to admit of any inferior amusement."

"O lud!" cried Miss, "I think the man is going to make love to a body, or do I take a compliment to myself that was not designed for me? Aye, aye, I believe 'tis so, for now I remember there were two ladies more in the same box, though I think they were not very handsome neither. Come, Sir John, if I am to be your confidante, only tell me the secret and I'll keep it—if I can."

"That *if*, madam," replied Sir John, "was a very considerable addition to your promise, but if a woman can keep a secret at all, it is certainly her own. Though, sure, it is none to tell you, I admire and adore Miss Friendly."

"Well, I'll swear now," said Miss, "I believe I shall grow grave upon this declaration, for I heard Papa say once that surprises, when they are a little over, set folks a-thinking, and you know, Sir John, we can't think without being grave. Hang gravity! It gives one's face an oldish cast, which makes me mad at you for setting mine into such a disagreeable form."

"Let not that give you uneasiness," returned the knight, "for there will be nothing displeasing in your face these twenty years, which I must tell you is a long reign as faces go now. But I have one question to ask you, madam: would you have me like your face?"

"Like it?" said Miss. "Well, I'll take my oath, I don't know whether I would or no. But I think I would not, because I have often heard you say you did not love rivals, and my face must have a very odd turn or Sir John Galliard a very odd fancy, if nobody likes it but himself."

"I own, madam," returned Sir John, "your remark is very just, and I should certainly be ashamed of a fancy that nobody jumped with but myself. Yet, though I would have a mistress generally liked, I would have her pleased with no adoration but mine."

"This," said Miss, "is just what my aunt told me yesterday when I was romping a little with my cousin William. 'Child,' she cried, 'leave off those girlish airs; you are now almost fifteen. Men love to take freedom themselves but don't care we should; they like to show their fondness to a hundred women, but expect we should only smile on one.' Now I would fain ask why we may not love variety as well as you. Yet your imperious saucy customs have made me perfectly ashamed of my own behavior. For there's Mr. Hatchet-face, a mercer from Covent Garden, and a rich one too, they say. Then there is Beau Spangle from the Horse Guards, and a trader from Exchange Alley worth a plum,[9] and a huge limb of the law, as big as one of an ox, from the Temple, with a man of quality to bring up the rear, which have all accosted me with equal ardor and complacency. And yet, the deuce take me, if I dare be civil to any of them because I don't know which I love best. So e'en let good nature and good manners shift for themselves, for I'll have nothing to do with either, where people are concerned that will take all for their own shares and leave nothing at all for me."

Sir John could have told her there was a vast disparity betwixt a modest woman and a man that lived at large, but his

[9] A slang term for the sum of £100,000.

present business was to get into her favor without disputing the matter and try (since she was perfectly disengaged) to make himself the happy man who might at last lay claim to her favor. He told her of his mighty passion, swore himself the humblest of her votaries, [said] though if she had a previous inclination, he saw no reason why she should not indulge it, though even to his undoing, for confinement he owned in any capacity was a thing intolerable to a freeborn agent.

"Even the beasts and birds," continued he, "prefer hunger and liberty to constraint and plenty, and shall man, that noble creature man, tie up his capacious inclinations and force them into the circumference of a mousetrap while he has the globe to furnish his desires with new and many joys. No, Miss," went he on,

> "Liberty's the soul of living
> Every hour new joys receiving."

"That," cried Miss, "is a piece of an old song, but pray what follows? 'Neither taking hearts nor giving.' So then, Sir John, you and I are just where we were and may wander at liberty till we lose one another."

"F—th, madam," said the knight, "you are grown so very witty I fear I shall lose you indeed for want of spirit to keep up with your repartee. And yet methinks it would vex me a little to be baffled by a woman, though I know you generally fight well at your own weapons, which are what we do not greatly understand. Come, no more disputes. Shall I wait upon you to the play tomorrow night?"

"Tomorrow night," said Miss, laughing, "nay then, you are in love without dispute. What, would you go to the play on Sundays? But if you have a mind to show your gallantry to perfection, you shall squire me to church if you please."

"Why f—th, child," replied the baronet, "if I were inclined to go to church with anybody, it should be with you, but I have too great a regard for the drums of my ears to come there among a parcel of unmusical bawlers that fancy God Almighty is to be charmed with noise. Besides, it is not above three months since I was there and then was absolved by half the parish, who no sooner heard the parson begin the absolution than they raised an audible voice and pronounced it as loud as he did."

"Nay," returned Miss, "I'll say something in behalf of our quiet congregation in the country, for they disturb nobody nor is it an easy matter to disturb them. The minister no sooner begins to pray than they begin a comfortable nap which always lasts till he has done, and then they wake and foot it home to dinner. Papa was rallying our parson one day and asked him why he did not speak loud enough to keep his congregation awake. He told Papa a natural stupidity could not be roused though even by the voice of thunder, unless they thought the lightning that attended it should set their haystacks on fire. 'Alas, sir,' continued he, 'religion is in a very dangerous condition, for men of low understanding have no notion of it and those of an exalted one are too apt to despise it.' "

"You have an excellent memory," replied Sir John, "but I doubt, madam, you have misplaced some of the good gentleman's words, because lightning is a forerunner of thunder, not an attendant on it."

In the midst of this dialogue Miss Friendly's aunt came to them with a letter in her hand and told her niece she had received a command from her papa to send her home. This news was not very agreeable to the young lady whose hankering inclinations after gaiety and the Town made her very unwilling to part with them, but to soothe her own disturbance she softly told herself every county in England was furnished with admirers of a fine woman, as she really was.

Sir John, however, began to ask himself how the remaining time was to be employed. Have her he must, if all his wealth or wits could furnish him with a scheme that would bear. His brain was fertile enough and produced a thousand plans, but every one was attended with a superior objection. The week after this was the time appointed for her journey. Sir John then took his leave and went to his lodgings where again he began to contrive. His greatest concern was to gain a few days more for her stay in town. The young one he believed might easily be persuaded, but the cunning lay in catching the old one. He therefore resolved not to visit her again till Tuesday that frequent attendance might give no suspicion. And when he did go, he made his application to the aunt as follows:

"Mr. Friendly, madam, has been gone from London some months and I, ungrateful as I am, have never made the least return to the many favors I received from him when here. I blush to think how Miss will accuse me when she tells her papa I have not so much as waited upon her to a play or any other diversion since he left her. I beg you will stand my friend and put off her journey home till next week, that I may conduct you both to the masquerade on Thursday night."

"Sir John," replied the lady, "I shall leave your request to be determined by my niece. If she has a mind to stay another week, I will not oppose it because I know the value my brother has for you, but hope that you will pardon me if I refuse your civility, for I have taken leave of the gay part of life ever since I was turned of forty."

"I'll assure you, Sir John," replied Miss, giving her head a toss of contempt, "if I had not a greater regard to my own pleasure than gratifying your desires, I would not stay, because you did not ask me first. But no matter: I am now going to the dull country and maybe Papa will never let me come here again, so for once I'll comply. And now let us consult about our dresses. Miss Wary will take the ticket you designed for my aunt and I daresay Sir John Galliard will change a matron for a girl at any time. For my part, I intend to personate a sea nymph and dress in moss and shells. You, Sir John, may appear like Neptune, because you know he is as much obliged to take care of the ladies of his own dominions as you are to protect me. As for Miss Wary, she has just finished a whimsical dress. So all you have to do, Sir John, is to go and bespeak ours."

Sir John accordingly went and they were sent as ordered. The night was no sooner gone than our young lady sent for her favorite companion, who was a near neighbor and the only daughter of Mr. Wary, a man of worth and substance. She had a frolic in her head which was soon communicated to Miss Wary and she asked her if she would join in it to cheat Sir John Galliard. The scheme was for the two young ladies to change habits and go to the masquerade before Sir John came. Miss Wary complied and in the evening they dressed in their several habits that they might not mistake one another when they came next night to the common rendezvous.

About half an hour before the appointed time of Sir John's coming Miss Friendly proposed going but desired her companion if the young baronet should chance to make love to her in her likeness she would use him well for her sake. "But," continued she, "if your inclination should chance to stand towards a little satirical raillery, never balk your fancy. It is no more than I should do myself and he will never distinguish feigned voices." Chairs were called and away the ladies went.

Sir John at the usual time came and was not a little nettled to find they were gone without him. He took it for a slight and resolved to mortify them accordingly. To complete his design he orders his chairmen to carry him to Covent Garden where he changed his dress, then followed the ladies, whom he soon distinguished from the rest but took no notice of them. They, on the other hand, kept a watchful eye towards the door and expected every enterer would prove Sir John, who was much nearer to them than they thought and followed them wherever they went, which at last Miss Friendly took notice of and, casting a side look at him now and then, she observed his naked hand going to convey a pinch of snuff to his nose and knew a ring he had on his finger, by which she found him out and told the secret to her friend but still behaved as before and seemed as indifferent as ever.

Sir John at last came up to Miss Wary, whom by the dress he took for Miss Friendly and asked her in a puppet's tone, "Do you know me?"

"Yes, better than you know me, and since we are deserted by

our guardian that should have followed us, we don't much care if we substitute you his representative, and. . . ."

"Hold, madam," interrupted Miss Friendly, still feigning her voice, "I will have nothing to say to him till he lets me into the secret of the ring on his finger, which I am sure belongs to Sir John Galliard, and for aught I know you are some ruffian that has murdered the man and ran away with his moveables. Come, come, sir, off with your mask or I'll send for a constable."

Sir John found by all this raillery his ring had discovered him and then began to say a thousand tender things to his nymph in double masquerade, who took all possible care to prevent any farther discovery. Some hours were spent in the common diversions of the place where wit and humor flew about like squibs, and when they came to the buffet, Sir John unmasked and would fain have had the ladies to do so too, but they were too full of the project of cheating the knight to end it so soon and therefore refused to drink anything, only put a few dried sweetmeats into their pockets which they eat as opportunity offered. But while they were yet at the buffet a little dapper gentleman came to Sir John and asked him if he would part with one of his ladies, for he thought it hard he should have two and himself not one. Sir John told him he could not guess from his looks that he wanted one, since they promised but very indifferently in his favor. However, if he could gain either of the ladies' consent to run away with a Tom Thumb, he should pity their want of judgment but that was a place of freedom and he could not use force to keep them.

The beau told him he wore a sword and should find a time. "I know not, sir," replied Sir John, "what time you may find, but I am sure mine would be lost if it were spent in killing a pigmy. And for your sword, if it be no longer than yourself, it will never make work either for a surgeon or an undertaker. Prithee, keep it in its peaceable scabbard and go thy ways for a little fool as thou art." At this the ladies laughed and the bauble went muttering away.

The variety this place offered of new diversion carried the

night insensibly off, and day began to break before the ladies were tired, at which time they desired Sir John to provide chairs. He went that minute and provided three but gave the chairmen the following directions: the two first were to go to the bagnio and the third to Mr. Wary's, the aforesaid father of Miss Friendly's companion. He then returned and conducted the ladies out, putting Miss Friendly (as he thought) into the second chair and Miss Wary into the third, who was immediately carried off, and Sir John got into the first himself and was as by order conveyed to the bagnio.[10]

As soon as they got to the door the well-designing knight got out and handed the following lady from her chair, who seeing another behind her (for one there was) thought it had been Miss Friendly and that the jest was now at an end. She pulled off her mask and, laughing, cried, "How do you like your sea nymph now, God Neptune, that should have been?" Then running to the other chair, "Come, miss," said she, "all is out." But what was her surprise when, instead of Miss Friendly, she saw the little gentleman coming out with whom Sir John had had a short contest at the masquerade. Sir John was now so mad at his disappointment that he was glad to see one on whom he might revenge himself. Turning to Miss Wary, he said, "Here is some mistake, madam. Those chairmen (who were then gone off) have brought us to the bagnio, I think perhaps by a bribe from this gentleman who I fancy has made a quarrel of what passed at the masquerade. I therefore beg you will take his dismissed chair and go home where you will find Miss Friendly for I ordered them all to your house. I would very fain wait upon you, but you see my honor is engaged and I know you ladies hate cowards. I will therefore conduct you to the chair and I wish you a good morning."

The young lady was soon at home where she found Miss Friendly full of wonder what was become of her and Sir John.

[10] The author may have a specific house of assignation—"The Bagnio"— in mind, though these bath-houses converted into brothels (cf. *stew*) were numerous in London. See Plate V of Hogarth's *Marriage à la Mode*.

I will now leave them a while to compare notes together, and step back to the bagnio to see what becomes of the two antagonists They were both got into the house before I came and the little gentleman began to bully Sir John, told him he had affronted him so far that his spirit could not bear it, and his design in following him was for satisfaction. Sir John, ashamed of such a combat, urged the folly of taking anything ill that was said in a place where a little good raillery was designed for the best part of the diversion. "And I farther know," continued he, "my sword and arm will meet with nothing but disgrace from so poor a victory. Yet if you insist upon satisfaction, I will give you all I can, but I think it your business to go and provide weapons since the place we come from admitting of none, we are unluckily both without. Another thing I insist upon is uncasing your face, for I never love to fight with a false one. Mine is bare and I expect yours should be so too."

"It will be of little service to you," replied the challenger, "to show my face since I am sure you never yet have seen it, but yet e'er I unmask I have a secret to disclose to you, and yet I must keep it, too. Know, then, I am a woman, a married woman, and I once thought a virtuous woman. My husband, too, is deserving of my love. He is young, handsome, rich and doats upon his wife, unworthy as she is. Nay, above the world I love him too, and all that's in it should never prevail with me to wrong his bed, were it not entirely for his own ease."

"I own, madam," returned Sir John, "I have often heard that women are riddles and sure you are come to confirm the assertion."

"No," replied the lady. "I shall soon clear up the matter when I tell you I have been eight years a wife yet have nothing to show for so much time spent in matrimony but a great estate without an heir to it. And there lies the bitter pill that takes away the sweets of life; that is the cutting blow, the smarting wound my husband always feels. 'Tis that, alas ... and could I ... but, O spare a farther declaration and guess the rest."

"No, madam," returned Sir John, "I can guess at nothing till

I see your face and if that proves good, I'll guess just as you would have me, though I think you have spoke so very plain that you have left no room for anything but certainty."

The lady unmasked and showed a face both fair and young, which our knight liked so well that nothing could be denied. No resistance is force against so fine a temptation, yet still he wanted to know the tempter's name. But that at first she was resolved to conceal, which proved no bar to his invited desires which were always too sharp set to want a poignant sauce. She told him, however, she was a woman of distinction; that she could not promise he should ever see her face again; but, by that honor she was now going to sacrifice, he should hear from her and have a just account of the success that attended the present undertaking. They retired, and I left them to go back to the ladies whom I found in much disorder at what had happened so lately to them.

Miss Wary, a cunning young baggage, would have it that Sir John Galliard had certainly some ill design upon the sea nymph and was sure it was more than chance that conducted them to the bagnio. Miss Friendly could not be of her mind for several reasons: first, she was sure that Sir John had too great a value for her papa to offer anything ill to his daughter; besides, her opinion in general was too good of him to believe he would do an ill action to anybody. And it signified nothing to enumerate reasons against a perfect improbability, since, had his inclinations been never so vicious, the bagnio was a place as improper for such an undertaking as a tavern or any other public house.

"You are mistaken, madam," said Miss Wary. "Those places for a small sum will find a thousand ways to avoid discoveries and prevent disturbance. My papa, when he was in commission for the peace, had several of those things brought before him. And I once heard a gentleman say a bagnio was no more than a tolerated bawdy house."

"Say no more, my dear Kitty," replied Miss Friendly. "I will hear no more of it till I see Sir John and hear what he says for himself. But come," continued she, "will you go with me and let us go to bed for an hour or two, for fear we should fall asleep at the play anon, where I am resolved to go at night, because it will be the last I shall see while I stay in town. Tomorrow you have engaged me, and on Monday I must set forward towards the West." They changed their clothes, and went together, got their breakfasts, and went to bed.

In the afternoon Sir John came to see how they did after their last night's diversion.

"O Lud! Sir John!" cried Miss Friendly, "I am glad to see you alive. I expected tomorrow's journal would have given some dismal account of your proceedings with the little gentleman. I hear he followed you for satisfaction. But as I see your arm is not confined to a scarf, I hope you came off with honor."

"Yes, madam," replied Sir John, "pretty well. We had indeed a little skirmish but it was soon over and we parted good friends at last."

"But the adventure of the bagnio, Sir John," said Miss Wary, "methinks I would fain be let into the secret of that scheme, which seems to have a sort of an unaccountable oddness in it that will not be presently answered for."

"L—d! madam," replied Sir John, "I am surprised that you that know the town should take notice of a few blundering chairmen. They heard the gentleman, I suppose, that dogged me give order to the bagnio and thought they were to go there too."

Miss Wary told him that would never hold, because it was plain he had given orders to the chairmen before the gentleman came out whose design was to dog them. "Besides, if it was a mistake, why did not Miss Friendly's chair go with the rest?"

"Well, well, Sir John," interrupted Miss Friendly, "suppose we leap over all those difficulties. How will you excuse yourself when you are charged with taking a couple of ladies to the masquerade and wanted both good manners and gallantry to see them safe home again?"

"Nay, ladies," said Sir John, "if ye both fall foul upon me at once, I must strike my flag and surrender. But be pleased to remember you denied me the pleasure of waiting on you there, which will a little excuse my behavior afterwards. Though I would not have lost the honor of seeing you back, had not that little trifler with his foolish punctilios prevented me. And yet methinks it pleases me when I remember how I revenged myself. But I now ask ten thousand pardons for all the faults you can charge me with, that so we may part friends. For my errand now is to take my leave of you, having engaged myself to accompany a friend who is going to take a trip to France. This afternoon we go on shipboard; so, ladies, if ye have any commands to that nation, I am at your service to convey them."

"O Lud!" cried Miss Friendly, "here's manners! Why, did you not make us promise to go with you to the play tonight? And now he is going to France. Pray go and tell the creature you have a pre-engagement upon your hands and you can't go till the next fair wind."

Sir John made some scurvy apology for his non-compliance and took his leave. He was now resolved to try another expedient to accomplish his design upon Miss Friendly and to lay it upon so sure a foundation that even Fate itself should hardly have power to baffle it. He went directly to his lodgings and sent for his apothecary, telling him he had now a very urgent occasion for his assistance, though of a different nature from anything he had ever served him in yet. He told him in very plain terms he had a mind to a certain young lady of whom he did not despair though he should use no clandestine means. But he had a reason for working with the mole underground and had rather have her unknown to herself than with her own consent, in order to which he desired him to make a private conveyance of some opiate into a few macaroons (which was what the lady greatly loved) to cause a lethargy for some hours and desired it might operate as soon as possible. This was no sooner proposed than complied with, because Sir John was an excellent customer and his bribe pretty large. The prepared macaroons were speedily brought, and in three hours after eating they were to begin their work.

He no sooner saw himself master of the soporiferous dose than he resolved to try the effects of it, which he did that night on a maidservant in the house where he lodged. He found it answered his expectations and in the morning he called for his groom, ordered him to saddle his horse which he mounted and unattended left London. He went to the inn where he knew the innocent sacrifice must lie the first night upon the road and thought it fit to be there two or three days before his victim, that he might have time to corrupt one of the servants to assist him in his base design against poor innocent Miss Friendly. He well knew a plebian mind was never proof against the persuasive power of tempting gold, a metal which insensibly diffuses itself into every sense we have and by a magic forces a liking, though death and ruin be its attendants.

Sir John, the base, ungenerous Sir John, is now got to the inn, where he soon singled out one of the wenches for his tool. He saw she thought herself handsome and knew the only way to get into her favor was to make her believe he thought so too. In order to which, he praised her beauty and told her of much more than she ever had, which with a kiss now and then and half a crown sometimes, made him the finest gentleman that ever came that road before. He soon saw he gained ground and at night, after having sat up pretty late with a silly landlord whom he made very drunk, he ordered Sarah, his chosen accomplice, to bring a pint of wine into his chamber and come up with it herself, which she readily did. Sir John had no occasion to make use of his opiate. The wench was very complying and he, to strengthen his interest in her, gave her leave to take share of his bed that night.

In the morning he began to think of letting her into the secret that brought him there. "Sarah," said he, "I am now going to trust you with a very grand concern, and after what has passed betwixt us, I hope I may confide in you. This night I expect a young lady to come to this house, with whom I had once an intrigue. A little misunderstanding happened betwixt us and I would fain make my peace with her again. Now, Sarah, what I have to beg of you is to convey me privately into some part of her chamber, where I may lurk till she is in bed. And when you have done this piece of service, you shall have a very suitable reward."

Sarah, who was too profuse of her own chastity to endeavor the preservation of that of another, not only complied with what was already proposed but promised her farther assistance if any more was necessary. Sir John, upon this promise, produced the macaroons and asked her if she could by some clean contrivance give one half to the lady and the other to her maid. At which the wench looked a little startled and told Sir John she hoped there was no poison in them, for she did not much care to be hanged neither. "No," replied the knight, "to cure your suspicion, see here I eat one of them myself," which he did. Sarah was satisfied, promised to assist, and then went to call up the guests to be gone.

O Man! How strong are thy passions, how exorbitant thy desires, and how weak, how impotent thy virtues! Here have we a person of birth, of fortune, of sense before us, a man who might have been a credit both to his country and species, had the early rudiments of that behavior which makes us value one another been timely instilled while his tender years were capable of impression. But, alas! the want of care in his education made him a perfect *Modern Fine Gentleman,* which, when we consider the sad ingredients, they made a very woeful compound. It is true if we abstract bad actions from folly (which in my humble opinion can hardly be done) Sir John was very free from the imputation of a fool, but then he had a double share of the rake to make up his *quantum* and finish a very bad character.

The close of evening brought in the stagecoach and in it the pretty lady expected. Sarah, that b — — — —, was ready at hand when she desired, as soon as she alighted, to choose her room. She conducted her to one which she knew fit for the design in hand, with two beds in it (for Sir John had told her before that the lady's maid always lay in her room but never in her bed). She pitched upon the first she saw and being a little weary with her journey and sadly tired of the dull company in the coach, she threw herself upon one of the beds and dozed till supper. Sir John saw her at some distance but kept *incog.* himself and felt a remorse for what he was about to do, but it proved too weak to conquer. While Miss Friendly was with her disagreeable company at supper, Sir John was conveyed into a closet which he locked withinside and there stayed till his time came of coming out.

Supper was no sooner over than poor Miss Friendly returned to her chamber with her maid who was just going to undress her lady when Sarah came into the room with a little salver of sweetmeats in her hand.

"Here, madam," said she, "I have brought you a present."

"A present!" replied the lady. "From whom, prithee?"

"Oh, madam," said Sarah, "from a very civil gentleman, I'll assure you. I am sure I have experienced his kindness more than once. He saw you alight out of the coach and bid me pay his devoirs (I think he called it) to you and beg you would please to taste two or three of the finest macaroons you ever tasted in your life."

"I believe," said Miss Friendly, "the gentleman is a witch, for I know nothing I love so well as a macaroon. Here, Jenny," continued she, "I know you love them as well as I. Take them three, and I'll eat the rest, for my supper lies on my stomach and I can master no more. As for the rest, sweetheart, you may either eat them yourself or return them with my humble service and thanks to the gentleman. And be sure you call me early, for I always take a deal of time to persuade myself to leave my bed in the morning."

The jade dropped her courtesy, promised obedience, and away she went. While Jenny was undressing her lady, "I wonder, madam," said she, "where Sir John Galliard is now? He can't be got to France yet, can he, madam?"

"I do not know," returned Miss Friendly, "where he is nor what time it takes to go such a voyage, but I think he left the kingdom very abrutly. And I daresay Lady Galliard will not be pleased with his ramble, but what is that to me?"

"Nay, madam," replied Jenny, "I know your indifference pretty well and dare lay my head to a row of pins you do not value one man upon earth, or name any for whom you have a superior esteem. If you could, you would certainly talk a little of young Mr. Wary. That's the man for my money—a man that has everything good in him, sober, virtuous, and rich, and...."

"Why, thy tongue's upon wheels I think," interrupted Miss. "What dost thou tell me of his virtue and stuff. I'll think of nobody yet. But when I do, for all your head to two or three pins, I can tell you I should value Sir John Galliard with all his faults much more than young Wary with all his fine qualities. Such a deal of reserve and gravity becomes a young man as ill as frolics and gaiety does an old one. And he that gives himself such exact airs will doubtless expect the same from his wife. And for my part, I love an easy, open, free behavior, guarded by innocence, and would not for the world be forced to sit primming and screwing my face into a prudish, hypocritical look. Oh, Jenny, I always suspect those sort of women and believe there are more faults committed under a sanctified phyz than are commonly found among such giddy girls as I am."

"Lord, madam," replied Jenny, "you talk like any angel tonight. I wish Sir John was a mouse in some hole to hear the declaration you have made in his favor. He would hardly sleep a wink all night for joy."

"You are mistaken," answered Miss. "Sir John is not much transported with women's favors; he is too well used to 'em to set any price upon them. Neither are my thoughts of him so free from reflections as they were once. I cannot reconcile the story of the bagnio to honor and am sometimes forced to think my own safety was owing to my change of dress."

"O ingratitude!" cried Jenny, "if that be true all mankind are monsters. But, madam, you forget you must be early up. Will you please to think of going to bed?"

"Yes," said Miss Friendly, "and to sleep, too, for I begin to grow drowsy."

Sir John was all this while snug in the closet where he heard all and sometimes wished it out of his power to ruin the lady. But his scheme was laid and all things succeeded to his wish. The time came, the lady asleep in one bed, her maid in another, and Sir John had all the opportunity he expected. As soon as he heard the least stirring in the house he got up, called for his horse, gave Sarah her reward, and away he rode to London as fast as his horse could carry him.

The guests at the inn were now calling up to be gone, but Miss Friendly and her maid could by no means be awaked. The whole house was alarmed and surprised; a doctor was sent for who, when he came, said they had taken some stupifying dose and all the art of man could not bring them to their reason till it was slept off. Sarah was frighted out of her wits and feared they would die, but kept her own counsel, as anybody else would have done. The coachman stood swearing and would fain have gone without them but not one of the passengers would go into the coach till they came. At last Miss Friendly came to herself and in a quarter of an hour more so did her maid. They were both surprised at what had happened but made haste to get on their clothes and proceeded on their journey, but continued drowsy and out of order all day. At night when they came to their inn, Miss Friendly ordered her supper to be brought up into her own chamber, the better to procure an opportunity of talking with her maid.

"Jenny," said she, "I am strangely embarrassed about this sleepy fit you and I have had and am entirely of the doctor's opinion that it was no natural repose. Yet where to place either the deceit or design of it I know not, but my whole thoughts have been chained to that one single subject all this day. Prithee, what is thy opinion of the matter?"

"Indeed, madam," replied Jenny, "my thoughts have had as little variety as yours, nor am I less perplexed to find out what I am sure has a secret in the bottom. But whence it sprung, or what drift they had is past my comprehension. I am only vexed I did not ask the maid at the inn from whom she had the sweetmeats she brought. For, if there was any design at all against you, it was certainly lodged in the macaroons because, madam, you may please to remember, neither you or I eat of anything else."

"That," answered Miss Friendly, "is what increases my astonishment, because they certainly came from somebody that knows how fond I am of them. But are you sure, Jenny, you locked the door before you went to bed, for there is a great deal in that one article."

"Yes, madam," answered Jenny, "I am very sure I locked it, but I doubt it was open in the morning, or how did everybody get in?"

"Perhaps," replied the poor lady in tears, "they broke it open when they could not awake us. But be it how it will, I fear I am ruined past redemption."

Jenny seemed confounded at what her lady said and was now sorry she had owned so much. But while she was striving to remove her lady's fears, a servant came up and said a gentleman below inquired for one Mistress Friendly. But her late disturbance gave her a new concern and she trembling answered she would see nobody.

"Yes, my dear," said a voice behind, "you will see me, I am sure."

She soon knew it was her father's, who, with a tenderness worthy of that name, was come to meet her, the sight of whom for some time banished her concern and she recalled her own pretty temper to entertain him with cheerfulness. After she had inquired after her mamma's health and such things, supper came up and as they eat Mr. Friendly kindly inquired after Sir John Galliard. Miss told him he went to France about three days before she came from London but believed it was rather a frolic than any desire he had to travel.

"Methinks," replied Mr. Friendly, "I feel pain for the mismanagement of that young gentleman, because, next to my own, I have a tenderness for him. And it would please me more to see him Old Sir John in behavior and principles than to increase my estate some hundreds in a year."

"Indeed, Papa," said Miss, "my brother and I have little

cause to thank you for that. But I hope there is a great deal more expectations of your doing one than seeing the other."

"Why, child," answered Mr. Friendly, "do you hope so? I have enough to make ye both easy in life. And should a luxurious superfluity take place against the good of our neighbor? No! I am so far from retracting what I have said that I would freely give some hundreds out of what I already enjoy to see him what I wish. It is a poor sordid spirit that is confined to itself only. A generous good man has an extensive fund of good wishes for all mankind in general, but in a particular manner for his friends and those he loves."

"Truly, sir," replied the pert chambermaid, "if Sir John Galliard goes on as he begins, for aught I know he may come to thank you for all you can spare him."

"Forbid it, Heaven," said the good old man, "that he should ever want my bounty! But if he does, while I have life and six pence, he shall share the latter." Too kind, too generous a declaration in favor of one whose black ingratitude made him the least deserving of such strict, such noble friendship.

The worthy gentleman and his darling daughter got safe home the next day, and Sir John was now again at London entertaining his five senses with every modish delight. But though he had always indulged himself in libertine principles and believed that man was made for nothing but to gratify his own sensual desires, yet the secret impulses of his mind (which he was very loath to call conscience) often gave him the lie and told him a curb was sometimes as necessary for man as beast. He could not reflect on the base action he had so lately done to an innocent virgin, the only daughter of a most worthy gentleman who loved him and had given him a thousand demonstrations that he did so, one whose seasonable counsels had once made an impression on his mind, given with all the sweetness, candor and affection in the world, though now worn off to make way for every contrary quality. He could not think on those things without remorse and short-lived pangs, which he always suppressed and stifled with some faulty new delight.

Drinking has too often been used as an amulet against troublesome thoughts, which for some time stuck pretty close to our knight, and which he endeavored to drown in burgundy and champagne. But as drinking was not his favorite vice, he soon left that off and struck into the Groom-Porter's,[11] where his worse luck pursued him close and in one hour he saw himself rooked out of all his money, watch, ring, and everything of value he had about him. He now in a rage flung out and called a coach to go home, though he had not a shilling left to pay the hire and, in compliance with a weak resolution, swore he would never go there again.

But in two hours' time the spirit of revenge took place of the fretful devil in his breast and he went for a new recruit. With which he pointed again towards the Groom-Porter's and though he feared he should not meet with the proper person on whom he would willingly vent his spleen, even he was the first man he saw, to whom he immediately gave a challenge to meet him, not with sword and pistol behind some old house but with box and dice at a public gaming table. The brave antagonist answered the bold challenger and to it they went again. Sir John set high and for some time seemed a favorite of Madam Fortune's. But her wheel turned of a sudden and in half an hour's time he lost an hundred guineas in ready money and double the sum to be paid upon honor in three months.

But all those amusements did not answer their end which should have driven the injured Miss Friendly out of his head, but on the contrary set him on thinking more than ever. And in

[11] "The Groom-Porter was an officer in the Royal Household, whose duty it was to tend the King's apartments and see that it was supplied with cards, dice, and other gambling appurtenances. At Christmas he was allowed to keep an open gaming-table. It was also part of his duty to supervise and license all gambling-houses and take action against those not conducted in an orderly fashion. Action was seldom taken, however, against ill-conducted gambling dens, and the utmost rioting frequently took place in the Groom-Porter's own gaming house." (Edward Ward, *The London Spy*, ed. Arthur L. Hayward [London, 1927], p. 200 n.) See also Pope's note on line 310, Book II, *The Dunciad*.

his intervals, when reason was admitted and a serious thought had leave to thrust in, he fancied all his ill-luck was sent him upon her account but that he presently stifled and cried to himself:

"Z – – – – s, fool, there's nothing in't. Conscience! D – – n the bugbear! 'Tis a cursed imposition forced upon man to keep his freeborn mind in subjection and make him a slave to the caprices of a whimsical priest. No, Galliard," continued he, "regard not what is past, but study to gratify the present, and to come. If our lives are confined to a few years, who would lose a moment's pleasure? We are sure of what we have, but what is to come is uncertain. Therefore, as an industrious tradesman takes daily care to provide for his family, so will I for my delights. He that wants courage to pursue his pleasures has lost the gust of life and like a tethered horse, sees his confinement to a fairy circle of the same food without the least prospect of dear variety."

This sensual soliloquy set our knight upon searching after new pleasures. He had heard very much of a goodly set of men who distinguished themselves by the name of the Hell-Fire Club[12] and thought if he could but made friends to get himself initiated a member of that glorious daredevil society, he should be a complete *Modern Fine Gentleman*. But before they would admit him, they resolved to try his courage and a small detachment from the whole body was selected to make the experiment. Sir John was ordered to meet them in St. Martin's churchyard about one o'clock in the morning, where on a tombstone were set wine and glasses with no light but a bundle of brimstone matches set on fire. And if Sir John could devoutly drink a health to the Devil without hesitation or being shocked, he was from that time to be reckoned one of them. If not, he was to be cashiered and fined twenty marks for the use of the club as a just punishment for his impudence in pretending to what he durst not go through-

[12] There seem to have been several of these clubs in the early eighteenth century. On April 28, 1721, George I issued a royal proclamation to stop the atheistical activities of a Hell-fire Club headed by the Duke of Wharton. The more famous Hell-fire Club of John Wilkes was founded about 1745.

stitch with. But Sir John most heroically saved both his money and credit, having the honor to begin the health himself.

Sure the liquor must be hot where the Devil's the toast, and the health very ridiculous where the Being is denied. But the saucy watch interrupted their diabolical mirth, or rather they disturbed the watch by giving the first onset, who, proving a parcel of sturdy fellows, fell on without many words and routed the whole herd. Some they took prisoners and some took to their heels. Sir John was among the runaways and made his escape saying the Devil might have had more manners than to see them routed by a parcel of scoundrels while they were showing so much civility to him.

He was now arrived at the end of his one-and-twentieth year and had by that time run the gauntlet through every vice of the town, which is not improperly so called since every vice has its lash and chastised him as he went. His drinking made him sick, his gaming made him poor, his mistresses made him unsound, and his other faults gave him sometimes remorse, though, as he had neither innate principles of virtue or the prejudices of a good education to wear off or struggle with, he in the main made himself very easy.

One day, as he was going through a certain street, he saw an old lady of his acquaintance called Mother N – – d – – m standing at her door.[13] She blessed herself (which was very rare) at the sight of Sir John Galliard whom she began to reproach for his long absence. He excused himself by saying he had now left off all those things, was resolved to live honest, and keep just one lady or two for his own diversion and have nothing to do with any more. But she, good creature, was not willing they should part so and therefore threw the old bait in his way. She told him she had a curious fine girl in the house that was just come out of the country, brought by a fellow that would fain have ravished her but she was resolved there should be no such

---

[13] Mother Needham, described by Pope (*The Dunciad*, Book I, lines 323–324) as "pious Needham." In the 1756 edition of the novel the name is changed to "Mother D – g – ns," whom I have not identified.

disorderly doings in her house. So she believed he was gone to take a lodging for her, and if Sir John would walk in, he should see her and try to gain her favor. This was a temptation too strong to be resisted by the knight. He struck in after the bawd who conducted him upstairs to a little room where, before they entered, they heard the poor young creature cry most pitifully. The old one entered first and after her Sir John. The girl in tears thought it had been her ravisher returned and cried: "Kill me, kill me, for I'll never be your wife. I had rather be torn to pieces than marry my brother's footman."

"No, my sweet child," said old Jezebella, "this is not the rogue that would have ravished you. This is a fine young gentleman that is come to help you."

At that the young lady turned her blubbered face towards him and on a sudden got up, ran to him with open arms and cried aloud, "My brother, my brother!" This was extremely surprising to Sir John, who knew her not because her face was so disguised with tears. He stood some time to consider her and asked her many questions before he could believe it really was his sister, all which she answered so pertinently that he no longer doubted the truth. Then he inquired how she came there and what rogue's hands she was fallen into.

She said one evening just after she and the rest of the misses had supped, Tom, that was once his footman and afterwards her mamma's steward, came to the boarding school where she was placed and told her mamma had sent for her to go home for a week or a fortnight.

"I was glad," continued she, "and got ready presently. He took me up behind him, nobody suspecting but that he was sent as he said and at night after he had rid very hard he brought me to an inn and said Mamma was gone to London and he was to carry me after her. I still was better pleased and never doubted but he told me true. So he brought me to this house three days ago and asked me if I would marry him? Then I spit at him and asked for Mamma. He told me she was at Galliard Hall and if I would marry him he would carry me back tomorrow morning, but if I refused him, he would ravish me and then sell me to the Turks. And he would have been as good as his word, if this kind lady here had not come to help me. He is now gone to get a lodging where he said he would do what he pleased with me and if you leave me, I am sure he will kill me."

"No," replied Sir John, "you are now very safe, but I would fain see how far this dog's villainy will go. I am resolved to abscond when I hear him coming and desire you will behave as if you knew of no help at hand."

"O," said the poor young lady, "I tremble to think I shall ever see him more. I hear his voice; he is just coming."

Sir John and the old woman stepped into a closet in the room and Tom came upstairs.

"Come, madam," cried he, "I am now provided of a lodging where I may do as I see fit and will now tell you 'tis neither love or lust that makes me desire either to marry or lie with you. It is sweet revenge that spurs me on and you alone are destined for the mark."

"Revenge?" she said. "Why, what have I done to you?"

"Nothing, madam," answered Tom. "You are innocent. So was my poor wife and yet she suffered by your mother's faulty hand and so shall you by mine. Make no noise; if you do, I shall find a way to silence it. Come, prepare. Put on your geers[14] and submit your neck to the yoke I have provided for it."

"Stay," answered Sir John, coming out of the closet, "and prepare your own for that halter which will certainly fall to your share. Villain, what has thou said and what are the grounds of thy accusation? Speak quickly or thou has spoke thy last. Dog, make haste; I cannot hold my hands."

Tom was so confounded at the unexpected sight of his late master that he stood like one struck dumb, but fear of losing a worthless wretched life gave his tongue its usual motion and he begged his master to suspend his just resentment till he could lay before him all his wrongs which required a more private place than they were now in. But Sir John, who could consider a little

---

[14] Clothes, possession.

upon occasion, feared he should hear more of what he knew too much already and that the fellow might have too just a cause for complaints and therefore thought good to dismiss him with no other chastisement than a broken pate. This was the first time Sir John Galliard ever commanded his passion and it must stand as a monument raised to his prudence, since a higher resentment would have set the world upon inquiring after the cause, which would only have spread a mother's infamy and brought a slur on a sister's character. He therefore stayed where he was. Night came on to favor the escape of the latter out of a very scandalous house, the principal of which (though a notorious bawd) he was now forced to have some value for, because her invitation (though a criminal one) had saved an only sister from a very black design.

As soon as it was dark, his footman brought a coach to the door and he conveyed the lady to his own lodgings, where she was no sooner arrived than she begged to go to bed, for her late fright and want of rest had left her no spirits. Her lodgings were immediately got ready and she as soon got into them, where a quiet mind lulled her to that repose which a troubled one had for some nights deprived her of. Sir John, after the young lady retired, sat a while to consider of the late adventure which soon worked itself off to make way for something more pleasing. His darling diversion was intriguing, which he carried on with so much address that he had a mistress in almost every street in town, which had impaired his estate as well as constitution and left both in a declining condition. But he is now undisputed master of a fine hereditary estate which he made a little too bold with in his nonage, yet a future good management will retrieve all.

He now sat considering with which of his madams he should spend the rest of the evening when his man came up and told him a lady in a coach at the door inquired for him.

"She is come," said he, "in a very good time to end my disputes. Pray bid her come up," not doubting but it was one of the fair ones he wanted. She no sooner entered than he saw it was Lady Galliard with a look that spoke the inward troubles of her mind and, ere he could approach her, she burst into tears.

It is certain that faulty lady's past behavior had taken away very much of that love and duty which is due from a child to a parent, but Sir John, conscious of his own innumerable faults, would willingly at that time have cried quits. And though his brutish way of living had almost unmanned him, he yet felt some returns of nature pleading in behalf of a disturbed mother, the cause of whose distress he knew and pleased himself to think he soon should end it. He ran to her and took her in his arms, saying, "Why, madam, are you thus afflicted? Am I the unhappy cause? Or does some new misfortune wait upon your hours? Believe me, madam, I will contribute to your ease if I have it in my power and beg I may share the heavy load in hopes of making yours the lighter." Lady Galliard's weight was great indeed, for she lay under the pressures of a wounded mind and often told herself the misfortunes that attended her children were heaped upon them for her faults.

"Sir John," said she, "my troubles flow from too many fountains and if I complain of your conduct, I shall doubtless hear of my own. I confess I am ashamed of one and grieve for both. I, wretched I, am destined to misfortunes. Your sister is irrecoverably lost, conveyed away, but spare my shame and ask me not by whom."

"No, madam," replied Sir John, "I need not ask by whom. I know much more of that affair than you imagine. Dry up your tears. Your daughter is safe and under my protection. Her better genius sent me in a very critical hour to her rescue, which saved her from a chain of ills designed her. But how were my ears filled with horror when I heard a mother accused of something that sounded much like murder."

"How!" said Lady Galliard, "and did my accuser go away with life?"

"F – – th, Madam," returned Sir John, "I was once going to stab the rascal but considered 'twas a pity to take his life for complaining of his wrongs. But no more—this subject must needs be ungrateful to us both and I beg it may drop. My sister is in this house, to whom I will convey you after some repast. In the meantime I must inquire after my country acquaintance. How does Mr. Friendly and all his family do?"

"Do?" replied Lady Galliard. "Have you never heard of their misfortune. I own I was not willing to send you word of it, because I would not spread the poor young lady's shame, but she has now a child. And to complete her wretched character and make herself a jest to everybody, she says and persists that nobody got it. And both she and her maid tells a most silly story of some sleepy sweetmeats sent by nobody knows who, with so many other circumstances that poor Mr. Friendly, when they first found out she was with child, went back to the inn where it seems the scene was laid to inquire a little into the matter, but the maid who brought the bait was gone away with child and nobody knew where. This was so far from giving our poor neighbor any satisfaction that it doubled his grief and he now languishes under such a profound disorder that the whole neighborhood is in pain for his life, which most people think will soon be ended."

At this account Sir John turned pale and trembled exceedingly, which Lady Galliard took notice of and said, "I see your gratitude to that good man in your concern for him and am pleased at it, because I know he loves you almost equal to his own, defends your faults when he hears you blamed for them, calls them the follies of youth which your reason, when grown a little stronger, will suddenly banish, calls you his dear Sir John and always names you with the tenderness of a father."

At this Sir John, in spite of manhood and his love to vice, dropped a conscious tear which, when he had wiped away, he thus proceeded: "But how, madam," continued he, "does the young lady behave under her misfortunes? Have you seen her lately?"

"No," returned Lady Galliard, "she has put herself into half-mourning, keeps her chamber, cries continually, and sees nobody but her brokenhearted parents, her maid and child. Her brother was sent to travel before the thing was known so that he is happily a stranger to it all."

"Would I were so too," replied the knight, "for I feel the utmost pangs of grief for that dear wretched family."

Lady Galliard now grew impatient to see her daughter, whom she was loath to disturb, but after a light supper Sir John conducted her to the young lady's bed. They met each other with a mutual joy and Lady Galliard took a lodging with her for that night.

Sir John returned to his own apartment and flung himself upon his bed where gratitude, humanity, good nature and pity began to have their places in his breast. "O Galliard," said he, "wretched Galliard, what hast thou done? And how hast thou for a few hours of brutal pleasure entailed an infamy upon a whole family, nay, upon a family that always loved thee even in spite of thy own demerits and with a tender care endeavored to wash out the stains of thy character? And hast thou in return of so much goodness branded theirs with an eternal disgrace? Had I taken the lovely creature's jewel by her own consent she had shared the crime with me, but to violate her honor without her knowledge is laying her under Cassandra's fate always to speak truth but never to be believed. For who will credit a woman that says she has a child which never had a father? So that, base as I am, I have not only laid her innocence under the character of a whore but have made her a jest to all mankind, when she asserts so great a truth as that she never knew a man."

But then as if he had a war within his breast betwixt his good and evil angels, he started up and cried, "Avaunt, ye tender motions of my soul, and leave me free as air to revel in some new, some fresh delights, the force of which may bear superior weight and crush the poor relenting thoughts of pity. It is more than sufficient I have destroyed their peace. I'll now endeavor to preserve my own. But then, the dear injured girl. . . . Why, what of her?" Again he cried, "Is she not a woman and was she not made for the pleasure and delight of man? Away, fond thoughts, I'll hear no more nor give a farther audience to thy impertinent harangues. Begone, I say, and trouble me no more." We may here see the struggles betwixt nature and a loose education, each armed with weapons to defend itself, and sometimes one and sometimes t'other's victor.

The next morning Lady Galliard, whose mind was much easier since the recovery of her daughter, would fain have persuaded Sir John to make her perfectly happy and go with her into the country to take a full possession of his fine estate, but that was a work required more than a little time to finish. A single persuasion was not sufficient nor any arguments strong enough to remove our knight which, when Lady Galliard saw, she resolved to take her daughter and be gone without him. But first she paid off his debts, both of honor and extravagance, after which she made the following speech:

"You are now, Sir John, set free in the world, both from debt and all restraint, sole master of a large and disentangled estate, which one would think impossible for one single person to encumber. But that I am forced to leave to your own discretion, for if you condemned my advice while you were yet a minor, I have little reason to believe it will meet with a ready acceptance now you are perfectly your own master. Yet if my entreaties could be of any force, I should urge them in your own behalf and beg you would not live without thought."

"Madam," returned Sir John, "if I make an excusive answer, it will certainly be attended with some reproach which I would fain avoid. It is certain that very few people's lives are concluded without some faulty scenes which may perhaps leave a sting behind, and yet for my part, I must grow weary of pleasure before I leave it, and to strike into rules of gravity while we are boys is to be born old and never know the pleasures of youth."

"I find, sir," answered Lady Galliard with some disorder, "the guilty are to be no instructors. Yet they that make a trip once need not stumble as long as they live, nor is it necessary that he who steals an egg for his dinner should be an accomplice with one who breaks a house. I am far from excusing my own failings of which I shall ever be ashamed, but you may remember when you convicted me how full of bitter invectives you were against me, and yet your behavior since has only shown that we are readier to spy small faults in others than great ones in ourselves. I am sorry there is any to be found between us, but since you would hint that example goes so far, let that of contrition find a place and leave your faults by the same example you act them."

"Methinks, madam," returned Sir John, "it give me a little pain to hear you call your actions small faults and hope you will please to consider the vast disparity betwixt both our ages and sexes. There are a thousand things perhaps not very innocent which I may act and no notice taken of them, which in you would draw the eyes of everybody towards them. Women are naturally modest, men naturally impudent, and, in short, there is no comparing the actions of one with the other."

This dialogue which admitted of something pretty sharp on both sides was interrupted by a voice below inquiring for Sir John. Lady Galliard withdrew and the stranger was introduced, on whose face Sir John no sooner cast his eye than he saw it was the little gentleman with whom he had had an intrigue at the bagnio some time before, and now again in man's apparel. Sir John received her with some transport and warmth which she returned with bare good manners and a modest indifference. The knight told her he was a little impatient to know the effect of their last meeting and whether it answered the wished-for intent. She told him no, she could not say it had, though there was a child, but it proved a daughter.

Sir John was not long before he kindly offered his service to get a son. The lady told him she was very ready to comply with only one proviso. "You are to know, Sir John, my errand to you now is very different from my last and, as I then tendered you my honor, I would now recall it and give you in its place my heart, which is now by the death of my spouse at my disposal. He has left me a very plentiful estate and the present question is do you like my person, face and fortune well enough to take me for your own with no other fault than what you are a sharer in. If so, you will find me mistress of fifteen hundred pounds a year and yourself master of both."

Sir John looked a little queer at the proposal and told the lady he had no objection either against herself or circumstance, but matrimony was a monster he should never have courage enough to encounter with, said he should be glad to serve her in any other capacity, and should take the sight of his child as a very particular favor. "But z – – – ds, madam," continued he, "a husband is a d – – – – d name for a man that hates confinement and loves variety as much as I do. Beside, marriage is the direct road to indifference, where we travel a few days and then strike into that of hatred, variance, strife, noise, and the D – – – l and all. No, madam, if we design to love, let us live single. A man may preserve an appetite that takes only a snack bye the bye, but a full meal very often gorges the stomach and turns to loathing and surfeit."

"Sir John," replied the lady, with some emotion, "I would not have your vanity swell too high upon this occasion, nor fancy the offer I have made you proceeds from any extraordinary liking I have to your person but entirely from the reflection of your being the undoubted father of my child, since I never came into a bed with my spouse after I had been with you. At my return I found him ill of a fever which increased till it killed him. I then forbore to write to you till I saw the event of the foolish action I had committed and then resolved either to be the lawful wife of Sir John Galliard or never know a man again."

"Why, upon my s – – l, madam," returned the knight, "I must own myself obliged to you that are so very willing to give up all your charms entirely to me. But as my person is not the inducement, I hope no violent action will ensue from my refusal. But prithee, widow, let me see the child. F – – – h, methinks I long to look at something that may prove my manhood. Come, I'll give it a whistle and bells."

"Your child, Sir John," replied she, "wants no whistle but is far from hence and so am I when I am at home. And since your principles hang so loose about you, I shall think it very fit to keep her at a distance lest their infection should reach the tender bud and blast each virtue as it grows up in her."

"O madam," replied the fleering knight, "the girl, I warrant you, will never want virtue while the father and mother are both so well stocked."

That answer cut the poor lady so deep that she burst into tears, told him his reproach was very just and what her folly well deserved, then left him. As soon as she was gone, Sir John called a servant and bid him dog the gentleman who was just gone out and find his lodgings but to keep at such a distance as that he might not perceive he was after him. The footman followed and the lady had not gone far before she called a coach, but the man being not near enough to hear the order where to go, as soon as the gentleman (which he took the lady for) was got in, he whipped up behind and the coach stopped at the Black Swan in Holborn, from whence stagecoaches go to more parts of the kingdom than one. As soon as the coach stopped, the fellow got down and slipped aside till it drove off and then returned and went to the inn. He pulled off his hat with an air of great respect to one of the drawers and desired a mug of Nottingham ale, which when he had brought, he desired he would please to sit down and take share on't. The drawer was surprised at all this civility from a footman, who seldom have any for those above them, much less for their inferiors.

"Pray, master," said Dick the footman, "what do you call the little gentleman who came in here just now?"

"I fancy," said the drawer, "by your manners and ignorance you are just come out of the country. Do you think we trouble our heads with the names of our guests? No, child, our business is to give them what they want and see they don't run away in our debt. But this gentleman you ask after came last night in the ——— ——— stagecoach and goes away again tomorrow morning. He is this minute with the bookkeeper entering his name."

"I was a drawer here myself," said Dick, "about—let me see— how long have you lived here, brother?"

"Lived here?" said the drawer. "Why, I have lived here come the fourth of June next just four years."

"Aye," said Dick, " 'tis just so long since I left it. And what

do you think I was turned away for? Egad! because I would not
nick my chalk and score two for one. A squeamish conscience
never does well in those public houses. But they repented their
parting with me, for I writ a very good hand and always put
down the passengers' names. Can you write, brother? If you will
fetch me the book out of the bar, I will show you my hand in
forty places of it, and I'll lay you a bottle of cider—you have some
profit in the cider, brother, have you not?—that you say mine is
the best hand in the whole book."

"Why," said the drawer, "as you say, I have some little
advantage from the cider and I'll bring the book on purpose to
win the wager, for there is a good deal of my own hand there
and the D – – – l's in't, if I vote against myself."

The book was brought and while Dick was looking for his
own hand which he was sure he should never find, he called aloud
for "The cider! The cider!" saying whoever paid for it he would
help drink it. And while the drawer went to fetch it, Dick turned
to the names and found the last set down for that county was
Mr. Venture-all.

"A Dutchman, I warrant," quoth Dick, "but here comes the
cider. Well done, brother," said Dick, "here take thy book, for
I had rather pay for the liquor and treat thee generously than
give myself any farther trouble to find out what you at last will
deny." They drank the cider which when out Dick paid for it,
and brother-drawer and he parted. Dick posted home (like
Scrub in the *Stratagem*) with a whole budget of news,[15] which
came at last to nothing, for Sir John soon knew the name was a
feigned one, but did his servant justice in owning he took a very
clever way to find it out.

Sometimes Sir John had a mind to go to the inn and inquire
for this Mr. Venture-all. But then he considered the lady had
frankly declared the greatest motive she had in coming to him

---

[15] George Farquhar, *The Beaux' Stratagem*, III, i, 55 ("Madam, I have
brought you a packet of news"). The scene, however, more closely resembles
Act III, iii, 1–116 of the same play, in which Archer drinks with Scrub to
get information about the ladies.

was to make herself as near an honest woman as her fault would admit, which he thought a very bad reason why he should hope for any further favors from her and, as for complying with her proposals, he found himself as inclinable to the other part of destiny where an halter cuts the thread and ends our woes at once. Lady Galliard tried a few more persuasions to get Sir John into the country for a while, but the wild oats he had so long been sowing came up apace and he resolved to stay and reap the crop. She then returned herself and took her daughter with her, leaving Sir John, because she could not help it, to trifle away both time and estate as the D – – – l and he could adjust matters.

Lady Galliard was no sooner gone than he began to think of setting up an equipage, which was no more than what with reason might be expected because every man, according to his ability, ought to support and maintain his own grandeur as well as to help and encourage the trading part of mankind in their honest labors and industry. But as most young heirs are apt to overdo things, his liveries were profusely rich, his attendants extravagantly numerous, to which I may add a train of lavish jilts, daily gaping for unreasonable supplies from his bounty or, to give it a more proper name, from his folly. Those sort of creatures know no bounds when they think they have a purse in view that will answer their impudent demands, an instance of which we may see in what follows.

Sir John, among many mistresses, had one who proved a sort of superior favorite and kept her ground much longer than any of her rivals had done, but she proved a very chargeable one, and Sir John at last found her bestowing her favors on somebody else which he would by no means believe she did. A little odd that a man should expect a whore to be honest. However, it incensed him so far that he turned her off and saw her no more for some months. But one day about Mall-time Sir John accidentally met her in the Park.[16] She soon saw him and gave herself some very grand airs as she passed by him which set the knight a-laughing and, looking after her, cried, "Madam, you have

[16] Late afternoon, in St. James's Park.

dropped your handkerchief," which was his own he had thrown down on purpose. She, resolving to lose nothing though she knew it was not hers and hoping to renew her acquaintance with him, turned about to take it up when Sir John with an air of gallantry stooped and presented her with it saying, "Madam, you know this is not yours. You once had the heart of the owner; why did you throw it away for a trifle?"

"A trifle, sir?" said Madam. "Why, 'tis my business to barter for trifles and if I was willing to part with your heart, why, that was a trifle too. And I would have you to know anybody's trifle that comes with money is as welcome to me as yours is. Beside, I never knew you had recalled your heart. It was so much a trifle indeed that I have not once asked myself what was become on't."

"Ah, Betty, Betty," said the knight, "this is all grimace, for if you had not been angry at parting with my heart, you would never have turned about to angle for't again. Come, I don't care if I dine with you today that we may talk over all with less passion and more love."

"Well," said the half-yielding nymph, "I am ashamed to think how tender my poor heart is which would not so readily soften into a compliance but that I have a mind to hear what you can say for yourself. So if we must dine together, tell me where and maybe I may come, but I won't promise neither."

Sir John, who once did like her and had been long enough from her to fancy her new again, told her he would meet her at the Fountain Tavern[17] and bid her go and bespeak what she herself had a mind to. They then parted and Madam went to the Fountain and ordered a dozen of the largest and fattest fowls they could get to be roasted for Sir John Galliard and his company, which was accordingly done.

The hour of dining being come, Sir John and his lady met as appointed when, to his great surprise, he saw two drawers

[17] The most famous Fountain Tavern was in the Strand, though another existed in Cheapside and Aytoun Ellis in *The Penny Universities* lists one at the entrance to Inner Temple Lane.

enter the room with each a dish and six large fowls apiece and, according to the lady's order, roasted crisp and brown. Sir John stood staring to see two such large dishes of the same food and told the drawers they had mistaken the room.

"Ye couple of blockheads," said he, "do ye think two people can eat up the dinners of twenty men? Or do ye expect the poor of the parish to come and dine with us?"

"Nay, nay, Sir John," answered the lady, "they have not mistaken the room. Set down the fowls," continued she, "and bring up some burgundy, a bottle of Rhenish, and another of German Spa."

The drawers ran to obey the lady while Sir John sat looking sometimes at her and sometimes at the monstrous feast without any manner of variety in it. "Madam," said he, "did you in reality order this dinner? For my part, I am filled with the sight on't and am in full study to find out the hieroglyphic, for certainly there must be one in it. What the D – – – l can it mean?"

"I'll soon explain the riddle," cried the luxurious monster. "You must know, Sir John, I have a great while longed to fill my stomach with the skin and rumps of fat roasted fowls, and that is all I shall eat of these. Now, as you bid me bespeak what I liked, I hope you will not grudge it now 'tis here. But they cool and then they are good for nothing."

So to 'em she fell and had got nine of them flayed before the drawers could return with the wine. Sir John sat with much patience, making some inward reflections upon the cursed extravagancy of such drabs, till he saw the eleventh fowl seized, without so much as one single invitation to him to taste. And seeing that flayed like a rook and the poor remaining one in danger, said, "I am sorry, madam, you did not bespeak two dozen instead of one that I might have dined with you. But since I find here are short commons, I beg you will let me have a wing of this unexcoriated animal and the next time we dine together you shall flay me. Sure the whole race of whores are the offspring of Epicurus."

"I do not believe," replied Madam, "he was any relation of

mine because I never heard of him before. But if he was one that loved a good dinner I am sure he has left a very numerous family behind him. Why sure, Sir John, now you are come to your estate you grow covetous or you would never make a stir about a poor forty shillings reckoning. I dare say that will pay it and if it won't, you may take your guinea again which you gave me a little while ago to help out."

Sir John told her he never clubbed with his wench, paid the house, and left her with a second resolution to see her no more.

The new coach was now mounted on the wheels, and the splendid knight began to make his appearance in all public places, the Drawing Room,[18] the Park, the Mall, the opera, the basset-table, the playhouse and everywhere (except at church) where there was hopes of being very much seen. It must be owned Sir John Galliard had many advantages both from nature and fortune that thousands wanted: his person perfectly agreeable, his sense much too good for the use he put it to, his temper flexible and easy, even to a fault, his dependence centered in itself, and his glaring equipage finished his charms. The young gay part of the female world had an eye upon him from every avenue and no art lay idle that had hopes or prospect of drawing him into the nets and purlieus which were spread in every corner to catch the game. But the bold knight stood armed cap-a-pie in his own defense, bidding defiance to all attacks and firmly resolving to keep his foot out of the stocks of dreadful matrimony. So that the poor ladies had the mortification to see all their artifices entirely baffled and their blooming charms despised. Sir John had now been a great while reduced to the low mercenary drabs of the town and was clogged and grown weary of them, resolving to leave them and hunt out nobler game.

He was one day at the Ring[19] admiring the ladies where he saw in her father's coach the young Miss Wary, formerly spoken of, accompanied by a beautiful young girl, whom he had never seen before. She pleased him much and he licked his lips and told

[18] The Royal Drawing Room at St. James's Palace.
[19] In Hyde Park.

himself he could be very happy in her embraces for a few hours, and resolved next day to visit her companion in order to find out who she was and how he might gain access.

Next morning before he was up, Sir Combish Clutter, an intimate of Sir John's, came to his lodgings or levee and finding him in bed cried, "Z – – – ds, Knight! What the D – – – l dost thou do between thy sheets at this time of day? Why, 'tis now six minutes three seconds past one o'clock, and it is impossible thou should'st get dressed by dinnertime. Besides, I would fain have your company in the afternoon to see my mistress who came to town but two days ago, though I must article with thee, Sir Jacky, not to rival me, and yet I am apt to believe thy persuasive faculty will hardly go much farther than my own. Gad, she's a fine creature, and if you do not say so when you see her, you are a son of a – – – – – ."

"Hold, Sir Combish," returned his friend, "and be assured I will do justice to the lady's charms. But if they prove too strong to be resisted, you must give me leave to try whose persuasive faculty has the most force. But he that does not like his friend's choice underrates his friend's judgment and that, Sir Combish, is worse than making love to his mistress. But where is this sunbeam? And what do you call her?"

"Thy questions," returned Clutter, "will meet with no answer. But get up and let us dine together; then follow me."

Sir John was always ready for a walk where a fine lady stood at the end on't, and therefore without hesitation got out of bed, was presently dressed, and away they went to dinner. Which, when over, and the hour of visiting come, Sir Combish conducted his friend to the lodgings of his mistress which proved to be at Mr. Wary's and the lady the same he had a design upon at the Ring. He secretly gave himself joy of his success and did not fail to promise himself a great deal from the happy circumstances of her being in a house where he had some acquaintance (though not much interest since the bagnio exploit) and being introduced by her lover, as a second good omen from his propitious stars, and resolved to ply her with love the first opportunity that kindly offered, which he swore should never slip through his fingers. He caressed her even before her lover with the extremest gallantry and she must have had a load of Cupid's dust blown in her eyes had she not seen a very considerable difference betwixt Sir John Galliard and Sir Combish Clutter, the latter of which shortened his visit not only to prevent the exchange of glances between Sir John and the lady but to humor his impatience which was in a woundly hurry to have Sir John's opinion of his choice.

They adjourned again to the tavern where Sir John told him his choice was his masterpiece and he had never shown his judgment to so much advantage before. "But I always understood," continued he, "that you were utterly averse to marriage, and yet I fancy the little angel expects nothing more than honorable love."

"Why, aye," returned Sir Combish, "there it is the D – – – l enters with his horns to push us from our easy happiness. 'Tis d – – – – d hard that if we lie with a fine woman once we must be forced to do so as long as we both live, but I don't know. . . . The pretty fool loves me and I think it a pity to break her heart, though I believe a month's enjoyment will change my mind, for a surfeited stomach does not care if the D – – – l had the dish that overcharged it."

"Nay, Knight," replied Sir John, "you outdo me abundantly, for as well as I love variety, I daresay I could be constant to that lady twice as long as you speak of and retire at last without one nauseating thought. But where the D – – – l didst thou pick up that lovely girl? Prithee marry her and let me (when thou art weary) have her a while. I'll show my humility by being content with thy leavings."

"Aye, b – G – –, Knight, so you may," returned Sir Combish, "for I have taken up with yours more than once, though it was through ignorance. For had I known it, I should as soon have taken a bone you had picked for a repast as a mistress you had discarded for my diversion. But what the D – – – l dost thou see in me to make thee fancy any woman that has once been familiar with me could ever have a taste for anybody else? No, no, Knight, I shall never have one uneasy thought about that affair. E'en win her and wear her, b – G – –. But I bar forestalling the market: no attempts till after consummation, and then. . . . But I must leave thee, Sir Jacky, for I have an assignation upon my hands at Greenwich, which I must answer this once though only to take my leave of a rare brisk girl, and if I thought the jade would listen to my proposal I did not much care if I resigned her over to thee. F – – – h, she has two good qualities—she is sweet and sound, but a little humorsome and pretty expensive."

Sir John thanked him, said he loved to choose his own whores, of which (Venus be praised) there was very good store. And then the two knights parted, one to Greenwich and the other to Mr. Wary's again, under pretense of inquiring after a stray snuffbox.

Sir Combish had with his conceited speeches a little piqued him, which when joined to the liking he had for the lady, made him very industrious to get into her favor. Nay, he was so set upon revenge that he resolved to offer marriage rather than lose the pleasure of it, as doubtless there is a great deal in balking a coxcomb. He found the ladies at picquet and told them if they would change their game he would make one at ombre for an hour or two, which they were pleased with, and to ombre they went. But while the knight's fingers were busied with the cards, his eyes had other employment and were hard at work darting a thousand kind things at the lady's breast, which aimed at nothing but her utter ruin. She understood their talk and returned as much as modesty and a short acquaintance would admit of.

Sir John, well-read in women's looks, beheld all hers with pleasure and being a little willing to sift her inclinations somewhat farther said, "I am glad, madam, I happened to return again and hope I have helped to drive away some of those melancholy minutes that sometimes hang upon a lady's hands in the absence of a favored lover."

"Sir," replied the lady (whom I shall call by the common

name of Belinda), "you would be kind in explaining yourself and telling us who you mean by a favored lover. For my part, I brought a heart to London entirely disengaged and till I see something of higher merit than it can hope to deserve, am resolved to keep it so."

Sir John was pleased at the favorable declaration and hoped it would join with his design, but made the following answer:

"If your heart, madam, be disengaged, what will become of poor Sir Combish, whose hopes of you I have some reason to believe is in a very flourishing condition, and do you now say your heart is disengaged?"

"Sir John," replied Belinda, "if you are well acquainted with Sir Combish Clutter, you must needs know him for a man of too much vanity to believe his offers can be rejected wherever he vouchsafes to tender them. I must own he has been so very condescending as to tell me he liked my person and temper, which doubtless he designed as a very particular favor. And when I have acknowledged it as such and given him my thanks accordingly, he has then all the return he must ever expect from me."

"I think, then," answered Miss Wary, "since you are so indifferent, you had best made a deed of gift to me of Sir Combish. Methinks 'your Ladyship' sounds so prettily upon the tip of every tongue."

"Aye, child," returned Belinda, "the sound is well enough, but if the man that gives us the honor is nothing but sound himself, in my opinion one had as good be tied to a drum. As for giving you Sir Combish, I am very glad it is not in my power, for I never give away anything but what's my own, and I here faithfully promise I will never have a title either to him or from him while I live."

Sir John was giving himself a vast deal of secret pleasure at the hearing of all this when Belinda's maid came in with a letter in her hand for her lady, which she looked upon and knew it was from her sister. She begged leave to withdraw while she read it. Sir John, with his usual gallantry, told her he had much rather dispense with a little breach in foolish decorum than lose the substantial pleasure of her company, though but the short time of reading a letter. "Besides, madam, I see it is a lady's hand which can neither raise a blush in your cheeks or jealousy in my breast."

"Jealousy, Sir John!" returned Belinda. "You surprise me greatly. I thought that silly whim had never taken place anywhere but in the breast of a lover nor there neither, unless he saw violent signs of encouragement given to a rival. But since you tolerate ill manners, I will read my letter which I own I am a little impatient to do." She opened it and found what follows:

"My trembling hand is now employed to tell you my dear child is extremely ill and you well know I share the malady. Fly to see it while alive and help to comfort a distracted sister.
P.S. Dear Bell, make haste."

Sir John, who with inward delight beheld Belinda's fine face, saw it alter and grow pale. He asked the cause of her disturbance. She made no secret of the contents of her letter, said she would be gone next morning but Miss Wary told her that was impossible unless she hired a coach on purpose, for the stage went not until the day after. She answered no consideration should retard her journey, that there were coaches enough to be had for money, which was a trifle compared to the peace of a sister.

Sir John had now an excellent opportunity of showing his compliance by offering his coach to the lady and himself to be her convoy, which he did with an air of so much sincerity and good manners that the young lady hardly knew how to refuse the compliment, though she urged the trouble it must needs give him and that so great a favor could no way be expected from one so much a stranger to her. She begged he would excuse her acceptance and give her leave to take a hackney coach, but Sir John liked the lucky opportunity too well to lose it and therefore most strenuously urged his coach might convey her home. She at last consented and Sir John posted home to give orders for a journey in the morning.

When he was gone the observing Miss Wary, who was no way

his friend, told Belinda she wished her a safe deliverance from him, said a woman's honor in his hands was in much greater danger than a ship in a storm, for there was a possibility of one being saved while the other must inevitably perish, and when she had said so much she told her the reason why she had so low an opinion of him. But Belinda was now prejudiced in favor of Sir John and thought Miss Wary's invectives proceeded rather from a little envy than any real demerit in the knight. She saw nothing in him which displeased her and was resolved to trust to her own virtue and his honor. But Miss Wary, who had not her name for naught, and who well knew the advantageous offers Sir John had often had if he would have resolved to marry, was in too much concern for her friend to let her advice drop till she had given it a little farther. She much feared Sir John's designs were not honorable and therefore proceeded thus:

"Suppose, Belinda, any misfortune should attend you in this journey. Do you not think your prudence would be a very great sufferer, which ought to tell you Sir John Galliard is, in the first place, a perfect stranger to you, and, next, that he is as much a libertine? Remember you have warning given you by one that has known him some time. And what danger may not a young girl, as you are, apprehend from the power of one who never denied himself any satisfaction in life? And what is your maid and you in the hands of him and all his servants? I tremble for the danger you seem to be in and beg you to stay another day and take the stagecoach."

But Belinda was now very sure that all Miss Wary's care proceeded from jealousy, that she had a mind to Sir John herself and could not bear the thought of his civility to her. She therefore answered thus:

"That I am a stranger to Sir John Galliard I readily own, but I cannot believe him a man of so much dishonor as to commit a rape. And I know myself too well to fear I shall ever consent to any action which cannot reconcile itself to virtue. I have, you know, but one sister in the world and she is very dear to me. Her only child, whose life is hers, is in danger, and can I be so cruel as to lose one hour in posting to her? No, I would, if possible, fly with the wind to her comfort, and I beg you will have no concern for my safety, of which you shall hear as soon as I get home." Miss Wary resolved to say no more, but when they had supped they went to bed.

Belinda was soon stirring in the morning and got ready by that time the coach and owner came to the door. Breakfast over, they set forward and Sir John had now time to make love without interruption, a work he was so well versed in that he knew how to model his tale to every taste and where he foresaw a difficulty, the hook was baited with a little touch of matrimony. But, how resolved soever Belinda was to reject Miss Wary's counsel, it put her, however, upon her guard and she kept a constant sentry at the door of her virtue armed with resolution to defend it forever. Sir John soon perceived it and began to fear he had a piece of work upon his hands which would take some time to finish. The introduction to his amour was an endeavor to raise her vanity by chiming continually in her ears the multitude of merits she was invested with and how impossible it was to view her charms without everlasting captivity.

"Sir John," replied the lady, "your love, like a thunder shower, comes on too violent and too hastily to last long; but I beg you will lay the subject by till I have seen my dear sister and know how her poor little girl does, for till she recovers, I shall never be in a humor gay enough to listen to love."

"Why, madam," returned Sir John, "do you enjoin me to a task impossible for me to observe? Do you imagine I can sit near Belinda and be insensible of her charms? Or...."

"No more, for Heaven's sake," interrupted the lady, "for who that has ever taken notice of a modern husband's behavior can with patience listen to a modern beau making love—the latter all adoration, praise, rapture and lies; the other jarring, discord, indifference, and downright hatred; one breathes nothing but darts, flames, and soft melting sighs; the other cries 'Damn you, madam, you are my aversion. We have been too long acquainted. A stale face is the D – – – l; prithee take it from my sight.'"

"That, madam," replied the knight, "is owing to our law-givers who force us into fetters and then expect we should hug them forever. No, Belinda! Love is a generous noble passion, values liberty, and scorns confinement and restraint. Is not a voluntary gift infinitely more valuable than one that is wrenched and forced from the donor? Come, my charmer, let you and I make a free-will offering of our hearts to each other. They will soon take root and fix in our different bosoms. And if yours, through the natural inconstancy of your sex, should ever desire to remove, mine shall break to give it liberty, as sure it must whenever it comes to know the fair Belinda is lost. Oh, come, my lovely charmer! Straight pronounce my joy and say I shall be happy!"

Belinda now saw with open eyes at what Sir John was driving, but thought it best to soothe his hopes, lest a resenting denial should make him desperate and, while he had her in his power, take by force what he could not gain by entreaty and stratagem. She therefore told him she saw nothing in him that was any way disagreeable but so short an acquaintance could not in reason expect a positive answer to the first request.

"Beside, Sir John," continued she smiling, "I would not have you engage yourself too far till you have seen another lady to whom I will introduce you at my journey's end, one of superior merit and a much better fortune than I can boast of."

Sir John told her he desired no greater merit than she was mistress of and, for women's fortunes, he never inquired after them because he never intended to trouble his head with them.

"The lady's person," pursued he, "is all I aim at, and that I'll use as love and gallantry inspires me. Come, Belinda, lay by these virtuous airs. Women were made to be enjoyed and I expect your inclinations will concur with mine and give you to my longing arms this night. Great is the addition to our joys which a ready compliance brings. It saves a man ten thousand oaths and lies, which are nothing compared to the loss of time spent in a fruitless attempt. Shall a bull or horse command a thousand mates while man, the reigning lord of all, stands

cringing at his vassal's feet, begging to be admitted to his own?
Would all mankind assume their own prerogative, we should
soon divest ye of your pretended virtue and let ye see your pride
and scorn are weapons only turned against yourselves."

"I am sorry, Sir John," replied Belinda, with a scornful
smile, "to find you take your example for plurality of mistresses
from the brutes. I always thought man a creature above them—
one that had reason to regulate and govern his inordinate passions, though, I confess, the comparison is very just in those
human monsters who neither can or will endeavor to subdue
them. But if every man were to choose as many women as he
likes and take them as his proper vassals, as you are pleased, with
much civility, to call us, I cannot but fancy it would destroy the
whole system of life and the best economy must be turned upside-
down. But, oh, I am now too sensible of my own obstinate folly,
which made me spurn at the advice of a friend whose kind persuasions would have kept me from the danger I now see myself
in. But I took Sir John Galliard for a man of honor, which I
now fear I shall not find him. I will therefore lay that aside and
sue for my safety to your pity and good nature. You know, Sir
John, the basest action in life is to assault an unarmed adversary."

"In such a case," returned the knight, "honor only is concerned and that you think me entirely divested of, and have
laid yourself under my pity and good nature for protection, which
qualities, when they have served myself, have certainly shed their
influence over you, but charity, my dear, begins at home. I must
first pity my own sufferings, which my good nature persuades
me to, and then, my child, I will consider of yours."

Belinda's maid, during all this discourse, kept nodding and
pretended to be soundly sleeping, though she heard every word of
her lady's danger. They were now arrived at the inn where they
were to dine and Sir John kept a watchful eye over his prey,
lest she should by any means give him the slip, nor would he
suffer the maid to come near her, who, having slept false all the
way, was now contriving her lady's escape from the ruin she saw
threatening her. She considered they had a six-mile forest to go

over in the afternoon, which would be too good an opportunity for the performance of any ill. She therefore went to the land-lord, who she had heard was a very honest man and told him the whole matter. He seemed to be much concerned for the young lady and advised to force her out of his hands by a speedy appli-cation to the first justice of the peace. But the maid opposed that and said such a thing would be too public and the noise of it would spread everywhere and blast her lady's credit. She rather desired he would try to provide four sturdy fellows well-armed and well-mounted to convey them safe over the forest, and they should have their own demands answered, let them be what they would.

The host told her he could easily provide her such a number of men but advised her to take them quite through the journey, for it was very likely if the gentleman found himself balked upon the forest, he would find some way at night to renew his attempt. She approved of what he said, begged him to lose no time and tell the men they should meet with a reward above their own wishes. While the maid was thus honestly and carefully employed for the good of her mistress, the poor young lady herself was in the utmost consternation and perplexity, being denied the sight of her servant, lest they should, when together, contrive their escape, which he was resolved they should not do till he had gained his point and then farewell love and all soft pleasure—till another fresh beauty presents itself and a fresh opportunity of acting the same villainy over again.

Dinner over, they again took the coach, which, as they were doing, Belinda's maid had the pleasure to see their guard well-mounted and ready to follow them, which they did at some dis-tance though none of the company knew their design but herself. An hour-and-half's riding brought them to the forest where Sir John had never been before, though his coachman had and knew the way exactly. He now began again to urge Belinda in favor of his own desires, at which she could no longer command her tears, which flowed from her eyes in a plentiful manner.

"Base and degenerate Sir John Galliard," she cried, "who has no sense of honor or even of the bare rules of hospitality, which you have most basely infringed. Am I not under your roof and protection, brought hither by the kindest invitation? And do you, at last, use me worse than a robber would do? Had I fallen into the hands of the veriest scoundrel upon earth, I might have hoped for better treatment. I only beg for a little time to consider before I consent to my own undoing."

He told her consideration was a perfect enemy to love, bid her look round, and see the very spot of ground they were then on—how many invitations (by privacy and solitude) it gave them to their joy—then bid his coachman stop. "I believe, sir," replied he, "we shall be forced to stop, for we are pursued by four men well-armed." Belinda was glad to hear of any interruption, though she expected to be doubly robbed both of honor and coin. Sir John was never in such haste to get rid of his money as at this juncture and much rather have parted with ten times the sum in his pocket than the promising opportunity that flattered his hopes. He therefore bid his coachman once more stop (which he did) and had pulled out a handful of gold ready to bribe their absence.

But when the coach stopped, the supposed pursuers did so too, which surprised everybody but the maid who knew the reason of their halt. Sir John then ordered the coach to go on, which drew the attendants after it. He made it stop again, and so did they. The experiment was tried several times and the same success attended it, till at last, provoked with the fear of losing so fair a prospect of bliss, he flung himself out of the coach, dismounted one of his attendants, and rid up to the fellows.

"Pray, gentlemen," said he, "have you any business with me or design against me that you dog my coach all this afternoon?"

"By what authority," said one of the men, "do you examine us? Have not we the same liberty to travel this road that you have? Can you say we have either assaulted or molested you or your company? And if we have not, go back and be quiet. We are resolved to go our own pace and either ride or stand still as we see occasion."

"Sir," said another of them, "to be plain with you, we have a very considerable charge under our care and keep up with your coach lest we should be robbed on't. Be assured we will offer no violence to any of you, provided you offer none yourselves, but we must have our liberty as well as you."

While Sir John was holding a parley with the men, Belinda's maid let her mistress into the whole welcome secret, which raised her spirits to so much courage that when Sir John returned she was quite another thing—and so was he too, though different reasons made the alteration. She was pleased at the very heart to think herself safe; he, mad at his, to see his hopeful project baffled. He stepped into the coach all cloudy and sullen, muttered some curses between his teeth, and sat for some time as if asleep.

"I fear, Sir John," said Belinda, after a long silence, "those men have robbed you, else whence proceeds this sudden chagrin? I thought the gay Sir John Galliard could never have been out of humor. Say, Sir John, what can be the cause?"

"You are very merry, madam, and have guessed right," replied the knight. "The dogs have robbed me of something very considerable, but I may yet recover it, perhaps."

"No matter," said the lady in perfect good humor, "though they have robbed you, I have escaped and I warrant I shall find money enough to last till tomorrow night, and then you shall be furnished with what sum you please."

He hardly thanked her or made any answer, he was so thoroughly vexed at such an unlucky hit in so convenient a place for his ill design, but sat some time with his eyes shut contriving new schemes. They were now off the forest, when Sir John hoped the four gentlemen would take another road, not once suspecting the truth of the matter. But they continued to follow the coach, which still increased his vexation. An hour before night he complained he was weary of sitting and asked the lady if she would alight and walk a quarter of a mile. She desired to be excused, said she was very easy and never loved walking in her life.

"Then, madam," said the knight, "will you not think me rude if I do?"

"No, Sir John," returned Belinda, "you cannot be rude, unless you repeat what is already past."

He went out and called his valet to alight and walk with him, to whom he gave order to ride before and take up the first blind alehouse he came at and to bid the coachman say his horses were tired and would go no farther. In the meantime the lady in the coach had leisure to talk a little to her maid.

"Oh, Nancy," said she, "I fear there is some new mischief hatching. Heaven, of its mercy, blast it and send me well out of the paw of this lion and may the next devour me, if ever I trust a strange one more!"

"Fear not, madam," returned the maid, "I have ordered the men behind to keep within sight and call, and when we come to the inn, if you please to go to bed, we will all sit up at your chamber door and guard you all night. But here is Sir John coming already. Let us not look concerned."

The knight re-entered his coach and seemed a little better-humored than when he went out, which added to Belinda's fears. About a mile farther, they came to a sorry hovel, at the door of which stood the valet, by way of signal to the coachman, who called (as ordered) to his master and told him his horses were tired and could go no farther that night. Sir John pretended to be in a very great concern that they should be forced to take up with such ordinary accommodation as such a pitiful hole could afford them but begged the lady to bear for once with inconvenience, since disasters would happen sometimes. This put Belinda and her maid a little to a stand and they knew not well how to manage. They were both assured the pretended accident was all designed and kept an eye upon their guard, with whom they saw Sir John's valet deeply engaged in talk, and to their great dismay and terror, saw two of them ride away. Belinda changed color, and Sir John conducted her into the house, such as it was.

"I hope, Sir John," said she, "you do not pretend to take up here all night. If your horses are a little tired, which must be false, an hour's rest will surely make them able to go two miles farther to an inn, where both they and we may have good entertainment. But I see too plainly what your design is. You are, 'tis true, a baronet by birth, but your mother has been some base, some faulty sinner, has violated a chaste marriage-bed, and you are the abominable product of her vice, the spawn of some of her footmen. Nothing but a channel, nay, a common-shore,[20] of base plebian blood, could put a man upon such low dishonorable actions. Villain," continued she, "for thou deservest no other name, hast thou left a shoal of common strumpets behind thee to persecute me with thy detestable love, as thou hast falsely called it? No, monster, ere thou shalt accomplish thy devilish designs upon me, I will let out life at ten thousand portholes and my last breath shall end with a laugh to see thy baffled disappointment."

Sir John was never so stung in his life before as he was now at her bitter sharp invectives. But that which touched him the nearest was her just remarks upon his mother from whence ten thousand vexatious thoughts crowded about his heart, and (as he afterwards owned) began to ask himself whether there was not more than a bare probability of his being what she at random called him. His supposed father he knew was a man of the strictest honor and virtue. "From whence then," thought he, "does it come that I am so differently inclined? And am I then," continued he to himself, "the offspring of a nasty curry comb or horse whip, at last? Why, if I am, I cannot but think I have many brethren in this nation that look as high as I do, and act exactly like me. Yet methinks I am not pleased to tell myself I am the son of a scoundrel."

His private meditations over, he again accosted the lady. "Why, madam," said he, "are you so very tart? Your words

---

[20] The term derives from "common sewer" and appears in Shakespeare.

touched me to the quick, and I now own to you they have given a turn to the design I had upon you. Yet methinks you had no cause to be so very apprehensive of danger while you had a guard so near you. It is true two of them are deserters bought off for a little money; the other pair seem to be honest and resolute. But trust me, Belinda, you shall have no cause from me to try their valor. You may now with the greatest safety dismiss them, for all the love I had for you is vanished, which, as you well observed, was false, and is now turned to esteem and respect, which shall for the future regulate all my actions towards you."

"No, Sir John," returned Belinda, "you have too much cause to blame my conduct already for giving myself up to the honor of a stranger, but you shall not have a new one to accuse me with by cashiering my only safeguard. But if you relent and are changed as you would persuade me you are, show it by leaving this dismal abode forthwith, and take the two men into your own retinue, for with me they shall go till I see the inside of my own habitation." Sir John with much readiness complied and they all went on to the inn.

Belinda's heart was now restored to its former quiet, and her fear and anger were both banished, for she saw the looks of the knight so much altered that she no longer doubted but his designs were so too. Her pleasant good humor began again to return, which Sir John perceiving, he suddenly threw himself at her feet and with a penitent look told her he would never rise till she kindly gave him her pardon for all the vile behavior he had been guilty of towards her. "Believe me this once," he said. "Though my words are invalid, I am ashamed of what I have done and which is more, you are the first woman that ever made me so. It would be a compliment to tell you if I could persuade myself to a whole life of captivity I should offer you marriage, which is, I own, what I am utterly averse to, and what I daresay you are very indifferent to, since a woman so well qualified as you are must needs have choice in every place you come at."

"Sir John," answered the good-natured lady, "do but forbear

to repeat your fault and you shall see I can now forgive it as well as thank you for the esteem you have for me. But when you talked of marriage you had not asked my consent, which I take to be pretty material, but no matter. We are now, or at least seem to be, upon very good terms, so I desire you will be pleased to order something for supper, since dinners uneaten never lie on the stomach."

"F – – – h, madam," replied Sir John, "you have starved my appetite and it would be but justice to do as much by yours. Yet, to show that good nature to which you once referred yourself, I will go myself and see what's to be had."

Sir John was no sooner gone from Belinda than poor Nan, who knew nothing of the reconciliation and good agreement that was betwixt them, came in to bid her lady have a good heart, for there was another coach and six just come to the inn. Belinda was just going to tell her how matters stood when Sir John returned, and said, "Madam, you will surely dismiss your two attendants now, because you have much better just come in quest of you. I believe I shall be forced to hire them for my preservation now, for I saw Sir Combish trip out of his coach as nimbly as a weathercock at the turn of the wind and with him Squire Cockahoop, as he always desires to be called, who will refresh your spirits after a harassed journey and give you some diversion. He is a thing just got loose from an old ill-natured governess who was first his nurse, then his maid, next his school-mistress, and at last his governante. The woman, it must be owned, has been very just to him and taught his as much as she knew herself, which was bad English, false sense, ill nature, and worse manners. They know not we are in the house but must ere long because both Sir Combish and his servants know my livery. And if Belinda, to relieve her late distress, will consent to a little sport, I dare answer she may have it from the comedians now ready to act their parts and I will bring both my rival and his ridiculous companion to kiss your hand."

She who had suffered more fatigue and disorder than she could well bear was very ready to consent to anything that would refresh her spirits and told him with some pleasantry that, since he had declared against matrimony himself, it was time for her to look out for one of more compliance and desired the new-comers might be admitted. Sir John, ready to atone for his past faults, ran to inquire for Sir Combish who was just bullying the cook because she refused him a brace of partridges Sir John had already bespoke.

"– – – – you, hussy," he said, "you deserve to be basted with all the dripping you save in a year to teach you how to use people of distinction. Here you are going to send up a brace of birds to some fools who perhaps may take them for crows and be angry if you reckon above three pence apiece for them. And we that know better things must take up with a neck of rotten mutton stewed till the bones drop out, which was ready to drop before the silly animal was killed. When they are [done] enough, I shall make bold with sword in hand to seize them, and show me the man that dare dispute the matter."

"Well said, my bully," cried Sir John, clapping him on the shoulder. "Come, knight, if you will be content with a limb or so, you shall have it without fighting for't, but thou knowest I am a true-born English cock and love to defend my own property."

Sir Combish, who knew the voice, turned about but did not readily know how to behave, whether as a friend or a rival, and putting on a solemn air cried, "Z – – – –s, knight, where's my mistress? And who the D – – –l desired so much of thy civility as to tramp after her a matter of seventy miles? Sure you did not expect to be overtaken or you would have made more haste. I thought you had been at your journey's end by this time and was posting after to see whose title was best."

"The last thing," returned Sir John, "that a man parts with is the good opinion he has of himself, and while Sir Combish keeps that he cannot fear a rival. Your mistress is in this house, and the reason why I tramped after her (as you call it) was because you were gone after a more inferior game and, as her occasion called her back sooner than either you or she expected.

I thought it a very good way of confirming our friendship, to show that respect to her which was due to you. Believe me, Sir Combish, your mistress is very safe and I have too great a value for her virtue to assault it. I wait your commands to conduct you to her and will with pleasure give up my care of the lady to one who must needs be more concerned for her safety."

"B – G – –, Knight," replied Sir Combish, "thy words are apocryphal and it is seven to four but I let thee keep thy charge, for I never knew thee willing to part with a woman till matters were fairly adjusted betwixt you. Now, though I might perhaps share a wench with a friend, I must insist upon keeping a wife to myself, because I should not care to mix my breed."

"I am sorry, Sir Combish," returned young Galliard, "to find your opinion of the lady runs so very low but am yet more surprised to hear you confess a flaw in your own merit, which you certainly do if you say it wants force to secure her to yourself. Come, don't be a fool and lose her by a groundless and false suspicion of her. By all that is virtuous, she is so for me and, I believe, for all mankind."

"A plague on't," returned Sir Combish, "I had much rather you had called her whore, for then I should have thought her ill-usage of you had raised your spleen but, z – – – – s, so much commendation is just as much as to say, 'Now I have had her, I'll bring her off as well as I can.' However, I will go to her and shall soon guess at her innocence by her looks. But where's my friend, Cockahoop? If the worst happens, she will serve him at last. Methinks I would not have her balked now she is set on a husband."

Cockahoop was called and they all went to Belinda, who saw them coming and met them at the door. Clownish thrust in first and, taking her about the neck, gave her a smacking kiss and said she was a good handsome woman, b – G – –, he would have another, which when he was going to take Belinda cried, "Hold, sir, 'tis ill manners to help yourself twice before the rest of the company are served. Besides, I am here by way of dessert, which always comes after a full meal and consequently should be used sparingly." Sir Combish, who was ready to boil over with jealousy, answered thus for his rustic friend: "How sparing you have been of your dessert, madam, to some that shall be nameless you know best; some perhaps are cloyed and some again don't care for sweetmeats, so you may as well give my friend Clownish another taste before they mold on your hands."

Belinda's true taste for good sense spoiled her palate for the relish of a fool and she told Sir Combish whoever she surfeited with her favors she would be sure to take care of overcharging his stomach, lest he should disembogue and they should all be lost. "But why, Sir Combish," continued she, "do you think me so very lavish? I am neither old, ugly, poor, or a fool, and a body may pick up a coxcomb anywhere who, if he prove not grateful for what we give, will at least receive it though only to brag of among his fellow puppies." Sir Combish told her with a fleering insolence he thought women's favors too low to be boasted of and when he offered her so great a one as marriage he did not see how she could make too thankful a return for it.

This made Sir John and Belinda laugh, and Cockahoop thought it a very good time now they were quarreling to set up for himself. "Come, young woman," said he, "b – G – –, I like you well and am resolved I'll have you, so never trouble yourself about Sir Combish any more, for though I am at present but an esquire, I intend to be knighted soon and then I can make you a lady as well as he. So let us strike up the bargain with a kiss," which he was just going to take when Belinda, not in a very good humor, returned his love with a sound box on the ear, which for aught I know the civil esquire would have sent back with interest had not supper interposed.

They had not half finished their meal when they heard a bustle at the door and a woman's voice say, "I will come in, you dog! I will see the rogue, your master!" Sir Combish heard and turned pale, at which time the virago entered and flying at him, armed like a cat, clapped her fierce talons into each of his cheeks, crying aloud, "Betty Dimple, revenge thyself and tear the villain's soul out!" Sir John got up and rescued the half-worried knight, though not without some danger to himself. Poor Sir Combish was no sooner relieved than he ran downstairs like fury, ordered his coach to be got ready that minute and drove away as fast as fear and six good horses could carry him, which in all probability he had not done so quietly but that Madam Betty, half-choked with gall, was fallen senseless into a chair and gave him time to make an easy exit.

Belinda and her company were very merry at the tragi-comedy and let her sit to recover at her own leisure, knowing that her distemper was nothing but passion which would soon work itself off. By that time supper was over and the cloth taken away. The furious Betty came to her senses again and looking wildly round her cried, "Where is the monster, the hell-hound that has robbed me, plundered me, and left me to misery, despair and ruin? O cruel man," she said to Sir John Galliard, "why have you put a stop to my design and hindered me from glutting myself with such revenge as suits the wrongs poor Betty Dimple has received? O, where is he? Show him to me! O, I rave, I die for my revenge!"

"You rave indeed," answered Belinda. "I would fain have you cool your boiling resentment and let us know the cause on't. Since your revenge is so public, your injury may be so too."

"Cool it, madam?" answered the woman. "It is not possible for me to cool my rage since every breath I draw heats and inflames it more. No, nothing will ever quench my burning wrath but the blood of him who first set it in flames. But, madam, as you are one of my own sex, perhaps you may have a little pity for me, and therefore you shall hear my tale.

"As for my father and mother, it is not at all to the purpose to tell you who they were or what they were, since they both died while I was yet an infant and left me to the care of a grand-father whose daughter brought me forth. While I was young, I had, I'll warrant you, forty flirting lovers with their fine speeches and filthy designs, who were ready enough to offer serv-ices they had little reason to believe would be accepted of, but what signifies that? I kept my ground as firm as a rock and stood stoutly to defend myself from them all.

"At last, one of the trouble-houses that was always after me told me if I would not comply he would take young Bateman's course and hang himself at his own signpost.[21] 'So you may,' said I, 'if you have a mind and lest your rope should prove too short, I'll lend you my garters to lengthen it.' 'Well, Mrs.,' said he, 'you'll meet with your match, I warrant you.' So off he walked, and I never saw him again or so much as heard he kept his word and hanged himself. The next was a lumping looby that weighed about eighteen stone[22] and he, poor man, was for drowning, but I persuaded him to stay till I got him a couple of bladders to tie under his arms for fear he should sink, and all the thanks he gave me was to call me a jeering bitch and went home as dry as if he had never been drowned at all. The next was a barber and a cunning shaver he was, for I as surely thought one night he had cut his throat as I was sorry afterwards I was mistaken. But the rogue deceived me as all the rest had done. The next was an apothecary's apprentice who had threatened so often to poison himself that I did not know but some time or other he might do as much for me, so I broke off my acquaintance with him as soon as I could before I began to swell. And yet a year after I saw the whelp with as wholesome a look as if his master had not a scruple of mercury in his shop.

"Well, I'll swear 'tis a melancholy thing to tell ourselves there is no trusting in man for anything but our undoing. When I had lived a year or two longer and had got more wit, a new sweetheart presented himself to me. He was a neighbor's child and one with whom I used to romp when I was a little girl, but he was grown so fine with his laced hat and shoulder-knot that I had much ado to know him. 'Humph, Will,' said I, 'you are very fine. I'll warrant your father is dead and you have given all he left you for those fine clothes. And what, are you married?'

[21] From a ballad beginning or entitled, "A godly warning to all maidens." A chapbook version appeared in 1710, *Bateman's Tragedy; or, the Perjur'd Bride Justly Rewarded. Being the Unfortunate Love of German's Wife and Young Bateman.*

[22] Now, legally, one stone equals fourteen pounds.

'Married?' said he, 'No, no, if I were married I should have no business here, for I am come to offer my service to you, as my master says to the ladies. My father indeed is dead and has left me his farm with a good stock upon it and I intend to leave my master and go and live upon it, if you will have me and help to manage it. I have lived these two years with one Sir Combish Clutter, who has lately had a honeyfall of a thousand a year dropped into his mouth. Some of your great wits call him cox-comb, but whatever he is, I have had a main good place on't and would not leave it but for thy sake, dear Betty. So take a short considering time and let me have an answer tomorrow.' 'Nay, nay, Will,' said I, 'you may as well take it now. What, you and I are no strangers to one another. We have no acquaintance to scrape at this time of day and the less we spend in courtship the better. But my grandfather must be told or else he will give me nothing and then, for all your fine speeches, you won't care a louse for me.'

"In short, my grandfather liked the match and promised to make my portion equal with his, so William gave his master warning and told him he was going to be married. 'A pox on thee for a fool,' said his master. 'Is not the D - - - l in thee to leave a place of plenty for a starving hole of thy own, with half a score naked bastards about thy heels, which in all probability will either go to Tyburn or a brothel-house?' 'No sir,' said Will, 'I hope not. I was not the son of a rich man myself and yet I have escaped the gallows. Beside, if there were no poor men in the world, who must wait upon such as you, sir? My wife and I betwixt us shall be better worth than two hundred pounds and that, with a little industry and good management, will keep our children from nakedness.' 'Why then,' returned Sir Combish, 'you are very rich I find, though your father was not. And pray, where does this wife-elect of yours live?' 'Why, sir,' answered William, 'your being a stranger in this country where your new estate is makes you so to all the pretty girls hereabout. She lives not far off and a titbit she is. If your worship will give me leave,

I will invite her to sup with us in the hall. She'll be no disgrace to the best among us servants.'

"At night I was brought to the house and the housekeeper conducted me in with as much ceremony as I deserved. But that devil, Sir Combish, was at a dining room window from whence he saw me and thought me worth a night's lodging, which he designed to honor me with. A day or two after, he asked Will when he was to be married. He said as soon as we were three times asked in church, which would be next Sunday. 'Well then,' said the knight, 'your wife may depend upon me for a father to herself and a godfather to her first child. And for thy part, since thou hast proved a good honest rascal, I will not only wish thee joy but I will give thee some by adding a good close to thy farm, which will make thee a freeholder and qualify thee for a vote against I want one. But before you leave me you are to do me a private piece of service which none but you are to be trusted with. You must know, as much a stranger as I am on this side the country, I have an intrigue with a girl not far off. That is, I would have one, but the jade is cautious; and though I do her an honor, she refuses it, unless I marry her. Now to gain my ends, I have promised to marry her, but d – – – me if I keep my word, though I intend to confirm it with a letter to her, which you shall copy, for you write a good, careless gentleman-like hand and I believe you spell like the D – – – l as well as myself. But she is no judge nor does she know my hand at all, so yours shall go for mine that if ever I am called to an account for it, I may with safety deny it and justly say I did not write it. Call upon me half an hour hence and I will give you what I would have you transcribe.'

"Will thought to himself that if the girl did not know his master's hand, he was sure she did not know his and, for the spelling part, it was perfectly indifferent to him whether it was right or wrong. The time was come when he was to wait his master's commands. He then gave him the following lines to copy, which are too well-impressed on my memory to lose one tittle of them:

'I thought, my dear, to have seen you this evening, but am prevented by company coming in. However, I cannot sleep till I communicate a secret to you, though I fear it will be late before I come. Let all be quiet and no light, for we have had the D – – – l to do here. But no more of that till we meet.'

"When William had writ this over, his master took it from him saying, 'Now have I a mind for a frolic and will go and deliver this letter myself. But if I do, it shall be in your clothes, Will. So slip on your frock and give me your livery.' Poor William obeyed without delay and was then sent on some sleeveless errand, which was to take up some time, while another servant was sent with the letter to me, which I made no doubt came from William, because I knew his hand, though there was no name.

"I was very impatient to know what the matter was and never wished more for my William's company than at that time. My grandfather and all the family were gone to bed except myself who sat, as ordered, in the dark till I heard some footsteps in the yard. I then ran and opened the door where by starlight I saw Will, as I thought, in his livery. He came in and whispered very low, asked if all were abed? I told him yes. He then told me I was false to him and he had reason to believe I was going to be married to another. 'Who? I, William?' said I. 'What do you mean by such a groundless suspicion? I love you too well to think of any man in the world but yourself and am so just to you that if your master would have me I would not change you for him.' 'Say no more,' replied the counterfeit William, 'for nothing shall ever convince me you are true unless you give yourself up wholly to my arms this night.'

"I loved my William and made no scruple to cure his doubts, though at the expense of a m – – – – – – – – d, which I had always kept for him. So we crept upstairs and to bed we went in the dark. But while we were there Will returned from the walk he had been sent and found all the servants very merry, but no master to deliver his message to nor could any account be had of him. He stayed awhile at home, and thought to himself Sir

Combish was gone no doubt to the poor deluded girl with the letter he had writ for him. And now, thought he, I will go for an hour or two to my Betty, who is doubtless in bed but I know she will rise and let me in.

"I was so eager to clear myself of the falsehood and stuff he laid to my charge that I went up to bed without fastening the house door, so that it being only on the latch, William came easily in and directly up to my room but, fearing he should fright me, he spoke just at the door and said, 'Do not be frighted, Betty; it is only I.' 'Only you!' cried I, trembling. 'Who are you?' 'What,' answered he, 'do you not know the voice of your William?' 'If you are William,' said I, 'who have I got here? Go fetch a candle, for I am undone forever.' He ran down to light a candle, while I jumped out of bed and got my clothes on. William no sooner advanced to the bedside with a lighted candle than Sir Combish threw his night-cap at it and put it out again. But Will was so enraged to have his place supplied by another that he ran to the bed and so jumbled his master that, after he had battered his face not fit to be seen a month after, he cried out 'Murder!' which roused my grandfather and all the house beside, who came with candles in their hands to my room and discovered the whole matter.

"Sir Combish lay still but cried, 'G – – d – – – thee, Will, thou hast given me a beating that no dog in England would have given a porter. Curse thee, go home and fetch my clothes. Take thy own and let me see thy dog's phyz no more.' But poor I had more than a double share of a plot I never helped to contrive, for when William came back with his master's clothes he refused to hear me justify myself, took a final leave of me just then, and I never saw him since. My grandfather, as soon as the knight was gone, refused to hear me likewise, turned me out of doors the next morning, and I never saw him since neither.

"Everybody believed I was designedly a whore, and I have lived ever since in the utmost contempt on what my needle and wheel could bring me in. I have an aunt in this town, to whom by an invitation I came three days ago, and was sitting at her door when I saw that infernal Sir Combish driven in, whose villainous soul I would have separated from his cursed corpse, had not this gentleman most cruelly prevented me. But I hope it is not yet too late. He is doubtless in the house still and it shall go very hard but I will have the other tug with his D – – – lship."

Sir John Galliard at this recital had two or three qualms and he often thought of poor Miss Friendly, whose wrongs only he felt compunction for. But Belinda was a little upon the smile and said, "You know not, Mrs. Betty, how well you have revenged yourself already, for I assure you Sir Combish by your appearance is driven from a mistress he followed from London, to which place I daresay he is by this time returning, for my maid whispered me in the ear just now and told me his coach and he were gone off. But let him go. He is a worthless animal and has used you basely. Yet I believe it will soon be in my power to do you some service. How long is it since William and you parted? And what sort of man is he?"

She then described him and said it was above a year since she heard of him. "Have you a mind," asked Belinda, "to be reconciled to him? If so, provide to go with me, for I fancy your William lives with a sister of mine. And I am the more ready to believe it is he, because Sir Combish came with his addresses to me soon after the time you speak of, and the fellow pretended to be sick all the while he stayed and would never appear. Now as I am almost sure this is the man, I am as well satisfied it will be in my power to make up the breach betwixt you, if you do but once meet." Mrs. Betty said she was willing to wait upon her anywhere but could never hope to see William again with any satisfaction.

Next morning they again took coach, Sir John and Squire Clownish who had slept all the while Betty Dimple told her story to Belinda and her maid. As for Mrs. Dimple, she came jogging after on a trotting horse who first dislocated her joints and then set them right again. After they had been some time in the coach Mr. Cockahoop asked Belinda when she designed to beg his pardon for the box on the ear she gave him and assured her that if Sir Combish had not been frighted out of the house and forgot to take him with him, he should hardly have been so civil after such an affront to wait upon her home. Belinda told him whenever he thought fit to ask her pardon for the occasion of the box, she might perhaps condescend to an answer of the same kind but, as for his company, she found no great reason to thank him for it, because it was a piece of civility forced upon him and yet she was glad of it, because Sir John Galliard must have gone back alone had not fortune left him behind.

Sir John sat all the morning with his head as it were in a cloud, gloomy and silent, his thoughts employed on different subjects which entertained him with no pleasing variety. Sometimes he was vexed he had missed his design on Belinda; sometimes ashamed he had ever attacked her honor. One minute he called himself a thousand fools for jaunting after a woman that would not be his harlot at last; the next he persuaded himself to marry her. But that raised a mutiny in his breast crying out, "Liberty! Liberty!" In short, he liked Belinda so well that he was forced to stand at bay with his own inclinations, keeping them always subdued, to divert them from what he had always declared against.

Belinda again took notice of Sir John's silence and said, "Have courage, sir. Your purgatory is almost at an end and a few hours will give you to yourself again."

"Madam," answered the complaisant Sir John, "it is my heaven that is near at an end and my purgatory will not begin till I leave Belinda, who, if she knew all, has more to boast than any of her sex ever had before her. For she has brought it to a single vote whether I shall marry or no."

"Nay, Sir John," returned Belinda, laughing, "a single vote can never do in a matrimonial affair. There must be a joint consent or we shall make a sad botch of what would otherwise be very clever. But I beg you will lay by all your gravity and consider travellers should be always merry, else methinks we look as if we were counting how many steps our horses take in an hour."

"By G – –," said Cockahoop, "and so we do, Bobs. I love to be merry. Come, Mrs. Bell, I will sing you a song I made myself, and a good one it is, though I say it:

> "My whoney Sue, give me thy haun,
> I love thee, as I'm an honest man;
> My hogs, my cows, my plow, my cart,
> To thee I value not a v – – t.
> And yet, Odzooks, thou art so coy,
> Whene'er I court, thou sayest me Noy.

Then Sue answers:

> Forbear your foolish suit, good John.
> For I must have a gentleman
> Can compliment and go more gay
> Than thou upon a holiday,
> Can kiss and à la mode can woo,
> While all your courtship's "hi-gee-ho."

Then he again:

> Aye, merry gep, are you so stout?
> In my heart I love for to jeer and flout.
> 'Ads watrilaits, were I in bed
> And wrestling for – – –   – – – – – – – – – – – ...."[23]

"Oh! for Heaven's sake," cried Belinda, "no more of your poetry, good Esquire Clownish. Beside, we are just at our inn."

"A p – – o' the inn," said he, "the best is to come and I am resolved to sing it out."

"'Ads watrilaits, you had best have a care, Cockahoop," interrupted Sir John. "The lady's fingers are as nimble as ever, and if your song does not please her ear, 'tis six to four but she finds the way to yours again."

---

[23] Squire Clownish's John sings with a Somersetshire accent. See Squire Western in *Tom Jones*.

"By G – –," replied Clownish, "but if she does, she sha'nt come off so well as she did the last time. And I am resolved I'll sing my song, too."

They were now all in the room together where they were to dine, when Betty Dimple, standing at the window, saw a coach coming and her old lover, William, riding before. "Madam," said she to Belinda, "I believe your sister is come to meet you, for here is my renegade—full well I know him." The coach drove into the inn and Belinda and Sir John ran out to see the lady alight. But oh, the ungrateful interview! When the lady in the coach knew Sir John Galliard for the father of her child then with her, and he the lady for the same he had had once at the bagnio. The confusion that appeared in both their faces was too great to be disregarded by Belinda, who looked alternately at them and whose share of amazement was equal to their surprise. Sir John saw it, and did all he could to recover himself, so he took the child in his arms and carried her into the house. The mother cried out, "Oh! my child, my child!" swearing Sir John would have taken her away from her.

"Pray, sister," said Belinda, "let us go in. Methinks I long to know the cause of your disorder." The lady got out of the coach but desired her child and a room to herself. And while she was going in, a thousand fears filled her breast. Sometimes she thought Sir John had not honor enough to conceal the intrigue betwixt them; sometimes again she thought Belinda and he was married. Then the fear of losing her child hurried her to despair, till she got into the house. And then she begged Belinda to bring her little girl to her, for she could not rest till she saw her again, because she had been so lately ill.

"Why, madam," answered Belinda, "are you so strangely ruffled? You give me at once pain and amazement. Have you ever seen Sir John Galliard before?"

The widow was a little nonplussed at that question but resolved to deny the acquaintance and therefore asked her who was that? Belinda said it was the gentleman that took Miss out of the coach, in whose hands she was sure the child was very safe.

However, she would go that minute and bring her from him.

She returned immediately with her, which removed one of the lady's fears, but there was yet two more which hung heavy on her mind. Nor durst she ask Belinda whether she was married or no, lest her answer should strike her dead. But as she knew it must come out, she trembling said, "Belinda, are you married?"

"Married!" replied Belinda, "what, in a week's time? No, sister. If your concern proceeds from your apprehension of losing me, calm your brow, for the gentleman you saw with me is too much a beau to be noosed, as they call it. And I would fain have you join the company or you will lose a very pleasant scene betwixt your William and a mistress of his, which I accidentally picked up. The story is too long for a present repetition and will serve to fill up a dull vacant hour another time."

While they were discoursing in one room, Sir John was considering in another and told himself with much ease the reason why the widow would not come to them. He therefore called for a pen and ink and writ as follows:

"It was an accident, madam, that brought us first together, and we are now met by another. I plainly saw your concern and showed too much of my own to be disregarded by the piercing eyes of your sister. If you would prevent her farther observations, look easy and view me with the same indifference you would have done had you never seen me before. And since nothing but a return of that indifference can secure us from being discovered, you shall find my behavior (as directed by prudence) answerable.

Yours."

When Sir John had writ his letter he gave it to a servant, bid him inquire where Belinda was and tell her he begged the favor of her company for a moment and, as soon as she left the room, to convey the letter into the hand of the new-arrived lady. Belinda answered the knight's summons and the servant delivered the letter as ordered. The lady read it and approved so well of the advice there given that she resolved to act accordingly. Belinda returned to her sister, told her dinner was just ready, and desired once more to know whether she would go to the rest of the company, or they two should dine there alone. The lady told her that since Sir John was so very obliging to give her his company so far, it would be highly rude to rob him of hers, and for that reason she would go with her. They went and Sir John received the strange lady with much civility but guarded looks. She used the same caution and managed hers so well that all observations were now at an end.

They were all sat down to dinner and the servants called in to wait, among whom was William so lately spoken of. He stood some time at his lady's back before he minded his Landabrides[24] at the table with them, who cast many a wishful eye at him unregarded. At last, Sir John drank to her, which drew his eyes that way. He no sooner saw her than he colored with resentment and was going to leave the room when Belinda said, "Stay, William, I have somewhat to say to you as soon as dinner is over." He stayed but with the utmost uneasiness, not being able to bear the sight of his unfaithful Betty, as he thought her. But when they had done and the rest of the servants dismissed, Belinda asked Will if he knew the young woman that sat there. He answered yes, he had too many reasons to know her for an ungrateful base baggage as she was.

"Hark ye, Mr. Rogue," said Betty, "don't you pretend to abuse me before all this good company, for, if you do, I shall make the house too hot to hold you, as I did for the rascal, your master, not long ago. Were you not one of the basest dogs alive to send me a letter writ with your own hand and then let your d – – – – d knight come in your clothes for an answer to it? And when you had done, came in with an innocent air to find me out in the very roguery you yourself had contrived. And now, forsooth, you pretend to put on a look of ignorance as if you knew nothing of the matter, that so your load of villainy might be heaped up at my door, like a base, treacherous whelp as you are."

"I cod," said Cockahoop, "you have got a d – – – – d tongue in your head which, if I were your husband, by G – –, I should

[24] Lindabride was a lady in the romance, *Mirror of Knighthood.* The name was used allusively for a lady-love, a mistress.

wish at the D – – – l. Why, what a p – –, you scold as if you got your living by it. And hear me, young man, if you know when you are well, by G – –, I think you have a good riddance of her."

"Oh no, sir," said poor William. "She has reason for all her anger, which I never knew before. My eyes are now open, and I plainly see both her wrongs and my own. Oh, my Betty! we have both been abused and let us pity one another."

"No," returned Betty, "I will neither pity you nor myself, till I have taken the law of that base transgressor of it. Why must a poor man be hanged for stealing a sheep, and a rich one escape that takes away by force or trick what is much more valuable from us? I am resolved to make both himself and the world know what a rogue he is, and I'll see him hanged before he shall wear the best jewel I ever had and not pay a good price for it." Here she fell a-crying and it wanted not much that William kept her company, till Sir John and Belinda laughed them out of countenance, and the latter told them she saw no cause for tears, since they were in so fine a way of recovering one another's favor, which in a little time they did.

Our travellers now began to think of finishing their journey, which a few hours completed. But how were they all surprised to find Sir Combish got there before them, who, resolving not to lose Belinda, crossed the country a little way and got into the road again, designing to be at her sister's as soon as she, and there to be free from the Fury that paid him so well at the inn for his past recreation. But what was his terror and confusion when he saw enter with the rest not only the cheated Betty but the wronged William, too.

"Z – – – – s," he cried, "I am haunted. Prithee, widow, dear widow, send for thy parson to lay these two infernal spirits and chain them down for life in the bonds of matrimony, or I shall never be quiet for 'em. Come, Will, consume thee, I'll give thee a farm of ten pounds a year for thy drab's m – – – – – – – – d and I think it is very well sold. But I will have it inserted in the contract that she shall never come within ten yards of my person, and the D – – – l take me, if ever I come within twenty of hers, if riding forty miles round it will prevent it."

"Why, by G – –, you are in the right on't," replied the squire. "Zooks, man," continued he, turning to William, "it will be a folly to wish you joy for if thou hast a soul in thee she will tear it out in a week's time. By George, our champion, I would not marry her if GEORGE our King would give me his crown for her portion."

"Well, well, sir," replied Betty, "you may give yourself as many scornful airs as you please, but, by G – –, I had rather have William with his own farm and that [which] Sir Combish has promised than you with your great estate. Everyone to their origin. I was never cut out for a gentleman, nor you for a milk-maid. So what say you, William? Shall we take Sir Combish at his word?" William scratched his head a little and then consented. So married they were and there I leave them, because after marriage (like cheese) comes nothing. "Yes," says a fleerer at my elbow, "children, noise, charge, discord, cuckoldom (maybe), and often beggary comes after." But this spiteful remarker had the misfortune to miscarry himself, and who would mind a preju-diced person?

When the wedding was over and the couple gone, Sir Combish began to renew his addresses to Belinda, who received them with a very cool indifference. For, as she never had any real value for the knight, it was not very likely his late behavior should make any addition. Being pretty well tired of his conceited imper-tinence, she resolved to give him a final answer in order to a speedy deliverance, which the very ensuing afternoon favored, for it happened to prove a very pleasant one and drew them all into the gardens. Sir Combish, resolving to take hold of the happy opportunity, conducted Belinda to a little shady grove which he thought a scene fit for love and, resolving to improve it while he was separate from the rest of the company, he first filled the lady's ears with his own profound merits and then told her how willing he was to bestow them all on her.

"Sir Combish," returned the grateful Belinda, "I shall always acknowledge the favor you have done me in acquainting me with your best qualities. Our worst, I must own, we neither love to speak or hear of. But as I am a person who must always be wholly disinterested both in your worth and demerits, all I have to do is to thank you for the honor you have offered me and to tell you without reserve I cannot accept of it."

"Now, may I be speechless," returned Sir Combish, "if I know whether I hear well or no. Did you say, madam, you could not accept my offer? I cannot credit my ears."

"I never eat my words, sir," answered Belinda, "but beg you will keep your temper, since nothing spoils the economy of a well-set countenance like resentment and anger. You know, Sir Combish, our passions are not at our command, and if we hate when we should love, it is owing to a depravity in our fancies, which we may strive against but can seldom master. This is just my case. I have tried to subdue my inclinations but a superior force keeps them under, and where our power is defective, submission is our only choice."

"Why, sure," returned the vain Sir Combish, "my ears or understanding must be defective, too. Did you really say you could not accept of my offers which is honorable love? and what I did not at first design, and perhaps more than some people deserve. But since your stomach is so squeamish, you may e'en try to strengthen it three or four years longer, and then coarser fare will go down."

"Nay, Sir Combish," replied Belinda, "my stomach was never sharp set towards nice bits, nor did it ever relish palates or coxcombs.[25] My taste lies towards cheaper food, which I think wholesomer, too." Sir Combish with an air of contempt wished her a good digestion and told her she that liked a neck-beef better than a pheasant might prefer a footman before his master.

"Why truly, Sir Combish," answered Belinda, "if we did but make some allowance for the paltry name on one side and the

[25] Belinda may be punning on "palate" and the tongue of a bird. The pun on "coxcomb" and "cockscomb" is evident. Both were supposed to be delicacies in French *cuisine* at the time.

good estate on the other, the man is very often preferable to the master. But here comes your friend, the esquire, with a hare in his hand. I see he has been a-coursing."

"Come," said he, "and tell me how you like my game. By G – –, 'tis better hunting hares than whores, for here have I in half an hour got one and was half a year in pursuit of the other bitch and lost her at last. So we will have this puss for our supper and let the D – – – l take the other for his."

"The D – – – l," replied Sir Combish, "owes thee not much for thy deed of gift, since thou hast offered nothing but what was his own before. A pox on thee for a fool, the whole sex was designed for him at the creation."

"Mercy on us!" cried Belinda. "Why, Sir Combish, what, do you mean? You make love till you grow perfectly rude. I beg you will be advised and when you leave a lady secure her good word by a civil exit, and then perhaps, though she despises you herself, she may have some worthless acquaintance to recommend you to."

"B – G – –," answered our friend Clownish, "you may talk of civility as much as you please, young woman, but I think you practice it as little as he does. Come, come, your tongue and your fingers are flippant alike. What a p – –, who is bound to take your blows and your fromps? B – G – –, if Sir Combish would stand by me, I would return both his abuses and my own with cent per cent, b – G – –." Belinda laughed at the fools and left them singing a piece of an old song, "Why, how now, Sir Clown, what makes you so bold?"

But while they like the cats were growling out love to one another, Sir John and the widow lady were doing it with more good manners at another part of the garden. He told her he was so out of countenance at the reflection of his own behavior to her when she was last at London that he wanted courage to ask her pardon, but begged that she would forget it, if only for the sake of his dear little girl, for whom he declared an affection and tenderness equal to what Nature gives us for our own.

"If you, Sir John," returned the lady, "are discontenanced at your behavior, what confusion and remorse must attend mine?

I do assure you without flying to any other interest than that of my own quiet, I have long since endeavored to forget my fault and had most happily banished the remembrance of you and my own weakness from my breast, when all was again recalled at the sight of you so near the side of my coach. I must own I had much to fear from the inward tremulous perturbations of my fluttering heart that a discovery would ensue, but I had a sister to deal with, innocent herself and loving me too well to think me guilty. And yet she had much ado to account for my conduct at such a perplexing juncture, but thanks to fate, it is now most happily over and if Sir John Galliard will but promise two things, I shall know no more distress."

"Name them, madam," replied Sir John, "and may I never know ease myself if I refuse (as far as my power goes) to contribute towards yours. Bar matrimony and command me in everything."

"As for that clause," answered the lady, " 'tis perfectly needless, and I promise never to put your good nature to that trial again. All I beg is that you will keep my secret and be my friend. As for a double state of life, I am now as much averse to it as you are, and it is because I believe you will never clog yourself with a wife that I do not add a third request to the former, which would be never to address Belinda, because abominable incest shocks my soul and gives my blood an ague."

Sir John told the lady he owned himself a man of pleasure but was not quite so bad as she unkindly thought him. Belinda, he acknowledged, was a fine woman. "But, madam," continued he, "she is your sister and rival only to your merit. I have already declared my sentiments of wedlock and for any other attempts I here faithfully promise to dismiss them. No, madam, I am now resolved to grant what you have asked and will for the future love you both with the same inoffensive love as if you were my sisters. And when I lay you open to the censure of the world, may I lose both memory and reason to prevent a repetition of my fault."

This promise was just made when Belinda came in some

haste to desire their protection, saying she was never in so fair a way for a good beating in her life before. "Pray, Sir John," continued she, "will you tell me (for you are his old acquaintance) how many degrees is Friend Cockahoop removed from a brute?"

"Nay, madam," answered Sir John, "if it was he that was going to beat you, I think you should ask how many degrees a brute is removed from him, since the very fiercest among them never fight their females. I confess he has put me a little out of countenance at being one of his acquaintance, and I would resent his rude behavior but that he is, in strictness, the guest of Sir Combish, not mine. Beside, I am sure Belinda would rather laugh at his ill manners than see it chastised, especially in this place.

"I will tell you, ladies (if you'll give me leave) how he once served me. When I was first acquainted with him I happened to have a slight intrigue with a lady whom I obliged more out of good nature than inclination because she had the misfortune of being a little stricken in years. She had one day invited herself to dine at my lodgings and, as she was a lady of some quality, I resolved to be very civil to her, when that rude monster came abruptly into the dining room and looking at her, cried, 'Why, what a p – –, Knight, art thou reduced already to the assistance of a bawd? Man, what doest thou do with this piece of frippery in her curls and her patches and her old coquettish airs, simpering and leering like a girl just come from her sweetheart, peeping into her bosom to see whether her withered bubbies heave or no. A young coquette is the D – – – l, but an old one is his dam, by George.'

"You may easily guess, ladies, how this blunt speech mortified the lady, who passed for a maid, too, and what confusion it put me into for an excuse. She colored so much with the extremity of resentment that it appeared through the varnish of her face, though none of the thinnest laid on. I was forced to shake my head and cry, 'Poor Mr. Cockahoop! I wonder how he has got loose from his confinement. Madam,' continued I, a little out of his hearing, 'this unhappy gentleman has for some weeks been disordered in his head and I beg you will take no notice of what he says.' 'O pray then,' said she, 'let me be gone and convey me safe into the street, for I neither love to be abused or converse with mad men. Sir John, you keep strange company. I wonder where you pick them up.'

"My rude companion catched her last words and answered, the D – – – l should pick her skeleton before he would pick up such an old ewe as she was, who for aught he knew was the first that rotted after the Flood. The poor lady made the best of her way downstairs and swore she should never come near me again unless I banished my mad man. I confess though Cockahoop's behavior vexed me and I let him know it did, yet at the same time it brought me a deliverance from one I did not much delight in, for which reason I forgave him his ill manners. And if Belinda will but consider that it is impossible to make a brute a man, I am sure she will do so, too. Tomorrow I design to set my face towards London and in order to your speedy deliverance will offer him a place in my coach, though I fancy he will hardly leave you till Sir Combish does. When that will be, you, madam, can best guess."

"If," said the lady, "one may guess at his stay by his treatment, I am of opinion he will not continue long after you and indeed it would be a little hard if he should, since nobody cares for the winnowed chaff when the substantial grain is separated from it. But do not grow vain, Sir John," continued Belinda with a blush. "I only hint at your superior share of good sense."

"I see no room for being proud of your compliment, madam," answered the knight, "since you only allow me a little more wit than a couple of fools."

"Nay, Sir John," replied the widow lady, "I think you are too severe. They are neither of them fools but the vanity of one and the ill nature of the other gives a turn of contempt to their words and actions which helps to rob them of the finest quality ever given to man, and I wish Sir John Galliard may always preserve his talent from every mixture that may rob it of its luster."

Sir John received the lady's kind wishes with a bow, though he knew they were attended with some secret reproach, and said he was too conscious of his own demerits to think he could deserve them. "But now, madam," said he, addressing Belinda (though what followed was designed for both), "we are now within a very little time of parting, possibly forever. I therefore beg an act of oblivion may pass betwixt us, and let us forget every disobliging thing that has been said on either side. Try to mend your opinion of me and I will endeavor to deserve it."

Here the widow lady left them to pluck a ripe orange she saw, when Sir John went on thus: "The world, you know, madam, is divided into four parts. So are the inhabiters of it distinguished by four characters: coxcomb, fool, knave, and man of sense. Now as we that live in Europe reckon it the least part of the world but the best, so must men of sense be allowed the superior character, though infinitely the inferior number. No wonder, then, if you ladies are persecuted with three intolerables for one agreeable. As for the coxcomb and the fool, I see them coming towards us, but which of the other two epithets will Belinda give to me?"

"Ah, Sir John," replied the lady, laughing, "I wish you could as easily acquit yourself of one of the remaining characters as you have an undisputed right to the other. But you cannot blame me if I say you have enough of the best character and too much of the worst. Yet, since you desire and I have partly promised that all should be forgiven, I will now go a step farther and endeavor to forget it too."

Sir John took her hand and kissed it as a return of thanks, which was all he had time to do before they were joined by the other two gentlemen. He then asked Sir Combish if he might expect his company to London in the morning? "Ask the lady," replied the knight. "Her vote must determine the matter. If she says I am welcome to stay, you go alone; if otherways, I am at your service. But I thought by the kiss you gave her hand just now, you had been returning thanks for leave to stay a little longer yourself."

"No, sir," replied Belinda, "Sir John Galliard need not ask leave to stay anywhere. His company will always be desired, but since he is resolved to rob us of it tomorrow, I think it pity he should want company, for it is dull travelling by one's self." Friend Clownish was just going to make some notable repartee when the lady of the house came to them and said she believed it was tea-time and so desired they would all walk in. How they employed themselves the rest of the day I know not, but next morning the two knights and the growling esquire returned to London, where everyone fell to the exercise and diversion they liked best.

Sir John had not been many days in town before he received a letter from Lady Galliard as follows:

"You showed so much concern when I was last at London for Mr. Friendly and his family that I imagine it will not displease you to hear farther from it. Last week I went to visit Mrs. Friendly but did not expect to see Miss, who has had a most melancholy time ever since she came from London. But as she is very young and of an easy, cheerful, sweet temper, she begins to recover her quiet a little and desired to see me. She told me I should see her little macaroon (as she calls the child) which, when brought, methought I saw every line and feature of Sir John Galliard's in his. You know best whether you are the father. Everybody believes you are, but the mother who says you were not in the nation at the unhappy conception of it. I wish you would come and see yourself in epitome, for, if you are not father to this, I am sure you never will be to one more of your own likeness. I should now reproach you for your long silence and twenty other things, but as I am fully determined to bury your faults, this shall be the last time I will (if possible) ever think of them, so you will but come to a mother impatient to see you and who will receive you with transport and pleasure. E. GALLIARD."

Sir John, who never heard Mr. Friendly's family named since the injury he had done it without some concern, trembled as he read the letter and could not prevent a sigh or two which forced their way from a disordered heart. "Sure," said he to himself, "this one action of my life must be the worst because all the rest wear off while this alone sticks to my mind and brings an ungrateful remembrance along with it. Poor Nancy Friendly, indeed I have done thee wrong and such a wrong as nothing can repay. At least I know but one way and that I never can consent to. No, Hymen forbid I should! And yet methinks the girl has vast desert, and I could wish my fault undone. Why? F – – th, I believe only to have the pleasure of committing it again. Well, what must be, must be, and I could gladly see this little likeness of mine. But how to face the charming mother? No, it must not be, for I should either discover myself by a foolish concern, or fall a victim to my own tenderness and marry the girl to redeem her honor while I entail a slavery upon myself for life. No, thank you, John," he said. "She, it seems, begins to be easy and I will be so too. May a separate blessing attend us both, and now I'll go to a lady that cannot marry me in order to forget one that would."

He had now an intrigue with a new h – – – – t, whose husband was very much a man of the town himself but was not very willing to give his wife the same liberty he took, which made him look a little displeased when a certain beau made pretty frequent visits to her. It was by this spark's interest that Sir John had gained admittance to her and he happening to be the finest man of the three, both husband and gallant were despised and Sir John fixed in her favor till something new supplanted him, as he had done his predecessors, for women are whimsical as well as men and sometimes love variety as well as they. But the poor ...c – – – – – d, must I call him? 'Tis an ugly name but it is much better than his wife's. He, I say, found his stomach grew squeamish and could not digest the gross proceedings of his partner, who had now cured his jealousy by certainty and made him resolve to chastise the interloper that shared his bed without his leave.

Poor Sir John, who was but just admitted and had never yet an opportunity of receiving one single favor above leave to make a present or two, fell into the trap and paid not only for his own intended faults but the repeated ones of him that showed him the way to it. The husband, however, knew nothing of Sir John Galliard nor had ever seen him. His design was laid against the notorious offender whose insolence grew so intolerable that he began to insult him in his own house, of whom to be revenged he let his man into the secret and by his assistance carried on the following design.

The lady was gone in the afternoon to the Park for air, when the good man, taking the opportunity of her absence, provided himself of an ounce or two of gunpowder with which he made about thirty crackers and placed them on a row on each side the stairs but so dextrously that they were not to be seen. As soon as he had done, he went to his closet and writ a few lines to be given to his spouse at her return:

"I am going, my dear, this evening with three or four honest fellows to eat fresh oysters at Billingsgate. It is very likely it will be late before I return. Let this desire you neither to expect me home or to be anxious for my stay. YOURS."

As soon as he had writ this kind epistle he gave it to his lady's maid and bid her deliver it to her at her return. And when he had given his man a key of a closet at the stairs' head where he was to act his part and farther directions about the affair in projection, he really went, as said in the letter.

The lady returned, read it, and immediately dispatched away her emissary to let Sir John Galliard know of the favorable opportunity that offered itself to promote their satisfaction. The knight who was never backward at paying his devoirs to a fine woman promised to be with her in an hour, being till then engaged. The man that was left at home to execute his master's revenge lay snug in the closet where he could hear the first step upon the stairs.

The hour was now expired and the visiting knock alarmed the scout who that minute made ready to fire his train, which, as soon as the punctual Sir John had advanced three or four steps, he did and made such a d ------ e noise about the poor knight's ears that he was not only scared out of his senses but he had his wig and linen set o'fire and his hands, face, and bosom very much scorched. He stood the shock of the ambuscade on the middle of the stairs till it had spent its force, not knowing in the fright whether he had best go forward or backward, while the expecting lady in the dining room stood staring and surprised at the unusual noise, full of wonder from whence it came. But it was now over and she ventured to the stairs' head, where she saw Sir John like a smoked flitch of bacon and burning his fingers to put out his flames, which were so perfectly extinguished that the poor lady never had any share of them, for the knight, supposing she had a hand in the contrivance, turned from her and went with the utmost precipitation out of the house to his lodgings, where he sent for a surgeon and was forced for some weeks to keep his chamber. O poor Sir John!

The lady, whom he left at the stairs' head when she saw her greatest beloved vanish, as it were, like the D---l with smoke and stink, began to inquire the cause and what it was that made such rattling doings in the house? But nobody could satisfy her curiosity. While she was disputing the matter among her maids, not a little vexed at her disappointment, the fellow in the closet made a shift to convey himself privately out of doors and went with tidings to his master, as ordered. He was both surprised and vexed when he heard the person that received his noisy revenge was not the man he expected. "I find," said he, "my wife provides against disappointment and lays in a stock of lovers against a dear year. Do you not know who the new stallion is?"

"I know no more of him, sir," returned the man, "than that he has been twice at our house and I once heard my mistress call him Sir John."

"Oh, very well," replied the husband; "she has been dealing among the officers and merchants ever since I married her, and now she begins to aspire to quality. Well, I hope Sir John, as she calls him, has got enough, however. Come, sirrah, since it is so, go you and fetch me a fresh w----. If she proves a fire ship, I'll carry her present to my dear wife, that she may disperse it among her multitude that so their crime may be attended with a certain punishment and everyone share alike. 'Tis a compendious revenge and reaches all, like a feast of poison to a crowd of rats." The man obeyed, brought the s – – t, and conducted her to a private apartment. The consequence I never inquired after but may guess it proved as intended.

The gentleman then repaired to his dwelling and was met by his wife in the entry. "My dear," said she, "our house is haunted."

"I know it, my life," returned the loving spouse. "It has been so a great while with the spirit of concupiscence, which I fancy you are too fond of to endeavor to lay."

"I know not what you mean," answered the innocent lady, "but I really believe the D – – – l has been here. He left such a stink behind him and for a minute I thought he had been taking the house along with him there was such thundering doings on the stairs."

"Good lack," said the tender spouse, "why, here has been sad doings indeed. But if the D – – – l had taken the house, so he would have but left the stairs and the stallion upon them, I daresay your good nature would have pardoned the rest of the damage and promised your soul as a reward for the great civility."

"Lard, child!" replied Madam, "you are strangely out of humor tonight. Indeed I did see a gentleman on the stairs, but did not know his name was Stallion, and I was so frighted I never asked it. Bless us! How came you to know on't? I am afraid you deal with the D – – – l and daresay he wanted you."

"I believe he did," returned the spouse, "for you and I are one. Pray, what color was he of?"

"Color?" said she. "He was so black I should have taken him for the Fiend that made the noise but that I saw a full-bottomed wig in flames, and I never heard the D – – – l was a beau."

"Verily, my fair one," replied the scoffing husband, "you grow strangely ignorant. I never took you for a downright wit, but methinks your small understanding begins to dwindle into nothing. Come, let us to bed and try if sleep can recover what seems to decay."

Poor Sir John was now doing penance and the fiery trial he had so lately gone through made him believe there was a purgatory in this world, whatever there was in another. He had had a long voluptuous reign without any considerable disturbance till this last engagement, which proved very mortifying and upon which he had leisure hours to make the following remarks:

He said to himself, "A common woman, like a common thief, was best to deal with because nothing worse than what we may reasonably expect can happen from either. But a sly lurking whore or thief steals upon us insensibly and draws us to ruin in the midst of security where we can have no defense because we fear no danger. Again, to intrigue with a married woman was (as experience had lately taught him) a very unsafe thing, because the love or jealousy or both of the husband often makes him watchful, while the policy of the wife, to establish her character in his opinion, sacrifices the lover to her own designs and bring him in the whole criminal, when he should only have been a sharer with herself."

These thoughts and some other of the same kind made the knight resolve against a married mistress for the time to come, though he often said that the best way to show a man his folly in running into matrimony was to lie with his wife and let him know it. While he was thus entertaining himself with thoughts, one of the servants brought him a letter which contained something a little unusual:

"Dear Knight: As partners are or should be always friends, I hope the sharing of a woman betwixt us will make no difference, at least when I am sole proprietor and yet willing to give up part of my right to one I never saw. Business, which you know must be done, calls me away for a few days, and as my dear wife may have business too, I beg you will assist her in it till my return. Women, you know, when alone are but indifferent contrivers, and if I leave my spouse a good assistant in the person of Sir John Galliard (for that I hear is your name) I shall expect at least your thanks for the favor and a positive answer per bearer, who will tell you how to direct it or at least convey it safe to the hand of your most affectionate, humble c – – – – – d."

Sir John had so many humble c – – – – – ds all over the town that, being a stranger to the hand, he could not possibly tell from whom the kind invitation came and was at a stand till he called for and examined the messenger who made no scruple (as by order) to let him know he came from the master of the last house he had been at. Sir John, being persuaded the wife was the contriver, at least an accomplice in the cracker scheme, was resolved by way of revenge to answer the letter as little to their satisfaction as the visit was to his. He therefore ordered the fellow to wait and writ what you may read:

"Dear C – – – – – d: Thou art certainly one of the civilest cornutes I ever had yet to deal with, and to let thee see I have some good manners, I here send my thanks for the kind invitation you have sent me but am forced to tell you the feast is too luscious and has cloyed me more than once. I therefore desire you will inquire after somebody that has a stronger stomach and a better digestion to eat up those orts you keck at yourself. And now, by way of postscript, thou art to know that I should have sent thee another sort of message but that I think it a little hard to lie with thy wife and then kill thee for it. J. G."

I might here tell the reader what effects this letter had upon the loving pair it went to. But as domestic jars are trifling to those that have nothing to do with them, I shall say no more of the matter but go back to Sir John, whose mortification daily increased when he considered he was not only confined to his lodgings but to a parcel of stale mistresses of whom he had long been tired and no present hope of dear variety. Besides, he saw himself a standing jest to them and every one made an invidious remark upon his misfortune though none of them knew how he came by it. "Lard! Sir John," cried one of the queens, "you look as if you had got a flap over the nose with a French faggot-stick." Another said he had burnt his fingers playing at hot cockles with the drabs of Drury. A third said she believed his heart had got a fever and his stomach had been blistered for it. All which, for the present, he was forced to bear but resolved to leave the town for some time as soon as his face was fit to be seen, which took up more weeks than he was at first aware of.

Sir John was no sooner in a condition to go abroad than he began to despise the thoughts of the country. He was now once more at liberty to cater for himself and seek out new game after a surfeit of the old. He had one choice companion among a great many more, whose name was Bousie and had been his adviser and assister in most of his irregular actions. This gentleman was one night at the Drawing Room with a good, clever, pretty woman when Sir John came there. And as he was always quick-sighted towards a new female, he presently singled her out for his own—that is, till he had enough of her.

He therefore made towards Bousie and, after the common compliment, asked him aside what lady he had got? Bousie told him it was his sister and hoped that information would be sufficient to prevent all farther inquiry after her, since he believed Sir John was too much his own friend to marry any woman and too much his to debauch so near a relation, but farther declared that if he ever did attempt her honor he should meet with all the resentment his sword or arm was capable of showing. Sir John laughed at his threats and said, "Why, how now, Bousie? I have often heard you say, nay swear, there was not an honest woman within the four seas. And what the D – – – l, is thy sister more than the rest of her sex? Or what is my fault that I may not have her as soon as another?"

"Keep your temper, Sir John," replied Bully Bousie. "While peace is the word, Bilbo sleeps,[26] but war will ensue if you rouse the dragon."

"You will have need of one," returned Sir John, "to guard your golden pippin, for you may depend on it, I shall attack and with some fury too." Bousie said the place they were in admitted of no dispute, turned away, and went again to the lady.

Sir John, on the other side, entertained the fine females of his acquaintance with his usual address and gallantry, which

[26] Originally, a sword made in Bilbao, Spain. By the late seventeenth century, a humorous term for the sword of a bully.

Bousie observed and took that opportunity of carrying off his sister, as he called her but who was in reality an innocent girl on whom he had honorable designs. However they did not get so cleverly away but Sir John's watchful eye catched their exit and immediately made his own to keep within view of them, though they knew it not or ever once imagined he was near them.

But mark the fate which curiosity and love of variety brings upon us. Sir John, fond of a new face which he resolved if possible to be better acquainted with, dogged both her and Bousie into a tavern. They took up a room and Sir John next to it, into which he conveyed himself without noise or light by a wink on the drawer who, by force of half a crown, was drawn to his interest and there heard all that passed betwixt them. But another of the drawers who saw him go in the dark and was in fee with Mr. Bousie, whispered him in the ear and told him where Sir John was. He nodded his head and bid the fellow be gone. He then took the lady to the other end of the room as if to show her something writ upon a pane in the window and there begged of her that when they returned to their seats she would seemingly comply with whatever he proposed to her and he would give her his reasons another time. She consented and they went again to the fire. Bousie then asked her how she liked the Drawing Room and the fine ladies she saw there. "Nay, Mr. Bousie," answered she, "that question ought to have been put to you. Mine should have been how I liked the fine gentlemen. But who was that you talked to while we were there? I think he was much the handsomest man in the room."

Bousie was not a little vexed to hear her say so because he knew Sir John did so too. But he told her that gentleman was a baronet, who had had a general fund of love for the whole female world and there is not a woman in this town that has youth and beauty to reconcile her to his notice but he either has had, will have, or would have an intrigue with. "I durst lay five pieces he is this minute at my lodgings inquiring after yours. For which reason, if you will oblige me in so small a matter, you shall change them this very night and lie in your Aunt Hannah's bed till she returns from Hampstead. But don't you dream of the knight, for them very lodgings were his once and it was there I knew him first."

The lady stared at what she did not understand but seemed to comply and when they had supped, away they went. But Sir John was beforehand with them, who no sooner heard how the lady was to be disposed of and preserved from him than he got out of his hole and went off in order to secure her.

When he lodged in the house Bousie spoke of, he lost the key of his bedchamber door (the same the lady was to lie in) and got another made. But he having left the first at a friend's house, he got it again and laid it by, lest he should happen to lose the other. The fair opportunity of getting to the lady soon reminded him of it and he went directly home, put it in his pocket, and then took his way towards Bousie's lodgings where, being well known, he went directly upstairs without any questions asked or notice taken, as if he had been going to Bousie with whom he used sometimes to lie. And by the help of the key he conveyed himself into the chamber where he expected the lady, laughing in his sleeve to think how he should mump poor Bousie with all his blustering, and when he had fixed himself to his own liking, he lay *perdue*, waiting for the happy approach of the lady.

Meanwhile Bousie, who well knew Sir John would leave no attempt untried to get to his mistress, conducted her safe to her own lodgings, and then went to an old madam of his acquaintance and desired her to put a girl into his hands that had not lately been under the surgeons. In short, he would have one, he said, that could pepper, though she was not pepper-proof. The b – – d understood him and accordingly supplied him. He gave the girl her cue, told her what to say, and conducted her to the chamber door, where he bid her good night and left her. It was now Bousie's turn to laugh, who knew Sir John had a key to that door and did not doubt but he had already taken possession, when he heard he had been upstairs and nobody saw him come down again.

This rencounter proved the very worst that ever poor Sir John was engaged in, for though he had had many skirmishes with the ladies, they had hitherto proved light ones. But in this last battle he was almost mortally wounded. And it gave him such a thorough mortification that he swore to himself if ever he got well again he would demand satisfaction of Bousie and then retire into the country where he designed to continue some time before he saw London again.

Bousie, on the other side, who knew a quarrel would ensue, played least in sight till Sir John was laid up pretty safe for a while and then got the girl's consent to marry her, which when over he went directly into the country to her father's house and I never heard Sir John and he met afterwards, for he thought it not worth his while to follow him, and so the breach healed itself. But the knight grew extremely impatient and, though he could not reach Bousie with the point of his sword, he sent many a curse after the cause of his sufferings and more intolerable confinement. But time recalled his former health and liberty, neither of which obstructed his design of going into the country because he began to be tired of the town.

The next post he sent Lady Galliard a very welcome epistle with his resolution of making her a visit in a few days. She immediately prepared for a sumptuous reception of him in the country and he in town for a speedy journey to her. In three days he arrived at Galliard Hall from whence he had been four whole years. His mother received him with open joyful arms and, making bold with a line or two of Mr. Cowley's, said

> " 'Go, let the fatted calf be killed,
> My prodigal's come home at last.'

May I, Sir John," continued she, "repeat the two next lines?

> 'With noble resolution filled,
> And filled with sorrow for the past.' "[27]

But before Sir John could make any return to what Lady Galliard said, the poor disconsolate Mr. Friendly, who expected

[27] The opening lines of "The Welcome," included in *The Mistress* (1668).

him much about the hour he came, entered the hall to make him a kind and early visit, but with looks so altered that Sir John, conscious of the cause, beheld him as well with a pitying as a guilty eye. He saw a man, once happy in his family and fortune, reduced to the utmost disquietudes and laid under the heavy pressures of a continued uneasiness. He observed his eyes grown languid, his cheeks pale and thin, the whole man wasted, lean and old with trouble, when at the same time he was forced to reproach himself and secretly say, "Ah, Galliard! thou art the cause of all."

"Mr. Friendly," said he, taking him to his arms, "I cannot say I am glad to see you because I can hardly persuade myself 'tis you. Believe me, sir, a good-natured tear steals to my eyes to see so great an alteration in you."

"Oh, Sir John," replied that worthy man, "you see in me a wretch deprived of joy, of ease, of comfort, one whose daily reflections on his own misfortunes make havoc of his peace and is in continual struggles with my heart to rend its strings asunder. I cannot look back to the happy time when I could have told myself none upon earth enjoyed more or greater tranquillity than I, none was surrounded with greater blessings. And when I tell myself how great a change succeeded all my bliss, it withers all my reason, blows a blasting vapor over my philosophy, and makes me wish I had been born wretched, to prevent the knowledge of what I have lost. I see, Sir John," continued he, "you pity your poor afflicted friend. Your eyes declare the sentiments of your heart for one who, if he has any remains of content, it is to see you again in safety of your own house. And may the return of your reason recall your scattered resolutions and force them to join in the firmest bands to make you my reverse. May kind Heaven shower down all those blessings on your head which it has seen good to deprive me of."

These words were succeeded by a pretty long silence and some tears on both sides, when Sir John, raising his eyes from the ground, found a sudden alteration in his breast. Honor, pity, gratitude, and every noble passion of the mind had seized the whole man, as if they had combined by force of arms to rescue his soul from all their own opposites. He could not hear such kind expressions from a man he had so greatly injured without the utmost remorse. And as he now began to look upon his past life with some contempt, he felt the dawnings of a secret impulse to do the injured justice.

"Come, Mr. Friendly," said the knight, "call up your courage to your own assistance and try to banish this corroding grief that preys upon your very vitals. I confess I am not much acquainted with the decrees of Heaven nor have I ever much concerned myself about them. But, if there be any such thing, they will certainly disengage your innocent heart from that black cloud which eclipses all your joy and taints all your morsels with the worst of bitters. You have often, and I believe with much sincerity, declared yourself my friend. I now give you here my hand as an earnest of a most faithful return and promise, in the presence of an Unseen Being, that I will do all I can to restore your ease. Nay, do not look surprised. That promise has weight and energy in it and will do more than you at present comprehend. Tell me, may I see poor Nancy Friendly?"

"Your words, Sir John," replied the father, "thrill through every vein and reach my afflicted broken heart. Oh say, but say it soon, are you the father of her child? And will you do her justice? Tell me, I conjure you, was she consenting to her own undoing and has she lied thus long in saying she knew not when her shame commenced?"

"Mr. Friendly," returned Sir John, "it is a little uncustomary as well as unnatural to accuse ourselves, but I dare venture to excuse her and believe her a woman of strict virtue and honor. Nor did I ever propose anything to her that could touch either, which I am satisfied she will confirm if she will give me leave to see her and that I earnestly desire to do."

"You shall freely have my consent to see her," replied Mr. Friendly, "but she has never seen the face of any man but mine since her child was born, who is now turned of two years old and has, I must needs say, the very face of Sir John Galliard. If you see her—at least, if she sees you—it must be by chance. She often walks in the garden which is her utmost limits and if you come in an afternoon and rush in abruptly upon us, she will have no time to abscond and then you must see her of course. But, Sir John, the answers you have made to my past questions seem a little ambiguous. If you are what you have promised to me, my friend, you will at once end those sufferings which I now must believe you have created and, if so, 'tis doubling your cruelty to procrastinate my ease."

"When we are once possessed, our malady is incurable," answered Sir John. "A few minutes make but a trifling addition, and there is no happiness so exquisite as that we are surprised into. I desire Mr. Friendly will dine with me tomorrow, and at your return this night take no notice of my design. Convey my service to your lady and daughter but give them no reason to expect a visit so soon."

Mr. Friendly, as desired, dined the next day with Sir John, whose impatience to see the young lady made him both hasten and shorten his meal, which when over Mr. Friendly went back to get his daughter into the garden and had not been there ten minutes before the knight appeared. Miss Friendly blushed extremely at the sight and looked with some displeasure at the freedom he took, which he would not mind but going up hastily to her gave her a country-kiss and cried, "Nancy, how dost, girl?" That very minute Mr. Friendly was called in to hear a cause (for he was a justice of the peace) betwixt two well-bred scolds whose tongues had given place to their fingers and bloodshed and battery ensued.

But the poor young lady was in double confusion when she saw herself alone with Sir John and said, "I cannot give you, sir, the common compliment of saying I am glad to see you because I am glad to see nobody, for gladness has left my heart ever since I had my little boy. I have got a little boy, Sir John. Did you never hear of it? But he is a fatherless one, for nobody will own him and I can lay him to nobody's charge. All people say he is like Sir John Galliard, but I am sure he is no way concerned in his being, because he was gone to France when my little macaroon was begotten."

"No matter, madam," replied Sir John, "where I was. Since he is so much my likeness I'll adopt him and take him for my own. Whoever is the father, Nancy Friendly is undoubtedly the mother and I will never be ashamed to father her productions. Will you give him to me?"

"Give him! Sir John," returned the lady, "do you think I want a charitable hand to take my child off mine? No! As you have already observed I am certainly the mother, though I can still say some unknown chance bestowed him upon me, and it is very possible that you, with the rest of the world, will laugh at me when I affirm it. Yet it is true, and perhaps he may yet live to recompense those melancholy hours his birth has given me. When he first made his appearance in life, I had an abhorrence to the very sight of him, but nature pleaded strongly in his behalf and I must own he is now so dear to me that the wealth of the universe should not buy him from me. But see where the little changeling comes."

Sir John, at nature's call, ran to meet it, took it to his bosom and embraced it with a father's love. "It is indeed my representative," said the real papa, "and what have you called him?"

"John," answered the lady, "after my own father."

"And after his own father, too," returned the knight, "for aught you know, since you are at a loss to find out who that is."

"That is too true," returned she. "I am so unhappy as to be a perfect stranger to him that wounded my honor, blasted my fame, and left my mind a continued chaos never to know either form or regularity more. Don't you pity me, Sir John? Yes, I am sure you do, for our fathers always loved, and you and I have never quarreled."

"You make me melancholy, madam," replied the knight. "Upon my s – – l, you do. But come, my Nancy, I'll get you a husband who shall banish all your shame and re-establish that peace in your mind which seems at such a distance."

"Ah, Sir John," returned she, "I do not want a husband for

myself but a father for my child, and till he is found I will never know a man. As for my shame, it is too well established to be displaced. 'Tis entailed upon my wretched days forever, and peace is become so great a stranger that if it were to make me a visit, I should look surprised and cry, 'I know you not.' "

"But suppose, Nancy," returned Sir John, "I should chance to be let into this grand secret and can tell you who the father of your child is. Suppose he should prove an inferior rascal and I, in pity to your wrong and instigated by friendship, should offer to marry you, which would you take?"

"Neither, sir," replied the lady, "for I have already declared against any but the father of my child and I should soon declare against him too, if he should prove what you have described. No, I'll never think of marriage; even that will never retrieve my lost credit. The good-natured world knows my fault, and it will be sure to keep it in continual remembrance."

"You wrong yourself, madam," answered Sir John, "when you own a crime you are not guilty of. You say you know nothing of the fault laid to your charge. How, then, are you culpable?"

"Alas, sir," answered she, "is not my child a living demonstration against me, and who do you think will believe me when I urge innocence and ignorance?"

"I will, my dear Nancy," said the knight, snatching her to his arms. "I know your innocence. I am the brute that wronged you of what you held dear, that plundered your honor and caused your shame, the father of your child and the ravisher of his mother, but...."

"Hold, Sir John," interrupted Miss Friendly. "You have said too much already to be believed. This condescending confession must proceed from your height of friendship. You love my father and would take a bad bargain off his hands. He, as well as I, ought to acknowledge the favor, but it would be the worst return in life to believe Sir John Galliard's soul could be guilty of so poor, so low, so base an action. No, in pity to yourself, unsay it all and keep up that good opinion I always had of your merit."

"Look'ye, Nancy," returned the knight, "this is too nice a

point to be entered into with much examination, and I have certainly done things since I was born which perhaps I should blush at now. But if I am willing to own my fault and make you restitution, I would not have you give yourself airs, but take me at my word when (liberty forgive me) I say I will marry you. And if your lost honor be what you lament, I will restore it with the addition of a ladyship and a good estate."

The poor lady trembled with resentment but, recalling her temper, said as follows: "Your barbarous usage, Sir John, might very well countenance a firm resolution of seeing your face no more, which I should certainly make were I only to suffer for it. But I have a child which is very dear to me, and in pity to him, I will close with your proposals, provided you will promise to order matters so that he may be the undoubted heir to your estate. I know it must be the work of a parliament, and you must expose yourself on such an occasion, but as you are the only aggressor, you must be the sufferer, too. These are the conditions, Sir John, if ever you and I meet again."

"Madam," said the knight, "I have promised to marry you and if I can but keep in that mind till the deed confirms my word, I shall never after deny you anything. Your child I am sure is mine, and it would be a pity to let him suffer for my faults. No, Nancy, I'll find a way without the legislature to make him heir to all. But here's your father coming, whose advice I will always follow for the future. Let us meet him and go in."

Miss Friendly's affairs looked now with a very propitious aspect. And Sir John, who had for many years indulged an aversion to a settled state of life, was now resolved to hasten his new design lest a returning qualm should rise to stop his generous and honorable intentions.

The very night before the nuptials Young Friendly returned from his travels, a most complete, clever gentleman, to the unspeakable joys of his glad parents. It was whispered that a love suit commenced betwixt him and Miss Dolly Galliard, but as they were the very reverse of one another I dare not affirm it, but shall leave their story to that grand telltale, Old Father Time, to begin and finish.

As for Sir John Galliard, I would have him acknowledge the favor I have done him in making him a man of honor at last. But, withal, I here tell him I have set two spies to watch his motions and behavior and if I hear of any false steps or relapses, I shall certainly set them in a very clear light and send them by way of advertisement to the public.

FINIS

A NOTE ABOUT THE EDITOR

WILLIAM H. McBURNEY is a native of Lake Charles, Louisiana. He was graduated from Southwestern at Memphis and received the M.A. and Ph.D. degrees from Harvard University. Dr. McBurney was on the faculty of the College of William and Mary for ten years, and he is at present associate professor of English at the University of Illinois. In addition to articles on Restoration and eighteenth-century topics appearing in scholarly journals, Professor McBurney has published *A Check List of English Prose Fiction, 1700–1739* (Cambridge, Mass., 1960).

PB-38841-SB
723-27T

DATE DUE

JAN 1 0 2005			
GAYLORD			PRINTED IN U.S.A.